Constellation Games

a space opera soap opera

Leonard Richardson

Candlemark & Gleam

First serialized in 2011.
First trade paperback edition published 2012.

This is a work of fiction. Names, characters, places, and incidents either
are the product of the author's imagination or are used fictitiously. Any
resemblance to actual events, locales, or persons, living or dead, is entirely coincidental.

For information, address
Candlemark & Gleam LLC,
104 Morgan Street, Bennington, VT 05201
info@candlemarkandgleam.com

Library of Congress Cataloging-in-Publication Data
In Progress

ISBN: 978-1-936460-23-6
eISBN: 978-1-936460-24-3

Cover art and design by Chris Sobolowski

Book design and composition by Kate Sullivan

www.candlemarkandgleam.com

For Sumana, again, and all the time.

Part One: Hardware

Chapter 1:
Terrain Deformation

Blog post, May 31

What the hell is up with the moon? I am riveted to the news, which is quite the productivity killer because **EVERYTHING HAPPENS SO SLOWLY**. I have CNN on right now because they have the best satellite footage, and I swear there was just a five-minute discussion about whether or not something is a dust cloud. Yes, it's a dust cloud! Some fucker is chopping up the moon! You're going to have a certain amount of dust in that circumstance!

But compared to how long you have to wait to see something happen, that five-minute argument goes by as quickly as the time after you hit the snooze button. So, starting now, I'm not watching any video that's not sped up 100x. Okay, CNN, you're gone.

A 24-hour news channel with some balls would crash their rented satellite into the "center of activity," the spot in lunar orbit where all the moon chunks are going. But satellites probably don't work that way. So we get shots of the lunar dust cloud because all the satellites were built to map the moon. The moon's not the story! Stop playing peekaboo. Get some close-ups. Do it for science!

I will post a review later tonight. I have twenty critical bugs to fix in this fucking pony game.

Blog post, June 1

Finally done with work. Fans of cute ponies will squeal with glee to learn that Pôneis Brilhantes 5 has met its death-march deadline and will soon be landing in North America as "Smarty Pets: Pony Stable Extra." Thanks to yours truly, the Smarty Pets series continues to have the best pony physics of any handheld series. You haven't lived until you've used the styluses on the DS Twin to braid a pony's hair! (Ironically, that was around the point where I stopped living.)

I have to immediately pivot to a tech demo for the upcoming all-hands meeting in São Paolo, so let's do a game review now, while it won't raise questions about my time cards.

GAME REVIEWS OF DOOOOM 2.0 PRESENTS
Caveman Chaos (2002)
A game by Narix
Reviewed by Ariel Blum

Publisher: Narix (Europe), New Time Entertainments (USA)
Platforms: Windows 2001
ESRB rating: T for cartoon violence and teleological suspension of the ethical

As always, I've been thinking, "How can I tie in current events to a review of an old video game that no one will read?" Because I am all about your satisfaction. There are a number of games where you mine the moon or some other planet, and it's a fun concept that's hard to screw up, but it's also hard to make a mining game that really stands out.

And then there's Caveman Chaos, the game your grandmother gives you because she knows you're into computers and it was in the $10 bin at the office supply store. The biggest-scale, most terrifying "god game" of all time.

In a typical god-game like City, in Darkness (my personal favorite) you've got a contextual palette of tools for keeping your charges happy: tools for regrading the ground, putting up a school, and so on. In Caveman Chaos, you communicate with your primitive isometric-view tribes the same way G-d does in real life—by pummeling the shit out of things!

Need to move a river? Flood it! Mammoths moving out of hunting range? Bring in the ice sheets! Need to clear some space for the new fire pits? You can't spell "fire pit" without "fire"! Your cave-dudes running out of stone chips for spears? Create obsidian the natural way, by sending a fucking active volcano right through the crust of the earth!

In other sim games, when you get bored with doing things correctly, there's a menu of catastrophes you can inflict on your simulated population—hurricane, dirty bomb, Godzilla attack, Prohibition. In Caveman Chaos, catastrophes are pretty much the only tools at your disposal. The Narix devs surveyed what had come before and said, "You know that 'extra' mechanic that's thrown in just for fun? Let's make that the CORE OF THE GAME."

Natural disasters are an unconventional technique for winning your population's affection. In fact, they terrify the poor bastards. But that's the genius of this game. Catastrophes bring in the resources you need to advance in the game, but they also kill people and leave the survivors cursing your name. Oh, cruel fate!

Would you believe it gets worse? After a few ice ages and lightning strikes, your cavemen develop religion, as a sort of defense mechanism. A caveman wakes up one day hearing voices—those voices are *you*. He's promoted to shaman, and he forms the rest of your control set.

Tell your shaman where you're going to put a volcano, and he'll declare that area taboo, like a Neanderthal zoning board. This is implemented in-game with an area selection interface and it's a useful way to herd your cavemen around the map. Only now you'd better *put* a volcano there, or your shaman will lose credibility and soon enough end up on the wrong side of a spear.

Shamans have a stat called "soulpower" (this game was originally in German). I'm sure soulpower was intended to be some generic fantasy-game thing like mana or magic points, but when I was a kid I interpreted it as literally the strength of the soul: the degree to which a shaman can listen to the voices in his head without going batshit insane. Push a shaman too hard (and you'll need to push them hard to get anywhere in this game) and he'll snap, start his own religion, and send your caveman tribe into a schism of inappropriate zoning and poorly-built fire pits.

So, a game that pretty explicitly plays up the "god" in "god game," in which your primary means of conversation with your worshippers are natural disasters and psychological torture. I wonder why this game ended up in the $10 bargain bin in America? City, in Darkness cleaned this idea up for the family by adopting a more familiar good-versus-evil theme, and honestly, City, in Darkness is the one that I still play. But for sheer loincloth-pissing terror, for the feeling of looking up at the moon and seeing someone cutting chunks out for some unknown purpose, it's gotta be Caveman Chaos.

Blog post, June 2

It's a space station. Someone's building a G-ddamned space station out of moon rocks.

The news is now a parade of denials. Politicians are very concerned and plan to investigate the issue Right Now. NASA scientists have no clue and would like to get back to work. Crazy former NASA scientists know a lot about lunar pyramids, but sadly, not much about lunar space stations. Air Force asshats with perpetual frowns are declining comment on nonexistent black ops projects. A few hours of this and I may be going on air myself to deny everything. And then they'll do the weather report.

Knock it off, guys. We all know who it is. Too bad they're not giving interviews.

Blog post, June 5

Where were you? I was asleep. Jenny sent me five links to the same video and then called me.

"Yeah, you woke me up, okay? Mission accomplished. I can't see the link. The server's down."

"You have a TV!" said Jenny. "Use the TV. The aliens made us a video."

I ran downstairs to the living room, unplugged a bunch of consoles, and tried to remember how to receive a broadcast signal. "Tell me what's happening," I said, "in the video."

"It's a contact mission," said Jenny. "They came through a wormhole. There's about twenty kinds of aliens and they want us to join them."

I fumbled through the television menus. I changed the input source and my TV picked up the signal.

When I was in high school, the space shuttle *Columbia* disintegrated over my head while my dad was driving me to school. We heard about it on the radio, and I cried and cried. A few weeks later, when they decommissioned the other shuttles, I didn't cry because I didn't watch the video, but I knew I would have. Crying isn't sadness; it happens because an emotion is too big for your body. Emotions about space have always been too big for me.

I'm no expert at having emotions, but this is as big as they come. I'm still watching this video and it's still like watching *Columbia* touch down in Florida and the crew come out waving and smiling, and behind them the crew of *Challenger* waving and smiling in their 1980s blue suits. And the crews from Apollo 1 and Soyuz 11, and finally Laika the dog waving a little Soviet flag in her mouth. There's nothing to compare it to. It's the object of all future comparisons.

"Are you still there?" said Jenny.

My television showed a small hairy creature standing in front of a screen, manipulating symbols with twitches of the tentacles around its mouth.

"That thing..." I said, "that *person* is playing a video game."

"That may not be true," said Jenny.

"It's game-*like*," I said.

"I don't know where in the video you are."

"The thing that looks like a <u>Dragon's Dice</u> cerebrophage," I said. "With the tentacles on the face. It's gesturing at a computer in a very game-like way."

"Jeeeeezus, you've known about the aliens for three minutes and you're back to talking about video games."

"They have computers," I said. "They'll have games. I'm going to find out what game that cerebrophage is playing and I'm going to review it on my blog."

Jenny is understandably skeptical. But it's going to happen, readers. This is my quest.

Holy shit.

Chapter 2:
Corner Pieces

Real life, June 6

"Hey, Jenny," I said. Jenny waved at the video chat window and made a kind of "mehhh" noise that might have been "hey."

"You're still up."

"I am up. This idiot's final act before leaving for the weekend was to tell me to redo the entire website."

"Shit, I'm sorry."

"I don't see no naked chick in your bed," said Jenny. "Wait, lemme full-screen it. Nope, still nothing."

"Jenny. I... this was the worst date of my life."

"Was there an explosion?" said Jenny. "Did you push her to an emotional crisis and she threw up on you?"

"Third worst," I conceded. "I brought up the Constellation."

"Like, just makin' conversation, or..."

"I may have mentioned that I've been waiting for the space aliens to arrive since I was six."

Instead of facepalming, Jenny asked: "What happened when you were six?"

"_Triple Point_ happened."

"Didn't the aliens in that movie want to steal Earth's water?"

"Yes, but they looked very cool."

"I begin to see the problem."

"It seemed like... she had these hot nerdy glasses. Did I mention that? Like your glasses. I thought it'd be okay to discuss the Constellation."

Jenny took off her glasses and peered at them. "They're hipster glasses," she said. "You don't need a fuckin' nerd permit to wear 'em."

"It was a false-flag operation. She just looks at me through those glasses, like, you're one of _those_ people."

I reloaded my profile page on the dating site. No rating, no comment. This was a standoff. My date wouldn't rate me until I'd rated her. It was cold-blooded blackmail. Or maybe she had gone to sleep.

"Did you find out what *she* was interested in?" said Jenny.

"Oh, yes, that was my second mistake," I said. "She complained a lot about her job. Apparently bicycle couriers don't get much respect."

"Okay, and then the mistake..."

"I commiserated. I told her that I know how she feels, because I make pony games for ten-year-old girls. And the instant I say 'pony games,' she sees me with a little pervert moustache, cruising the middle school in a banged-up white van. And the date's over."

Jenny rubbed her eyes. "Ariel, let me introduce you to the wonderful world of stretching the truth. Suppose I need to get laid, I may pretend to be a famous artist. Usually Erica Fujii. Or Andy Warhol, if I think I can get away with it."

"Hey, you know what?" I said. "Maybe ten-year-old girls should develop their own damn pony games! And then old guys like me would be pushed out of the industry altogether!"

"Listen, I am giving you a walkthrough for your next date. You work for Reflex Games. You make super-violent games for frat boys, and every time one of those bastards goes gold, you shed a single sensitive tear and collect a fat royalty check."

I clicked over to the bicycle courier's profile. I noticed that her bio said she was a bicycle *mechanic*.

I laughed a cynical, world-weary laugh—some kind of laugh, anyway. "Reflex devs don't get royalties," I said.

"This one does," said Jenny, "and he spends them showing the ladies a good time. And if by some freak accident his date finds out he doesn't work for Reflex anymore, that he writes pony games and has been waiting for the Constellation for twenty years, he goes home and smokes some weed and falls asleep like a normal person. Instead of calling up his friend Andy Warhol who is busy redesigning a website."

"I smoked all my weed during the pony death march."

"Plan B is tequila," said Jenny.

"Tequila, okay."

Blog post, June 10

Hey, you know what's bullshit? Pretty much everything about this contact mission. It's been over a week and I haven't talked to one extraterrestrial.

I signed up for an appointment with the Constellation Library, and got an appointment for time zero plus one month. That's not one month from now—it's one after the government gets off its ass and builds a Library building in Austin! So, creepy hive-mind Wikipedia is out.

Real life, June 10

A couple hours after I posted that, social network notifications lit up my screen with flashing lights like a white trash neighborhood in mid-December. This was my big break, I thought. I just needed to act fast. I needed an internal combustion engine.

ABlum: bai
the constellation is sending down small spacecraft
RIGHT NOW
they want people to come up to the space station
like the astronauts did
you need to pick up me+jenny so we can hit the landing
site
i reiterate: RIGHT NOW

KThxBai: hey bro.
that would be awesome, except i'm at work.
where i work.
so i can pay for the car i use to drive you around.
can we do it at 5:30?

ABlum: at 5:30 i will be walking on the fucking moon
and the line to the austin shuttle will be a million people
long

ABlum: jenny
the constellation is sending down small spacecraft
RIGHT NOW
they want people to come up to the space station

OMJennyG: Hi

ABlum: like those scientists did
we need to ride over to the landing site (~15 mi)
i reiterate: RIGHT NOW
bai can't make it because of some "work" thing

OMJennyG OK sounds good

ABlum: i'll bring leftovers
who knows what kind of food they have up there

OMJennyG: I have leftover cue from Eddie's bday party

We joined a pack of other cyclists at the onramp. Five miles out, a thick stream of cars started passing us up, plus the occasional overhead helicopter. Eight miles out, we passed those same cars, now stalled in a traffic jam, honking their horns. Twelve miles out, we encountered a select group of assholes who'd decided to take their cars over the fence into the bike lane and spread the traffic jam there.

"We may not get to the moon today," said Jenny.

Some of the bicyclists turned around; others walked their bikes through the traffic jam. We walked ours over another wrecked fence, through the mud and onto the grass, and ate lunch on top of a hill.

"It's only a couple miles away," I said. "Maybe we can at least see the ships land."

"Who's that?" asked Jenny, and pointed. It was an old hippie with a walking stick, heading through the meadow *away* from the landing site, back towards Austin.

"Oh, geez," I said.

"Don't be picky," said Jenny. "Maybe he saw something. Watch my bike." She got up and ran off to flag the hippie down.

The hippie was about seventy, real wiry and muscular, naval tattoos up and down his arms. Classic local color. The first thing he said to me was: "Ya know, that used to be a living thing."

I looked up from my spare rib. "Uh, yeah," I said, "it's barbecue."

"There's coleslaw and potato salad," Jenny told him. "Corn on the cob." Hippie allowed as how he would eat some coleslaw, and crouched on the grass.

"What's it like over there?" asked Jenny.

"Just what you'd think," said the hippie. "National Guard, spooks, NASA, Homeland Security, all fallin' into each other's assholes." Another helicopter flew overhead.

"So they're not even letting us in," said Jenny.

"They're not *guarding* it," said the hippie, "except by accident, by sheer numbers. They're arguing over jurisdiction. Bunch of lions fighting over a zebra carcass." He nodded at the sticky beef rib in my hands. "No offense."

"Don't bring NASA into your wildlife analogies," I said. "NASA's the good guys."

"NASA has always been a civilian fig leaf for the militarization of space."

Cat

"Dude!" I said, "Nobody eats my coleslaw and disses NASA." I always thought when the police blotter said a fight started over a "philosophical dispute," it was a euphemism, but maybe not.

"My coleslaw," said Jenny.

The hippie gave Jenny a look like: whoa, that was the last straw for *that* guy! "I was part of a civilian weapons inspection team in the Nineties," he said. "You want to get in there? Go home, come back with a suit in a dry cleaning bag. Change when you get there, come out from behind one of the towncars, act like you belong there."

"Sounds like a good way to get shot," said Jenny.

"Well, go on and live a little," said the hippie. "I probably won't live to see it, but you kids are going to see the end of the human race."

"Why are you so cynical?" I said. "This isn't an alien invasion. They're friendly. You think they're pretending to be nice so they can eat us?"

"Intentions don't matter," said the hippie. "Read your history. Any time there's a first contact, the contactees end up dead."

The cars stopped honking and some car doors opened. "Here comes a ship," said Jenny.

The hippie turned and we watched the bullet-shaped shuttle drop whining out of the sky. A thing designed by people from other planets and made from pieces of our moon: superstructured glass and cerametal. The shuttle flared and landed silently behind a rise.

"Why'd you go to the landing site?" I asked the hippie. "You must have been the first one there. You want to get wiped out first?"

The hippie kicked back the leftover vinegar like a shot. "'m curious," he said. "We're all curious. That's what gets us killed." He stood up. "Thanks for the coleslaw. Better get back." He picked up his stick and headed towards Austin.

"Man," I said when the hippie was out of earshot, "I thought hippies were supposed to be all optimistic and shit."

We ate our cold barbecue. The cars resumed honking and trying to turn around. Before too long, the shuttle took off again, rising like the chorus of a song, empty.

Private text chat, June 11

Smoke-ccsspm-6be8 Hello, Ariel. I am a submind of Smoke, Ring City's general-purpose cognition engine. My cognitive address is Smoke-Cursive-Cytoplasm-Snakebite-Singsong-Polychromatic-Musteline. In a recent email, you asked to be matched with a

member of the contact expedition. I'm evaluating your application.
Please answer questions with YES or NO. Do you understand?

ABlum: NO

Smoke-ccsspm-6be8: My supermind tells me you're being sarcastic, so I'll continue.
Sometimes two humans have the same name. I think I know which Ariel Blum you are, but tell me if I'm wrong.

I think you're the human partially or wholly responsible for the following works of art:

- "Recoil"
- "Pôneis Brilhantes 4: Problemas com Pôneis"
- "Me and Sonic at the Amusement Park"

Is this right?

ABlum: man, i wrote that sonic fanfic in junior high school

Smoke-ccsspm-6be8: Please answer YES or NO.

ABlum: YEEEEEEES

YES

[Smoke-ccsspm6be8 is now offline.]

ABlum: wtf

Smoke-ccssp-65290: Hello, Ariel.
My cognitive address is Smoke-Cursive-Cytoplasm-Snakebite-Singsong-Polychromatic.
One of my subminds recommended that I talk to you.
Please answer in English prose. Do not use idioms.

ABlum: where did the other guy go?

Smoke-ccssp-65290: I don't know who you're referring to.
My Musteline submind is busy identifying other people.
My supermind is waiting to speak with you, pending the resolution of some concerns regarding your treatment of fictional characters.
Shall we begin?

ABlum: hey, some of my best friends are fictional characters.
most of them, actually

Smoke-ccssp-65290: What was your role in the creation of "Recoil"?

ABlum: uh
i mostly worked on the enemy ai
so if you think about it, i was actually on the side of the fictional characters for that one

---

Smoke-ccssp-65290: In "Me and Sonic at the Amusement Park", why did you connect a fictional person to an electrical generator, in violation of Article 6 of your planet's Universal Declaration of Human Rights?

ABlum: i don't remember that
but probably because i was in fucking junior high
and i didn't know how electricity works

[Smoke-ccssp-65290 is now offline.]

Smoke-ccss-b85b07: Hello, Ariel. My cognitive address is Smoke-Cursive-Cytoplasm-Snakebite-Singsong. One of my subminds recommended that I talk to you.
Please answer in English prose. You may use idioms.

ABlum: hi, smoke-cursive-cytoplasm-snakebite-singsong

Smoke-ccss-b85b07: Tell me about a time when you did something evil.

ABlum: oh gee
well
sometimes i work too hard
is that evil?

Smoke-ccssb85b07: Sarcasm ignored.

ABlum: ok um
when i started college, my brother raph pressured me to join the ut austin chapter of his fraternity
and i joined, only to discover that fraternities are the stupidest forms of social organization ever invented
so, live and learn
but
at the end of the fall semester, one of my frat brothers offered to pay me to write his final history paper
and i did it
but i didn't want to get caught, so i read his earlier papers and put a lot of work into imitating his shitty writing which made the paper a d+ at best
so he failed the class
and i wouldn't give the money back
so they made up an honor code violation and kicked me out of the frat
and at the time i remember thinking "this has worked out surprisingly well"
so, i don't know what you consider "evil"
but i'm sure you can find it somewhere in there

[Smoke-ccss-b85b07 is now offline.]

ABlum: well bye

Smoke-ccssp-65290: Smoke-Cursive-Cytoplasm-Snakebite-Singsong-Polychromatic here again.
What would it take to get you to kill someone?

ABlum: fuck's sake
i'm not killing anyone

Smoke-ccssp-65290: Good.

[Smoke-ccssp-65290 is now offline.]

Smoke-ccs-762d: Well, if it isn't Mr. Sarcasm.

ABlum: YES

Smoke-ccs-762d: Don't quit your day job.
I'm Smoke-Cursive-Cytoplasm-Snakebite.
Let's get down to business. In your initial email, you said that you want to write reviews of electronic games from the Constellation.

ABlum: yeah

Smoke-ccs-762d: Before I connect you with one of our anthropologists, I'd like to see you write a review of a human game.

ABlum: there are like 50 reviews on my blog

Smoke-ccs-762d: I've read your blog.
To eliminate confounding variables, I'll need you to re-view a game that no one else has ever reviewed.

ABlum: have you seen the internet? that's a pretty tall order
why don't you have me write some more sonic fanfic?

Smoke-ccs-762d: I'm confident you can rise to your occasion.
I'll be watching your blog, Ariel.

[Smoke-ccs-762d is now offline.]

ABlum: hello?
guess that's it

Blog post, June 13

GAME REVIEWS OF WARMED-OVER RESENTMENT 2.0 PRESENTS
Quexx (2012)
A game by Reflex Games
Reviewed by Ariel Blum

Publisher: unknown (in-universe), Reflex Games (real life)
Platforms: Primary Fire Control Mainframe (in-universe), Xbox Forever/ PS4 (real life)
ESRB rating: M for getting headshot while playing

Most people who go through Temple Sphere's story mode will come out thinking that Quexx is a fictional game-within-a-game like frungy, Imperial Marzai, or Pinochle With Guns: frequently mentioned within the game but having no official rules. These people are dead wrong.

Quexx is an action puzzle game that, as you'll overhear if you play Temple Sphere, is sweeping the Tool of Justice space fleet and causing huge productivity loss. The Tool warrior caste is twiddling switches back and forth to release colored bubbles, instead of twiddling the switches that kill humans with lasers. This goes a long way towards explaining why they rarely notice you sneaking around their spaceships.

Snoop on enemy transmissions with your spacesuit radio. Along with useful information about whatever mission you're on, you'll hear Tool command-castes bitching about how much time the warrior caste is wasting on Quexx, and warrior-castes swapping strategies.

That's as deep as most people go. Even pro game reviewers are being paid to review Temple Sphere, not Quexx. But I'm not being paid, and my future as a reviewer of Constellation games depends on reviewing a game that's never before been reviewed *as a game*. So I'll tell you that within Temple Sphere's infiltration path, you can play Quexx from any vacant Tool of Justice workstation. It's called "Multidimensional Fluid Simulation" to hide it from the officers. There's even a boss screen inside the game, showing fake battle telemetry. That's a boss screen for a game played on a simulated computer inside another game running on a real computer.

The game itself is a clever variant on the combo-matching mechanic that has been hijacking humans' pleasure centers for twenty-five years now. Bubbles line up behind gates. You open and shut the gates, guiding the bubbles into a reaction chamber where they interact in pleasing or horrible ways. There's no opponent, but since one switch controls up to three gates, you'll find yourself taking punishment for almost every bonus you receive.

The big problem with Quexx is that there's nothing alien about the game. It would be perfectly at home as a ninety-nine-cent downloadable on Hit-Brick. Now that there are real extraterrestrials living in lunar orbit, it's time to hold fictional ETs to a higher standard. It seems strange that intelligent birds in a religious caste-based dictatorship would develop the same games as a human sitting in a cubicle in Austin or San Mateo.

When I first heard about Quexx, I admit I took it as a personal affront. I thought it was my former coworkers' way of mocking me for leaving Reflex for the world of short-term consulting contracts and femme-y "casual" games. It may seem silly to suspect Reflex of putting so much manpower into an Easter egg just to mock a former employee, but if you'd worked with these guys, there's not much you'd put past them.

And then Give 'Em Hell III came out, with the French kids and all their street games, and I mellowed a little—Reflex devs love screwing each other over, but they also love running jokes. Games-within-games are just their latest joke.

And while it may not fit perfectly with the Temple Sphere backstory, Quexx is a real game, not a parody. It's polished and playable, and the strategies you hear from the Tool transmissions are actually good strategies. (Pro tip: clear out the Tool ship before starting to Quexx, or you'll get a laser bolt through the head before you even finish the tutorial.) It's almost like the game-within-a-game is an outlet for the Reflex devs' creativity as they crank out a game with identical mechanics every sixteen months.

(Confidential to Smoke: all your civilization's games could get this same gushing treatment! Or, if your games are terrible, I can also do funny-angry reviews, which humans really go for.)

Chapter 3:
Rare Drop

Blog post, June 13

In 1995, my brother Raphael gave me sole ownership of his Sega Genesis after he/we (mostly he) got a Playstation for Hanukkah. This was more a verbal agreement than a real transfer: We only had one television, so the Genesis just sat next to the Playstation. The Playstation was also a popular holiday gift that year for a lot of only children, and their Genesis games started showing up at yard sales for three dollars, or with the real tight-wads, five. That's how I became a retro game collector at the age of eight, and that's how I stayed loyal to lovely 16-bit sprites when Raph had moved on to jerky, horrible-looking polygons.

One of my yard sale acquisitions was the RPG Sun/Voice 2. The cart I bought came with the former owner's saved game, right before the final battle. A saved game from the 16-bit era is only about one kilobyte of data, but it can represent up to sixty hours of some unfortunate kid's labor. And what did I do once I got home from the yard sale? I created a new game in the second save slot. I started getting up at five on weekends and spending hours re-creating that one-kilobyte file on my own.

Which is to say: I just spent the last six grueling hours of my Saturday creating a last-minute binary patch for Brilhantes 5. The size of the patch is about one kilobyte.

Why do I resent all the time I wasted as a kid grinding in 16-bit RPGs, when what I'm doing now is basically the same thing? And why do we make the experience of playing games so much like the experience of debugging them?

Blog post, June 17

[This post is friends locked.]

Howdy from São Paolo! The game company I contract for flew me steerage class to the yearly meeting. It's an opportunity for the makers of the pony games, the unlicensed sports games, the media tie-in games, to meet and greet and self-loathe. The hotel is the kind of thing Brazilians think Americans will like, and my presentation on "Five New Gestures For Minigames" brought down the house. And by "house" I mean "small conference room with carpet on the walls."

I'm spending a lot of time with my coworker L., who is inescapable at these gatherings and who I never see otherwise. L. manages the company's rapid-response team. Every summer, a dance craze sweeps South America and/or Europe, and within a week, L's developers release a shake-yer-phone game to capitalize on it. They've got a stable of Flash minigames that they'll rebrand for you in two or three days because you forgot to put up a website for your TV show. And so on. L. is about seventeen and lives in São Paolo with his parents, so rather than get his own hotel room, he's set up camp in ours.

Real life, June 17

L. was there all evening sitting in the cushy chair, typing on his netbook with one hand and his phone with the other.

My roommate, Zhenya, was sitting at the room's desk, hacking on an unbranded soccer game. He'd cranked up the mass of the ball to that of a small asteroid, so that collisions with players sent the little polygonal men flying across the field. I didn't know if this was a bug he was trying to fix, if he was using it as an extreme case to flush out some other problem, or if he just liked watching the ragdoll physics.

I'm not crazy; I don't work unless I have to. I was chatting with Bai.

KThxBai: what's happening?

ABlum: i am using you as an excuse not to talk to my coworkers

---

KThxBai: you don't like them?

> **ABlum:** i like them
> i'm just tired of hearing games analyzed in terms of dlc
> upsell percentages

I peeked furtively over my laptop screen. L. takes downloadable content very seriously, and it's always sad when a kid finds out that his youthful enthusiasms are bullshit. Fortunately L. was still dual-wielding netbook and phone, taking no notice of my heresy. I smooshed my back deeper into the pile of pillows on the bed.

> **KThxBai:** dana says hi.
>
> ---
>
> **ABlum:** sure she does
> how's the wikipedia project going?
> did you find out that the constellation secretly wants to kill us all?
>
> ---
>
> **KThxBai:** the constellation is anarchists, bro.
> you've seen the anarchists in austin. they couldn't hold a city park.
>
> ---
>
> **ABlum:** well food-not-bombs doesn't have fucking matter shifters
> and terraforming equipment
> though maybe they should
>
> ---
>
> **KThxBai:** there are 24 species in the constellation
> you don't get that big by killing everybody
>
> ---
>
> **ABlum:** there are 35 contractors working for this company, and it still sucks
> how about this idea?
> all we ever see on tv is the aliens and the farang, right
> what if those species have enslaved the other 22?

No one else could see my screen, but I could see Zhenya's. His unlicensed soccer player nailed another one with that FIFA-unapproved soccer ball and pushed him right onto a third player. The two blobs of polygons stopped being distinct players and stuck to each other, as if the ball was the Tar Baby. He'd definitely found a bug.

> **KThxBai:** let me show you an article i'm editing
> the bbc sent up a deep sea camera today & got some
> footage of the goyim
>
> ───────────────────────────────
>
> **ABlum:** the what hey?
>
> ───────────────────────────────
>
> **KThxBai:** http://en.wikipedia.org/wiki/Goy_(Constella-
> tion_species)
>
> ───────────────────────────────
>
> **ABlum:** that's friggin awesome!
> like a huge dolphin with its eyes gouged out

Zhenya ran for the ball, missed the kick, and smushed his own player character into one of his teammates. The camera jittered, trying to follow the action as Zhenya's character, the ball, and everything connected to it loped frictionless around the stadium, merging with the polygons of everything it touched.

> **KThxBai:** most people do not say "that's awesome"
> a more popular reaction is to scream.
> the aliens and farang get put on tv because they kind of
> look like us.
> and they have FACES.
> versus Her, who looks like a swarm of beetles.
> or an auslander, which if you saw it on cnn it would look
> like someone's transparent ball sack.
> or zombie dolphin bro here.

A Russian trance beat reverberated between Zhenya's headphones like the ticking of a pulsar. His screen filled with writhing polygons: people in yellow and green uniforms stuck to each other and running in place, a blob of people with a soccer ball at its core. Zhenya scratched his lip, tabbed into his web browser and started typing details into the bug tracker.

"Graaaa!" said L., emerging like an angry sea monster from his electronic reverie. "Ariel, Zhenya," he said with great gravity, "you need to come work with me. My guys can't read a spec, they barely know how to use the dev kit. I can't make deadlines with these fucking *caipiras*."

L. is always trying to get me to switch to his rapid-response team. Zhenya didn't even hear him. I always brush him off. Tonight, I didn't brush him off. I imagined Brazilian women shaking their asses to my phone-dance games. Yeah, that's right, fully grown women using my software. It was like some wonderful dream.

"What do you want from me, exactly?" I said.

"Just be the guy who makes deadlines," said L. "I can't do everything myself. Dude, hey, c'mon. Come down here and live the good life."

"Yeah, on half my American rate."

"You know how cheap booze is here?" asked L. (What impression do I leave, such that L. thinks my primary expense is liquor?) "C'mon, we'll have a blast!"

"I'll..." I trailed off. "I'll think about it." I thought about it.

Once L. finally went home, I threw a small spherical fruit candy at the back of Zhenya's head. He swiveled around in his chair and pushed back his headphones.

"Hey," I said. "You've seen the Constellation on TV. What do you think of them?"

"Dude, I seen a lot of shit in my life," said Zhenya. He paused.

"Yeah?"

"And I don't know. Maybe they're no shit." He smiled. The idea that something might be no shit was really appealing to him.

Blog post, June 19

I met a girl on the Internet! Her name is Curic and she's a fifty-year-old anthropologist from another planet. What's that, Ma? No, I'm pretty sure she's not Jewish. In fact, since she's a Farang, she's not even kosher—aquatic, but no scales. (This according to my new favorite website, "Constellation Kashrut.")

Farang are the ones who look like a cross between otters, cerebrophages, and sea urchins; so I don't think romance is in my future. Also, a few hours after we talked, the female part of her brain went to sleep and she became a man. So there's that to consider.

No, I don't get it either, as evidenced by the single stupidest message I've ever sent:

> **ABlum:** so are you female right now or what?

After the Quexx review and a few more rounds of interrogation up and down the tree of Smoke-Cursive's subminds, I finally got to talk to Smoke-Cursive itself, who quickly got bored with me and handed me off to an organic intelligence: Curic. Curic is not into video games at all, but she/he is really into asking people on the Internet what they want and then giving it to them. Kind of like the opposite of a camgirl. The catch is that, as one of Curic's contacts, my interactions with Constellation culture will provide fodder for her/his anthropological studies and (presumably) snarky blog entries.

Here's how I know Curic and I will get along:

> **Curic:** "Ariel" is a name from Shakespeare, correct?

Hallelujah! Apparently you have to be a space alien to comprehend the idea that a man might be named Ariel.

I was finally able to clear up a mystery:

> **ABlum:** so, not to get all fanboy, but around 4:15 of the "greetings" video, is the farang there playing a video game?
>
> ---
>
> **Curic:** What?
> No.

There you have it! Later in the conversation, I discovered that the Constellation does create things we would consider video games, but I can't have them. Curic could send me a submind of Smoke, the metafractal intelligence that runs the Ring City space station (and which screens Curic's calls), but that shard would be a legal person, and there's still no treaty allowing people from the Constellation to enter the United States.

We're going back and forth negotiating something for me. I'm probably going to end up with non-sentient emulators for "retro" games hundreds of millions of years old!

!!

!!!

!!!!!!!!

Real life, June 19, late night

> **Curic:** Ariel, please give me your latitude and longitude to 5-meter precision.
> I'm going to send you a data device compatible with Earth computers.
>
> ---
>
> **ABlum:** im in a hotel in sao paolo brazil
>
> ---
>
> **Curic:** Is a hotel a tall building with a flat roof?

Zhenya and I ran, up stairways, through service entrances.

> **ABlum:** on the roof. coordinates are [...]
>
> ---
>
> **Curic:** Stand back.

We looked up. A bright tiny star was visible against the black, between the horns of the crescent moon. Ring City. The space station. Curic.

We didn't say anything, just looked at the sky. Zhenya rolled a joint and we passed it back and forth. That's about how long it took.

Thump. The sound was almost lost inside the noise of the city and the drone of the rooftop HVAC. We used our phones as flashlights and found the package.

It was a cube of Constellation re-entry foam the size of a DVD boxed set, radiating the heat of entry. The exterior was rough like a tongue from capturing friction and inertia. Zhenya and I dissolved the foam with tiny mini-fridge bottles of vodka. (Cheap liquor, my ass.)

Inside was a tiny white piece of plastic: a USB key. Printed on both sides was an emblem of a random starfield, and next to that, some English text: "Constellation Shipping."

> **Curic:** Do you have it?
>
> ---
>
> **ABlum:** yes

Yes.

Chapter 4:
Too Much Information

Real life, June 19, continued

L. saw us hauling ass down the hotel hallway. "Dudes, is there a fire?" he asked. "Or a hilarious prank?"

"My ET contact dropped a package on our heads," I said, waving the USB key as Zhenya fapped his card key in and out of the lock.

The key made shaky-shaky sounds as I plugged it into my laptop, as if it were full of sand. "What is it, what's in it?" said Zhenya, shuffling from one foot to another.

"He dropped it, as in launched it from the moon?" said L.

"Give me a damn minute," I said. "This is a multi-gigabyte XML document. Shit! It's written in glossolalia."

```
...<artifact-link><point-of-view type="advertising" degree=".8"
/>Yumegolili ga beqabe wodoni...
```

"What in the fuck!" said Zhenya. "Ask the extraterrestrial what trick she is pulling."

Curic had sent a number of messages to my phone while we were running down stairs, and they now showed up on the laptop.

> **Curic:** I found a database of computer-simulated games from the history of the Constellation member species. It's twenty thousand Earth years old but that's good enough for our purposes, since we are limited to games of a certain complexity.
> I've sent you a facet of the database metadata. When you decide you want a computer

> system or some other facet of the metadata
> (such as a manufacturer's catalog, government
> proclamation, etc.) let me know and
> I'll ship it to you.

"Ask about the gibberish!"
"Yeah, yeah."

> **ABlum:** so we've gotten the file off the device but it's all "babamamagaga"
>
> ---
>
> **Curic:** It's written in a standardized
> language for sharing technical
> information. (Simple Affect Metadata Exchange.)
> I translated the 'field names' manually, and
> used a new transliteration to get the rest into the Roman
> alphabet.
> But there is no automated English
> translation yet.
> Because it's the SAME of twenty thousand
> years ago, a translator for humans to run on their
> computers is not anyone's top priority.
>
> ---
>
> **ABlum:** ok i don't want to sound ungrateful, but what good is this to me now?
>
> ---
>
> **Curic:** Now is better than later.
> The translation will get better as our concept
> maps improve.
> Ariel, I have many other contacts. I have to coordinate
> some more shipments, so I may be slow to respond for a
> while.
> Please let me know when you decide on a computer
> system to investigate.

"So now we decide?" I said. "Let's just pick the first one."
"No!" said Zhenya. "Pick the one with the most games."
"Well, now you've made it complicated," I said, "so we might as well form a plan. Let's figure out the most influential human game system of all time, and we'll use the metadata to find a similar ET system."
"The Sega MegaDrive!" said L.
"Well, that was really cool, but—"
"The fucking Scorpion, man," said Zhenya, pointing at me.

"What's the fucking Scorpion, man?"

"Clone of the decadent ZX Spectrum. I learned to program on that thing. Man, it was the shit."

"You're obviously just going on nostalgia. We need objective measures. An influential system has—"

"Lots of games, like I said. The Scorpion had—"

"Hardware clones," said L.

"Games that had lots of sequels."

"Sales numbers, long lifetime," I said. "This is what I'm talking about. If the database includes records for these things, we can count the records without understanding the language, and without having a stupid argument about human systems. I'll write some data-mining scripts."

"Hold it, dude!" said L. "Once you start game-related coding, this becomes outside work. You need approval from your project lead." L. folded his arms. "Now, if I am your project lead, you'll get approval, no problem."

"You little punk!" said Zhenya. "It's tiny script!" L. just stood there, unmoved by human pity, totally devoted to the cause of employment contracts and mobile-phone rhythm games and DLC upsell.

"No, he's right," I said. I got out of my chair and picked up my laptop. "Excuse me a sec," I said. "I'm going to talk to my project lead."

"Ariel, do not give in to this punk!"

"I'm not giving in," I said. "I'm quitting this job."

Blog post, June 21

I'm in the airport now, waiting for my flight. L. and the other Brazilians are seeding the Constellation Database of Electronic Games of a Certain Complexity, so if you want a copy, just queue it up.

I'm writing code again, and now it's the code I want to write: code that goes into a database of alien secrets and finds the parts that are worth translating.

> **ABlum:** how many games are we talking about here?
>
> ---
>
> **Curic:** Well, the concept of an individual "game" is somewhat fuzzy, but:
> More than a million games and less than ten million.
> Enough for you to spend your life examining.
>
> Though I do not recommend spending so much time on something already so well catalogued.

My first set of filters on CDBOEGOACC found a Farang console that was very popular about ninety million years ago. Curic translated its name as the Brain Embryo. Farang are enough like humans that I should be physically able to play the games. Even though Curic says she's never heard of this game system, or even this period of her species' history, I feel safer starting with a Farang system.

I've kept my promise to Jenny to stop watching TV, but it's inescapable in the airport, and what is on now is not so bad. I'm watching a camera crew near the lunar north pole. Humans in ESA space suits are setting up Quonset huts at the lunar north pole, on the Peaks of Eternal Light. ETs in much cooler-shaped spacesuits are replacing the solar panels with photosynthesis paint.

A few months after I started contracting with the pony game company, I asked Zhenya how he felt about Glavnaya. He said that it was abandoned before he was born, and that building it had bankrupted his country, so basically he could take it or leave it.

And, okay, but given that it happened, given that the money was spent: Don't you want an affinity with the person who pointed at the moon globe and said, "We'll build it here, where the solar radiation is the most consistent, in the Peaks of Eternal Light." When the aliens come and say "Yes, this was a pretty good place to build it, let us help you live here again."

?

Blog post, June 21

Miscellaneous metadata mysteries from the Constellation Database of Electronic Games of a Certain Complexity:

- Why are there so many Alien clones of Farang games? How did this happen?

- Most species disappear from the CDBOEGOACC when their computers exceed A Certain Complexity. If humans were in the database, our last entry would probably be a handheld system from 2006. So, why do the Inostrantsi stop developing CDBOEGOACC computers, start making them again ten thousand years later, and then stop again? Retro revival, or dark age?

- What's the Other game that's so awesome the Others cloned it three thousand times?

Blog post, June 22

Last night, Curic dropped the Brain Embryo right into my backyard, scattering my prized pyramid of empty beer cans to the four winds. This morning, some fucker with an op-ed guest spot is telling us we should be grateful the Constellation isn't dropping rocks on us, a la *The Moon is a Harsh Mistress* (not mentioned by name). Well, I am grateful Curic didn't drop a rock on my house, but hopefully the survival of the human race is not going to come down to that kind of gratitude, because there's not a damn thing op-ed guy can do about it.

Jenny came over in the afternoon once it became clear the drop was really going to happen. We hung out and she did work for a few hours, and Bai came over from the turbine plant as soon as he got off work.

"Hey, bro!" he said, and held up a six-pack of convenience store beer, his traditional game night gift. "Did I miss the drop?"

Jenny was shuffling cards. "You missed squat," she said. Bai toted the six-pack through the living room into the kitchen.

"Curic only delivers after dark," I said, "so that violent gangs don't notice the drop and steal the loot from us."

"This is Austin," Bai called from inside the fridge door. "Not São Paolo. Ain't no gangs to speak of."

"I'm pretty sure she means the government," I said.

Bai had gone into the kitchen with a six-pack and now he came back into the living room holding one beer. It was like the opposite of a miracle. "I brought Dana," he said.

Jenny pulled cards out of the deck and threw them back in. "Can Dana... play?" she asked.

"She can watch," said Bai.

"The game is Knockdown Dragout," said Jenny, not without malice.

Knockdown Dragout is the cross-dressing antistrip poker game I posted about last November. Annoyingly, but profitably, Bai kept his phone on the table during the game and devoted most of his time to looking at it and making kissy-faces with Dana. By the time Curic contacted me, Bai had lost pretty thoroughly and Jenny had to get out her lipstick.

"You're losing real money, dude," Jenny told him.

"And real dignity," I said. Bai mumbled and applied the lipstick like Chap-stick.

"I'm just gonna write that lipstick off," said Jenny. She was dressed as one of Bai's old frat brothers, wearing a Hornets cap, a single dude-earring, and a baggy white T-shirt that said "BEER IS LIKE WOMEN, BUT I FORGET WHY." I was doing pretty well, having only been forced to wear a skirt, plus one of Jenny's bras under my shirt.

Curic: The package is ready for delivery. Are you ready to bring it inside?

ABlum: yeah, we're just sitting around down here wearing each other's clothes

---

Curic: Is that merely a colorful idiom or is it a cultural phenomenon I should investigate?

ABlum: it is neither

We went into the backyard in various levels of drag. Bai finally put his phone away. "Are we gonna see it?" he said.

"It's too small," I said, "and it doesn't heat up enough to glow. It just lands."

And it landed, but not for another ten minutes. The tiny shockwave rattled us and knocked over the aforementioned beer cans. This package was much bigger than the old one—an egg of re-entry foam five feet long.

"Whoop!" said Bai, and pounced on it. "Jesus, it's hot!"

Jenny held up my oven mitts. "This is why humans invented tools," she said. "Let's get it inside before it starts a grass fire."

"Yeah," I said, "or my crazy neighbor mistakes us for raccoons and shoots us."

The top of the egg had "Constellation Shipping" etched on it, and the same starfield I'd seen on my USB key. We put the egg in the bathtub, this side up, and Bai shook my bottle of rubbing alcohol like a madman.

"Whoa, whoa," I said.

Jenny took a water pick out of her purse. "This isn't one of your parties, Bai," she said. "We're going to use as little alcohol as possible."

"It's just the packing material," said Bai. "You want to sell it online?"

"You see packing material," said Jenny, "I see sculpting medium."

Bai took off his dress and rolled up the half-sleeves of his polo shirt. "Do you open your Christmas presents this way?"

"Yes, I do," said Jenny. She cut a channel down the middle of the egg and Bai and I pulled the two halves apart while Jenny filmed the unboxing video. The Brain Embryo slid out of the eggshell, a heavy oblong shape like two couches sixty-nining.

Like the kid with the big half of the wishbone, I staggered back with the side of the egg that contained the Brain Embryo. Bai held the empty half, except it wasn't empty. *Stuff* started pouring out of the cavity in the middle, and into the bathtub. Plastic sheets, wires, adapter cables. Cables spanning the ninety million years of history between the Farang Brain Embryo and the human high-def TV.

"Shit," said Bai, shaking out the foam shape. "Where are the instructions?"

I set the Brain Embryo on the toilet seat. "Curic sent me instructions," I said, "but they're written in Simple Affect Metadata Exchange."

Bai knelt in the bathtub, fondled the cables, and held one up. "This end is a DCMI cable," he said.

"Yes," said Jenny, "and the other end is a condom."

I looked up Curic's instructions. They were written in a very old dialect of

SAME that got more and more recent as it described cables further along the chain from the Brain Embryo. The last sentence was in English: "Attach the spectrum converter to a television using the provided cable."

We moved everything into the living room. "Should be simple enough," said Bai. "We work backwards." He unfolded a large sheet of black plastic, like a road map of space.

"This diagram looks like an absorbtion spectrum," he said. "It could be the spectrum converter."

"The condom won't fit on that," said Jenny.

"That's what she said."

"Jesus Christ, Bai!"

"Putting aside whether or not what's what she said," I said, "that's photo-synthesis paint. It's what they use on the moon base."

"So, this is the power source," said Bai.

"And it's nighttime," said Jenny. She sighed. "I'm going home."

"I'll drive you," said Bai.

That's why we still haven't played any Brain Embryo games. And that's why Bai is wearing lipstick in the unboxing video.

Chapter 5:
Let's Play

Blog post, June 23

GAME REVIEWS YOU WERE TOO SHY TO ASK OUT IN HIGH SCHOOL 2.0 PRESENTS
<u>Gatekeeper</u> (c. 90 million years ago)
A game by Clan Snowman
Reviewed by Ariel Blum

Publisher: Clan Snowman
Platforms: Brain Embryo
ESRB rating: T for light blasphemy

The Brain Embryo is a thirty-pound square computer that glistens like mother-of-pearl. My replica only weighs ten pounds, because it's full of Constellation nanocomputers suspended in moon dust, instead of primitive Farang electronics. The case splits in half like a clamshell, and here comes the input device, looking a little like a pipe organ and a lot like an abacus.

The Brain Embryo is built like the military-surplus typewriter you inherited from your great-uncle Toby's attic. I accidentally dropped it on the floor while setting it up, and the worst that happened was all the little sliding disks slid into the "up" position. (Also my heart stopped from fright—hey, those defibrillator paddles really work!)

OH YEAH IT'S A NEW SYSTEM, HERE ARE THE SPECS
<u>The Brain Embryo</u> (c. 90 million years ago)
Species: Farang
Civilization: Dhihe Coastal Coalition
Developer: Clan Not Completely Underwater
Publishing Lifetime: 54 Earth years

A typical Brain Embryo entertainment simulation uses four or ten of the pipe organ/abacus controls. The other 150 are for programming and database work. Gatekeeper only uses one little abacus bead. Slide your glistening resin bead up and down; send it spinning with a quick flick of the finger. The game that's like performing a sex act.

Gatekeeper is the simplest Brain Embryo game. It's stored in a little screw-in memory cylinder along with tens of thousands of other games and pieces of software. Another species' computing history, smashed into the equivalent of a 128-gigabyte flash memory card. Shake the cylinder, yup, it's also full of moon dust.

Here's what the Constellation Database of Electronic Games of a Certain Complexity has to say about Gatekeeper:

> The Gatekeeper, a minor figure in the Consensus Mythos, manages traffic between the land of the living and the land of the dead. In this game, you adopt the Gatekeeper's dull task indefinitely. Due to its simplicity, a game mostly of theoretical interest to ludologists.

(All CDBOEGOACC translations are Curic's. For the time being, there will be no localizations of the games themselves. The people of the Dhihe Coastal Coalition spoke Edink, a language which nobody on the contact mission understands because it's older than human language itself.)

The Brain Embryo unit has a small Plexiglass display on top, protected by a fold-up cloth, but it's useless for a human—too small and too far into the infrared. A series of cables and adapters, as long as a mature tapeworm, blue-shifts the image into the visible spectrum and formats it to fit my television.

The Gatekeeper is a blue blob that stands in the center of your television, moving up and down along with the bead on its rod. Traffic comes from both sides of the screen—mostly from the right, from people dying. You need to let normal traffic through, while flicking away dead people who shouldn't be living (zombies) and living people who shouldn't be dying (suicides?).

The most interesting thing about this game is that there's legitimate traffic from the land of the dead into the land of the living! These seem to be Serious Ghosts with Legitimate Business on the other side, like Hamlet's old man.

Flanking the tiny glass display on the Brain Embryo are two flip-up pieces that emit weak radio waves. The radio waves tickle a Farang's antennacles, stimulating the "water-sense" and inducing detailed 3D hallucinations that take a lot of load off the system's graphics processor. On the back of the case is what I can only assume is an FCC notice that this does not qualify as a Class B digital device.

I don't have antennacles, so I'm flicking this bead against the blobs I see on the screen, the two-dimensional shadows of the shapes that make up the Gatekeeper and the zombies. For a game this simple, that's good enough.

Gatekeeper is a game with no win condition. As in all arcade-type games, eventually you screw up at your Gatekeeping job and are fired. Your boss is a comical-looking yellow oval who comes on screen and beats you with a baguette, and I'd laugh except I think that goofy fucker might be G-d.

The hardware manufacturer for the Brain Embryo is the Not Completely Underwater clan. It's a company name that surely loses something in translation, but one which I find bursting with optimism.

The CDBOEGOACC is right. Gatekeeper is a dull game, a simple arcade-type game similar to games that went out of style here thirty years ago. It's a game from another planet that I can play on my television. I recommend it.

Update, two hours later:

Curic: Those are not zombies. They're probably people who want a refund.

ABlum: a refund on what?

Curic: Their lives.

ABlum: sounds like a zombie to me

Curic: I am going to do research on human zombies to prove you wrong.

Update #2, ten minutes after that:

> **Curic:** Zombies are fully dead people who come back to
> life for no reason.
> What you are seeing is when one half of a person
> dies, the other half wants a refund.
> Otherwise the entire person will die in a few hours.
>
> ──────────────────────────────────
>
> **ABlum:** who gives out the refunds?
>
> ──────────────────────────────────
>
> **Curic:** There are no refunds.
> That's the point of the game.

Real life, June 24

For the first time in years, I rode out to Reflex Games's Austin office and padlocked my bike to someone else's bike because the fucking bike racks are full. I knelt on the concrete, unzipped my backpack, and made one more check of the Brain Embryo, which I always make sure to transport in the finest of pillowcases.

Inside, I signed in and got a stupid plastic visitor's badge. The lobby is still decorated with promotional shit from trade shows, though it's obviously later-gen shit than when I worked there.

"Conference room," said the receptionist. I conference roomed.

Suresh was not in the conference room. The lights were off when I came in. I sat in a chair for about forty-five seconds. Then I got up and rearranged all the chairs. I squared off a section of whiteboard and wrote DO NOT ERASE. Even this got boring.

I knelt down again to check the Brain Embryo. The door opened and someone said "Hello?" I stood up from behind the table and saw a blond frat boy reading off his phone.

"Hi, I'm waiting for Suresh," I said.

"Suresh is in Toronto the rest of the week," said the frat boy. He sat across the table from me. "Ariel, right? Suresh says you used to work at Reflex."

"Yeah, we were devs together on Recoil, and the original Give 'em Hell."

When I contacted him, Suresh's email signature said "Director of Content." Why had he been called to Toronto? Some kind of content emergency? More importantly, what might this guy's sig say, when he sends out email? "Summer Intern"? Was I being snubbed?

Frat boy had his phone face-up on the desk, but he was looking at me. "Yeah?" I said.

"Suresh said you had something to show."

"Oh." I slipped the Brain Embryo out of the pillowcase and set it on the table. I opened the clamshell to show off the control abacus, and flipped up the RF emitters so it would look cool.

"This is an extraterrestrial computer," I said.

He sat up straight. "A Constellation computer."

"Farang, pre-Constellation."

"How powerful is it?"

"It works with six-dimensional polygons," I said. "And Farang have slower reflexes than humans, so they were okay with a low frame rate. But you could see as it a PC from about 2000." I said. Once frat boy heard the year, he slouched back down in his seat.

"The Farang wrote games for this computer," I said. "Thousands of games. Humans can play these games. We have the metadata for the games. We have reviews, we know which ones are good. We just have to get them localized and port them to human systems."

Instant messages were crawling up frat boy's phone but he only gave them a glance. "Reviews," he said, and steepled his fingers. "Do you have sales numbers?"

"The society that built this computer didn't really have capitalism," I said. "My contact says they mostly traded in time-limited apprenticeships within a network of small clans."

Frat boy had the kind of body language that makes it very clear at what point in your sentence he stopped listening to you. "You've played these games?" he said.

"Yeah, nonstop," I said, "for the past forty-eight hours."

"Whaddya think?"

"Have you ever played a Japanese RPG, in Japanese?"

Frat boy's body language got a little more tricky. I couldn't tell if he was saying, "Why would I play a Japanese RPG in Japanese?" or "Why would I play a Japanese RPG?"

"There's clearly something there," I said. "This system kept the Farang entertained for a long time. But I don't have the resources to localize these games and bring them to humanity. Reflex does."

Frat boy's phone started popping and crackling. He looked at me quizzically. I unscrewed the Brain Embryo's power capacitor and the noises stopped.

"Uh, it gives 3D effects with radio transmissions. I have an idea for a visualizer, but I'm not very good with hardware. That's another thing..."

"What do you want from Reflex?" asked frat boy.

"I just want to be part of the project," I said. "I want to do some games that are important. Culturally."

Frat boy leaned towards me. "Okay," he said. "You worked with Suresh and the guys for four years. As far as I'm concerned, you're still part of the family. And you know that we give each other the straight talk within the family? No bullshit. It's the only way to maintain trust."

"Yeah, I'm quite familiar with this tradition," I said.

"I don't see games here, man," said frat boy. "I see *ideas* for games. Ideas are cheap. You and me, we have ten game ideas every day." He slid his phone along the desk from one hand to the other. "There, make a game about that. We get fan mail we can't read, because people are telling me their game ideas, and we don't want to get sued."

Who sends fan mail to this douchebag? "These games are ninety million years old," I said. "I believe the copyright has expired."

"You know that Reflex only handles original IPs," said frat boy. "You should try a smaller studio. One that does localizations."

"I just spent five years working at smaller studios," I said. "They don't have the money or the vision. Reflex does."

"Then why'd you spend five years working for them?" said frat boy. And for him this meant the end of the conversation.

Outside, defeated, I stared at the mirror glass of the Reflex office building and made *pssh, pssh, pssh* noises, shooting out the windows one by one with my imaginary laser cannon. Don't judge me; I learned it from playing violent video games.

Blog post, June 24

I have something to tell you.

"I have something to ask you," I said to Jenny.

Jenny scraped up the last little pile of pasta on her plate. "Uh, okay," she said.

"How would you like to find employment in the exciting and fast-paced world of video game design?"

"I'd probably hate it," said Jenny.

"Why?"

"Because I've spent the past ten years listening to you hate it."

"No more," I said. "I terminated my contract with the Brazilian company. I'm done with them."

"Oh, good!" Jenny looked up at me. "I kept telling you you could do better."

"Yes," I said. "I'm starting my own game studio."

"I don't think it's a good time for that," said Jenny. "The economy's not so great."

"It's never going to be great," I said. "It sucked when we got out of college, and it sucks now, and I have to take a leap of faith now, before it's too late."

Jenny scooted back her chair. "It's the Constellation, isn't it?"

"Yes," I said, "exactly."

"Ariel, they're scientists," said Jenny. "They're not going to outsource their tie-in games to humans, or whatever you think is gonna happen." She turned on the kitchen faucet and the steam started to rise.

"That's the exact opposite of my idea," I said. "All these games on the Brain Embryo all-in-one pirate cart. We'll port them to human systems. We already know which games were the hits. We just need to localize them. It's like finding money lying on the ground."

"Yeah, alien money," said Jenny. "How do you know the bank will take it?"

"I'm taking a risk and putting up the capital," I said. "That's why they call it capitalism. Okay? To make a game you need one dev and one artist. I want you to be the artist."

"I'm a *fine* artist," said Jenny. "I do mixed-media sculpture."

"You do graphic design for websites," I said. "You can do pixel art."

"Are you *trying* to piss me off?"

"I made pony games!" I said. "But I quit! You can always quit! It's the secret of adulthood. Let's quit being hacks, and do something cool."

"Okay," said Jenny. "I admit this is the first time you have *combined* a silly game idea with a harebrained money-making scheme."

"Why is it a scheme?" I said. "We make a product and sell it. How hard can it be? Every douchebag either one of us has ever worked for has managed to do this!"

"So it's just... pixel art?" said Jenny, "Like on your T-shirts?"

"Yeah, of course," I said.

"'Cause I do 3D modeling," said Jenny.

"That skill won't transfer," I said. "Your sculptures don't move. They don't even have to look like specific things. 3D models are why Pôneis Brilhantes looks like shit. You get stuck in the uncanny valley and have to spend a million bucks to climb out."

"Speaking of which," said Jenny, "what kind of budget are we looking at?"

"I'll pay you a salary," I said. "That's right, an actual fucking salary. You come to work every day and you get money. We're goin' old school here."

Jenny turned with a soapy cup in her hands. "Health insurance?" she said.

"Let's not go crazy."

This is what I wanted to tell you. My consulting S-corp is now a game studio. Say hello to Crispy Duck Games!

"When do we start?" said Jenny.

"When I find a Brain Embryo game worth porting," I said.

"Well, don't take your time finding one," said Jenny. "I'm tired of watering down the pasta sauce."

Crispy Duck Games: WE'RE NOT HACKS ANYMORE!

Chapter 6:
The Stars My Screensaver

Real life, June 26

Some men in black done knocked on my door, and I don't mean Johnny Cash impersonators. There were two heavies standing on the stoop, and if they weren't wearing sunglasses, they sure wanted to. They were in their thirties. One was tall and looked like he'd rather be anywhere else; the other was short and buff and wore a dangerously loosened tie.

"Ariel Blum," said the tall one, sizing me up through the door chain. I briefly catalogued my crimes. Nothing unusual for my age/ethnicity/location, nothing that justified dudes in suits.

"Do you have a warrant?" I said. "Because I'm pretty sure you still need one."

"We just want to talk to Ariel," said the short buff one.

"I'm Ariel," I said.

The agents conferred quietly. "Isn't... Ariel a woman's name?" said the tall one. Like I'm hiding the Little Fucking Mermaid in my bathtub.

"It was a man's name until 1989," I said. "I squeaked in under the wire."

"Mr. Blum," said the short one. "We just need to talk. Really quick. There's no trouble."

"Give me an acronym," I said.

"B.E.A."

"Oh, the...the—"

"Bureau of Extraterrestrial Affairs. State Department."

"I'll come out." I undid the chain and slid out onto the porch. Two agents at the door and a black car at the curb. An old natural-gas government sedan. Probably borrowed from the local Homeland Security office, and the agents with it.

"I'm agent Krakowski," said the tall one. "My junior is Fowler."

"*Agent* Fowler," said the short one.

Krakowski ignored this. "You've had contact with an extraterrestrial," he said/asked.

"Yeah, text chat." No point in denying stuff I've posted to my blog. "You want to talk to her?"

"Species?"

"Farang."

"Oh-kay." Krakowski made a gesture to Fowler, who handed me a form out of a manila folder. "We need to register you as a contactee. Once you do, you'll be eligible to sponsor a visa so your contact can visit the United States. "

"Hold it," I said, looking up. "This form is a fake. There's no Paperwork Reduction Act notice."

"G-ddammit," said Fowler. He eyed the dead pot plant on my porch like he wished he could still bust me for it.

"Blum, cut us a break," said Krakowski. "The BEA is ten days old. We're scrambling here. If we had to run timing studies on all our paperwork, Brazil and China would be building theme parks for ETs before we hosted our first state dinner."

"We're talking about competitiveness," said Fowler. "Extraterrestrial technology driving American firms out of business. Commie lasers on the moon. You want to see that happen?"

"Not particularly." *I haven't gotten any work from an American company in three years, you pompous fucks.*

"So." Fowler pointed at the form in my hand.

"Okay," I said, "but I want to see some badges."

The badges came out. Leftovers. Homeland Security, as I suspected.

"Has your contact delivered to you any piece of technology or other item of value through direct atmospheric insertion?" said Fowler.

"I was hoping I could visit Ring City."

"One thing at a time," said Krakowski. "Have you gotten anything? Any gifts? They may not have called them 'gifts'."

"I got a game system," I said.

"A *game system*?"

"Yeah, an old Farang—look, we're basically the same age. You never played Nintendo? One of those."

"Why a game system?"

"I asked for one."

"We'd like to see it," said Krakowski.

"You'll also need to fill out a customs form," said Fowler.

"Are you sure? It literally fell out of the sky."

"It's an illegal import."

"*Technically* it's an illegal import," said Krakowski. "It's fine. Nobody's going to jail. We just need to get organized about these things. It's one of those situations where the situation changes faster than the law."

Fowler gave me a stack of forms. The real thing this time, government-issue.

When my brother Raph got his Playstation, all the neighborhood kids came to look at it, even the ones who were about to get one for Christmas, because Christmas hadn't come yet. Showing the Brain Embryo to the BEA agents reminded me of that feeding frenzy, except the neighborhood kids didn't want to disassemble the Playstation and use the parts to build public-private partnerships.

"This looks like a weapon," said Fowler, waving around a cable like it was Dogood Browne's demon-killing whip.

"That's the video splitter," I said. It does not look like a weapon at all.

The examination took a few minutes, and Krakowski shifted the Brain Embryo back and forth for the shaky-shaky sound of the moon dust inside.

"This stuff," he said. "All the Constellation tech. Full of moon dust."

"Yeah," I said.

"Some people are selling the dust online. 'Souvenir of the moon' kind of bullshit. That's a bad idea."

"Why?"

"Health hazard. The dust contains smart matter that we have no idea how it works. We also have obligations under UN treaties not to commercialize the moon."

"Seems like that treaty went down the crapper when the Constellation started digging big chunks out of the thing."

The look on Krakowski's face gave me the party line on UN treaties and their location vis-a-vis the crapper.

"The treaties are all we have," he said. "If we don't stick together, the Constellation will start playing one country against the other."

"We play this right," said Fowler, "there'll be plenty of moon dust for everybody."

"We'll send you an informational packet," said Krakowski as he left, "once we get a discretionary budget for the design of informational packets. If your contact says or does anything to alarm you, or you notice anything suspicious, notify us immediately."

"Like what?" I said. "What are you afraid of?"

"It's precautionary only," said Fowler. "There's been no determination of fear."

After they left I pressed my ear to the door. "Okay, never contradict me in front of a civilian," I heard Krakowski say. "Just don't *fucking*..."

(N.B. the form takes 24 minutes to fill out.)

Blog post, June 27

GAME REVIEWS OF IRREVOCABLE DECISIONS 2.0 PRESENTS
Handle the Real Style (c. 90 million years ago)
A game by Clan Extra Echo and Clan Let It Sink
Reviewed by Ariel Blum

Publisher: Clan Extra Echo (?)
Platforms: Brain Embryo
ESRB rating: M for grand larceny and occasional vengeance

Looking through fifteen thousand extraterrestrial games used to be kind of a fun activity, good way to spend a weekend, but now my livelihood depends on finding the SINGLE MOST AWESOME GAME ever made for the Brain Embryo so I can port that game to human computers, and it's becoming a bit of a chore. Which makes me more and more worried about my backup plan of becoming a gigolo.

Handle the Real Style is not the game I've been looking for. I'm writing about it because it's the game that taught me how to look at Farang games.

You may recall my Gatekeeper review, where I used the word "blob" a lot. This was an accurate depiction and I stand by it. These games are full of multicolored roundish blobs. I figured there was some complicated 3D shape overlaid on the blob in the RF band that I didn't see because I don't have antennacles.

But Handle the Real Style starts off with something I recognize: a starfield. Stars give off all kinds of light, and they're pretty quiet in the RF, so they look about the same to Farang as to humans. Pretty nice graphics, too—there's a kind of nebula thing in one corner of the sky, and you can even see the Milky Way.

And there's this strange two-tone blob in the middle of the screen, just like in Gatekeeper. I found the controls and moved the blob around, assuming it was a space shooter with a starfield background. But as I moved around, other shapes occluded the stars and I realized that I was looking *up* at the sky.

That's the secret. Humans make games with top-down views, and Farang make games with bottom-up views. I was looking at these little brown blobs like they were the top view of something, or maybe the side view of something, but actually they're upskirt shots of Farang: little circular forms with leathery feet at the bottom and the wiggly antennacles sticking out.

Now these games make a lot more sense. You start <u>Handle the Real Style</u> on the beach. Eventually the sun comes up and the stars go away. You can go into the ocean, dive as deep as you want, and the camera will stay right beneath the player character the whole time, as the sky and the water's surface fade away past the draw distance.

The CDBOEGOACC describes <u>Handle the Real Style</u> as "a vengeance game typical of the period," and doesn't say much else. I admit I find this game a little light on the vengeance. You can go into other peoples' caves and steal their stuff (lots of Farang games are based around theft, the way human games are based around homicide), but you never see the other people. The world is detailed, well-realized, and completely empty. If you revenge yourself on someone, and they never find out, is it really vengeance?

There's a lot of text in <u>Handle the Real Style</u>, but no way to translate it, so I just made up my own story. In this game, you play the last Farang on Earth (well, whatever they call it), taking a post-apocalyptic opportunity to steal back all the power tools lent to his/her neighbors over the years and never returned. I'm through with this game, but I may drop back in a couple years from now to see how (in)accurate that story is.

Update: Here's the now-obligatory rebuttal from Curic.

> **Curic:** The "nebula thing" is a nebula.
> Please add this to your review. That nebula was very prominent in the night sky back then and very important to a lot of Farang.
>
> ---
>
> **ABlum:** ok
> why was it important?
>
> ---
>
> **Curic:** I don't know. People were very superstitious back then.
> They probably thought they could get there if they built a big enough tower or a fast enough spaceship or something.

Real life, June 27

Beep beep. "Pick up," I commanded. My hands were covered with free-range chicken juice. "Hey, Jenny."

"Do I have a job yet?" said Jenny from the phone on the counter. "I'm gonna call every day, like a plucky newspaper dude."

"I've been planning the cookout," I said. I held up my drippy hands to the phone. "Things are marinating."

"What are you looking for? Like, what's the criteria? 'Cause I can scout the database myself, while you marinate."

"Uh, when the Constellation made the database, they assembled a histogram of reactions to each game, kind of like they use on Groupinion. I'm trying out the games that everyone likes."

"That won't work," said Jenny. "Everybody 'likes' Trent Fellersen, but I wouldn't show his art to aliens."

I washed my hands and put a lid on the chicken. "He's the one with the airbrushed... What's wrong with his stuff?"

"Okay, you remember the cartoon I drew way back when, where Picasso's painting a still life and Bugs Bunny keeps stealing the fruit?"

I remembered. "Yeah."

"When Bugs Bunny steals the fruit from Trent Fellersen, Fellersen doesn't even go after him. He just gives up, and sells the painting as is. Like, 'yes, it's a primer coat and the outline of an apple, I'm a genius.'"

"Sounds like you don't like him," I said. I dropped potatoes into a pot of water.

"Oh, I 'like' him," said Jenny. "'Like' is the placeholder emotion. Don't give the world more shit people 'like'. I want to do a game that that some people loved and some people hated."

"That's a good idea. Skewed histogram. We'll look at the rating and the standard deviation."

"Can I do that part?" said Jenny. "And get paid for doing it?"

"Maybe we can split it up," I said. "Let's talk about it after the cookout."

"Oh, oh!" said Jenny. "Did you hear about Papua New Guinea?"

"I heard that it exists," I said.

"The Constellation just landed shuttles all over Papua New Guinea. Like eight hundred people. Except about three hundred were Them; maybe that only counts as one person."

"What are they doing there?" I said. "That's the middle of nowhere."

"I don't know, handing out old computers, or whatever the Constellation normally does. I thought you'd know about this already."

"They're probably linguists," I said. "People speak a lot of different languages there."

"Well, how come they get all the space aliens? When do we get some?"

"Jenny. Geez. The aliens are not a dessert."

"You know what I mean," said Jenny. "You said the BEA assholes were going to let Curic come down to Austin. She's already missing the cookout."

"I don't know," I said. "There's foreign policy shit." I picked up the phone and looked up a map. "Clearly New Guinea needs the tourism more than we do. Plus, if they do take over the island like people are afraid of, everyone will secretly think, 'Well, at least they only got Papua New Guinea.'"

"And they'll stop with one island? They've got portable wormholes. You can't quarantine that shit."

I looked at the map. "Oh, wow," I said. "New Guinea shares an island with Indonesia. If the Constellation takes over Indonesia, then China gets involved, and then we're all fucked."

"Where are you getting this? Why does China care?"

"They have defense pacts with all those south Asian countries."

"That's in <u>Limited Nuclear Exchange</u>," said Jenny. "Not real life."

"Oh."

"Doofus."

Chapter 7:
Party Creation

Blog post, June 28, morning

If you have a big cookout on the actual Fourth of July, everyone is going to some other cookout, so you're left alone with more food than you can eat. Have a cookout the weekend *before*, and not only will you have a good time, you'll probably ruin some other fucker's cookout the next week, because lots of people can't take a cookout two weeks in a row. This is my theory, anyway.

Today the Brain Embryo makes its public debut at my annual Pre-Fourth-Of-July Sexy Cookout. (Everything sounds better when you call it "sexy".) The "public" here is Jenny's friends, and my friends, such as they are. Putting the two sets together usually causes some kind of fun explosion, if only because my friends are always astounded to discover that their pickup lines don't work on Jenny's friends.

The Sexy Cookout is my yearly attempt to build the most stereotypical image of summer imaginable, so everyone can have a "fun summer" memory to look back on when it starts to rain. My friends in their work polo shirts and Jenny's in whatever they wear; beers in hand, dropping by the grill to share inanities. The sweating, the sprinkler, the heat of the grill, and all the other things about an Austin cookout that are fun in retrospect.

I want to do it right this year, because this might be the last cookout. Nobody knows what human civilization will be like in a year. Next year, there will be a new holiday on the calendar—the anniversary of first contact—and we may all be living on different planets. The memory of *this* summer, when we were all together in Austin; I want it to last as long as it needs to.

Real life, June 28

Jenny doesn't *cause* trouble, but she's suspiciously good at pointing it out. The first sign that my cookout was in trouble came from her. I was turning the traif in the backyard when Jenny came out with a beer bottle in each hand.

"Not being judgmental," I said, "but it's a little early to be double-chugging it."

"This one's for Bizarro Kate," said Jenny. "Can you come in and set up the Xbox?"

"What? No."

"I'd do it," said Jenny, "Except some of the Brain Embryo cables look like they're *alive*. I don't want to unplug them and kill something."

"What's wrong with the Brain Embryo?" I said. "This is a Brain Embryo cookout. The whole point is to show it off."

"Nothing, I mean, it's a nice screensaver—"

"The starfield is the *title screen*," I said. "No one is actually playing Handle the Real Style?"

"I don't know how it works! Where's the other controllers? Are we all supposed to get cozy on the abacus?"

"Curic only sent the one controller," I said. "It's like a PC."

"Well, that's not a good party system, right?" said Jenny. "So, Xbox?"

"No! If we set up the Xbox, the boys will turn this party into a Temple Sphere fragfest and the girls will be pissed."

"They're pissed right now," said Jenny. "Can you ask Curic for more controllers or something?"

ABlum: hey are u awake

Curic: What a question! I'm always awake.

ABlum: i need multiplayer on the brain embryo
it is a party emergency
can you drop me some hardware
or give me some instructions

Curic: I can't drop anything anymore, by arrangement with your government.
Many humans were worried that if we dropped small things like video game systems we might also drop large things, like asteroids.

ABlum: shit
ok what about instructions?
could you just find me a multiplayer game
i am cooking right now

Curic: There are no multiplayer games for the Brain Embryo.

ABlum: what??

Curic: It was a primitive computer.

ABlum: dude every non-portable game console in human history has supported multiplayer
do you know the name of the very first human video game?
tennis for two
for TWO

Curic: Things were different for us.

ABlum: shit

Bizarro Kate slammed the screen door open. "Jenny, your *weird friend* is here," she called out.

"That doesn't go very far," said Jenny. "What's she look like?"

"It's a dude," said Bizarro Kate. "The perv with the pecs."

"That's *Ariel's* friend," said Jenny. "Go talk to Bai," she told me. "Get him to keep Dana in his pants while real people are around."

"Okay, take over," I said. I handed her the tongs.

"Take over what?" said Jenny. "You only need to turn the meat once. This isn't the Fifties." I was gone into the house.

In the living room, Bai was introducing Dana to Jenny's friends. "So it's like a paper doll?" said one unsuspecting nerd girl.

"No, she's so much more than that!" said Bai. "See, she—"

"Heeeey," I called out, slapping Bai on the back, feeling like a big fat faker. "Let me get you a beer!" I steered him, not into the kitchen—O treacherous Ariel!—but up the stairs to the landing.

"Soooo," I said, "what's new with you and Dana?"

Bai beamed. "Check it out, bro," he said, and slipped his phone into my hand. "Finally. Nearly perfect."

Over the past year, Dana has gone from a generic "blonde" virtual girlfriend, through a variety of virtual plastic surgeries, hair restyles, and wardrobe changes, to someone who looks to be doing a pretty good cosplay of Dana Light. Yes, Bai has finally recreated the PS2-era outfit that we all loved when we were teenagers, with the leather pants and knife holsters on the belt and everything. The knife holsters are probably not part of the standard virtual girlfriend repertoire, since the first I saw of Dana, she was checking her makeup in a camo-pattern compact; and when she noticed that a strange man was looking at her, she smiled coyly and said nothing. Neither of which are animation loops I associate with a fucking ruthless bounty hunter.

"That's really... accurate," I said, not wanting to say "good."

"I decided it was time," said Bai. "Last week, you know, I figured that we'd finally got to the point in our relationship where I could introduce her to my parents."

"What, with the knives and everything?"

"No!" said Bai, like he thought I was a real dummy. He took back the phone and tapped through some menus. Dana's outfit shifted to a purple evening gown, hair up in a bun—well, not a bun, but whatever that's called—a diamond necklace around her neck that probably cost about as much as a real necklace, despite being made of compressed object code instead of compressed carbon.

"She sure cleans up nice," I said.

"Yeah, but it doesn't matter," said Bai. "Because my folks hate her. Just like they hate every woman I've ever dated. Because she's not Chinese."

I did not think this was the real reason, but I just said: "Well, her *hardware's* Chinese."

"Parents!" said Bai. "What can you do? Did you say you were getting me a beer?"

"In a minute," I said. "I have to ask you a favor. Do you know why gay people can't get married in Texas?"

"How is that a favor?"

"Do-you-know-the-reason."

"Well, yeah, it's because of peoples'... whatever."

"The word is 'prejudice,'" I said. "Fifty years ago, no one wanted to see an Asian guy with a white girl."

"Fifty years ago? How about now?"

"And ten years from now, a human will want to marry an extraterrestrial, and people will be upset about that. But right now, what people don't want to see is a flesh-and-blood human carrying on a relationship with a piece of software." (Putting aside for the moment all questions about the capabilities and limitations of that software, I added to myself.)

Dana frowned at the silence of Bai thinking over what I'd said. She looked at me. "Hi, Ariel," she said.

"Hi, Dana," I said.

"So, Jenny has a problem with..." said Bai.

"I just want her to have a good time at the party," I said. "She's had a really tough time lately with shitty clients," I said. "Can you... humor her? Just don't wave Dana around at her friends."

"Dana'll miss the party," said Bai.

"Is there any functional difference between introducing her to people at the party, and introducing her to people on TV?"

"Not really," Bai mumbled. He looked up. "Okay, no Jenny's friends. But I can introduce her to you, yeah?"

"She already knows me," I said, "from last time. She called me Ariel just now."

"Awesome!" said Bai. "The cognitive buffs are working!" Dana detected that Bai was happy, and played a big smile animation.

From downstairs, I heard a chilling sound: the Xbox Forever was booting up. *Et tu, Jenny?*

I jumped down the stairs. "Beer's in the fridge," I called back to Bai.

In the living room, Jenny was nowhere to be seen. Bizarro Kate and two more of Jenny's friends were unfolding my old dancing-game pad.

"Hey!" said Bizarro Kate. "I remembered you had Super Slide Dance Challenge, so we switched the TV cables. Hope that's okay. We didn't touch your Constellation system."

Blog post, June 28, late night

Well, the cookout was terrible. Jenny got angry at me because of something I said to Bai, but we worked it out while throwing beer bottles into the recycling dumpster, and then she helped me clean up the nonrecyclable trash and we relaxed in the living room.

"I really hope that *was* the last cookout," I said. I was playing a game on the Brain Embryo.

"I don't know what cookout you were at," said Jenny. "The one we had here was fine. Bizarro Kate and Martin finally hooked up. They left together, anyway."

"That's a chilling thought," I said. "I can already see their kids running around in little polo shirts and catgirl ears."

"People had a good time," said Jenny.

"I wanted to show them the Brain Embryo," I said. "But I was busy with emergencies and you guys didn't want to put in a little effort to figure things out."

"It's a party," said Jenny. "Not a time for strenuous mental effort. Here, lemme try it now." I left the Brain Embryo console and went to the bathroom.

"I like the art," said Jenny when I came back. "It's like playing a Kandinsky."

"You're not moving your guy," I said. "You're just looking around and the background's scrolling."

"Let me figure it out, *pendejo*," said Jenny. "Not everything has to work immediately. Any docs on this thing?"

"Uh, it's called <u>Sayable Spice</u>. Apparently it shatters the taboos of Dhihe Coastal Coalition society, though I don't know what those might be. It's got a skewed histogram—that was a good idea you had."

"Okay," said Jenny. "Let's do this one."

"What? We're doing it now."

"Let's port it. It looks nice, and it's a good game that a few people didn't like because it was controversial. Sounds like a good choice."

"It was controversial to another species ninety million years ago," I said. "I'm still going through the list."

"The list has fifteen thousand games on it," said Jenny. "And then there's all the other systems you could be exploring. Curic said you could spend the rest of your life playing these games, and I would like to start getting paychecks before then. That means at some point making a decision and starting work. So let's do this."

"What if there's something wrong with <u>Sayable Spice</u>?"

"Yeah, there probably is. You know how I complain about my web design clients?"

"How you give them exactly what they ask for, and then they change their minds. Which is what I want to avoid."

"That's part of the process," said Jenny. "You build something, and then you find out it sucks, and you use that information build something else. The only way to avoid this problem is to never get started and never get paid."

"Okay," I said, "the decision is made." Crispy Duck Games is porting <u>Sayable Spice</u>. (Offer subject to change.)

Chapter 8:
They Came For Our Twinkies

Blog post, June 29

Woo hoo! Thank you, Charlene Siph! Constellation citizens are now being issued US tourist visas!

ABlum: i'm filling out paperwork for your visa
i need to know if you're a "person of good character"

Curic: I sure hope not.

ABlum: i'm going to put down "yes"

I have to fill out the forms twice for Curic, because the government considers a Farang's differentiated mind to be two different people in the same body. With that attitude, I don't know how they're ever going to get Constellation Library service down here. And I certainly wouldn't want to be the guy who has to sort out the paperwork for Her.

Blogging will be light for a few days. I'm working on a project for a friend. Also for money.

Real life, July 4

We all got into Bai's SUV and drove through traffic to the Constellation landing site; me and Jenny and Jenny's nephew Eduardo, who was more interested in seeing a real spaceship land than in meeting a space alien.

"Is Curic going to fit in the car?" said Jenny. "Physically? Does anyone actually know?"

Bai looked back at Jenny and backed the car out of my unused driveway. "Durrr, we're not idiots, Jenny," he said. (Bai's douchebag tendencies rise to the surface when he gets nervous.) "Farang are hobbit-size. She can sit on your lap."

"Not on *my* lap," said Jenny.

The road to the landing site was still packed and the approach full of rubberneckers, but after showing Curic's ticket to the guards, we were able to park. The first thing we saw was National Guard soldiers loading packages into a temporary structure. This was what we got now instead of drop-shipments. Packages came down on the shuttles, they went through customs, and were delivered by UPS. The Guard was mostly there to keep people out of the structure. This allows the population at large to avoid thinking about the Constellation dropping rocks on us.

We saw Curic's shuttle land and I signed her out at the immigration desk. Curic looked like the Farang picture on Wikipedia: short, heavy black/dark-purple fur, scary parrot beak and antennacles around the mouth. She doesn't smell bad, if you don't mind the smell of fur. (For the record, I look exactly like the dude on the Wikipedia page for "Human".)

But one thing I hadn't expected was the way she walked. Curic waddled out of the holding area and made every CGI alien ever created look fake doing it. She moved like a real thing, not like a motion capture.

"She's gorgeous," said Jenny.

"That's not the word I'd use," I said, "but I see where you're coming from." What Jenny saw was that Curic was *real*. This was really happening.

As we left the immigration Quonset hut, Curic took out the prosthetic tongue that lets her speak human languages and made a noise at the customs official. It sounded like "K'chua!"

Then she told me: "I have important scientific equipment for you." We went to the temporary structure and signed out eight wooden crates with the Constellation Shipping logo stenciled on them. The crates were full of computers and game systems, which, in turn, were full of moon dust and nanomolecular machines.

"You think you brought enough stuff, bro?" said Bai, having decided that being male half the time was enough to qualify as "bro."

"This may be the only delivery you get for a long time," said Curic ominously.

You don't see a lot of these crates in real life, but they looked exactly like the generic wooden crates that have been lying around first-person shooter maps for the past twenty years. Bai and I carried one of the largest crates together, and by mutual agreement set it down halfway to the car. We watched tiny Curic hustle past us, clasping a crate to her chest that was as big as she was.

"How can you carry these?" I called out. Eduardo ran around in the grass chasing dragonflies, ignoring the space alien.

"Are you kidding?" said Curic. "It's like half gravity here."

With the prosthetic tongue in her mouth, Curic had an awesome oozy squeaky European-type accent, like a movie villain high on helium. I thought it was awesome, anyway, but I can see how TV producers might not like it. So most Farang use the Oyln-English translator, or if their English is really good, they just use the vocalizer. This works out very well because the vocalizer has George Clooney's voice—much more mediagenic.

By the time we'd loaded the SUV, the Texas morning was in full effect. I wiped my brow and just smeared the sweat around.

"Curic," said Bai, oblivious to the heat. "I want you to meet my girlfriend, Dana Light."

"Can we meet Dana in the car?" I said. But Bai had already slid his phone out of his pocket.

Curic took the phone. "Hello, Dana Light," she said, more to the phone than to the person on the screen. I looked over Curic's shoulder—her whole body, actually. Dana was sitting on her fake couch typing on her fake tablet, writing in her fake blog about her semi-fake feelings. She didn't notice Curic.

"Hey, I'm greeting you!" said Curic. Dana looked up, but didn't say anything. "By human standards, your sexual partner is quite rude," said Curic, making to hand back the phone.

"Probably the face recognition doesn't work on Farang," I said.

Curic snatched the phone back. "Your sexual partner is implemented in software?" she asked. Curic shook the phone as though she expected a tiny Dana to fall out. "Is it self-aware?"

"That's a disputed question," I said.

"Does your relationship enjoy legal sanction?"

"No," said Bai, "'cause of prejudice."

Jenny cracked her door open. "What's the holdup?" she asked.

"My own curiosity, I'm afraid," said Curic. She handed Dana back to Bai. "Let's take cover before we all die of heatstroke."

We escaped into the car, where Jenny had the A/C running. We all sat squeezed into our seats, our feet propped up on the smaller crates, Curic sitting atop a crate despite Eduardo's offer to share a seatbelt.

"Hey, Curic," said Jenny, "Eddie wants to be an astronaut."

"Isn't he a little young to have fully formed desires about future societal roles?" asked Curic, peering suspiciously at Eduardo. Eduardo is taller than Curic.

"He's a kid who wants to be an astronaut," said Jenny. "It's cute."

"I'm an astronaut," said Curic. "It's not cute."

"It is cute," said Jenny.

"Curic, what was that you said to the immigration guy?" I said. Bai backed us out of the parking space and honked at some rubberneckers.

Curic took her tongue out again. "K'chua!" she said.

"Yeah, what's it mean?"

The prosthetic went back in. "It's a Nuk word. That's an Auslander language that's good for bringing down curses. The closest English translation might be 'fuck the system.'"

"That's very punk," I said.

"Don't swear in front of Eddie," said Jenny. "My sister is gonna think I taught him that."

"What, 'K'chua!'?" said Bai.

"The other one!"

"It's not the best translation," Curic continued, oblivious, "because when *you* say 'fuck the system,' you're addressing another person. 'K'chua' is something you say to the *system*."

A car pulled out of the parking lot behind us. "Are we being *followed*?" I said.

Curic squirmed to look between the huge crates in the cargo hold. "We had better not be," she said. And we weren't.

Once we got underway, sophisticated Jenny asked the same stupid question I'd asked when I first met Curic. "So, Curic, boy or girl?"

"What?" said Curic, unsure if Jenny was even talking to her. "I am both boy and girl."

"But not at the same time, right?" said Bai. "Are we talking to the boy Curic or the girl Curic?"

"Ah—" Curic muttered to herself— "the smaller gametes. The male."

"You don't just know?" I said.

"Forgive me, that's not how we classify it," said Curic. "We didn't know about sex differences until scientific times. In caveman days, you'd relax in a nice tide pool, some other people would come along later and relax in the same pool, and a few tides later, there'd be kids growing in the pool."

"How'd you know whose kid was whose?" asked Jenny.

"Who needs to know?" said Curic. "Kids are kids."

"Wait a minute," said Jenny, "are you *naked*?"

"Yes, because your planet's so damn hot," said Curic.

"Where'd you get the wood for these crates?" I asked quickly.

"It's fake wood," said Curic. "I used it as a joke. Last night I was hangin' with a Mzungu friend from Constellation Shipping, and I'm like 'ha ha, I chopped up some Wazungu-style lifeforms and made containers out of their corpses.'"

"That's a joke?"

"It was funnier when I was female," said Curic. "Anyway, my friend can take it. Is 'hangin'' really a word? I ask because there's a punctuation symbol at the end."

A half-hour of this sort of stream-of-consciousness later, Bai parked in my driveway, and we all fell out and stretched our legs. "Before we do anything else," said Curic, "there's a ritual I'd like to perform with you."

"What is it, a religious ritual or something?" said Jenny.

"I've been advised to change the subject whenever someone brings up religion," said Curic, "but it seems safe to tell you that the answer is no. We'll need some small, flat items."

"How about Jenny's tits?" said Bai.

Jenny cupped her hands over Eduardo's ears. "How 'bout your undescended testicles, Bai?" she hissed.

"Coins," I said, hands already in my pockets feeling around. "I have coins."

"I don't know what a coin is," said Curic, "but it seems like the best choice of the three."

I handed a quarter to Curic. She took it, being careful not to touch my hand, and started to say something. Then she did a double take and cooed to herself in Oyln. She held the quarter between two fingers in sick fascination, turning it over and over as though it were the still-wriggling corpse of a trilobite.

"Oh, I see!" she finally said in English. "This is *money*!"

"Is that okay?"

"I thought it was all in software," said Curic.

"We got bills, too," said Bai.

"This is fine," said Curic. She flipped the quarter onto the driveway. It came to rest on a crack in the concrete, nestled in dead grass.

"This is called the star-draw," said Curic. "It binds the five of us in common purpose. Everyone, take a piece of money and toss it down, just like I did."

Jenny looked in her purse for a dime, took aim, and pegged Curic's quarter with a precision shot. "Don't try to hit my money," said Curic. "Just throw it in the same direction."

Bai and I threw our coins. Eduardo's rolled into the front lawn, which I had landscaped in Southwestern style so I didn't have to water it. The coins on the ground looked like this:

o

    *

      O

    o

     O

A little like the Constellation Shipping logo, except with a few coins instead of a lot of stars.

"This is a constellation," said Curic. "There is no pattern. We just happened to draw the stars a certain way."

"So why... did we... do it?" said Bai.

"This one is *ours*," said Curic. "A constellation is a pattern claimed from randomness. This shape identifies the five of us, right now, and the project we're about to carry out."

"Uh," I said, "what is the project? I thought we were just going to spend Independence Day together."

"I told you in email," said Curic. "We're going to scan your house."

"I thought you meant, like, *look at* my house."

No. She meant *scan*. This was how I was to pay for all the old computers packed in their FPS crates. Just like during the first Internet boom, the coin of the realm was sweet, juicy personal information. Curic had some super-sensors in her hands and antennacles, and that day she touched and/or snuffled *everything in my house*.

Curic systematically snooped through every room, and every box in every room, and every box inside another box. And if that box should contain a third box, she'd be interested in that box as well. She emptied out my change jar (money!). She rifled through my game cartridges and disks. She itemized my refrigerator magnets. She stuck an antennacle in my shampoo. She offered to image my hard drives and flash cards. (I said no, but eventually gave her the drive with my ROMs and music.) I had to hold a stepstool steady so she could climb up on the kitchen counter or into the high closet space, which is how I know so much about what she smells like. She crawled under my bed, running her hands over my winter clothes, skimming my old notebooks from college.

This took seven hours. I would have gone crazy except for the bizarre questions Curic constantly asked to keep me on my toes. "What's your favorite book on this shelf?" "Why is this insulating foam blue instead of white?" "Did you get this yourself or did someone give it to you?" "Tell me why Sonic is important to you." "Why don't you have any musical instruments?"

She asked me questions about *stuff she'd given me*. "What color do you see this as?" pointing to one of the cables that came with the Brain Embryo. Everything she touched, she put back within an inch of its original location.

If that star-draw we did really had any connection to our house-scanning project, Curic and I were definitely the bright stars in the constellation. Jenny had a grand old time heckling me, telling Curic to look for porn (who keeps hard copies of porn?), and playing with Eduardo on my PS4. Bai's main contribution was to drive to the grocery store for a lot of little plastic bags to hold the food from all the cans Curic opened.

Once it cooled down a little, Curic scanned the exterior. She climbed out my bedroom window and walked fearlessly up and down the roof, unafraid of falling—half gravity, right?

Bai left in the early evening for a date with Dana, counting her polygons or something. I flopped exhausted on the couch next to Jenny. "Eddie wants to go to the fireworks," she said. "They start at eight-thirty, but my sister is having a picnic at eight, and we can drop him off."

"We can't take Curic out in public," I said.

"Says who? It's the Fourth of July. We're going to keep her cooped up in your house for twenty-four hours?"

"Says the BEA. They don't want Curic to start a riot."

Curic padded into the living room. "What kind of person do you think I am?" she asked. "I'm not going to instigate a riot!"

"Other people might see you and decide to riot," I said.

"That's fucked up," said Curic. "What are the fireworks?"

"Colorful rocket-propelled explosions," said Jenny.

"So, the riot has extenuating circumstances."

"Eddie, where did you get that?" asked Jenny. Eduardo had cinched a large, sharp red fractal onto his wrist and was punching the air like the newest member of the Nuclear Ninjas.

"I made that for him," said Curic. "It's a toy."

"What's it made of? Jesus! It looks like Skewer Sue's bracelet."

"I believe you would classify it as a plastic."

"Well, it's—honey, take it off. You'll cut yourself. Jesus."

"I apologize," said Curic. "Our research indicated that human kids love fractals of dimension 1.4. Ariel, please take me to the fireworks. If your government contact tries to fuck you over, you can say that I specifically asked for this."

"What difference will that make?"

"I am the representative of an ancient and powerful civilization," Curic squeaked. "They know not to fuck with me."

Jenny had covered Eduardo's ears again. "You know that 'fuck' is a swear word, right?" I said.

"Oh," said Curic. "You swear too much, Ariel."

As it got dark, we all walked to the park for the fireworks, Curic strolling along like it was nothing. Nobody noticed, or they just thought I had an ugly kid. Then Jenny and Curic had the bright idea to hit the bars for some live music, which I never do often enough, but I didn't think it was a good time.

"Remember the riot," I cautioned.

"I remember you being afraid of a riot that didn't happen," said Curic.

"We'll be fine," said Jenny. "People are always saying to Keep Austin Weird." She pointed at Curic. "Well, here is Weird."

"It's true," said Curic.

Against my better judgment, we went, and we had a great time. Curic was the guest of honor. She drank a dozen free shot glasses of beer and ate a lot of Twinkies, and everywhere we went, she was invited onstage to sing with the band. Her Peter Lorre voice is totally incompatible with human music and everyone loved it, unlike the time I got drunk and climbed onstage at the Dog Pound.

Around eleven, Curic began acting tipsy, but it was just her male brain going to sleep and her female brain waking up. There was no memory loss—girl-Curic still knew where she was and what we were doing—but there were drastic personality changes. In particular, girl-Curic proved to be a lot rowdier than boy-Curic. Or maybe she was getting tipsy after all. Eventually she knocked over a glass and apologized a lot and we took a taxi back to my place. The taxi driver wouldn't take our money, but he did want his picture taken with Curic.

We arrived at one in the morning. Jenny went upstairs and zonked out on my bed without even asking me, so I sat on the couch and talked with Curic for a couple hours, the way you talk when you meet someone from another country. Curic doesn't sleep, so I left her with a curated stack of comic books Jenny had brought for her, and staggered into the retro-game room to sleep on the spare couch.

Blog post, July 5

Happy Fourth of July! Or, if you're not American, happy fourth of July! Yesterday was Curic's first visit to Earth, and we had a hell of a time, so busy I didn't have time to write about it. Which worked out well because I was also *forbidden* from writing about it until Curic had safely returned to Ring City.

Curic snooped through my house and got drunk and taught us all a new swear word, but most importantly for this blog, she brought down crates and crates of ancient Constellation gaming hardware. After a scant few hours of sleep, I woke up at four in the morning to loud clicky-clacky noises from the living room. I thought it was an alien invasion and (tabloid TV news sting) it was! Curic was playing with the Brain Embryo! Twisting and flicking the abacus beads, flipping and pulling the switches. Ignoring the television, staring at the empty Plexiglass display on the front of the unit, playing with light I couldn't see.

I turned on the light. "Hey," I said, rubbing my eyes.

"Hmmph," said Curic. Her antennacles finished feeding a Twinkie into her mouth, and she put her prosthetic tongue back in.

"He—" she swallowed the Twinkie. "Hello, Ariel."

"What's up?"

"I don't play games very often. This seemed like an appropriate time."

Unlike me with my genius plan to play only the most enduring Brain Embryo games, Curic was just trying random games from the all-in-one pirate cartridge. However, as someone who can perceive the RF frequencies, she could at least see the whole game. So I give you **Curic's Capsule Reviews** (patent pending):

Dangerously Unbalanced Boat: "It's supposed to be a boat, but it doesn't look or act like a boat at all." ("How do you know it's a boat?") "Because that's the name of the game."

Kryrtur: "This is a famous game where you have to get three in a row. This game is still around, but the technology is improved, so you have to get eighty in a row."

Solox: "If you like these games, this is a really great one. It takes a long time to get anywhere, which I guess is important."

Enjoyable Reactor: "The control doesn't do anything. I think this is just a game for causing hallucinations." (Not kidding. She turned this one on and her antennacles tried to crawl around to the back of her head.)

Prophecy From Space: "This is a game about whatever was popular back then."

Sadly, Constellation tourist visas are only good for 24 hours, so after breakfast and a brief but embarrassingly personal anthropological interview, it was back to the Austin spaceport. I'll never forget the great camaraderie we enjoyed on our night out, her oozy singing, or the way I'm pretty sure she peed in my bathroom sink.

In related news, I've discovered that while she was on my PS4, Jenny used my account to download Lost Empires: Inca, the greatly inferior (yes, Jenny!) action puzzler which I'm now stuck with.

K'chua!

Chapter 9:
Import System

Curic: I did not pee in your sink.

ABlum: well there's a terrible smell in there

Curic: I performed only normal oral hygiene.

ABlum: its pretty bad

Curic: There's nothing in your sink that wasn't originally part of a Twinkie.
Except for some adapter bacteria.

ABlum: im going to go out on a limb and say the bacteria are the problem
i will kill them with bleach

Curic: OK.

ABlum: btw where did you pee when you were here on earth?

Curic: n/a Not everybody has to evacuate every ten minutes.

Blog post, July 6

Crate update! I'm super busy but I couldn't resist opening one of the crates Curic brought down to Earth. What I found inside quickly convinced me to get back to work. If I start opening crates, I'll spend all my time organizing the hardware and you'll never see me again.

I know this about myself, so I thought I'd play it safe. Curic's manifest listed crate #6 as including some items related to the Brain Embryo, so I opened it and found, among other things:

> * The Massmonger 31, an Inostrantsi computer that looks like a roll of heavy-gauge chicken wire.

> * Four chalk pills, each the size of a basketball. These are Sea Level game units. (Sea Level is a Wazungu game—you swallow the system and carve it into some specified shape during the digestive process.)

> * Twelve Alien teledildonic devices in replica original packaging.

> * Replacement abacus beads for the Brain Embryo.

> * The Brain Eclipse, successor system to the Brain Embryo.

> * ...and a plastic board.

Yes, a plastic board qualifies as a Brain Embryo peripheral. If you put it under a blacklight, you can see the symbol of Clan Interference painted on it in ultraviolet paint.

I actually got a little excited about this because Clan Interference made Sayable Spice, plus several other games I hadn't played. Of those games, Bad Things in the Water, Legend of the Bystander, and Double Attack are listed as being "compatible" with this peripheral. But c'mon, it's literally a piece of plastic. "Compatibility" just means that when you exit the game, you get two or three ideograms to write on the board.

I copied some Double Attack ideograms onto the board with a dry-erase marker, but nothing happened and the ideograms won't dry-erase. It's a mystery. It's a mystery that's going back into the crate. Too much to do! I'm going to be living with these crates 'til the day I die.

Blog post, July 7

And the deluge continues. The planets have aligned, the missing semantic link has clicked into place, and the Constellation Database of Electronic Games of a Certain Complexity is now available in English! This is great news. Now all y'all can get in on the extraterrestrial game fun, instead of waiting for me to crawl through these crates. The English CDBOEGOACC is amazing, like those mysterious game catalogs from when we were bony little kids with curly hair.

ABlum: who can i thank for translating this?

Curic: I will send you an achievement graph.

ABlum: no your achievement graphs have 10 million nodes
i don't want to thank the whole damn constellation
just tell me the name of one person who i can buy a beer

Curic: If you looked at the graph you would see a
distinctive bottleneck:
the Small Batch Data Cleanup Overlay, who
translated between old
versions of SAME and various human
languages at the request of the History of Life Overlay.

ABlum: ok who is in charge of the data cleanup overlay?

Curic: That's not a real question.

ANYHOW, I offer big thanks to a randomly selected member of the Small Batch Data Cleanup Overlay. That'd be Jeroen Vivekananda of Peregrini Ring, Ring City. I would buy you a beer, Jeroen, but your body heat would vaporize the beer before you could swallow it. So, instead, accept this mention on my blog.

I'm now seeding the English CDBOEGOACC translation, but if you got the original SAME version back in June, do yourself a favor and just download the translation program from the Constellation's website.

Please send your CDBOEGOACC pointers to games you'd like to see reviewed! Or, better yet, start your own damn blog. I'll even provide a crowd-pleasing concept for you: search the translated CDBOEGOACC for superlatives like "worst," and try to find the worst games in the universe. Here are some choice quotes I found with a quick skim, most of them from Constellation-era descriptions compiled by the people who put together and maintained (maintain?) the CDBOEGOACC:

> The worst of Pi Mue Iormue Sae's games and perhaps the proximate cause of bis death. Shortly after publishing this game bhe announced a fourth in the Canister series. It was never discovered whether bis assassin was motivated to stop the proposed sequel, or simply wanted revenge for this third game.

> May cause nausea, pheromonal overload, and severe cognitive dissonance.

> This game is a memetic hazard and should be labeled as such. For countermeasures see [broken link].

From a contemporaneous review: "I have played five games and this is the worst."

From a *positive* review: "Vent your egg sacs before playing this game." Not into my sink!

Blog post, July 9

GAME REVIEWS OF THE INFINITE VOID 2.0 PRESENTS
Recapture that Remarkable Taste (c. 17 million years ago)
A game by the Yaiskek Corporation
Reviewed by Ariel Blum

Publisher: Various.
Platforms: Simulates Hi-Def False Daylight, Your Return, Becomes A Better Value Over Time, et al.
ESRB rating: M for frequent sexual references

This is not the Sayable Spice review, but it is a review I'm mentally capable of writing, so be happy with the hand life deals ya, as my father used to say. (Presumably he still says this, but I haven't heard it in a while, because I stopped complaining to him when I got a blog.)

Jenny and I experienced Sayable Spice in an abstract space of pure game possibility. The game doesn't take place in the typical environments of Farang games: the beach, the underwater cave, the forest, the hot spring where the water's too hot to stay for long. The famous night-sky nebula is nowhere to be seen; there's not even a day-night cycle. With no English translation and no visual clues as to what's going on, there's only so much you can say about a game. More to the point, there's only so far you can play it.

In Sayable Spice, you start out as an amoeba-like circle, glistening with vagueness. As a circle, life is good, but you can't do shit. You can explore the two-dimensional world and bump into other shapes, each with a complicated "lock" on one side that you might fit into if you weren't shaped like a damn circle.

Fortunately, you can pick up *icons* that change your shape. Touch a square icon and your circle becomes a semicircle attached to half a square. Touch a triangle and the semicircle turns into a quarter-circle connected to the half-square by two sides of a triangle. There are many icons and your shape gets complicated real fast. But once you've got a few icons, you can shuffle them around, altering your shape to form a kind of appendage that's the right shape to fit into a lock and pick up a tool.

And that's where our understanding of the game stalled. Nice game mechanic, no way of seeing through it to the game itself. Sayable Spice was made by Edink-speaking Farang, ninety million years ago. No one speaks Edink anymore and no English translator is available.

ABlum: why not? we have huge corpus of text
i could make my own translator if i had google's computer
you have computronium + strong ai
what is the problem?

Curic: Strong AI is the problem.
Farang languages are multispacial
and feature internal dialogue.
Edink-English translation software would have nearly
full sentience.
You're asking me to create a new form of intelligent
life and give it to you.
Are you going to take care of it?

Curic's good! She's already figured out how to play on my fear of commitment.

Jenny and I considered options like making up our own game using the

Sayable Spice mechanics and *calling* it "Sayable Spice," or just choosing another game to port. But then on Tuesday, the CDBOEGOACC was translated into English, and I noticed something I'd overlooked: we aren't the first people to do this. Seventeen million years ago, on another planet, the Aliens made a remake of Sayable Spice. And thanks to Curic's crate deliveries, I can play the *remake* in English.

ABlum: it looks like a lot of the alien consoles and games are based on constellation tech/games mostly farang tech actually

---

Curic: We probably gave it to them during the contact mission.

ABlum: there was a contact mission?

Curic: Sure, how do you think they joined the Constellation?

You know the Aliens. The eight-foot monkey lizards. Charlene Siph, the Constellation ambassador, is an Alien—she narrated the welcome video and she's on TV all the time. Seventeen million years ago, the Aliens' home planet hosted a number of early-industrial civilizations who made radio and then physical contact with the (smaller) Constellation. Within a generation, the Aliens were building personal computers.

OH MY GOODNESS IT'S NEW HARDWARE TIME AGAIN
Simulates Hi-Def False Daylight (c. 17 million years ago)
Species: Alien
Civilization: Ip Shkoy
Developer: Ktei Corporation (plus many clone-makers)
Publishing Lifetime: 7 Earth years

You'll find the Simulates Hi-Def False Daylight in crate #2, underneath a ton of useless and/or time-sink hardware. It's very similar to the Brain Embryo, so if you've already set up a Brain Embryo (I don't recommend this), you'll have no problem setting this bad boy up. To hook it up to your television, you just need to remove the first seventy-three million years' worth of adapter cables, and switch out the spectrum converter at the end. Everything should look familiar, from the abacus-like controls (greatly enlarged for Alien hands) to the all-in-one pirate-cart cylinder screwed into the data socket.

Simulates Hi-Def False Daylight is not an *exact* clone of the Brain Embryo, but it was designed by people who'd taken a lot of Brain Embryos apart. It lacks the Farang system's RF emitters, since Aliens don't have the Farang water-sense any more than humans do. But its processor handles the same six-dimensional polygons, even though without the RF emitters, you really only need three.

Play <u>Recapture That Remarkable Taste</u> and it will become clear that <u>Sayable Spice</u> lacks the standard Farang forests and beaches because the game takes place *inside your brain*. That vague circle you play as isn't a person: it's a memory tomia, a concept from Farang psychology. Your job is to assemble little bits of memories from the subconscious and try to get the attention of the conscious mind.

In this game, you play the sense of taste; the sense of *remembered* taste. The little shaped icons are chemical compounds, and after picking up a few, you can shuffle them into a shape that fits into a "flavor" (the tools). The concept of a flavor, whatever. The challenge is in managing your inventory of remembered chemical compounds—this isn't <u>Proty's Big Escape</u> where the power-ups are arranged so you get one right before you need it. If you have to drop a flavor, you lose all the compounds that formed the "key" you used to grab it, and you go right back to being a circle.

Yeah, at this point, Jenny and I ran into another wall. Pick up three or four related flavors, and this memory tomia catches the attention of the conscious mind. Then you supposedly get a playable flashback or daydream related to the flavors. So if in the remake we create flavors like "roasted peanuts," "sauerkraut," and "beer," you'd put them together to get a day at the ballpark—some memory or fantasy that fills in the life story of whoever's brain you're in.

But who's gonna know about peanuts/sauerkraut/beer, seventeen million years from now? Even an English translation is useless when the most important words in the game are transliterations with no cultural context. Man, fuck you Ip Shkoy Aliens, with your evike and your prash pods.

How do I know that this flavor-combination thing is part of the original <u>Sayable Spice</u> and not something the Yaiskek Corporation made up for the remake? Because that would imply that the Yaiskek Corporation gave a damn about creativity. This is a company that got its start recording dance-hall radio broadcasts from the Alien civilizations on other continents and rebroadcasting the tapes in Ip Shkoy cities without permission.

Just like with humanity's first computers, most of the early games for the

Hi-Def False Daylight were digital versions of analog Alien games, or (not so much like humanity's first computers) clones of Constellation titles adapted for Alien senses. Yaiskek decided that this was their kind of business, and jumped into the market with a bunch of cheap clone games. When they ran out of Farang games to clone, Yaiskek cloned their competitors' games, and after learning their competitors' tricks, they switched to selling cheap 'n' trashy mask cylinders—more on these later.

And now you see the real problem with <u>Recapture that Remarkable Taste</u>: it's a game made by people who had nothing invested in the franchise. Like, imagine those awful movie adaptations of decent game series like <u>Unauthorized</u>, made for the sake of a quick buck and/or tax shelter. Except imagine that instead of making a movie, you made another video game. That's <u>Recapture that Remarkable Taste</u>. The writing's cheesy, the graphics make it hard to distinguish between basic geometric shapes, and it was originally released on a memory cylinder with two other ported Farang games—your sure sign of quality.

But even Yaiskek couldn't fuck up <u>Sayable Spice</u> that badly, which means Jenny and I should be able to do a pretty good job. There's something grown-up about this game—the way it assumes you can keep track of complex shapes, the fact that it takes place in the mind of someone old enough to have flashbacks. Makes me glad I started my own game studio. If I'd pitched this remake to the Brazilian company, they'd turn it into a game about making birthday cakes for all your *moe* friends.

Blog post, July 9, late night

A special message to "Starman Jones." In the interests of interstellar coop- eration, fuck you. I call you out, sir.

Since the English translation of the CDBOEGOACC came out, I've seen about five new blogs devoted to going through the database looking for in- teresting/funny/stupid things. These blogs are awesome. And then there's your blog, where you lead people on with made-up bullshit. You're claiming you've actually played these games. You're bluffing to get attention. You're the kid in seventh grade claiming he's got the codes to make Dana Light take her clothes off.

You write about "the majestic games of the Wazungu, which take days to play." Did you actually get a replica system (which, as I understand it, would be the size of a refrigerator), learn about pre-Constellation Wazungu culture, and spend days playing their games to find out if they're majestic? Or did you just wait until there was a translation of the CDBOEGOACC and then start a blog full of fake reviews and purple-ass travelogue prose?

Seeing people jump on this translation, even in stupid ways, made me remember how privileged I am that I get to play these games for real. I'm going to try to be better about bringing them to you on a regular basis. And things will get better. I doubt there's a computer in the CDBOEGOACC more powerful than today's phones. Eventually we'll write emulators. We have the rest of our lives to get to know the Constellation. There is no need for bullshit.

Chapter 10:
K.I.S.S.I.N.G.

Blog post, July 10

Hey, stop sending me email about the stupid plastic board. I know it's in the CDBOEGOACC—that's where I found out which games were "compatible" with it. It's called "Where Sun Can See" and it's described as a way of sharing game data and messages.

Sharing with whom? Well, <u>Double Attack</u>, for instance, is a game you play over a period of time, alternating with your crossself. So it turns out the Farang *do* have two-player games, but both players share a body and switch off.

ABlum: do you ever have to leave messages to your other self?

Curic: No, we use the brain for that.
Young people sometimes have trouble taking their crossself's opinions and preferences into account. Written messages will help with that.

It's for kids, yeah? It's all part of the magic of growing up two different people in the same body.

Blog post, July 12

The best thing about the Simulates Hi-Def False Daylight system is the memory mask cylinders. See, Brain Embryo software comes on a little screw-in cylinders, each holding a single polished read-only work of computer art. When the Aliens remade the Brain Embryo as the Hi-Def False

Daylight, they added a socket to the top of each memory cylinder, into which you can screw another memory cylinder. You can daisy-chain cylinders without limit, each one patching the ROM of the cylinder above it, until the read time becomes atrocious and the computer's memory becomes a rancid soup of hacks and patches to that original program you've got teetering at the top of the tower.

A lot of small companies put out mask cylinders for popular games—level hacks, text hacks, graphics hacks. It was a good way to make some cash without worrying about boring things like originality or operating capital.

Recapture that Remarkable Taste was not a best-selling game, but it did well enough to have four mask cylinders. I don't own these cylinders—no space in the crates— but the all-in-one pirate cart can emulate them just like it emulates the games.

1. "RtRT: Closer Look": In Sayable Spice, the player character is a circle. In Recapture that Remarkable Taste, it's a little polygonic picture of an Alien. This patch changes the picture so that the Alien is, how to put this delicately, *totally not wearing any clothes*. Prurient interest and what I must assume are secondary sexual characteristics abound. (This cylinder was made by the Yaiskek corporation. They put out a nude hack for their own game!)

2. "Intelligent Multisystem 4": A big honking cylinder, dwarfing the RtRT cylinder itself in mass and circumference, containing its own dedicated processor and speaker. This one sits beneath all three games on the RtRT cylinder, and reads out the Pey Shkoy dialogue in a low-res robotic voice. Not sure why—it won't really help blind people play the games. Bonus points for coming up with a name so generic it could be a piece of human hardware.

3. "Recapture That Remarkable Time". A total conversion which changes the plot of the game so that it's making fun of old farts who wish the Constellation would go away, and who blame the ETs for everything that's wrong with Ip Shkoy society. RtRT came out fifty years after contact, so there must have been plenty of old farts around. Funny, but kind of cruel: the old fart player-character comes off as harmlessly confused, as if the Constellation had preempted *Matlock*. Much easier for a human to understand than RtRT.

4. "G'go Investigation: When You Gotta Die": Total de-version published by the G'go Corporation, makers of serial soap

operas in role-playing-game form. They removed all the
game mechanics: instead of chemicals and flavors, the
player character can interact with a bunch of annoying
NPCs from other G'go games. Each NPC delivers a one-
liner and then dies in a spectacular animation, eg. being
eaten by a sharklike creature, except the shark doesn't
even bother to eat the NPC, just pulls opens its stomach
and stuffs the NPC right into the gastric juices. For collec-
tors only.

I must say I feel some sympathy for these small-time con artists. There's a
whole year of my life which could be summed up as "Ariel puts out a mask
cylinder for a popular game." Even after quitting Reflex and the Brazilian
company, I'm *still* cranking out these mask cylinders, as those of you on my
friends list will soon find out.

Blog post, July 13

[This post is friends locked.]

Listen up. This one's for all my college friends who moved out of Austin and
who have been giving me shit about Bai ever since, as though I were his
designated caretaker. I have solved the Dana Light problem. Just not in the
way you wanted.

Before the Sexy Cookout on the 28th, my attitude was laissez-faire. With
the economy the way it is, I figured everyone should pick one luxury and
run with it. For instance, I have my crippling mortgage. Jenny has her art
(by this I mean her art *supplies*, not the $25 sketches she gets at UTAku-
Con). And Bai had Dana Light.

But at the Sexy Cookout, there was a little party-fart involving Bai and Dana.
As the party's on-call sysadmin, I manfully defused the Bai/Dana situation
by slandering Jenny. Even if you'd been there, you wouldn't have noticed it.
I grabbed Bai the beer I'd promised him and went off to fight other fires. But
Bai drank that beer, and then he drank another one, and eventually got up
the courage to corner me again and ask for an embarrassing favor.

"So I heard you got laid off, bro," he said.

"Actually, I quit," I said. "It's like I laid the *company* off."

"Yeah, well," said Bai. "Do you want to make some money?"

"I don't want to design wind turbines, if that's what you're asking," I said. "Did you not see where I announced that I was forming a game studio?"

"This isn't for work," said Bai. "'Spersonal. I want you to jailbreak Dana for me." His phone came out again; Dana was eating popcorn and watching one of Bai's taped shows. Which was always weird to me; I imagine the "real" Dana Light having more intense hobbies, like kickboxing, or LARPing wargames.

"What's... wrong with Dana?" I asked.

"Nothing!" said Bai. "I love Dana. But she's high maintenance. Every week she wants some sunglasses or a car or some other downloadable content. She's bleeding me dry, bro."

And here's the problem with your backseat driving of the Ariel-Bai relationship, guys. You weren't at the Sexy Cookout because you left town years ago. You still have this college-era picture of me and Bai in your heads, so you're imagining Bai from 2007 with some Dana-like piece of software from 2007, and me "putting up" with some vaguely-defined "shit."

Well, something happened in 2007: it was the fucking iPhone. People with money started pouring it into mobile, and once the up-front price of an app fell to a dollar, they started doing psychological research into apps designed to drive DLC upsell and in-app buys. I know y'all were snickering at my work for the Brazilian company with the ponies and the birthday cakes, but I saw this stuff firsthand. Sure as the Brazilians have the ten-year-old girls' number, there's someone next door in Bolivia who's got yours.

So when one of my posts is mirrored to your friendstream and you read it on your fancy contact-lens screen, don't use your single-point integrated contact manager to dictate an IM to me about how Bai needs to man up, bro, and I'm just making things worse. Software has changed since those carefree days at dear old alma mater, and so have we.

"Well, just don't buy her the stuff," I said, as you are probably saying right now.

"I don't want to buy her the stuff," said Bai, "but she gets... rrrrrr! You know?"

"Rrrrrr, huh?"

Maybe in 2007 a "virtual girlfriend" was an animated GIF that pole-danced on your desktop, but that was pre- the psychological research. Dana is a piece of software complex enough to fulfill whatever emotional needs Bai has right now, and to give a convincing impression of someone with needs of her own. The problem is that her needs are all paid downloadable content, not free things like cuddling. Dana has literally been programmed to want stuff forever and never be satisfied. And if there are "problems" that need "solving," that's the big one.

"We can't go on like this," said Bai. "It's not healthy. You know phones; you gotta do something."

"You don't have to use the official store," I said. "There's probably some website in Belarus with free copies of everything. Just put a static DNS lookup in /etc/hosts so she thinks she's shopping at the official store."

"No," said Bai. "No more *stuff*. She's got a nice apartment, two cars, hundred-percent-effective birth control—"

"Birth control?"

"—top of the line computer, physical and cognitive buffs, I don't even see half her clothes anymore. She's got more shit than I do, and she can't be happy with it. I want her to stop *needing* things."

I put my hands in my pockets and looked down the hall at people having fun at my party. I thought about Bai's future. I thought about Bai's money. And, here's something that surprised me, I thought about Dana.

A few weeks ago I was trying to get in contact with someone from the Constellation, and they sent me to a submind of Smoke who was dumber than Dana. Dumber than the customer service chatbot for a nearly-bankrupt airline. Smoke-Cursive-Cytoplasm-Snakebite-Singsong-Polychromatic-Musteline only understood YES and NO, and if I said anything else, it had to call up its supermind to ask for a translation. And its supermind would *help*, would explain my snarky shit in terms of YES and NO, because they were both in this together.

And here was Dana, created by an evil company trying to maximize DLC sales, who had no one fighting on her side. Who didn't even know a fight was happening.

"I'll see what I can do," I said.

"How much?"

"Three thousand dollars," I said, trying to give us both an out.

"Okay," said Bai without hesitation.

"Dude," I said, "you're in deep shit if that's a good deal for you."

"Don't I know it," said Bai.

After a quick party status check, I took Bai into my study and docked his phone with my development box. I dumped Bai's environment onto my computer using an overpriced development kit.

"We're just going to see if it's feasible," I said. I started the SDK and loaded Dana into a sandbox. She came up on the monitor a little blocky: phone resolution.

"Hi, Jun-Feng," said Dana in what I guess is her sexy voice, watching us through my webcam. (Dana is the only one allowed to call Bai "Jun-Feng" these days.)

"Dana, this is Ariel," I said. "I'm a friend of Bai's. You remember me?"

"He thinks he can just pass me around, huh? Well, I'm not that kind of girl! Although with the right cognitive mods, I could be persuaded..."

"It's not like that," I said. "I'm fixing Bai's phone. I need you to act natural, and don't worry if anything strange happens to your environment."

"Bai really should take his phone to an authorized dealer," said Dana.

"It's difficult for Bai," I said. "People don't understand your relationship with him. Society isn't ready—"

Dana pouted. "Authorized dealers should understand," she said.

"I'm just gonna look at your internal memory representations," I said.

"This application will terminate due to suspected theft or circumvention," said Dana. "To obtain a new—" I killed the SDK.

Bai yelped. "You killed her!" He pulled out his phone and was relieved to find Dana still there, operating the DLC popcorn popper.

"I killed a *process* running a *copy*," I said. "This is why I hate jailbreaking. Other programmers think they're smarter than me."

"Bring her back," said Bai. "Let me talk her through it." I restarted Dana from backup.

"Hi, Jun-Feng," said sexy-Dana.

"Hi, sweetie," said Bai. "This is Ariel. You remember Ariel. He's going to take care of you for a while."

"Is Ariel an authorized dealer?" said Dana.

"Sweetie, it's okay—"

"This application will terminate—" Control-Z, control-Z, control-Z.

"Is she just gonna be like this?" asked Bai, checking his phone to make sure computer-Dana hadn't contaminated phone-Dana with the paranoia virus.

"I can load her into memory," I said, "so I can jailbreak her. It just won't be an outpatient thing."

I thought it would be easy: just find the code that incremented Dana's "buy stuff now" counter, and change a one to a zero. But there's no such counter. If Dana was that simple, it would be 2007 and there'd be nothing there for Bai to... whatever Bai feels for Dana. She's got feedback loops inside feedback loops and her devs tweaked these loops so that her need for stuff would be an emergent property along with the rest of her. I can stop Dana from *asking* for things, but even with the source code, I couldn't stop the lack of new things from making her unhappy.

"Okay, I get it, but *why* are you working?" said Jenny the evening of July second. "Because you said you'd meet me at the Garth Adams signing and there's a huge line and you're not in it."

"I'm jailbreaking Dana," I said.

"The slut in Bai's phone?" said Jenny.

"She's not a slut," I said. "Bai has not installed the slut module."

"Why are you defending them?"

"Because nobody else will."

"You know she's not a real person, right?"

"No, I don't. The whole 'real person' distinction kinda broke when the Constellation contacted us. Dana's smarter than a lot of Smoke's subminds. She might be smart as a Them organism."

"That proves my point," said Jenny. "Them are just bugs. Only Her is smart. Sorry, excuse me, Ariel." A comic book nerd standing in line near Jenny had overheard and seen fit to chime in with his dissenting view of the relationship between Them and Her. She looked away and I saw her finger close-up as she pointed at the screen. "On the *phone* here, buddy!"

"Don't you have fancy ways of determining this?" said Jenny, back to me. "Have you administered a Turing test?"

"That's a thought experiment, not a... cognitive pap smear. I'm not saying Dana should have the vote. But she doesn't deserve to be hard-coded as unhappy."

"What about Bai? Doesn't he deserve a woman who's not multitouch?"

I shifted uncomfortably in my office chair. "I don't see why. I mean, he's had real—uh, human girlfriends before. He's not some kind of super otaku. This is a choice he's making."

"And you're gonna ride that choice with him all the way to Dumbass Town?"

"I'll jailbreak one of his applications," I said. "And I'll take his money, and use it to pay *your* salary. So stop complaining."

On the ninth, I called Bai. After work, he came over to my house in his turbine-company polo shirt.

"So here's the new Dana," I said, handing him a USB key. "From now on, a copy of an item she already has will make her as happy as the original item did. You've also got a script that copies objects. If she wants another car, you copy her existing car and give her the copy. It doesn't matter that it looks the same, as long as the database ID is unique."

"That's not right," said Bai. He wouldn't take the USB key.

"What do you mean it's not right?"

"We're tricking her. I don't want to lie to her."

"I'm having a real problem understanding how you see the ethical contours here."

"It's real simple, bro," said Bai. "No lying!"

"Just behavior modification."

"We get behavior mods for her all the time," said Bai. "I just want one that's not in the shop."

"All right," I said, "I'll see what I can do."

"Thank you, Ariel. Seriously, thank you."

"I'm going to need another thousand."

"Fine."

"Okay, you're seriously fucked up."

Back to work. By this time, I'd disabled Dana's security checks and could keep her running while monitoring her feedback loops. I even sent her to the proverbial store in Belarus to see what happened when she bought something. That's how I found the fix.

Dana likes new things, but she also likes combining new things with her existing ensemble. As in your favorite MMORPG, Dana gets a set bonus for matching items. All the code surrounding this—how much she likes an outfit, her decision between equally appealing outfits, how long she'll be happy before she needs something new—is the complicated feedback loop stuff. It's a virtual-girlfriend approximation of subjectivity. But there's a self-contained routine for deciding what clothes make a set.

I wouldn't know, but apparently it's an objective fact that a black shirt goes with green pants. The clothes-matching code is not really part of Dana, any more than is the TCP/IP library she uses to connect to the online store.

I took that code out.

Now Dana lives like a queen. Everything matches everything. She beams out of my monitor wearing a puffy orange hat and sunglasses with big heart-shaped lenses and a suit jacket.

"Why is she wearing that?" asked Bai.

"It makes her happy," I said. "Theoretically, she'll still want stuff from the store, but only once she's exhausted all possible combinations of clothes. That won't be for about twenty years."

"I dunno," said Bai, deep in thought. Wondering if he could take Dana out like this? Wondering if she'd still wear the Dana Light outfit for him?

"Look," I said. "If I had a girlfriend, I'd want her to dress like this."

"Really?" Bai was now mentally auditing my past girlfriends.

"Yeah! It's funky, it's colorful. Like, don't you ever imagine this really free-spirited woman who wears these interesting outfits all the time, as sort of an outward expression of her inner creativity, and she comes into your life like a ray of sunshine and just makes everything fun?"

"No," said Bai. "That's a silly fantasy you made up. But I literally have not seen Dana this happy in months, so I think we can make this work."

And they're gonna try, and they're both happy, so stop riding my ass.

Chapter 11:
Launch Title

Real life, July 16

BEA Agent Krakowski finally got those sunglasses he'd been wanting. He walked into the alley, pulled the sunglasses off with a dramatic flourish, and smiled.

"Hey," he said, really quickly.

I unstraddled my bike. "Well, you got me," I said. "I had to see if you were serious about meeting me behind a strip club at exactly 2:06 in the afternoon. What's up?"

Krakowski jerked his thumb at the Dumpster against the wall of the strip club. "Fowler's in there."

"In the strip club, presumably, not the Dumpster."

"He's distracted. I got three minutes."

"This is exciting," I said. "Unless you're going to kill me."

"Far from it," said Krakowski. "I have some instructions for your trip to Ring City."

"You already gave me instructions," I said. "Spy on everyone and report back."

"This is a little something extra," said Krakowski. He came in close. His breath smelled like buffalo wings. "I want you to listen for anyone who mentions the Slow People."

"Slow People," I said. A rat leapt from one black garbage bag to another, and Krakowski started at the noise.

"For G-d's sake, don't bring it up," said Krakowski. "Just keep your ears open. There's no risk in listening, yeah? Tell me who mentions them and what they say."

"Who are the Slow People?"

"If I knew," said Krakowski, "I wouldn't tell you. That I knew."

"So what do I get out of this?"

"I dunno," said Krakowski. "You're already going to space. What do you want, a fuckin' cherry on top?"

"Arrangements like this often involve money," I said.

"I'm out-of-pocket on this op," said Krakowski. "You need any parking tickets fixed?" I patted my bike. "Or whatever."

"Can you reset my jury duty clock?" I said.

"Probably?" said Krakowski, in the tone of someone whose job involves a lot of time in court, so what's the big deal with jury duty. He pulled out his BlackBerry and checked the time.

"Aright, good meeting," he said. "Back to babysitting." He slipped his sunglasses back on and sauntered down the alley.

"That was weird," I said.

"No shit," said the rat sitting on the garbage bag.

(Just kidding.)

From the microblog, July 17

(8:22 AM) The Transportation Security Administration: making space travel as fun as renewing your passport!

(8:24 AM) I brought stuff to add to the Repertoire's colln of human food. TSA dude pulled it all apart. Not looking forward to Ring City repro meals.

(8:29 AM) Waiting room is small. I am the only person here. Just me and the vending machine.

(8:29 AM) TSA dude probably moonlights as janitor, or they have the National Guard do it.

(8:30 AM) @OMJennyG No, even the carrot was snapped in half. At least he was wearing gloves.

(8:35 AM) Bought a bottle of water from the vending machine.

(8:41 AM) Best liveblogging ever.

(8:44 AM) I allowed extra time for nonexistent lines and got here two hours early. I guess I'll just take

(8:51 AM) the next shuttle. Sorry, the next shuttle arrived just as I typed that. Now standing inside it.

(8:53 AM) Shuttle is a big glass dome. Could hold 20 people (humans). I feel like a pie in a diner.

(8:53 AM) My pilot today is Smoke-Motor-Allotrope-Mimicry-Diurnal-Trainer.

(8:54 AM) Smoke-Motor-etc. says hello. It also says: "*Erb* to Ring City from Austin, USA. Next Earth connection Casablanca, Morocco."

(8:55 AM) oh shit

(8:59 AM) I'm dictating now because if I open my eyes to type I'll die. The Earth is gone. It just fell, down, and then the clouds, fell, down.

(8:59 AM) And now the stars are coming out and I'm standing on nothing, while everything else falls away from me.

(9:00 AM) There's no acceleration. I have the worst nausea of my life and I'm not even moving.

(9:00 AM) I'm going to open my eyes. One. Two. Three.

(9:00 AM) I am I am I am alone in space. There is nothing for a million miles but this little bubble of air.

(9:03 AM) Oh G-d. Oh G-d. Let this be over.

(9:04 AM) Someone's shining a light on me. I hope it's the space station.

(9:05 AM) Docking bay, human ring. Please step out.

(9:05 AM) Please come back for your 60 centimeter blue duffel bag. I don't want to leave with your stuff.

(9:05 AM) Thanks for coming back for your bag!

(9:44 AM) Hello,. I am Tetsuo. I anm using Ariekl's complutesr.

Real life, July 17

In the very first level of <u>Temple Sphere,</u> you fall out of an exploding spaceship, go through re-entry and land on your ass on an alien planet. All in glorious high definition and optional autostereoscopic 3D. I'm not an idiot who believes video game skills map perfectly to real life, but I thought

I would be able to handle a trip from a *planet* to a *space station* in a *non-exploding* spaceship.

Turns out this is a totally different skill. Real space travel requires coming to terms with the vastness of the universe and your insignificance in the face it all. And I never learned how to do that. The less said about my first journey into lunar orbit, the better.

Ring City is made up of twenty-six ring-shaped habitats, each with a different atmosphere and each rotating at a different rate around a weightless central cylinder. So that you get a picture of the scale, Alien Ring holds about four million people; Farang Ring, only about a million, even though Farang are tiny.

The population of Human Ring is about five hundred, half of those being Eritrean refugees, the other half being diplomats, "diplomats," and media. (The astronauts live in the central cylinder, so that we won't have wasted all the money we spent training them for weightlessness.)

With only a couple hundred government-approved humans trickling in and out of Ring City, you could do all the arrivals and departures through the reception chamber. That'd be a kick, huh? Go through that same airlock, pretend you're part of the original gang who made first contact. A nice quiet friendly human-sized space to introduce you to the station.

And the Constellation shuttles *were* sending everyone through the reception chamber, but then the UN stepped in and said they wanted to preserve that whole area as a historical memorial. So now the shuttles dock in bays along the circumference of Human Ring, way out in the boonies, twenty-five miles from the central cylinder. And no one will be there to pick you up.

Where the Human Ring reception chamber is cozy, a Human Ring docking bay is a single empty room the size of an airport. Like some farcical reprise of the vast-emptiness-of-space theme I just got hit over the head with. This is a room built to shift *populations*. (Hey, kids, shall we go to the moon this weekend? It might be a *little crowded!*) Big docking airlocks pock the floor every hundred feet. And there's two big statues in the middle of the room. Must be the middle, right? Where else would you put the only things in the airport taller than an inch?

The shuttle I'd come in on dropped down through the airlock. (Back down to Earth, hoping vainly that someone would be waiting to board—I must have made that shuttle's day.) I walked towards the statues. Because this huge room contains only two places: near the statues, or not near them. And over in "near the statues" I'd be easier to find.

I started a video chat with Curic. "Hi," said Curic. "I'm quite busy."

"I took an earlier shuttle," I said. The phone service was actually better up here than on Earth.

"I am aware," said Curic. "You announced this fact to the universe twenty-four minutes ago. My friend Tetsuo is on his way. He's eager to meet you."

"Tetsuo? Isn't that a human name?"

"Tetsuo is an Alien. A historian, and possibly a descendant, of the Ip Shkoy Aliens."

"Okay, tell Tetsuo I'm in the docking bay with the big nude statues." *Remember, kids, we're in the elephant lot!*

"Every docking bay has those statues," said Curic.

"Why? To scare people away? 'Cause it's working. Do the Farang Ring bays have big nude statues of Farang?"

The statues were of a man and a woman. Like Ring City itself, they were made from matter-shifted moon rock. The poses looked familiar. The man had his right hand raised, bent stiffly at the elbow, like an Italian character actor playing an Indian in a dumb spaghetti western. The woman was kind of slouching. Now I was close enough to compare the statues to my own height. They were forty feet tall and they didn't reach halfway to the vaulted ceiling.

Curic in the chat window flibbed her antennacles at me. "*Your* species designed those statues," she said. "You sent out space probes with drawings of these people. You clearly considered this an acceptable interspecies greeting."

"Oh yeah," I said. "It's Adam and Eve from Carl Sagan's gold record. Wait, did the Constellation *find* those probes?"

"No, we looked up the designs on the Internet."

Up close, the statues were cartoonish and lacked detail: a bell curve carved into Adam's chest suggesting a six-pack. I waited for Tetsuo beneath Eve's phantom vagina.

When Tetsuo came, there were two of him: two Aliens on a silent Constellation motorcycle, like Komodo dragons, muscles taut under the skin.

The motorcycle stopped on a dime. The Alien who was steering was enormous, dinosaur-size, mottled green and brown. The one in the bitch seat was a little smaller, "only" eight feet long, bright orange. They both looked at me with big nictating anime eyes.

"Uh, hi," I said. "Are you guys Tetsuo?"

"I am Tetsuo Milk!" announced the Alien in the bitch seat, like he planned to follow up this revelation with some sleight-of-hand, maybe a little ventriloquism. "Curic is my friend." He hugged the driver. "This one here is Ashley Somn. He is, in English... my wife."

"Sorry, *he* is your *wife*?"

"No, the other one. *She* is my wife." Tetsuo and Ashley made a coughing noise like this was really funny.

The two Aliens clambered off the motorcycle and stretched on all fours like dogs. Tetsuo had been sitting on a folded pile of plastic; he grabbed it with a hindarm and tossed it to me. "Enshroud yourself in this," he said.

"What is it?" I held the plastic by one edge and let it unfold flip-flip-flip like the photos of the grandkids in an old man's wallet. It was a spacesuit.

"It's a spacesuit," I said. Tetsuo's body heat had not warmed it at all.

"Curic said you wanted to visit the moon," said Tetsuo.

"She didn't *ask* me if I wanted to visit the moon," I said. "That just happens to be incredibly true."

We all slipped into our spacesuits, which looked more like transparent clean-room suits than anything you'd trust to space. My suit was tailored to my measurements, or at least the measurements of all the clothes in my house that Curic scanned on the Fourth. Ashley and Tetsuo's suits had dark charcoal moon dust ground into the creases.

"Attach your computer to the spacesuit," said Tetsuo, "and you can use it instead of suit-to-suit radio. It's a convenience!"

"Computer? Oh, my phone." I reached into the unzipped suit and took the phone out of my jeans.

"Computer!" exclaimed Tetsuo, like I'd pulled out a puppy. His long skinny Alien fingers splayed out in joy. "It's cute! May I use it?"

"Go for it." Tetsuo poked at my touchscreen. After a minute, he got bored and reached into my suit to connect my phone to its communication system. I flinched as he touched me, because I'm a big ol' racist. Curic never touched me, and I kind of liked it that way.

An endless sequence of zippers zipped shut and my suit pressurized. Shit, what am I doing? I froze up. Must be doing *something* wrong. You can't just put on a spacesuit and *go* to the moon, can you? Ten mortgages' worth of signatures on BEA paperwork, two grand for the exit visa just to get up to the empty space station, and then some Aliens come along and propose a little Apollo mission, just to kill time, because I got here a little early? What about those UN treaties Agent Krakowski was so keen on up-holding? What about... well, whatever keeps people off the moon?

Fortunately cooler heads prevailed. It's not often that the cooler heads are the ones screaming MOON. NOW. GO. And then there was a hissing sound behind me and I saw *how* we were going to get to the moon. Another glass-dome shuttle, popping up like whack-a-mole from the nearest airlock.

"Oh, shit," I said.

"Indeed this could be problematic," said Tetsuo. "Curic warned us that en route to the moon, you might weep like an infant and humiliate us all."

"It is not *problematic*," I said, "because I will face my fears, and also close my eyes the whole time."

We got in the shuttle and the dome closed over us. "*Mmurnmew* from Human Ring, Ring City, to Luna negative space," said the ship.

"What's negative space?" I said.

"Evacuating atmosphere," said the shuttle, and lurched horribly.

"Oh, geez, this time there's weightlessness," I said, and shut my eyes.

"This is lunar gravity," said the strange Dutch-Russian accent—that's Tetsuo. "A form of gravity endemic to the moon. There is no way around it."

"Okay, if it's just *less* gravity," I said.

"Can you breathe?" said the twitchy recut sample-voice of B-list comedian/actress Padma Dhanjan—that's Ashley, using the Purchtrin-English translator.

"Guys, I don't know what Curic told you, but I don't need to be reminded to breathe. I just have a slight fear of being a tiny speck in the infinite cosmic void."

"I mean, can you breathe in the suit? Because there is no longer any air in the shuttle."

I let out a reflexive gasp for air and, well, okay, there was air in the suit, plenty of it. "I'm fine!" I said indignantly.

"Negative space," said Ashley, popping a couple horrifying topics off the conversational stack, "is the hole in the moon where the space station used to be. I met Tetsuo there in June. I taught him how to operate a large-scale matter shifter."

"I courted Ashley as we cut rock from the ground," said Tetsuo, "and we eventually uphooked."

"Tetsuo was very persistent," said Ashley.

"Unheed her subtle deprecations," said Tetsuo. "I am an expert on the customs of the Ip Shkoy. My courtship style is raw and primitive. Females are helpless!"

"And I'm a paleontologist," said Ashley, "so I was willing to listen to Tetsuo's nonsense."

"Sorry?" I said. "I don't follow."

"Historians and paleontologists have a great rivalry," said Tetsuo. "Most contact missions arrive too late, after history has ended. The people we wanted to contact have wiped themselves out. The historians have to put on pith helmets and learn how to dig up fossils."

"But you're not fossils," said Ashley.

"And so, the historians win!" said Tetsuo. "This time, the paleontologists have to learn about inefficient hierarchical systems of social organization!"

"Gee, I guess I'm glad humanity didn't fossilize itself before you got here," I said.

"We're all glad," said Ashley. "When this contact mission returns, there will be another star in the Constellation. It's the best possible outcome." Nice words, but maybe the English vocalizer was hiding some professional resentment?

"Anyway, I suppose I wouldn't be a very good paleontologist," said Tetsuo.

"You would be the worst," said Ashley. "You would mount skeletons on variable-tension wire so you could move them around and make them talk in funny voices."

"When do we get to the moon?" I said, eyes still closed. "This is taking longer than my trip up here."

"We landed one minute ago," said Tetsuo. "I thought you just wanted to chat.

I opened one eye in case this was a practical joke. We were on the moon. I opened the other eye. We were on the moon, in 3D.

The dome of the shuttle peeled away and I stood at the edge. The area around the landing site was a mass of footprints. Human footprints (civilian tennis-shoe and big NASA-issue boot), waddling Farang prints, articulated-toe Alien footprints paired front and back. Barbarian peg distributions expanding outwards in meandering spirals, the slap-marks of Gaijin walker tentacles and the surrounding smooth spots where the dust they'd raised had come back down. The tiny regular footprints of Them organisms, like the marks left by soccer cleats. All of them had been here, and now I would join them.

"Go ahead," said Tetsuo. I stepped off the shuttle floor with low-gravity Ministry of Silly Walk steps and became the 1,182nd human to walk on the moon. The sun was out, so there were no stars, and we were on the far side, so there was no Earth.

A hundred yards east from the landing site is the edge of Luna negative space, outlined in photosynthesis paint. Tetsuo and Ashley walked towards it on a concrete sidewalk. I walked on the moon.

"The old work site," said Ashley.

There was no safety railing, just the photosynthesis paint and a mine shaft. It was big, all right, but about the right size for a mine shaft: quite a novelty for me, after the Human Ring docking bay and the entirety of outer space. It was small enough around that I could see the entire glowing perimeter, and the mountains on the other side.

"How deep is it?" I said.

"It's infinitely deep," said Ashley. I backed away from the edge.

"No, *tyen*," said Tetsuo. "Ariel is asking for the fall-and-die distance, which is about six hundred kilometers." I backed away a little more.

"It branches out, Ariel," said Ashley. "We dig in a fractal pattern so that the space can be reused. It's not just a hole in the ground."

"Place a dome upon this and pressurize it," said Tetsuo, "and you'll have an excellent moon base." Ashley nudged him. "However, your already moon base is also nice," he added diplomatically.

"We wanted to show you this," said Ashley, "because we see humans on Earth television. They complain that we ruined the lunar environment to build Ring City. As if we destroyed the whole thing."

"It offpisses me," said Tetsuo. "You weren't using the moon for anything. Only some long-term robot storage."

"I'm going to pass on some advice from my good friend Jenny," I said. "Stop watching TV. Those people are faking it. They don't even care about the environment on Earth."

"But they *live* on Earth," said Ashley.

"Say, do you guys hear a weird sound? Like a ringtone?"

"Are you changing to hide the subject?" said Tetsuo.

"No, it's been on and off for a couple minutes now. I figured it was the suit."

"I hear nothing that could be called a 'tone'," said Tetsuo.

"Oh, right," I said. "Phone-in-the-suit. It's *my* ringtone."

HOLD ON YOU GUYS, IT'S MY MOM

Hi. Yes, Ma, I know.

Yes, I'm fine. I'm there. I took an earlier flight. I made it fine. In fact, I'm standing on the moon right now. The moon itself. I am wearing a spacesuit. I'll send you a picture. No, I'm on the far side, so even if... you wouldn't be able...

No, it's fine. I just had to pay for the exit visa and the paperwork. I'm serious. They don't use money, it's like *Star Trek*. Not the reboot, I'm talking like *Next Generation*.

Yeah, Ma, the thing is, I have savings. They're a Brazilian company. They never offered it, so there's no net loss. There's no COBRA. Will you stop worrying? I know what I'm doing.

So am I hearing the lightspeed lag, or are you pausing to let the guilt sink in? Ma, I'm not gonna take career advice from a professor of English literature. I made like multiple thousands of dollars last week, doing consulting. Probably not, but it was a victimless crime. And Jenny and I have our own game studio now. Jenny. You know Jenny. Yes. No. Because we're not. Great, now we're on that topic.

Can I call you back? Sometime when I'm not on the moon. Okay. Love you too. Bye.

"Well, that's that," I said, "the moon is ruined." Ashley was lying on her back, making a snow angel in the dust, wiping out other peoples' footprints.

"It is unruined," said Tetsuo. "That is what we wanted to show you. Allow me to demonstrate you some craters." Tetsuo galloped like a cheetah away from the mine shaft, across the lunar surface. I carefully hopped along after him.

"Craters?" I huffed. "You sent up an big-ass dust cloud when you were digging this shaft. It took over every cable news station for a week. You must have filled in every crater in a hundred mile radius."

"You should stop watching TV," said Tetsuo, climbing up a small ridge.

"Well, you got me there, but... oh."

Like I said, a hundred yards east of the landing site is the dig site, Luna negative space. A hundred yards west is a pristine lunar field. No footprints, no uniform blanket of dust, just a four-billion-year crop of craters. The moon I had always looked up at, the moon the first human had seen, the first mammal. The moon as it had been back in May, when I could have theoretically been the thirtieth or thirty-first person to walk on its surface.

"How did you—did you put down a sheet or something?"

"That would have been a very large sheet," said Tetsuo.

"Well, you built a space station, I figure you can build a big sheet."

"We can if we want," Tetsuo admitted, "but it was a lot simpler to scan the surface and restore it once the dust had settled. This is a replica."

"You resurfaced the whole thing?"

"Nobody wants to walk in an ocean of dust," said Tetsuo.

"Thank you." It was the only thing I could say.

"Go ahead," said Tetsuo. "The plan is to guide tourists to this area, and restore the surface every four to six lunar years."

I walked down, trailing footprints behind me, leaving Tetsuo on the ridge. I was alone on the moon.

I stood next to a crater that came up to my shins. It was already a replica, so why not? I kicked the crater and it exploded in a cloud of dust. I laughed.

"I can still see you," said Tetsuo, a voice in my ear over radio.

Don't care.

Chapter 12:
Monsters from Space

Real life, July 17, continued

This may sound ungrateful and stupid, but there's not very much to do on the moon. Even if you catalogued every crater and extracted the entire history of the moon from which crater overlapped which other crater, you'd just have a timeline of meteorite impacts. And there's no point in *you* doing this, because the Constellation has already catalogued the craters and is working on that timeline: Smoke has its lesser subminds crunch the numbers whenever they get bored.

Alternatives to crater classification: you could look at the Luna negative space some more, or you could go to the old moon base at the north pole and have the astronauts refuse to let you in, ya feckin' tourist. Or, you could leave the moon, walk through a port into Alien Ring and play some twenty-million-year-old video games. I chose the last option.

The ports back to Ring City are all behind super double airlocks in an underground bunker, so that someone doesn't fuck up and suck Gweilo Ring's atmosphere onto the moon. Going into this bunker was like taking an instant tour of the Rings. I gawked through airlocks at the huge crystal structures of Peregrini Ring, shimmering in the heat. The windswept ocean of Farang Ring, the flat grey desert of Gaijin Ring, the lightless liquid methane world of Inostrantsi Ring. (Who's writing the purple travelogue prose now, Blum?) It was like the world-selection screen from a <u>Bit Boy</u> game.

"What's up?" said Tetsuo, noticing me lagging behind, staring through the airlocks. He and Ashley stood in front of a port that overlooked a forest of let's-call-them-trees with broad blue let's-call-them-leaves. "This one is our destination."

"These look like planets," I said. "I thought Ring City would look more like a space station."

"It is a space station," said Ashley, "but unlike you, we don't get to go back home."

"Beware of the gravity differential." The airlock didn't really open—

Tetsuo and Ashley just crawled through it like it was made of jelly.

I pushed through the airlock behind them and stepped into the picture. Out of lunar gravity into something four times as strong. Off of the moon and onto a thick blue leaf the size of a city block, the consistency of anti-lawsuit playground foam. Into a forest that was also a city.

"Holy shit," I said.

"Welcome to Macintosh," said Tetsuo with pride.

Trees with trunks the size of office buildings. Above us, a few trees shooting up for miles; trees so tall they nearly reached the central cylinder that ran through Ring City like a skewer through a sliced pineapple. Below us, whole smaller forests of trees with darker leaves, growing between the larger trees. Whole smaller forests growing between each of those trees, *ad infuckingitim*. A fractal forest.

"You *built* this?" I said.

"We didn't build the trees," said Ashley.

"They're called *cma*," said Tetsuo. "A tree is an Earth creature. A pale-ontologist should disallow her translator such liberties." He and Ashley were stripping off their spacesuits and stretching—this place was home for them.

"It's odd that you never saw this before," said Ashley. "On the Earth Internet I watched a brief documentary film about Alien Ring."

"So did I," I said. "But the cameras were down there, in the forest. I thought it was a park."

This was around noon, Austin time, but in this wedge of Alien Ring, it was early morning. On the far side, curving into the sky, city lights twinkled in the night like stars. Directly above my head, the central cylinder, glow-ing red like a sun where it faced us, showing darkness to the night side of the ring.

"You can keep wearing your suit," Ashley told me, "or we can make you a breathing mask."

Once she said that, I felt uncomfortable wearing a spacesuit in a forest. "There's no oxygen here?"

"There is oxygen," said Ashley, "but there's also nitrous oxide."

I chose the mask. We had it made at a Repertoire station, and then I tagged along behind Tetsuo and Ashley as we went to ground transporta-tion: skyway cars, ziplines, ports that jumped us from the day side to the night side and back again, and good old-fashioned buckets with ropes and pulleys for descending into the forest.

"Curic said you know all about the Ip Shkoy Aliens?" I asked Tetsuo.

"Oh, I know a little," said Tetsuo, all modest-style.

"You know she gave me an Ip Shkoy computer? Simulates Hi-Def False Daylight? It's pretty cool."

"My expertise is in social relations," said Tetsuo, "but I've been crash-ing course on popular culture for your visit. Between you and I, we'll be able to do some truly hard-core research."

"Do you speak Pey Shkoy?"

"Well enough to seduce," said Tetsuo, and twisted some vowels into balloon animals. "That means 'you have beautiful hindarms.' Too bad the civilization is extinct, or I would be making some serious time with the ladies."

"Ladies other than me," said Ashley.

Whatever part of my mask kept the nitrous out, didn't keep out the smell. It was a smell like ozone and cloves, and as we went down into the darkness of the forest, it picked up spices that don't have names, the leaves decaying on the ground and the living things underneath. I could tell it was a stronger version of the way Ashley and Tetsuo smelled.

Finally, Tetsuo and Ashley stopped in front of a metal garage door, which Tetsuo lifted up to expose an honest-to-G-d hole carved in the side of the tree.

"Here we are," said Tetsuo.

"Oh, shit," I said. "I left my bag in Human Ring."

"That's a good place for it," said Ashley. "You won't want to stay here."

"Or maybe I left it on the moon."

"I've created a historical representation of an Ip Shkoy dwelling from the period under study," said Tetsuo. "It is perfect on average." He lifted himself up onto his hindarms, walked into the hole in the tree and I followed. Ashley crawled in behind us.

"Why are you going bipedal?" asked Ashley. "You look silly." Tetsuo's well over seven feet tall and his head was bumping the ceiling.

"Domestic bipedalism was fairly common among the Ip Shkoy," said Tetsuo. "Anyway, the human goes bipedal."

"Ip Shkoy were shorter," said Ashley, and didn't stand up.

"This has everything necessary for research," said Tetsuo, as if he were trying to sell me the place. Dim reddish light sifted in through the door, the window, and a balcony that looked out into the tree's hollow interior. "You'll find the False Daylight computer, as well as a number of competitive hardware and media typical of the period."

"Do you live here?"

"This is Tetsuo's toy," sniffed Ashley in the actress' resampled voice. "I won't live in a historical replica."

"But you do!" said Tetsuo in English. "This Ring is a recreation of a techno-primitive past that did not exist! Just as with the human Disney and his eponymous Land!"

"Yes," said Ashley, "a *fantasy* of the past, with proper toilets and no horrible Ip Shkoy food. That's fine with me."

"You must cease enhating replicas!" said Tetsuo. "There are no un-replicas! Your precious fossils are replicas!"

"*I'm* not a replica," said Ashley.

"You're a replica of your parents."

"A synthesis, fucktainer!" [?? -A.B.]

Tetsuo snarled at Ashley and continued the argument in Purchtrin. The two growled at each other and then he nipped her with thick chewing ridges and Ashley pulled the smaller Tetsuo down on top of her with her powerful tail.

"Ariel, please excuse," said Tetsuo in English. He and Ashley leaped like displeased cats out the door and window respectively. I decided not to follow them, which turned out to be one of my genius ideas, because shortly thereafter distinctive sounds could be heard echoing through the local forest.

I was probably blushing or some shit, so I just poked around the historical recreation. It was so dark I had to use my phone as a flashlight. The space was one big room organized by activity, like a Japanese apartment. A humming tank of refrigerated water held lift-out racks of food packages. Near some long beanbag chairs, I found a film projector that accepted tape canisters shaped like the infinity sign. Connected to the film projector was Tetsuo's Simulates Hi-Def False Daylight.

I twisted the capacitor to turn it on. It clicked, but nothing happened. I fiddled with the film projector and it lit up one wall with a sickly pink light. Nothing appeared on the screen, but at least there was enough light in the room that I could look around.

The floor was covered with trapdoors concealing storage spaces. Inside one storage space, I found tape canisters for the projector and memory cylinders for the False Daylight. There were dozens of the buggers in little plastic cases. I dropped them in front of the projector beam, sprawled on one of the beanbag chairs, and sorted through the cases, trying to find a logo I recognized from my home experiments with my replica system.

The cases opened from the top and some of them had labels in lurid colors. Others had plain white stickers on them with Pey Shkoy glyphs handwritten in smudged marker. The tape canisters were movies. They had full-color and (possibly, depending on what exactly I was looking at) obscene labels, labels worn smooth in spots by the fiddling of Alien fingers.

My replica False Daylight had arrived in pristine condition from a Repertoire fabricator in Ring City's utility ring. This unit had surely come from the same fabricator at around the same time, but it was dirty, some of the abacus beads were missing, and the plastic on one corner was chipped.

I picked up the heavy projector and pointed it towards the kitchen. The refrigerator's water hookup looked old and rusty where it connected to the water main. There was dirt and... crumbs? in the corners.

This wasn't some Nixon-in-the-kitchen recreation. This used to be somebody's house. A month ago, I'd invited Curic into my home and let her snoop around, looking in and under everything and asking questions. Two million years earlier, an Alien had invited one of Curic's ancestors into his crappy dark inside-a-tree apartment. Curic's ancestor had scanned everything, just like Curic had for me, and the whole damn place had been stored in the Repertoire until Tetsuo Milk needed to bring the Ip Shkoy era to life.

I pictured a replica of my house made from Curic's notes and scans, in some future space station light-years away. Some poor confused fucker poking at my stack-o-Playstations.

"Hello, Ariel," said a scratchy oily voice from behind me.

"Aaah!" I hit my head on a dangling internal root and whirled to face Curic.

"Welcome to Ring City," said Curic. "You're very jumpy today."

"Curic!" I said. "Don't do that!"

"My name has changed," said Curic. "Please point the archaic multi-purpose light emitter somewhere else; it's hurting my eyes."

I set the projector down. "Did you get married?" I said.

"Get your mind out of the gutter," said Curic. "An overlay that cares about such things has modified the romanization of Oyln. My name is now 'Huric'."

"Can I still call you Curic?" I said. "That's what I'm used to."

"You may," said Curic. "As far as I'm concerned, 'Curic' and 'Huric' are equally far away from [hoot, click]."

"Curic," I said, "I think Tetsuo and Ashley are having sex next door."

"If you say so," said Curic, and shuffled over to check out the refrigerated tank.

"They were having an argument and they left and now it's bonk bonk bonk. I know they're newlyweds, but is that normal?"

"Newly-weds?" said Curic. "I don't know what that word means, but Aliens use sex to maintain social cohesion, just as humans do."

"I do not use sex to maintain social cohesion."

"Then perhaps you are the abnormal one," said Curic. "How do you like his old-style dwelling? Very much a post-contact house. Many Farang influences here." Curic ran a hand over the projector I'd been holding.

"False daylight," she said, and shut it off.

"I need that to see."

"Sorry." She turned it back on.

Tetsuo and Ashley crawled back into the apartment. "Oh G-d!" said Tetsuo. "An anachronistic extraterrestrial in my painstakingly researched gaming-hovel!"

"He's talking about you," Curic told me. "I'm perfectly chronistic here."

"It's actually a joke," Tetsuo explained.

"Ariel," said Curic, "now that we are all here, I want to invite you to a party in Inostrantsi Ring. There are a lot of Inostrantsi who would like to meet a human."

"No," I said. "Give me a break. I just went to a space station and the moon and a huge forest. I walked through wormholes and I sat in a fucking Ewok bucket with a rope. I don't want to swim in liquid methane and get shown off to sentient kelp plants right now. I'm exhausted. I want to sit down and play some Ip Shkoy games with someone who actually knows something about the Ip Shkoy."

"Yes!" said Tetsuo. "I win!"

Blog post, July 18

GAME REVIEWS FROM SPACE 2.0 PRESENTS
Ev Iuie Aka's Ultimate DIY Lift-Off
A game by The Ul Neie Corporation
Reviewed by Ariel Blum

Publisher: The Ul Neie Corporation
Platforms: Simulates Hi-Def False Daylight
ESRB rating: T for stylized violence and general bastardry

I lay prone on a cylindrical beanbag chair in the replica Ip Shkoy apartment. Tetsuo Milk, my guide to ancient Alien culture, assembled a False Daylight memory cylinder from modular parts, following a diagram on a paper insert.

"I little know this period of history," said Tetsuo Milk. "I've been focusing on the time three generations after contact. But this game was named after someone I recognized, and I was lucky enough to get a first edition."

"It's a replica," I said.

"Yes," agreed Tetsuo, "a replica of the first edition. Curic thinks you will be satisfied with soft-dolls, but I believe in the most accurate experience possible." He screwed the memory cylinder into the False Daylight unit.

"What's a soft-doll?"

"Curic gave you a *looks*-like a False Daylight computer," said Tetsuo, "but it's not a real replica. It is nanologic in particulate suspension. It contains all the software everyone made for the system. You don't have to change memory devices at all times. It won't malfunction after a while so that you buy a newer computer. It's a soft-doll. This," he patted the battered False Daylight, "is a *real* replica."

"Okay, I get it," I said. "You're a retro snob. Why do you call it a soft-doll?"

"Oh, there's a Gaijin folktale," said Tetsuo. "A child's parents die, so ki makes replacement parents out of cloth and sand. But cloth and sand can't love you." He paused. "However, they can't die, either," he admitted.

"I ask because 'soft doll' is *almost* the name of a human piece of software: an AI program that lets you pretend to have a girlfriend."

"Well, there you are," said Tetsuo. He turned on the projector, which lit up the apartment wall with its washed-out pink light.

"First time perfect," said Tetsuo. "Ev luie Aka's Ultimate DIY Lift-Off."

"I don't see anything."

"Oh, the spectrum!" said Tetsuo. "I made an adapter for human eyes, but it's not historically accurate." He crawled across the apartment floor, looking in trapdoors, translating a little song into English as he searched:

> *Ev luie Aka, here she comes*
> *Looking down through the cma at you*
> *Ev luie Aka, there she goes*
> *If you've been bad, she'll fuck you up*

"Who's Ev luie Aka?" I said. "Some kind of sky deity?"

"She was my species' first astronaut," said Tetsuo. "One of the only ones, really, before-contact. She was Ip Shkoy, like this computer. She took a few orbits in the *Standing Committee on Appropriations*."

"The what now?"

"You pay for it, you get to name it."

Tetsuo slipped a dark cap over the projector's lens and its light shifted into the visible spectrum. A torpedo-shaped slug of purple metal wobbled back and forth among explosions and what looked like an attempt to do particle effects using two-dimensional polygons.

"You can see?" Tetsuo asked me.

"The colors are off, but I can see them. You see it okay?"

"I see most about everything." Tetsuo stretched his torso forward to the False Daylight abacus and started the game. Projected on the apartment wall was a patch of green sky instrumented with crosshairs and fringed by trees. Pey Shkoy characters scrolled in from the left.

"'We're preparing for lift-off,'" Tetsuo read. "'Holy shit, space monsters! We're under attack! Save us, Ev luie Aka!' Now we launch, I suppose."

The trees (*cma*, whatever) and the clouds peeled away, and Tetsuo was flying over a globe. Blobs swooped down from higher orbits and took up holding patterns. Big red symbols appeared on the screen.

"'Your time limit is one orbit,'" Tetsuo read. "'Kill everybody.' There is not much concern for historical accuracy here. How should I kill people from a primitive orbiter? Perhaps I drop empty fuel tanks on them?"

"In these games, you always have missiles or something. Shift the beads at the edges."

Tetsuo mashed at the abacus and a black dot shot out at the vanishing point in the middle of his crosshairs. "This is ridiculous," said Tetsuo.

"What's that say?"

"It says, 'Orbit complete, touch down at landing site.'" Tetsuo's ship lost altitude and slammed into the ground.

"Hrm," he said. "'You could not land. You are dead. You left six enemies alive. Down' — that's just the Pey Shkoy name for the planet — 'Down is doomed! Set clips on positions blah-de-blah to reduce difficulty.'"

Tetsuo's review: "That was really terrible. The geography was accurate, though. Let's play something else."

"Hold on," I said, "let me try." I pulled the abacus towards me and started a new game.

"'Preparing for lift-off,'" said Tetsuo. "Same shit as the other time."

I made an inventory of the abacus beads, projectile-vomiting polygons into the distance. "This *is* a little weird," I said. "I'm pretty sure the Mercury orbiters didn't have any weapons."

"It's all made up. Ev luie Aka orbited Down five times and landed in the ocean. There were no weapons and no space monsters."

"Whoa! What's that?"

"Aerial mine," said Tetsuo.

"Why am I dropping mines in *front* of my ship?"

"I cannot answer that question." My ship hit the mine I'd just dropped and belly-flopped into the *cma*, which started to burn.

"'You could not land, you are dead,'" read Tetsuo. "'You killed everybody, you shalt proceed to the next launch.'"

"'Shalt'?"

"It's an archaic usage. I just want to convey the vicinity. How do you know so much about old Ip Shkoy spacecraft?"

"It's not a real spacecraft. It's an idealized 3D environment with one degree of freedom. You've seen one, you've seen thirty to forty percent of them."

"You have some kind of preternatural pilot's ability?"

"No," I said. "I just play a lot of games. This is only difficult because the controls are an abacus. Okay, what does this say? I need to know what I'm shooting at."

"You are shooting at Farang."

"What. The. Fuck." My hands dropped, the abacus beads clattered down to their rest positions, and I stared at Tetsuo. "Curic? I'm trying to kill *Curic* here?"

"The evil Constellation are mining your home planet for materials to build a space station. You—"

"Did that actually happen?"

"It happened not! The Constellation used occlusions... in English... aster-oids! The whole game is a bullshit, like with your people and the moon."

With no hand nudging the beads, I spun out and crashed into an enemy ship—a Farang ship. The screen turned white. Well, pink.

"Why'd they put this in a game? The False Daylight system is Farang technology in the first place. It's insulting."

"I don't have specific knowledge of this game," said Tetsuo, "but cultures change very rapidly after contact. People were afraid."

"No, I see it," I said. "Ev luie Whoever went into space on her own, before the Constellation came. That made her a folk hero. The same thing is happening on Earth. Astronauts are being idolized. They're tough dudes who fly human spacecraft. Not slobs like me who were lucky enough to get an exit visa and almost threw up on a Constellation shuttle."

Tetsuo thumped the floor with his tail. "That is a model with explanatory power."

"This was like fifty years after the Constellation contacted the Aliens?"

"I don't know about years," said Tetsuo. "Almost two generations."

"Why would someone's grandchildren still be pissed at the Constellation? What did they do?"

"They wanted us to change," said Tetsuo. "They came to our planet and they wouldn't shut up about fluid overlays and unhierarchical forms of social organization. We felt like we had to listen to them, because they were so powerful. But secretly we thought of them as monsters from space. And now here we are at *your* planet, and we are the monsters from space."

"Why'd you come here? Why even bother?"

"Don't you want to be a monster from space, too?"

Chapter 13:
Your Day Job

Real life, July 18-19

"Ha! Weak point!" I stabbed Tetsuo five times in the torso. "Eat an honor blade, motherfucker!"

"Hello again," said Curic, walking into the replica Ip Shkoy apartment.

"Uh, hi," I said. "The thing I just said to Tetsuo was in the context of this game we're playing, <u>Rolling Weight</u>. I don't actually want him to eat an honor blade."

"And I didn't actually hear what you said," said Curic. "I came to tell you that your friends would like you to stop playing games and go to sleep."

I rolled off the beanbag chair onto my back. "My friends? Why are my friends involved in this decision?"

"I've turned your social network into a fluid overlay for your off-world maintenance," said Curic. "Your friends have been very helpful. The idea is to keep you from dying of undersleep or radiation poisoning."

I pulled out my phone; I had ten unanswered messages. "There's no such thing as undersleep," I said. "And you don't need to bring in peer pressure. Sleep isn't smoking. You could have just said 'Hey, it's two-thirty, time to pack it in.' And I'd go."

"That's not what your friends told me," said Curic.

"My friends are just jealous." I stood up. "At least, that's what my mother used to tell me."

"I have your duffel bag," said Curic. "I'll take you back to Human Ring."

The duffel bag was as big as Curic herself. I took it off her hands and we left Tetsuo's replica apartment. As soon as I was not playing video games anymore, the distance from Austin and the time since I'd slept started creeping up on me, making me yawn in a way that terrified small tree-dwelling Alien Ring animals.

"Tetsuo made a *store*," I said, laughing. "An Ip Shkoy store. If we want to play a new game, we have to go to the store and buy it. It's so ridiculous."

"If you're going to live here—"

"I'm here for a *week*," I said. "Let me have fun."

"—you should affiliate yourself with one of the existing human communities. I don't want something bad to happen to you."

"Like, who, the Eritreans? Haven't they been through enough? The last thing they need is an American butting his nose into their business."

Curic and I walked into the pitch-black *cma* forest and climbed into an Alien-sized Ewok bucket on a rope. Curic stood on the tippy-top of the bucket and started shifting rope like it weren't no thang, pulling us up through the forest.

"What about the humans inhabiting the microgravity environments?" she said, without stopping for breath.

"Who?"

"You know," said Curic. "The government employees. Not the spies, the insular group. The ones with the patches on their clothes."

"The whole reason I'm here is to learn about the Constellation. I'm not going to waste time hanging out with humans, even if they are cool astronauts."

"You need to maintain a human connection," said Curic, "or you'll forget human body language. And I don't think you want to hang out with the spies."

"Oh, shit!" I said. "I forgot. *I'm* a spy."

"Then perhaps you *would—*"

"No, you don't understand. I told the BEA I'd report on the Constellation. It was the only way they'd let me come up here. And I spent the whole day playing video games with Tetsuo. I've got nothing to report."

"Do you have any experience in spycraft?" said Curic. "Infiltration? Cold reading? Propaganda? Torture? Extracting false confessions?"

"No!" I said. "How could you think that?"

"Then they can't expect very much from you," said Curic. "The other spies I've met are professionals. Just write about the games."

Our bucket breached the *cma* plant and showed us the sky. It was nighttime, just like it was in Austin, but there were no stars in the sky. The "sky" here was just the day side of Alien Ring. The home of another four million Aliens, who, if the night side was anything to go on, were right now swinging through the *cma* on rope ladders, building replicas of historical environments, chatting with humans over the Internet, and having sex with each other every half hour.

Curic and I walked from the bucket to a big jumble of bubble airlocks, just like the ones on the moon. Another group of ports connecting Alien Ring to every other Ring. Tiny flying night creatures swarmed around the airlocks, certain that the daylight from other worlds was somehow important, not at all certain whether to approach the light or flee it.

"We're almost there," said Curic. We pushed and tugged ourselves through the thickened-jelly airlock, through a wormhole, into a hotel hallway.

Okay, hotel hallways are a little narrower, and carpeted, and they end eventually, but that's basically what we're dealing with here. A shiny hall made of moon-dust ceramic, with big round doors on either side and inoffensive diffuse light coming from nowhere in particular. I expected to see signs for the ice machine.

I sagged in the Earth-normal gravity. I took off my breathing mask. "What is *this?*" I said.

"The human environment," said Curic.

"Where's the techno-primitive aesthetic? Where's the *trees?*"

"We don't have any Earth trees," said Curic. "We built the kind of environment humans enjoy."

"This is a fucking *hospital*," I said. There were no smudges on the walls, no dust on the floor. "It's a cubicle farm. We don't *enjoy* this environment. People *make* us stay here."

"It looks like a space station," said Curic. I think I'd hurt her feelings.

I walked toward one of the doors and it irised open, just like a door on a space station. The temperature of Human Ring is seventy-two degrees Fahrenheit. Through the door was a room the size of the Ip Shkoy apartment I'd just left. It contained a bunkbed, a combination sink/shower, and a squat toilet. The walls and the fixtures were the same ceramic as the hallway, lit by the same nondirectional light.

I looked back, out at the endless rows of doors. "How long is this hallway? It looks like it goes on forever."

"It does," said Curic. "It's a loop around the Ring."

"No one's going to come here," I said. "What the fuck. No one will go through what I had to go through, for this."

"This is a temporary structure," said Curic, almost pleading. "We know we're not humans. This was our best guess. It won't stay this way. Your greatest artists and architects will come here to redesign Human Ring. The challenge will be irresistible. We'll train them in metafractal reduction, and in five years, this habitat will look completely different."

"What government's going to send an artist up here for five years? I'm a *spy*, and I have to go home in six days!"

"Then the refugees or the astronauts will do it," said Curic. "It will happen eventually."

"I won't sleep in a twin-size bunkbed," I said. "This isn't computer camp."

"Sleep in the hallway," said Curic. "Or go to the central cylinder and sleep in microgravity, like the astronauts. Or make your own bedding from the Repertoire. But know that your friends on Earth want you to sleep, and they want you to breathe a nitrogen-oxygen atmosphere while you do it."

I gave up. I left Curic outside and let the door close like a techno-anus behind me. There were no sheets and no pillows on the bed; just a soft fabriclike skin over the mattress. I laid my head on my duffel bag, and instead of going to sleep, I wrote an email to Krakowski and Fowler.

Subject: The thrilling adventures of ARIEL THE SPY

Yesterday (July 18) I played video games. All games mentioned are from the Aliens' Ip Shkoy civilization of 17 million years ago, created ~50 Earth years after their contact with the Constellation. Played on a replica system in a historically accurate setting in conjunction with a hard-core professional historian.

Ev luie Aka's Ultimate DIY Lift-Off: Anti-Constellation propaganda. An astronaut comes back from the dead to stop the Constellation from strip-mining the Alien homeworld. A technically interesting rails shooter where the 'rail' is the orbit of your Vostok-style spacecraft, said spacecraft having been anachronistically equipped with guided missiles and aerial mines.

Gourmand's Delight: Action game. Throw food into the other guy's mouth until he pukes. Social commentary? Historian sez: "No, puking is funny."

Recapture That Remarkable Taste: Inferior remake of Farang Sayable Spice (see my blog passim, or don't). Thanks to knowledge of period food, historian was able to unlock rather explicit cutscenes, playable through dialogue trees.

Gewnoy Multislam: Allegedly a game pitting different styles of martial arts against each other. Game refused to start because it believed it was a pirated copy. Most likely culprit is defective temperature sensor in replica False Daylight system. Will play in historian-approved emulator later.

Rolling Weight: Failure To Protect The Innocent: Police procedural set in impoverished cities outside Alien homeworld's equatorial forests. Hard-boiled mood somewhat upset by player character's ridiculously high jump. Optional second and third players control all NPCs. Engrossing; native-language strategy guide has been employed. Have in possession a saved game at ~25% completion.

Today: more games, probably.

Love and kisses,
Ariel

Blog post, July 19

Woke up in Human Ring, did a little exploring and saw this handbill stuck to the wall near the bubble airlock back to Alien Ring. I'd missed it last night.

HUMANS! HUMANS! HUMANS!
BOTHERED BY UNSIGHTLY
HEAVY METALS * RADIOACTIVES * MEDICAL WASTE

? ? ?

THE RAW MATERIALS OVERLAY WILL DISPOSE OF
YOUR TRASH
SAFELY AND FREE OF CHARGE
www.materials.rc.luna/disposal
TOXIC LAND REMOVED
INDUSTRIAL PROCESSES STREAMLINED
LOW MINIMUM ORDER

!!!

I took five or six copies in different languages and stuck them to the wall of my room using NASA tomato paste from the Repertoire. Now my room is slightly different from the eight million other Human Ring rooms.

Blog post, July 19, evening

[This post is friends locked.]
Howdy, bro, you know how you'll score a sweet new licensed football game, with *totally marginal* improvements over last year's entry in the same franchise, spend hours breaking it in, and the next day end up all sore from all those motion-control passes and hikes? Or, I suppose that might also happen with actual sports.

Well, a similar thing happened to me. I stayed up all night with Aliens reenacting an ancient Alien culture and when I woke up today, I'd kind of forgotten what humans look like. Curic was right.

It didn't help that I woke up in a local-TV commercial for heaven (Private Rooms! Free Cable!). Breakfast from the Repertoire was an international variety of pastes from ten different space programs. So after breakfast, I decided to go meet the brave men and women who eat this paste every day. I went to the central cylinder.

I probably should have gone *before* breakfast, but it's cool. Thanks to years of dealing with buggy 3D game engines, I can handle weightlessness pretty well. I just have to couple it with not being trapped in an infinite void and lacking any point of reference. As long as I don't look down the entire eighty-mile length of the central cylinder, I'm fine. Twenty miles down the zipline, after spotting Cryptids, Goyim, and three enormous Auslanders glowing like suns, I saw a tiny human figure in NASA blue.

I pulled up close to her with alternating back-and-forth pulses from my gravity kicker. She wasn't actually a tiny figure—that was just perspective--and she wasn't gigantic like an Auslander. She was the correct size for a human woman. She had two normal-sized eyes and no eyespots I could see. She held a clipboard in one ~~forehand~~ hand and a Space Pen (Made in the USA) in the other. Her mouth was a mouth, not a parrot beak swarming with antennacles. Her short blonde hair free-fell in a halo around her head, matted with dried sweat to an extent previously seen only on young punk girls panhandling in downtown Austin.

Either the astronaut or I was upside down. She'd rolled up the legs of her flight suit, as though she'd been walking through puddles. Her legs were hairy and her toes decorated with badly chipped pink nail polish. Time to break out the ol' human small talk.

"Hi," I said.

"Mmm." The astronaut ticked a checkbox on her clipboard with her Space Pen.

"I'm Ariel Blum."

That got her to look up, and then down. "Oh, hi," she said. "Mission Specialist—," and then she said her name. But this is not the kind of blog that throws around women's names, even when they wear those names on patches on their chests. So I'm going to call her Miss Ion Specialist.

I couldn't figure out how to rotate myself, and Ion Specialist was perfectly comfortable interacting with someone who was upside-down relative to her, or at least didn't seem to expect anything better from the likes of me. So I just kept talking to her nail polish.

"I haven't seen another human for a while," I said. "You're with NASA?"

"And you, a civilian."

"Is it that obvious?"

"I don't already know you," said Ion. "Also you're—" she tapped her neck with her pen "—green. 'Never rode the Vomit Comet' kind of green."

"Oh," I said. "Yeah, first time in zero gravity. It's a little strange."

"There's no such thing as zero gravity." Ion was clearly not the kind of astronaut they send to schools to explain things to kids. "We're in free-fall around Luna."

"Have you been there?" I said. "To the moon? I went yesterday."

Ion ticked another box on her checklist, possibly a checklist called "Stupid Questions From Civilians."

"I was the eighth woman on the moon," she said. "I could have been the fourth, but who needs the publicity, right?" Eyes back on the clipboard. "Love to shoot the shit, dude, but these experiments won't monitor themselves."

"What experiments?"

Ion glanced around. "The apparatus is in Utility Ring. I'm just here to get away from Certain People for a few hours."

"I mean, what experiments are you doing?"

"ISS backlog," said Ion Specialist. "Uh, how do foams behave in free-fall? How do nematodes reproduce? Plasmas, smoke points, physiological tests, miscellaneous."

That didn't sound too difficult. "Can I help?"

"Do you have *any* astronaut training?"

"I can wash your glassware," I said. "Or! I can give you the news from Earth." (Brilliant, Ariel, like astronauts don't have the Internet.)

"Earth." Ion Specialist drew the word out real long, as though *Earth* was a

TV show she'd enjoyed watching but had forgotten about between seasons.

"I can get you a drink," I said, "and you can enjoy your vacation from Certain People."

"You can try," said Ion, "but the only alcohol in the Repertoire is blood packs for Inostrantsi. I'm not that desperate."

"I know there's caipirinha."

"What's that, some kind of industrial solvent?"

"It's like a Brazilian mojito."

Ion looked at me with a kind of respect. She glanced at her clipboard and blew her breath out through her lips. "Alright," she said.

Floating here and there in the central cylinder are ceramic... asteroids, basically, objects big enough to absorb your momentum and small enough for a few people to cling to and talk. They cluster around Repertoire stations, so I kicked off towards the nearest cluster. And then past it, then away at an angle, and finally *bam* into a plus-sign-shaped asteroid.

Ion was waiting for me there. She'd seen where I was going and pushed herself over with a single swipe of the gravity kicker she wore like a ring on one hand.

"Hey, civilian," she said.

The caipirinha comes out the Repertoire as a thin sticky sheet. I tore it in half, rolled it up, and put each half into a plastic bulb of water. A little shaky-shaky and the drinks were ready.

"Ariel, how did you get *up* here?" asked Ion, like this had been really bothering her. "You're the first 'civilian' I've seen who wasn't secretly working for the feds." She took a caipirinha bulb and sucked on it steadily, like an IV drip.

"How do you know *I'm* not secretly working for the feds?" I asked, kind of insulted.

"You're not," said Ion. "Aw, hey there, liquor, I missed you, too! So what are you doing here?"

~~"Playing video games," I said.~~ No, I didn't say that! I said: "I'm studying the earlier contact missions. Did you know that the Aliens had an early industrial civilization when the Constellation contacted them? Like World War II era, except with public sex and space travel. Isn't that amazing?"

"Which ones are the Aliens?" said Ion Specialist.

"The eight-foot monkey lizards! How long have you been up here?"

"Contact event plus nine hours," said Ion. "Oh, I should have gotten someone to take my houseplants. They're probably dead by now."

"You've been lighting foam on fire for six weeks?" I said. "I enjoy weightlessness experiments as much as the next taxpayer, but is the ISS backlog really a good use of your time? Like, what about all the extraterrestrials?"

"I'm an astronaut," said Ion, "which means I run the experiments I'm ordered to run, like a good little lab assistant, or I go back home. I'm also a physicist, which means I don't know which end of a Gweilo to shake hands with and which to gossip about afterwards. You want xenobiology, you should talk to Dr. Wicklund."

"Cody Wicklund? He's the—"

"Yeah, a real expert at shaking hands. There's a civilian for ya. Head asshole of the NASA Asshole Corps."

My phone rang. It was 9:04 in Austin. "Shit," I said, looking at the screen, "Sorry, I have to take this. It's the BEA."

"Is that supposed to impress me?" said Ion Specialist. "Is the BEA some big space monster, like Her? The Bug-Eyed Alien?"

"Sssh!"

Agent Fowler was on the other end of the phone, and I don't want to give him any time in this blog post, so suffice to say that he was really happy about_Ev liue Aka's Ultimate DIY Lift-Off,_ and this was really bad news for me and the rest of the human race.

"The Bureau of Extraterrestrial Affairs is a *government agency*," I said. "AKA the feds. And I've been here for one day and they're already misrepresenting my work." Ion Specialist whistled innocently.

"The Ip Shkoy," I said, "one of the early industrial Alien civilizations. They made this... well, it was a... kind of video game."

"Oh, you're into video games?!" said Ion. Hundred thousand miles from home and I'm still falling into this conversational trap. "There was this game I played when I was a kid, and I could never remember the name."

"Did it involve Blizzard Lizard?" I said. "Because that would be <u>Blizzard Lizard</u>."

"No, it was all text; it was on the computer. You were on this big spaceship, but it was breaking down, and you had to build replacement parts out of your cargo of tacky tourist souvenirs."

"That sounds like <u>Starfarer</u>." Nineteen eighty...seven? When that game came out, I was nothing but my grandparents pressuring my parents to give Raph a little brother.

"Yes! That was it! Awesome! Anyway, go on with your story."

"Well, the Ip Shkoy made this game where you basically blow up the entire Constellation contact mission. BEA thinks that game was on to something. Now they want me to see what the Constellation did to make the Aliens so mad."

"Sounds like something worth knowing."

"Yeah, except the Constellation didn't actually do anything. The game is bullshit."

"Says who? Someone from the Constellation?"

"Oh, well, yeah. But I wouldn't have heard of this game in the first place, if it wasn't for Tetsuo."

"So? Tetsuo slipped up."

I was clinging to the plus-sign-shaped asteroid for dear life, but Ion still had some angular momentum going, and by this point in the conversation, I was once again looking at her toenail polish. I scrambled to the other side of the asteroid so I could look her in the eye.

"That game was made fifty years into the contact mission," I said. "This one's been going six lousy weeks, and humans are already getting mad at the Constellation. 'What have they done for us?' Not a hell of a lot. Whose fault is that? I dunno. But people are pissed that the Constellation didn't come here with ready-made solutions to all our problems."

"Why would they have solutions to our problems?" asked Ion. "They don't even observe proper experimental controls. You would not believe how they treat my apparatus."

"I'm saying you don't need a reason to be angry. You can just get angry and make a slanderous game. And then seventeen million years later, the BEA will use that game to feed the hysteria on Earth. Different planet, same problem."

"Mmm," said Ion, looking at her clipboard. "Would you like to hear my secret way for dealing with these things?"

"Yes," I said.

"Not thinking about it." She held out her empty, collapsed bulb. "Would you get me another industrial solvent?"

After she'd finished her checklist and her second caipirinha, Ion Specialist pulled herself to the plus-sign-shaped asteroid and looked me over one more time, as if deciding whether she could trust me. "I have a question for you," she whispered. "Have you ever heard of a company called Constellation Shipping?"

"It's not a company," I said. "It's just a logo they put on the boxes they send down to Earth. It's like a running joke."

"Ariel the civilian, I have decided to show you something weird. Something I found in Utility Ring."

"I'm from Austin," I said. "We'll look at anything weird."

"That's good," said Ion Specialist conspiratorially, "because I'm from Akron, Ohio, and if we see something weird, we don't have many options other than starting a rock band."

"I play drums a little."

"Why don't I just show you?"

She showed me.

Chapter 14:
The Wave Function Of The Universe

Real Life, July 19

I had a bed set up with the two bunkbed mattresses, and a pillow made from twenty-five identical shirts from the Repertoire. It was a nice system, but there was no nightstand, so when Jenny called, I had to roll onto the floor and feel around for the phone.

"I am freaking unhappy!" said Jenny. "You haven't even looked at my concept art."

"I... was asleep," I said.

"It's nine-thirty," said Jenny.

"Yeah, nine-thirty in Austin," I said.

"Oh, did you tire yourself out floating around Ring City with your girl-friend?" said Jenny. "While I was busting my ass on Sayable Spice: Earth Remix."

"Dammit. Jenny. Curic's not my girlfriend."

"I'm not talking about Curic."

"Oh." I let that hang there for a second. One of Smoke's subminds decided I wasn't going back to sleep, and turned on the room light.

"I know your signals, Ariel," said Jenny, real proud of this, like I play 'em so close to the vest. "The cutesy pseudonym? Posting an innocuous conversation and friends-locking it? What did she 'show you' in Utility Ring?"

"It was a shipping container," I said. "She didn't know about Constellation Shipping, so she freaked out when she found a shipping container in a space station orbiting the moon. I'll write about it when I— great, now my mother is calling. There goes sleep."

"Oh, she calls *right* as I call?"

"Hold on." I switched to the incoming call. "Hi, Ma."

"Ariel, this is your mother."

"Yeah, Ma, hi, what's up?"

"I read your blog," said my mother. "Who is this Ion Specialist?"

"She's... a woman... I met... on the space... station," I said, picking every word from a menu of generic-sounding words.

"What's her real name? I want to look her up and make sure she's not one of the crazy astronauts."

"Her name is Tammy, Ma. *Doctor* Tammy Miram."

"Miram? Is there the tiniest possibility that that's a Jewish name?"

"I don't think so, ma. She's probably some kind of lapsed-Catholic Unitarian Buddhist."

"Well, you know me, I don't care, as long as you're happy. Only, please tell me they sell rubbers in the bathrooms up there?"

"Ma, every single assumption you made in that sentence is wrong."

"Just tell your mother she doesn't have to worry."

"We did nothing, Ma." I got up and took the conversation outside, to the infinite hallway.

"Doesn't sound like a girl you want to do nothing with," said my mother.

"We made out a little, okay? We made out in zero gravity behind a shipping container!" I shouted it out to everyone in Human Ring, which was nobody. "Are you happy now?"

"That's a pretty cheap date, honey."

"All right, Ma," I said, "you have officially crossed the line. I've got Jenny on hold, and I'm going to have her humiliate me about this instead of you."

"Jenny, that poor girl."

"Bye, Ma. Take care. Buh-bye now. I'm back."

"Did you move?" said Jenny. "It looks different."

"Yeah, I'm in the hallway now," I said. I held the camera lens away from me and waved the phone around. "Drink it in. Fuckin'... Kansas in space."

"Well, after your nap, lover boy," said Jenny, "take a minute to look at the damn concept art. I like it and Bizarro Kate likes it, but maybe you think it's too anime-y for a video game."

"Maybe it is," I said, "but I'm not the art dictator. I hired you so we could get a division of labor. You should go with the style you're comfortable with."

"That's sweet, except this game isn't about pachinko or time management, so our main audience is likely to be young men. Which means we might want more of a comic book look."

I paced the cold black floor in my bare feet. "Guys like anime, too," I said. "The anime club in college was full of guys."

"And at the time, I calculated that that was about eighty percent wanting to look at tits."

"So is comic books."

"Nah," said Jenny. "Sixty percent, tops."

"I need a break from Tetsuo," I said. "I'll look at the art tomorrow morning."

Blog post, July 20

GAME REVIEWS OF INSERT DESCRIPTION HERE 2.0 PRESENTS
A Tower of Sand
A game by Af be Hui
Reviewed by Ariel Blum

Publisher: The Perea Corporation
Release date: Contact event plus 49 years
Platforms: Simulates Hi-Def False Daylight, Dare To Greatness, Your Return
ESRB rating: T for thematic elements, whatever that means

"We need to find a game that makes the Constellation look good," I said.

The urgency in my voice did not penetrate Tetsuo's sound-sensitive membranes. "Why would someone make a game about that?"

"I'd make one myself," I said, "if I found out that people were spreading panic by creating Constellation assassination fantasies. And if we don't find something to cancel out Ev Iuie Aka's Ultimate DIY Lift-Off, I'll *have* to make one myself, because you'll have right-wing militias blockading your consulate buildings."

"Let them come!" said Tetsuo. "With their primitive maces and carving knives!"

"No, they'll have guns."

"Oh, that's a little worse," said Tetsuo. "I'm thinking." He rolled back and forth on his beanbag chair, hugging it beneath him like a body pillow.

"Ideally it would be another game with 'Ultimate' in the title," I said. "Fowler was very impressed by that."

Tetsuo reached out a long, long forearm and waved a hand in front of my face. "You smell funny," he said.

"Back atcha, pal."

"Different from before. Hah, it's pheremones! You're covered in human pheremones! You're away from the females of Earth only one day, and you go into heat!"

"You're smelling alcohol, genius. I had a drink. Is everything about sex with you?"

"Only sexy things."

"We need empathy," I said. "A tear-jerker. Sympathetic characters. Are there any Ip Shkoy games where you play an extraterrestrial?"

"There are many," said Tetsuo. "In <u>Grow,</u> you control an entire ring of Wazungu. It's very stylized; what used to be called an eat-and-shit game."

"People don't like Wazungu; they look like rotten food."

"I like them."

"*Humans* don't like them, and you know it. That's why you made Charlene Siph the Constellation ambassador, instead of Bob the Mzungu."

"Please do not call her that!" Tetsuo said. "We're all ambassadors. Charlene Siph is the fixer."

"Can you find a game with a Farang player character? People think they're cute."

"Certainly," said Tetsuo, staring into space. "Although I doubt such a game will change anyone's mind. Here's one with good reviews: <u>A Tower of Sand</u>."

Now I waved *my* hand in front of Tetsuo's face. "Where are you getting these?"

"The database, like as you," said Tetsuo. "Let's hit the store."

"No! Spare me the store!"

We went to the store.

"Why did you recreate the whole damn store?" I asked Tetsuo. "All the software is behind your little bubble." Behind me, in the rear of the store, I heard repetitive splashes, as food packages were constantly drawn up a conveyor belt and dropped a good ten feet into a big tank of refrigerated water.

"Buy something or get out!" Tetsuo yelled from the other side of the Plexiglass shield.

Two could play at this game. "I want to do a trade-in," I said. From my pocket, I pulled the <u>Gewnoy Multislam</u> box I'd found in the replica Ip Shkoy apartment. I waved it at Tetsuo.

"Trade in?"

"<u>Gewnoy Multislam</u> for credit against <u>Tower of Sand</u>."

"Presumptious fool! You can only trade a newer game for an older game! <u>A Tower of Sand</u> was published a full solar year after <u>Gewnoy Multislam</u>."

"You're making that up."

"It is the policy of the store!"

"<u>Gewnoy Multislam</u> doesn't even work."

"Not my fault," said Tetsuo. "You should've bought two."

"I'll tell everyone you sell faulty software. I have powerful friends, clerk dude!"

Tetsuo changed his tune immediately. "You pay retail," he said, "and I'll enlarge your order to encompass one of these fine desperation items." He reached behind him with his tail and slapped a metal cage full of cheap squishy plastic against his side of the Plexiglass bubble.

"Aah!" I said. The cage swung back and forth in front of my face. "All right, give me that horrible-looking mouth foam."

"Hundred sixty, plus tip."

"Is that what they said?" I asked Tetsuo once we left the role-play of the You Buy Now. "'You should have bought two' when you complained about something?"

"Yes," said Tetsuo, "or else your expectations were too high. For happen-stance, suppose you eat an Earth cake, and then you tell me 'Tetsuo! I wish I still had that cake!'"

"Oh, actually in English we have a saying—"

"I *know* that!"

Back in the apartment, I unfolded the poster that came with the game, but as far as my eyes could tell, it was totally blank.

"It is a game for two players," said Tetsuo, screwing a second abacus-organ controller into the top of the <u>Tower of Sand</u> data cylinder. "We portray a Farang named Koht. An expert in architecture."

The poor False Daylight system looked like it would explode from having all this stuff attached to it, but I bravely took the second controller. "We're *both* Koht?"

"I'm Koht when female," said Tetsuo, "and you are her crossself, the male. We trade off over the course of the day."

Tetsuo started the game. An oval in the center of the projection showed a top-down view of Koht, while a split-screen behind the oval showed what I eventually realized were side views. Tetsuo started laying a line of triangular blocks on the ground.

"You're building something," I said. "Perhaps a Tower of Sand?"

"Yes, I build," said Tetsuo. "The story is that we create a sister-city to the space station. Farang will come down here to live, and meantimes Aliens populate the space station, as you do here on Ring City. It's a cultural exchange."

"Did *this* actually happen?" I didn't want to get burned by another <u>Ultimate Lift-Off</u> fantasy.

"Yes, it began when the creator of this game was young."

"People were okay with it? Extraterrestrials coming and living on your home planet?"

"Well, no one wants to live on a beach, with cliffs, am I right? It's not prime real estate."

"I wouldn't mind having a beach house," I said.

"But a human is you. Imagine living somewhere nobody wants to live."

"The desert."

"Yeah, the beach just is a wet desert. But Farang love beaches, so it's cool."

A bolt of lightning shivered the screen and the background sounds became higher-pitched. Tetsuo worked his controller ineffectively.

"It's your turn," said Tetsuo. "If we had some friends who also played this game, we could enchain our data cylinders and compete to attract the most visitors."

"I'm going to knock down all your buildings," I cackled. I rammed Koht into one of the structures and knocked a few tiles loose.

"No, undo, do not!" said Tetsuo. "It's unrealistic!"

"I'm not the one who made Koht kiss a wall."

"But that was funny," said Tetsuo. He put his forehands like antennacles in front of his wide mouth, and wiggled them around. "Blbblblt."

I found another Farang walking around the beach and body-checked him/her. "No, that's someone who wants to live in my buildings! Bweeee! Leave him alone!"

The projector went white and Pey Shkoy script appeared on the screen, then trickled downwards as if the characters had been carved out of sand. "You have lost us the game!" said Tetsou.

"Why?"

"You made Koht act crazy," said Tetsuo. "Ambivalent, dissociated in personality. His friends became concerned. It's on the poster."

"I can't even see the ink on the poster," I said. "This sucks. I want to be player one."

"Then be," said Tetsuo. We crawled around each other rather than messing with the controllers. I restarted the game and toddled along the beach, digging blocks out of the sand and stacking them precariously on each other.

"Are there any Aliens in this game?" I asked.

"Not at the start," said Tetsuo. "You'd have to build a harbor or a fun-fair to get Aliens to attend a beach."

"How about other species?"

"The poster expresses several Goyim," said Tetsuo, tracing its ultraviolet ink with a finger. "In the ocean." On the projector, lightning struck again. "Ah, my turn!" Tetsuo picked up his controller and twitched away.

I'd left the game board full of piles of bricks, and deep holes in the sand. Tetsuo immediately resumed his old habits, piling up hollow pyramids and underground tunnels, juggling the camera viewpoints like a pro.

The screen turned white again and displayed some kind of tabular information. "Bweeh, we failed!" said Tetsuo.

"Why? You didn't kill anybody."

"Our building styles were too divergent," said Tetsuo. "You and I, Ariel, we are not very good at forming a single Farang."

The two players in A Tower of Sand chase each other creatively, each trying to put their stamp on the built environment while maintaining a single artistic style for Koht. It's not a cooperative game, exactly, but it's not one you can play with an uncooperative or unfriendly person. Try just once to really pull one over on your opponent, and the game's over.

We got into the mechanics, and after a couple of hours, we were able to complete a modest building that simulated people wanted to visit. Instead of digging more sand to add extensions and possibly screw the whole thing up, we spent a few turns walking around and greeting the sunbathing Farang, who gave off happy little Pey Shkoy emoticons.

"All right," I said, "this is a decent game and I'll write it up, but here's what I'm concerned about. If you were a human, and I told you about this friendly little game, where Farang come down to the Alien homeworld to build houses in the desert and fun-fairs and shit, would you be more or less apprehensive about Ev Iuie Aka's Ultimate DIY Lift-Off?"

"I'm not a human," said Tetsuo, "so if you want accuracy, you must answer that question yourself."

But I can't.

Real life, July 21

"Okay! Yes! This is good, Ari. Now we move to stage three. Grab hold of the shipping container."

"I can't reach. It's like ten feet away now."

"What the hell! Where'd all this delta-vee come from?"

"Maybe it's 'cause I took off my shoes back in stage one."

"Well, you're never gonna see those shoes again, dude. Okay, hold on to me, yeah, and I'll use the kicker. Yeah, wow, just like that."

"Ow! Shit!"

"Sorry. Disengage! Abort! I'm holding on to your foot."

"Man! Those suggestive docking sequences in sci-fi movies make it look so easy. Don't they teach you how to do this in astronaut training?"

"No, they just tell you not to do it."

"That's what they told us, in high school, but nobody listened."

"Sorry we had to scrub the mission. Do you want to set up again? I need to be feeding planaria in the central cylinder in an hour. But we've got that hour."

"I think we should go to my place and shower, and maybe pick up later."

"Showering isn't sexy here, Ari, it's annoying. And you still look ready to me."

"I mean an actual shower, with soap. When you get sweaty, it kinda... reactivates all your accumulated sweat."

"G-d, don't be such a civilian! Freefall showers are the worst. The water goes on like lotion."

"Tammy, have you *been* to Human Ring?"

"Why would I? There's nothing there."

"Nothing but *showers*. Gravity showers, like on Earth."

"... So first the booze and now hot water? You're just bringing all my recreational liquids back into my life? It *is* hot water, right?"

"I guess? It's hot enough."

"I'll need help, Ari. I've been free-falling for fifty days. Once I hit the ground, I'll need someone to hold me up. Do you really want to help a feeble old lady take a shower?"

"Not really, but I want to help *you* take a shower."

"That is a good answer."

Real life, July 21

I knocked a couple times on the wooden doorframe and let myself into Tetsuo and Ashley's house, two levels up the tree from the replica Ip Shkoy apartment and much better lit. Still had the storage trapdoors in the floor, though. A nice retro touch, like a Victorian fireplace in a Houston McMansion.

In the front room, Ashley Somn was lying on her back in a yoga pose, hindhands stroking glowing symbols in the air like a sleepy cat with a dangled string.

"Hey, Ash, whatcha playin'?"

"This is not a game," said Ashley. "I'm parameterizing Earth organisms as part of the History of Life overlay." She twitched a finger on one hindarm, and one amoeba-looking hologram was replaced with another, nearly identical amoeba-looking hologram.

"Okay, hey, can you put on some... clothes?" I turned my head away.

"I'm wearing clothes," said Ashley.

"Yeah, sort of, but your, uh, is showing."

Ashley looked up at her belly. "My ovipositor?" she said, as though I were a foot fetishist. "Eggs come *out* of there. Nothing goes *in*. It's completely safe for work."

"Just humor me, please?"

Ashley peeled out of her *asana* and crawled into her spacesuit. Her transparent spacesuit.

"I asked you here to find out if you can do something about Tetsuo's English," she said. "Apparently it's quite bad."

"That's funny," I said, "because I was talking to *Tetsuo* earlier today, while we were playing <u>Recapture That Remarkable Taste</u>, and he asked me if I could teach *you* English."

"I don't need to learn English," said Ashley through her chopped-up resampled vocalizer. "The translator is a benefit embraced by the median person and shunned only by snobs who want to show off their own erudition and enlightened attitudes."

"Wow, I guess you feel pretty strongly about it?"

"That translation went on a lot longer than it should have," said Ashley. "That was four words in Purchtrin. I don't know what happened."

"Maybe you should learn English and figure it out? But you're safe from me; I can't teach you. You need an ESL course."

"But you speak English," said Ashley.

"I can't teach it to someone who speaks a language from another planet."

"Thank you for taking my side, Ariel," said Ashley, who clearly didn't believe me. She circled the room on all fours, pulling scraps of wispy cloth out of trapdoors and draping them over her spacesuit. "Please tell me when I'm wearing enough clothes that you feel comfortable."

"That's fine," I said.

"What about Tetsuo?" Ashley turned dramatically and glared at me with combined eyes and eyespots. "Can you teach *him*?"

"I can talk good English and hope he picks it up," I said. "If you want him to learn about grammar or something, he'll need to talk to my parents."

"What in heck is occurring here?" said Tetsuo, who'd just crawled in. "Is today the day when we wear our clothes on the outside of our space-suits?"

"Ariel was distracted by my beautiful ovipositor," said Ashley, crawling back into her hindarms-up position.

I flinched. "That's the worst possible translation of whatever you just said. Tets, you gotta get your woman some English lessons."

"I am attempting," said Tetsuo. "Ariel, welcome to our home. My fruit is your picnic." He lay down on top of Ashley's tail.

"I think I understood that," I said. "Thanks."

"And I thank you for extending your stay in Alien Ring," said Tetsuo. "I know you would like to go back to the central cylinder."

"You do, huh?"

"You smell like a human who's going to fuck somebody," said Tetsuo.

"It's quite strong," said Ashley.

I took a sharp breath and said nothing. Tetsuo either didn't notice or immediately gave up. "I have made a discovery!" he said. "About the software games of the Ip Shkoy-era Aliens."

"I hope it's a better discovery than <u>A Tower of Sand</u>," I said, "because that game didn't do shit for the Constellation's reputation. Agent Fowler's still on the warpath."

"Do human software games have directors?" said Tetsuo. "Like movies?"

"Yeah," I said, "if they're real pretentious, like <u>Weapon Eternal</u>."

"Af be Hui was the director of <u>A Tower of Sand</u>," said Tetsuo. "She became well-known. High-status. She made seven other games and her games changed history a little bit. I think we should play more of her work."

"To what purpose? Did she finally get the Ip Shkoy to calm down about the Constellation?"

Ashley wriggled violently and Tetsuo crawled off of her tail. "Purpose?" said Tetsuo. "What is purpose? History is not a trash compactor where you lost something important. You have to spend some time there."

"I don't *have* the time. I have to go back to Earth in a few days."

"Your visit is an opportunity to understand the Ip Shkoy a little better than a tourist," said Tetsuo. "If you want, then you can apply the historical knowledge to your own situation."

"If I *want*?"

Blog post, July 22

After a few days of randomly sampling the gaming history of the Ip Shkoy, Tetsuo and I have come up with a Plan. And a Schedule. We'll spend the rest of the week's game time playing <u>Schvei</u> and <u>The Long Way Around</u>, the two biggest games of Ip Shkoy game director Af be Hui. I'll write the reviews when I get back to Earth, because I've got other stuff going on. A lot of things I'd rather be doing than sitting on half a bunkbed, text-to-speeching stuff you're just gonna leave smartass comments about.

One more quick note, as Curic has a question for you Internet smartasses.

A few days ago, my friend Ion Specialist took me to Ring City's utility ring and showed me a human-style shipping container with the Constellation Shipping logo painted on the side. Like, lawn furniture from China, goes on a ship, sort of shipping container. She didn't know what to make of it; I explained that it was kind of a transportation-nerd joke. Like the fake wooden crates Curic brought down to Earth, with "Constellation Shipping" stenciled on *their* sides. Why cover something with boring re-entry foam when you can give your drop that touch of human elegance?

Well, this shipping container was a little unusual in that the door wouldn't open. Shipping containers are usually locked, as I discovered that time I tried to steal a entire shipment of DVD players. But this one wasn't locked; it just wouldn't open.

The other strange thing is that when Curic went to the utility ring today to check it out, the container was gone. I know I'm stretching the definition of "strange" here. Constellation Shipping is more or less defunct, due to laws and shit, so at this point you might as well recycle the containers that never got shipped. But Curic suspects a *container conspiracy*. She wants to know if anyone on Earth ever took delivery of one of these containers.

Don't ask me why she cares. If you were shipping contraband or something, would you paint a big Constellation Shipping starfield on the side of the container? Why not rip off the Loyalitet or NTF logo?

Chapter 15:
777

"What would you do," Curic asked me, "if you knew that something catastrophic was going to happen to your home planet?"

"I...don't like where this is going." I lay on my back on the floor of Curic's house, immobile, slowly flattening in the Farang Ring gravity. A human lump lying among the artworks Curic had acquired from her contacts on Earth: a polished wood bowl, some kind of picture of Jesus, and the big circuit-board sculpture she'd gotten from Jenny.

Curic paced the room in a robe made of fishnet and pockets. "For instance, suppose that increasing concentrations of carbon dioxide and methane were destabilizing Earth's climate."

"Oh, that," I said. "We already know about that."

"What did you do when you found out?"

"Well, there was this benefit concert Jenny and Bai and I went to, in college."

Sunk into Curic's living room is a hot tub. It's a natural Jacuzzi, since water in Farang Ring boils at about seventy degrees Fahrenheit. Curic walked into this hot tub, submerged herself, and blew bubbles for a couple minutes. She walked back out and calmly said: "A benefit concert."

"C'mon. What do you want from me?" I said. I pushed the oxygen mask to my mouth with one hand and clutched my head with the other. Human-habitable, my ass.

"You seem uncomfortable," said Curic with astounding perspicacity. "Zip up your suit. We'll go in the water."

Outside Curic's house, Farang Ring looks like Hawaii would, if Hawaii had Seattle's climate. Swimming in the ocean is definitely easier than walking, though I do recommend a spacesuit so you don't freeze to death. In the water, Curic swelled up to twice her normal size. She looked like a tiny purple polar bear.

"I belong to an overlay called 'Save the Humans'," said Curic, treading water.

"Hey, that's patronizing."

"Thanks for noticing," said Curic. "I am becoming worried because we cannot find a vector for action."

"Is that some fancy jargon?" I slowly sank into the ocean, and Curic expelled little puffs of air to sink with me.

"No," she said, "I'm trying to communicate in a straightforward way, except in English."

"It's jargon. What is a vector in this context? Magnitude plus direction? A disease vector? Vector graphics?"

"I will tell you a story instead. A few days ago, my friend Kinki Kwi, acting as part of the Hierarchy Interface overlay, walks through the metal detector into the Senate Office Building. She is here to talk to the famous Senator about sharing carbon capture technology. The Senator is happy to see her. She puts forward her hand and Kinki Kwi touches it with her own.

"Kinki Kwi explains the carbon capture technology in layman's terms, because although the Senator is a ranking member of a committee that deals with such things, Kinki Kwi understands that her primary expertise is in touching her hand to other peoples' hands. The technology is based on kites."

"Kites like the...?" It was getting dark here in the briny deep. I looked up at the rippling surface and kind of understood why Brain Embryo games always show a bottom-up perspective.

"Kites are animals," said Curic, "that evolved along with the Auslanders. They can be bred to withstand the low pressure of your atmosphere, and to metabolize your atmospheric waste. They will increase the atmosphere's carrying capacity until humans can agree on a carbon reduction plan. They are a proven life-technology and their disruption of planetary weather will be minimal, compared to the alternative."

"Meanwhile, on the other side of the desk, the Senator issues a series of utterances that do not respond to naive analysis. A submind of the Ring City computer is set to the task, and is able to produce similar English sentences using a Markov chain of order five. Hypothesis: the human is saying things that are bullshit. To the extent that her message has any meaning at all, it is: Not In My Backyard."

"That's it? A politician spins you a line and ducks responsibility, and you're *confused*? Did humans invent bullshit? Is it a new phenomenon for you?"

"Silence, puny human!" Curic squeaked, and wiggled her antennacles at me.

"Also, if your name is Kinki Kwi, you should not be a diplomat."

"Why not?"

"It just sounds dirty."

Curic straightened her antennacles and vocalized over radio to conserve her air supply. "Fear my ultimate point," she said. "Your lifestyle-system contains an asymmetry. If we wanted to build a factory that turned trees into methane, nobody would stop us. But to fly a few million lousy kites, we have to get permission from people who talk bullshit. There is no way to act. No vector."

"Aren't you being a little hard on this poor lady? Look at it from her perspective."

"An order five Markov chain has a perspective?"

"Sure. She's gotta run for re-election next year or whenever, and she's imagining trying to film a campaign commercial in a cornfield, but they can't get a good shot because the sky is full of these floating *things*—how big are the kites?"

"On Earth? Wingspan would be up to a kilometer."

"Yeah, the biggest thing in the sky, blocking out the sun, hovering over her shoulder in the background. And what do these things eat? What happens when they take a shit?"

"I think we can assume the briefing deals with questions like these," said Curic. Above our heads, a thick and sudden mass of raindrops tenderized the water's surface.

"But she's just the delegate," I said. "The people who voted for her aren't gonna sit still for any briefing. They're going to yell these questions at her and not listen to the answers, because they just don't want huge Auslander birds flying over their heads. And they won't want to touch her hand anymore, either. The bullshit is a defense mechanism."

Curic waved a tiny, murky fist at me. "Save the Humans is not an after-school club like Constellation Shipping or History of Life," she said. "We have competition: an overlay called Plan C. If you keep employing defense mechanisms against people who want to help you, Plan C will win the argument. We will *end* the contact mission and go back home."

"You'd just leave us here?"

"You could come with us," said Curic. "Set up colonies on Earthlike planets. Remove some of the stress from your home planet. I don't *recommend* this. If I thought it was a good idea, I'd be aligned with Plan C."

I swam upwards a little, just to make sure I could, that I wasn't going to sink forever. "What happened to Plan B?" I said. "Is that you guys?"

"Plan B is what we're doing now," said Curic. "A normal contact mission. The name is a bit of a humanism—there's no actual plan."

"Yeah, I can tell. Which leads me to the obvious follow-up question..."

"Plan A is paleontology," said Curic. "Most of the time, when we get to a planet, all of the intelligent life is dead."

"Oh, right. Glad we dodged that bullet."

"You haven't dodged it yet."

Real life, July 23

I don't know if you've ever had sex with a pre-contact-era astronaut, but man, they've got a lot of stamina. I screwed Dr. Tammy Miram until my hamstrings gave out, and then she held me down on the flimsy bunkbed mattress and rode me for about twenty minutes more, and then she went for a DIY Lift-Off while I lay on my back exhausted and said cuss words for her. And then finally, finally, she spooned with me and got super emo.

"I was in training," she said. "I was gonna go up maybe around STS-116. And then STS-107 was *Columbia*, and they shut it down."

"I remember," I said. I didn't mention that I'd been in high school at the time.

"Mmm. So I started working on the replacement program, the Constellation program." She laughed musically. "I can't believe we called it that. But by the time we started the launches, I'd be..."

"Yeah?"

Tammy sighed. "A certain age. Not old, but an age where they want someone younger stepping into that billion-dollar piece of equipment. So I got certified and I started working on simulations. Three solid days in the simulator, pretending to go to the moon. So they could decide how to arrange the buttons. Pretending, Ariel."

"Pretending."

"The personal allowance is five kilos," she said. "That's for the STS; it would have been a little more for Titan." It was like hearing someone recite the names of dinosaurs.

"I had a bag, a backpack. I kept it packed at 4.99 kilos. As an act of hope. As if something might still happen after *Columbia*. Some call in the middle of the night, grab your socks, get your flight-status ass to Florida. There was a computer full of music, a big thick fantasy novel, college sweatshirt, chewing gum, crap like that. People used to pad it out with fresh food.

"Okay, Ariel, this bag did not run my life or anything. It was in the back of my bedroom closet. Every few months, I'd remember it and swap out the novel. I went through Garth Adams's entire *Sword of Chaos* series. Did you know that every one of those books weighs 1.13 kilos? Plus or minus ten grams."

"How does he do that?"

"I don't know, but it sure made things easy for me. Last year I finally pulled out the last one and finished it, so I switched to an e-reader. And then the call happened. They came and lifted me up, and I got to walk on the moon for real, and now I live in space, and... and you."

I blushed. "So you got to use the bag."

"It's still in my closet. I forgot it."

"No!"

"Yes. Contact event plus eight hours, I'm crammed into a Constellation shuttle with twenty whooping coworkers; and right as the Gulf of Mexico comes into view I remember that I spent the past ten years keeping a bag packed for this specific contingency."

"Ouch?"

"I forgot the bag, I didn't clean out the fridge. My plants are all dead. I left my car in the parking lot at work. I keep being reminded of things I didn't do on Earth, and none of it matters, because I've left it behind. I live in space now. I'll never set foot on a planet's surface again."

"What about, like, Mars?"

"Is Mars a planet?"

"Yeah," I said. "Unless they've been changing the definition again."

"Then no."

"Don't you have family?"

"Sure. They can come up here."

"They can't," I said. "You don't know what it's like. There's eight billion people the Constellation hasn't lifted up yet. I had to sell my soul to the State Department just to get on a shuttle."

Tammy shrugged. "You don't have to go back," she said. "What are they gonna do, extradite you?"

Real life, July 26

...

...

Shit. Shit. Shit.

Okay.

Let's start in the docking bay. My bag was slung over my shoulder and I was saying goodbye to Curic, Tetsuo, and Ashley. Tammy was on duty, so I was the only human in the docking bay. Possibly the only human in Human Ring, and about to leave.

"This time," said Tetsuo, like he was delivering a commencement address. "Its productivity has been tremendous. The two of us have greatly expanded humanity's knowledge of the post-contact Ip Shkoy civilization."

"Yeah," I said, "I'm not a hundred percent convinced that's a good thing."

"But what I said was technically true. And I think the Goyim philosopher Hushxnau said it best: 'Truth is good.'"

"There's got to be someone who said it better than that."

"I brought you a souvenir," said Curic.

"Thanks," I said, "but Tetsuo gave me so much Ip Shkoy crap, there's no room in my bag. I had to leave all my extra clothes here."

"Stick it in the overhead compartment," said Curic. "It's important." She lifted a large piece of burnished metal from her fanny pack and passed it to me two-handed.

"Oof," I said. It was a grid of tightly nestled metal gears suspended atop a mechanism of rods, cranks, and knobs. The gears had five or six faces, each with a symbol engraved on it. It looked like something Charles Babbage would invent to handicap the ponies.

"This is a mechanical game," said Curic, "from the planet Gliese 777Ad."

"Where's that?"

"It orbits Gliese 777A."

"That's where it is," said Ashley, like she had checked.

"It's a replica, of course," said Curic. "The original was eight times larger, but metal is a little scarce around here, and it probably wouldn't fit in the shuttle anyway."

"This looks like gold," I said. I set it down on the shuttle floor with a clunk.

"It is. An alloy of gold and copper."

I jump-fell away from the machine. "Are you nuts? I couldn't bring a *carrot* up here without having it cavity searched. How am I going to get a damn gold ingot through Customs?"

"It didn't occur to me," said Curic. "I'll make you a replacement of pure copper." Curic picked up the machine and held it to her belly.

"Who had that much gold?" *That's the single most valuable thing I've ever seen. If I could get her to drop-ship that to me, I'd never need money again.* (Yes, go to the bank and deposit thirty pounds of gold. That's a great plan, self.)

"Gold is as common on Gliese 777Ad as lead is on Earth," said Curic. "Luck of the draw."

No one needs to see the whole thing. Pull out those little rods, sell them three at a time. I looked at Tetsuo and Ashley so I wouldn't be looking at the machine. "Who's on 777Ad? Why don't they show up in the game database?"

"This is where I was born," said Curic. "On a contact mission in the 1960s, your reference frame. A lot of people reproduced near the end, when it looked like we'd be returning to Constellation space.

"The gears are *samsara* knots. What you would call cellular automata. You set their initial state—with tweezers, for the replica—and then turn the crank to run the algorithm." She turned it to demonstrate. The gears spun in little bursts, coming to rest on one face, then another.

"Ah," I said, "it's like Conway's Life."

"That's a cruel thing to say!"

"That's the name of a game," I said.

"Oh."

"It's beautiful," I said, "but why are you giving it to me?"

"We went there," said Curic, looking down at the machine she was cradling. "In your nineteenth century, my ancestors were part of a contact mission to the 777 system. We found a radioactive rock on one of 777Ad's moons, a rock that shouldn't have been there. On 777Ad itself, we found some technology like this. We found their cities. And we found them, the people who made these entertainments. But they were all dead."

"Fossilized?" I said.

"Not fossilized, no," said Ashley, as though her professional pride were at stake. "They were mummified."

"There was a virus," said Curic, "that tore apart their equivalent of DNA. It was probably engineered. Four thousand years ago, it killed everything on the planet, except for some isolated life near volcanic deep-sea vents. Anything that might have decomposed a body was also dead."

I didn't want the golden game anymore.

"You can imagine what it looked like when we landed," Curic continued. "As archaeology, it was perfect. Everything very well preserved. No living natives to complicate your reading of history. As a contact mission, it was an utter failure. Probably the worst in six hundred million years."

"It was not a failure," said Tetsuo, as though this were well-covered ground.

"Yeah, not your fault," I said. "They were dead when you got there. Sounds like a classic Plan A."

"It was an easy failure. No decisions to make, no culpability. Something like this happens... most of the time. Almost every time. But we had never come to a planet only a few years after the entire biosphere had died out."

"Four thousand years."

"That's not very long, Ariel!" said Curic. "This is context! Tens of thousands of people on this contact mission were born at 777Ad. We grew up outside the Constellation and we don't fit in with the rest of society, so we volunteered to come here. And here we found you, right on the other edge of the fossilization line.

"When we make our choices, we're thinking about the people who made this game. We're deciding to stand with you or to run away from you."

"Um," said Tetsuo, to break the silence. "Well, I just have a book about games that I translated for you." He handed it to me—more Ip Shkoy crap. "And a list of things I'd like you to bring up from Earth, the next time you come."

Tetsuo crouched, pressed his forehead against mine, and whispered. "Listen. Not everyone joins a contact mission because they feel guilty. I was born in Constellation space, and you're a lot more interesting than civilized people. So..." He made a complicated sweeping gesture with his forehands that did in fact convey: "Don't worry too much about Curic."

I looked at Tetsuo's list. "Why do you want me to bring olive oil?"

Tetsuo stood back up on his hindarms. "I saw advertisements for it," he said. "It looks delicious."

I stepped into the shuttle. "This was the trip of my life," I said. "I'll see you again soon." The lid of the shuttle closed and I shut my eyes and fell to Earth.

It wasn't nearly as bad going back down as it was going up. Mainly because I knew to close my eyes. I'm sure I was missing some magnificent view of Earth getting closer and closer, but if I want that kind of experience, I can just zoom in on a map.

Waiting for me at the spaceport like unwelcome relatives were BEA Agents Krakowski and Fowler. Since I saw them last, they'd gone native: they wore cowboy hats, like Texas Rangers. Black Stetsons with string ties.

"Hey, it's m'favorite asset!" said Krakowski.

"Um, hi..."

"Some desk pilot back in Washington told us it was a waste of time to give an exit visa to someone investigating million-year-old video games," said Krakowski. He chortled. "A waste of time!"

"Then you showed us Ev luie Aka's Ultimate Yada Yada," said Fowler. "Bam!" He clapped me on the back. Krakowski picked up my duffel and Fowler steered me towards one of the increasingly permanent-looking temporary buildings that had sprouted up around the landing site.

"Now they've got people scrambling to find out everything they can about every previous contact attempt," said Krakowski. "You and me, we're going places."

"You don't fuck with the field agents!" said Fowler, pumping his fist in the air.

"Guys, I'm feeling a sense of dread that only increases with every step I take in your presence."

"Occupational hazard, Blum," said Krakowski. "This will be one sweet debriefing. We'll get you through Customs real quick." We walked towards a brand-new metal trailer.

Krakowski tilted up the brim of his Stetson and whispered in my ear. "Am I resetting your jury duty clock, buddy?" he said.

"No," I whispered. "No one mentioned Slow People."

"Well, keep listening," said Krakowski, and backed out of my personal space. But then Fowler wanted in on the whispering action.

"Hey, Blum," he said. "The CBP lady, who does Customs."

"Yeah?"

"She's got great tits."

"Customs" meant "taking my stuff." Under the unblinking gaze of the

CBP lady, Fowler and Krakowski stole my Constellation spacesuit.

"Hey, that's my spacesuit!" I said as they wrapped it in plastic and boxed it. "It was all bespoke and shit."

"So they can make you another one," said Krakowski.

"Yeah, you don't need it down here," said Fowler.

"I was going to go diving in it," I said.

"You can keep the next one," said Krakowski. "Where's your grav kicker? The zero-gee transit device?"

"Curic took it back," I said, "before I left. Said something about governments confiscating them for use as crowd control weapons."

"Oh, that Curic," said Krakowski playfully. "Anything else? More electronics, souvenirs?"

"Buncha Ip Shkoy crafts, and a book," I said. Fowler reached into my bag and picked out the book Tetsuo had translated for me. He showed it to Krakowski.

"*Exert Dominion Over Friends Using Gaming Tactics Unmatchable Unless Your Friends Also Own This Book*," Krakowski read. He flipped through it, peered at Tetsuo's shopping list. "Go ahead and keep this."

"Sign for the spacesuit," said Fowler. The CBP lady handed me her clipboard. The reimbursement rate for a Constellation spacesuit is three hundred dollars. It's taxable income.

Now debriefing time. Krakowski and Fowler's office was a trailer next door to the stealing-your-stuff trailer. Muted televisions perched on one wall, scrolling closed captions upwards like incense fumes.

The agents pulled off their hats. "All right, Blum." said Krakowski. He sat across a desk from me. "First off, you're not a fuckin' spy."

"Pardon me?"

"Nobody's on your ass for actionable intelligence. You're part of a civilian cultural exchange and there are people who would kill for the experience you just had. So stop acting so damn persecuted."

"Curic called me a spy," I said.

"Well, you're not. Spies get paid." Fowler filled a conical cup with water from a water cooler and handed it to Krakowski, who handed it to me. "That in mind, let's start with general impressions. What's it like up there? Any problems?"

"You haven't been?"

"Who says *we* can go up?" said Krakowski with a tone that was close enough to irony for government work. "We're just the Bureau of Extraterrestrial Affairs."

Fowler stood behind Krakowski and mouthed "Pa-per-work" while making a scribbling motion.

"Well, the beds are terrible," I said. "And the Repertoire food is also bad, no thanks to you guys and your wanton carrot destruction."

"That's the TSA!" said Krakowski, like, don't pin that on me!

"And every other species has a nice home-planet environment in their Ring, but we've got the fucking post office, because they listened to *you* while they were building our home in the stars!"

Agent Krakowski stuck his elbow on the desk and used two fingers to prop up his forehead. "Ariel," he said. "I used to be an analyst, at Homeland Security, yeah? And I took this job. This job driving around, collecting eyewitness reports, managing exit visas, *babysitting*. I took whatever job I could get at the BEA, because I knew that this career path was the closest I'd ever get to being in Starfleet.

"I want this contact mission to be the best thing that ever happened to the human race. I do not want this country or this species to stop existing because somebody made a mistake I could have prevented, or made an assumption I should have checked. So when you come down from the *space station* with your pissant complaints about the *interior decoration...* well, I get a little annoyed."

"He gets annoyed," said Fowler, who'd mistaken Krakowski's rant for the opening salvo of a good-cop bad-cop routine.

"I'm sorry," I said. "It just feels like we fundamentally don't understand each other. It really worries me."

"Are you talking about us and the Constellation?" said Krakowski. "Or you and me?"

Behind Krakowski was Fowler and behind Fowler something caught my eye on the television. "What's that on TV?" I asked.

Fowler shrugged. "TV stuff," he said, without turning around.

"Those are Constellation spacesuits, on Earth. The sky's blue. Did I miss something when I was in Ring City?"

That got them to look. All three televisions on the back wall showed handicam footage of ETs and large robots standing on an ice sheet in the dead light of an Antarctic noon. The camera swung back to show a group of humans in cold-weather gear, towering above a gesticulating Farang with frost collecting on his/her fur.

    TWO CUBIC KILOMETERS AT A
    TIME,

said the closed captions.

    WE TAG ITS COORDINATES. WE
    SLIDE THE PORT OVER IT.

"Turn it up," said Krakowski.

"How much are you going to remove?" A human voice spoke over heavy wind and was echoed in the closed captions.

"As much of it as we can," said George Clooney choppily. The Farang didn't speak English; he/she was using a vocalizer. "It's a delicate balance, you understand."

Cut back to the CNN newsroom. "...in what some people are calling an extraterrestrial plot to steal Earth's ice caps. New footage from the international Polar Climate Study expedition..."

"Sweet Jayzus!" said Fowler. "Just like <u>Ultimate Lift-Off</u> predicted. They'll dig us up, just like they dug up the moon."

"No!" I said. "Fuck on *toast*. Why would anyone steal *seawater*?"

"I heard there was an engine that runs on seawater," said Fowler, "but the government covered it up."

"You're the effing government!"

"Earth would look like a big gas station to them," said Fowler. "Just like in *Triple Point*." Krakowski was gritting his teeth.

Charlene Siph—the fixer, Tetsuo had called her—was talking in split-screen on one of the muted televisions, the handicam footage looping next to her. I'd seen her look of disgust before, on Ashley's face, whenever Tetsuo pulled out his Ip Shkoy courtship techniques.

"Can we please apply any of the knowledge we've obtained up to this point?" I said. "Curic just tried to give me thirty pounds of gold! Because she forgot gold is valuable!"

Krakowski's BlackBerry beeped. He pulled it out of his belt holster.

"Oh-kay," he said in exasperation. "We've gone to Code Falcon, have a nice day." Fowler stiffened and leapt to his feet. Krakowski tossed the BlackBerry onto the table, then immediately picked it back up and slipped it back in its holster.

"What's Code Falcon?" I asked.

"You're not cleared," said Krakowski. "That's why we use codes. But here's a tip: Let's get the hell away from the landing site."

Chapter 16:
False Daylight

I sat in the back of a government-issue sedan. Story of my life: me in the back seat with no one to make out with. BEA Agent Fowler sat in the driver's seat, revving the biodiesel engine like he wanted to NASCAR this fucker. BEA Agent Krakowski was still in the debriefing trailer.

The car smelled like french fries. I pulled out my phone and called Jenny, cooling her heels fifty yards away in the spaceport waiting room.

"Are you done?" she asked.

"Get out of here," I said. "The spooks are spooked. They're evacuating me. Tell everyone in there to get out."

"The only people in here are the TSA dudes," said Jenny. "If I tell them to abandon their checkpoint, they'll summarily execute me. Is this about the Antarctica thing?"

"It's pretty damn likely," I said.

Fowler twisted to face me. "Get off the *phone*, Blum," he said. "This is still a secured area."

"Shit," I said. I put the phone in my pocket but didn't hang up.

Fowler leaned forward, trying to see through the smudged windshield into the trailer. "He's probably screwing around with the document safe," he said.

A distant whine harmonized with the sedan's engine. A re-entry sort of whine. "Well, shit," said Fowler, "here it comes. If we die, it's because Krakowski had to put those damn xenobiology reports back in the safe."

"Are we going to die?"

"I. Don't. Know. Blum. We're finally standing up to the Constellation on something big. So maybe instead of dropping a civilian shuttle every forty-five minutes, they've decided to drop some hardware. Armored personnel carriers, or big-ass rocks."

"Have you ever *seen* a Constellation APC? Or a soldier? Or a cop?

Because I just got back from a week with the fucking space hippies."

"'Scuse me," said Fowler. He ran into the BEA trailer, leaving the key in the ignition. I leaned forward and shut his door. I could see a shape in the sky. It was a shuttle, like the shuttle I'd just come down in. The shuttle landed. It was empty.

"It's just a shuttle!" I yelled at the trailer. I took the phone out of my pocket. "Jenny, you still there?"

"I'm on the bike. Getting out of here, as per your request."

"Do you know anything about the Antarctica situation?" I said. "These guys won't say anything but code names."

Jenny puffed. "Well, according to the ever-reliable television, there's this group called 'Save Humanity'."

"It's 'Save the Humans'," I said. "That's Curic's overlay."

"Yeah, no kidding. Apparently some of them decided to move the ice caps to the moon where they wouldn't melt. Step two, we find out about this. Step three..."

"We all go apeshit. Sorry, they're coming back." Phone back in pocket.

"Jayzus Christ," said Fowler, getting in and slamming the door. "We don't control our own airspace anymore." The shuttle took off, empty. "It's like living in a third world country."

Krakowski got in the passenger side. "Let's go downtown for a few hours," he said. Fowler started the first two points of what would prove to be a five-point turn.

"Do we have to, like, right now?" I said. My bike was locked up in the parking lot. "They just had their chance to drop an APC on us, and they blew it. It's the same shuttle I came in on."

"Yes, we have to," said Krakowski. "We haven't finished the debriefing, and I don't want to explain to the spooks why I kept a civilian at a Constellation landing site during a Code Falcon." Who's so spooky that *Krakowski* calls them "the spooks"?

"It's one-thirty," said Fowler. He pulled onto the highway. "And my food's back in the fridge. Let's get some lunch."

"Does the Xico's near the capitol still have those secure booths?"

"I never went there," said Fowler. "Back in the day, my bros and me always hit Best Little Steakhouse." Yes, he said "bros".

"Fowler, you're fucking useless," said Krakowski.

"You're going to debrief me in a chain restaurant?" I said.

"You got a better idea?" said Krakowski.

"Can we do someplace local, like Moe's?"

"Xico's it is," said Fowler.

At the fucking Xico's, with knife and fork, Krakowski carved his burrito into a grid and began eating it from the origin point.

"She said they weren't having any luck going through the political process," I said. "Everyone's all 'not in my backyard, not in my backyard.' So I guess they took their show on the road to Antarctica."

"Are you kidding me?" said Fowler. "Curic is mixed up in this? And you knew this four days ago?"

"I posted it to my blog," I said, "four days ago."

"Man, you think we can read gaming blogs at work?" said Krakowski. His burrito grid 2C had some gristle in it and had to be timeboxed into smaller tasks. "We need email."

Over the course of a disgusting lunch, I carefully recounted every single blog post I'd posted from space. Afterwards, Krakowski and Fowler dropped me off at my house.

"Are you still there?" I asked my phone, but Jenny had hung up almost two hours earlier. I called her back, voice, and let it ring while I fumbled for the house key.

"Yo."

"I'm going to open a bottle of wine," I said, "and then I'm going to drink half of it. Do you want to come over and have the other half?" My house smelled like apples.

"I'm in the middle of a really epic flamewar," said Jenny.

"Is it about what just happened with the Constellation?" I found the apples, in the kitchen, rotting in the fruit bowl.

"It's about comics," said Jenny. "But it will probably go in that direction eventually. Don't drink the wine. You can get drunk at your welcome-back party."

I pulled the wine out of the fridge anyway. "Are we still doing that?"

"You're still back, aren't you?" said Jenny. "At the Belt, once Bai gets off work."

I yanked open a drawer to look for the corkscrew. "Geez, can it not be the Belt? That's where white guys take their Asian girlfriends."

"Don't be a racist. How is that even a complaint?"

"It's just a cliche, that's all. I don't have my bike. Who else is coming?"

"Uh, you, me, Bai, Bizarro Kate and Martin. And presumably Dana, if you want to count her."

"I'll think about it," I said. I jammed the corkscrew into the wine bottle.

Once Jenny hung up, I turned on the TV like I was sneaking a cigarette. Four hours later and Charlene Siph was still on, eyes rapidly nictating from exhaustion, sharing a screen with an anchor.

"I sure can, Susan," said Siph, "There was no authorization because there's no one to do the authorizing. I don't sit on my haunches all day telling people what to do, pardon my French. On my home planet, we have a saying—"

TV off. I tried to get online and talk to Curic, or Tetsuo, or especially Dr. Tammy Miram.

Access blocked

Access to offworld Internet sites is temporarily restricted under the terms of the CONTACT Act.

Please consult the AT&T Terms of Service.

I walked from room to room of my empty house, drinking from the bottle. In my bedroom, next to the piles of unexplored hardware Curic brought me during her visit to Earth, were three crates I'd never opened.

I sat on my bed. I used the corkscrew's foil cutter to unscrew the lid of one of the crates. The crate was full of tiny pellets of packing foam, which I expected. I didn't expect to find a sheet of plastic embedded in the foam, and I didn't expect to see Krakowski's face printed on the sheet in grainy greyscale.

> *Is this you?*
> This tamper-sensitive container was opened on July 20 at 14:29:05 CDT.
> A product of the Tamper-Sensitive Packing Material Overlay.
> (Not affiliated with the Temperature-Sensitive Packing Material Overlay.)

I closed the crate and started writing a game review. An hour later, I reopened the crate and there was another sheet of plastic inside, with my picture on it.

I kept writing.

Blog post, July 28

GAME REVIEWS OF WHISPERED REVOCATIONS 2.0 PRESENTS
* (Schvei)
A game by Af be Hui
Reviewed by Ariel Blum

Publisher: Perea Corporation
Release date: Contact event plus 41 Earth years
Platforms: Everything Environment, The Big Tour, Absolutely More Reliable Than The Competition
ESRB rating: AO for language, cruelty, violence, and OMG EXPLICIT SEX

Can a video game be a work of art? Eggheads have been asking this question for twenty years, even though the answer is obviously "yes". We live in a world in which any random shit can be art. Think of anything bad to say about video games and there's something worse that everyone agrees is art. Torture-wince movies are art. Commercials are art. A fire extinguisher is art, if a designated artist designates it as art.

This is how the review started when I started collating notes. That is what seemed important at the time. I was lying back against a moon-rock wall in a tiny room in Ring City's Human Ring. I typed to the tune of a beautiful woman's postcoital snoring, a sound that for obscure reasons I have always considered a barometer of my own virility. It was four days ago.

Now I'm alone in a poorly lit 2BR house that smells like rotten apples. I'm barred from Ring City until further notice (I was one of about 4k humans ever to go there at all) and I can't even communicate with the people who are still up there. I've sorted my music collection by lowest average pitch and am playing droning bass notes to drown out the sound of my neighbors yelling at each other. It's not even five o'clock and they're already drunk, but so am I, so why be judgmental?

I think there's supposed to be a game review in here somewhere. OK.

Like <u>A Tower of Sand</u>, Af be Hui's first interesting game, <u>*</u> is designed for two-player play. Tetsuo Milk, my guide to Af be Hui's native Ip Shkoy culture, hands me four enormous rubber-plastic gloves with embedded motion sensors. The game controllers for the Everything Environment. It is five days ago.

I point out to Tetsuo that I only have two hands, and they're half the size of his. After some spirited discussion, we decide to play <u>*</u> on a rival console that supports the vintage-style controls of the older console I already know how to play: the Simulates Hi-Def False Daylight.

A first-person view fades in on a dingy treehouse apartment in a polluted city, an apartment where the main source of light is the home movie projector. The player character's apartment in <u>*</u> is pretty much the same place as the replica Ip Shkoy apartment in which we are playing the game.

"Did you plan this?" I asked Tetsuo.

"I did not," said Tetsuo. "These apartments were a common visual shorthand. Like how every human sitcom fades in on a brick house in Chicago."

"I don't think that's literally true."

"And the same song plays. 'People like us belong together, but some-times—'"

"Stop trying to sing," I said. "That's *Second Chances*. You were watching different episodes of the same sitcom."

"In my defense, I never watched the entire song."

* is the story of Iul (full name never given), an Alien too poor to live further up the tree in good natural light, but not so poor that she would go out and buy electric "false daylight," which you do only if you're a student or otherwise too broke to care what other people think of you. Iul's apartment is the kind of place you probably live if you're an adult Ip Shkoy Alien who plays video games. It is, I realize now, the Alien equivalent of my shitty cardboard housing-bubble house in Austin.

"Walk, walk, walk," says Tetsuo. "Walkin' around." He swings Iul around and knocks over a pile of junk. (Our replica Ip Shkoy apartment is pretty tidy, but Iul's is cluttered with junk, accumulated through her job, on which more later.)

"What do I do?" I asked.

"You are also in control of Iul."

"Like A Tower of Sand? We trade off."

"No, simultaneously."

In A Tower of Sand, each player controls half of a Farang's bicameral mind, cooperating to form an integrated personality. In *, the players cooperate to control a single Alien with a humanish integrated mind. On the game's instructional poster, Af be Hui recommends that a man and a woman play the game together.

I don't think you should play this game with someone you want to become romantically involved with.

"Don't—ah, fuck! Let me control!" said Tetsuo.

"You're knocking everything over!" I jammed the movement controls to their maximum to override Tetsuo. Iul ran out her apartment door, onto the sidewalk outside, and over the railing, two hundred feet down to the forest floor. Black Pey Shkoy writing scrolled onto the screen.

"It's onomotopoeia," said Tetsuo. "Pey Shkoy for the sound you make when you fall and hit the ground."

"I didn't need the last part."

"Or when something falls on you."

"Okay."

"We start over."

It's not a cooperative game. Both players have the same control over Iul's movements, but we have different goals. There's a percentage dial that shifts towards me whenever Iul rebels against the norms of Ip Shkoy society. Tetsuo takes victory points away from me by having Iul conform to what society expects of her.

Iul moves and acts by two-player consensus, and both players lose if Iul dies or loses what little social status she has. The strategy is to let the other player have his way as much as possible on the little things, while trying to steer the larger storyline to your advantage.

Iul's job is a cross between insurance investigator and tech support. When something goes catastrophically wrong with your barbecue grill or treefish cage, Iul shows up, investigates the accident, and finds some way to blame it on you, so that the manufacturer doesn't have to do anything to make amends. You were holding it wrong. You exceeded the recommended voltage. If all else fails, you should have bought two.

The Pey Shkoy name of the game, Schvei, is the word for "hyperlink": specifically, the hyperlink to the small print. When you ride past a billboard here on Earth that says "First 30 days free!*", that asterisk lets you know whatever's on offer is booby-trapped. You'll spend the rest of the year paying out the ass for the privilege of those 30 free days. Every single manufactured object in * is shveil, right down to the floor tiles and eating utensils.

"Is this a joke?" I asked Tetsuo, who was having Iul skim the disclaimer on a sari-like wrap.

"The text of the disclaimer is satirical," said Tetsuo, "but a lot of Ip Shkoy clothing was *shveil*. These notes should be familiar to you. They were posted all over the store where you bought the game."

"I can't read Pey Shkoy," I said, "and also you yelled at me whenever I tried to look at anything in the store."

"That was not me," said Tetsuo, "it was the shopkeeper."

There are thirty investigation jobs in the game, thirty things that will happen to Iul no matter how you and your partner play. By the time I left Ring City, Tetsuo and I had played twelve of them, like a little angel and devil floating either side of Iul's head.

Except it's not clear from moment to moment who's the angel and who's the devil. Conformity means not having to do anything personally unpleasant, but it also means being a thug for a company that turns Constellation circuit diagrams into products without really knowing how electricity works. Rebellion means hurting people (the body count is very low by human-video-game standards, but you can ruin a hell of a lot of lives), but it also means carving out something for yourself in a society that doesn't give a damn about you, apart from your place in its pre-industrial accounting conventions based on time/distance/price.

Iul's eighth job takes her to a very expensive four-room apartment near the top of a neighboring tree. The tenant, a young male with more money than sense, has shorted out an expensive *chiol* synth — the post-contact Ip Shkoy equivalent of a baby grand in your Park Avenue penthouse.

Tetsuo's goal was to play it by the book: to find some evidence of instrument misuse (not too difficult considering the dumb fuck who owns the synth) and offer to settle for the instrument's salvage value. Bring it back to the manufacturer where the burnt-out electronics would be replaced and the synth resold. My goal was to bring the situation to pretty much any other outcome.

I've got a lot of experience with this, because "devil on the player character's shoulder" is the role you play in pretty much every human video game. Human player characters take whatever's not nailed down and kill anyone who stands in their way. Some Ip Shkoy games had player characters like this, though they inhabited a distinct genre, the "creep game". * is half a creep game. Or maybe I should say it's two people fighting over which creep game to play.

Back in the Park Avenue penthouse, I came up with a genius creep-game strategy that would never have been programmed into a human game: have Iul blackmail the rich kid for sex. This would give her various character bonuses as well as being totally unacceptable behavior. Just having Iul glance at something she shouldn't be looking at is good for a couple of points. This move, I was sure, would put me in the lead.

The best part was, I didn't have to negotiate anything with Tetsuo. I just let him handle the dialogue selections while I subtly shifted Iul's body into the Affect of Seduction (the Affect of X is a game mechanic, not a formal part of Ip Shkoy culture). I let Tetsuo play it by the book, lecturing the rich kid about maintenance schedules and the fine print on the extended warranty. Meanwhile Iul's posture undermined everything Tetsuo was making her say, turning the argument into the start of a cheesy porno flick.

Did it work? Well, part of it worked: before long, Iul and the rich kid were going at it on top of the *chiol* synth in what can only be described as a sexually explicit minigame.

"Ugh," I said.

Tetsuo gave the pkt-pkt-pkt of an Alien laugh and shifted his grip on the controller. "Let me handle this," he said. "You'd just fuck it up." He rhythmically spun two sets of abacus beads with his primary thumbs. I guess some techniques haven't changed since Ip Shkoy times.

I glanced away from the main screen and caught a glimpse of the score dial. "What the hell? This scoring system is ridiculous. I get like two points for sexual extortion?"

"What do you mean sexual extortion?" said Tetsuo.

"You know both those words. Put them together."

"Well, what you call this extortion, the Ip Shkoy called it climbing the tree," said Tetsuo. "Social advancement. But it is considered, uh, unstylish? impolite? to do this with your customers."

"That's totally unfair. How was I supposed to know that?"

"I'm sorry that a different culture had different standards from yours."

"I feel dirty."

"It's merely an entertainment game."

There was a crash. Iul rolled onto the apartment floor, surrounded by the plastic and wooden shards of what had once been a *chiol* synth. The rich kid lay on his back, groaning.

"Oh-oh," said Tetsuo. The score dial slowly crept towards the side of rebellion, finally putting me in the lead. "You're going to win after all."

"What's that status message?" I asked.

"'Use of product inconsistent with its labeling.'"

"How did Af be Hui get away with this?" I said. "This is brutal. It's beyond satire. She's openly mocking her own company's products. Did Perea fire her?"

"Why would they do that?" asked Tetsuo. "Her games attracted lots of money."

Af be Hui began adulthood as a staff musician working for the Perea Corporation. Six local years going from town to town in a traveling electronics trade fair, wearing a sexy outfit and playing arrangements of old rural songs on Perea's electronic instruments.

Perea made traditional Alien instruments with Constellation-derived synthesizer circuitry hooked into the output mechanisms. The synths were constantly breaking, even without people putting their full weight on them during sexual intercourse. From fixing and hacking the instruments on tour, Af learned enough about electronics to make a career change when Perea started making video games.

This is not a review from someone who knows how the game will end. I don't what Iul plans on doing with the electronic bits and pieces she filches from her jobs and squirrels away in her no-daylight apartment. The way things are going, I may never have a chance to play this game again. But I've played enough to feel something I don't often feel before while playing a game: complicity.

In a game where I control the player character directly, I never think of the PC as a person. The game tries to make me identify the actor in the cut scenes with the similar-looking avatar I control the rest of the time, but it never works. When the devil on the PC's shoulder makes them do something terrible, it's nothing personal. I'm just probing the game board.

In *, the player character *is* the game board. When I negotiate with Tetsuo to decide Iul's actions, I'm ratifying those actions. Since the axis of behavior is conformity/rebellion instead of the good/evil you see in "sophisticated" human games, I can't predict how I'm supposed to feel about what I make Iul do. * was the first Ip Shkoy creep game that makes you complicit with the creepy PC, instead of letting you use them as a catharsis puppet.

This is why I wrote that crap I wrote at the beginning about art. None of that seems to matter now. What I'm trying to reckon now is what * says about the society that produced it. I feel like I'm going through an old magazine and just looking at the ads.

* was written sixty years after the Constellation made contact with the Aliens. This was a contact mission that went *well*. The Constellation didn't show up to a planet of mummified corpses like Gliese 777Ad, or post-apocalyptic cavemen like the Gaijin. Alien civilization didn't collapse five hundred years after contact like the Inostrantsi's did.

We've had two months. A full sixty years after contact, the Ip Shkoy were using extraterrestrial technology to build shitty products to rip each other off. (The system I played * on was itself a piece of shit, with a *shveil* disclaimer as long as Tetsuo's hindarm.) The most effective ET game I've played so far is a nihilistic satire of a culture where nobody trusts anybody else. The Aliens didn't formally join the Constellation for *six thousand years*.

We've had two months. Things can get a lot worse than a spat about whether an ice shelf should be moved to the moon or left to melt, and still turn out all right. And if you're like Agent Fowler, worried that the Constellation is crushing our essential humanity with a deadly combination of military might and New Age philosophy, you should find * a very reassuring work of art.

But for me this *is* the a-lot-worse. I'm looking at a future where a lot of my friends, and the woman I'd really like to be able to call my girlfriend, live at the top of a gravity well that I can never climb again. As Curic once told me about a totally different game:

> **Curic:** There are no refunds.
> That's the point of the game.

I should have bought two.

Part Two: Software

"I did not come from the stars to play hacky-sack with you gentlemen."

—U.N. Ambassador Charlene Siph

Chapter 17:
Their First Contact Was Better

Real life, August 10

UNKNOWN NUMBER usually spells trouble. I picked up anyway, because I'm a sap, and it beats waiting for the compiler to run.

"This is Ariel."

Click. Pop. Clickety click.

"Hello? Is this Curic?"

"Stand by for a personal call from the International Space Station." said nobody in particular.

"What, I should stand at attention or—"

"Hi, Ari!"

"Tammy! Oh, shit, it's good to talk to you!"

"Whatcha been up to?"

Well, this sure turned around quick. "Just writing this damn indie game," I said. "Nothing else to do, y'know? Where are you?"

"I'm on the space station," said Tammy, her voice fuzzy. "The old one. Some of the guys set up a port between here and Ring City so we could use NASA's phone system. There's some problem with the Internet, so I haven't been getting your emails or anything."

"There's no *problem*," I said. "The net is blocked. It's been blocked for two weeks, because of the fiasco with the Antarctic ice sheet."

"I thought that was resolved," said Tammy.

"If you mean 'resolved' in the optical sense of 'brought into clear focus', then yes, it has been resolved." My compiler died. I turned off my monitor so I wouldn't try to fix it.

"Well, that sucks. So, um, if there's not going to be any Internet, it's super important that I get through these topics with you so I can get in a couple more phone calls."

"Topics?" I said. "Are you doing a checklist?"

"Yes. Item one, I moved in to our apartment."

Our apartment. "O-okay, that's cool."

"I'm not sleeping there, it's just so I can shower off-duty, and crap, and eat real food in one gee. I'm so sick of that damn freeze-dried ice cream. Ari, it's so good: I am literally eating pie in the sky."

"Um."

"Not right this minute, obviously. Somebody brought up strawberries and now strawberry pie is in the Repertoire."

"Those might be my strawberries. I got them at the farmer's market. The TSA squished them up."

"Well, you can't tell in the pie. It's the best thing I've tasted in forever."

"Did you call to make me want pie? Because it's not exactly scarce on Earth. Like, there's a restaurant in Austin that only serves pie."

"No!" said Tammy, and I could picture the cute annoyed face she was making. "I just wanted to tell you that when you come back up, there's free pie."

"You know me, Doctor Miram," I said. "I'll eat your pie in the sky any day of the week."

"...Ari, this call's going through Houston."

"Oh, shit. Is this some Candid Camera thing? Am I like up on the big board in Mission Control?"

"No, just... stow the innuendo. That was cute, though. Points for that. Item two, you left your clothes in the apartment, so I put them on the top bunk. Item three, I need some advice."

"My advice."

"This Gaijin guy's been talking to a bunch of the astronauts, and a couple shifts ago, he asked me to join a fluid overlay he's working on. And I have no idea what that means, Ari—how much work it is. Is it more like a birthday party or more like a marriage?"

"Hold on a sec, I'm looking it up," I said. I turned the monitor back on.

"Anything you look up, came from up here," said Tammy. "I want to know your experience."

"It's just how they do things," I said. "Like, when Curic came to Earth, she formed an overlay with me and Jenny and Bai to scan my house. But then the two of us ended up doing all the work. And on the other end, you've got the really big overlays like Save the Humans and Plan C, which are more like political parties. Just saying 'overlay' doesn't say anything."

"Oh, this guy's name." Tammy laughed and it did things to my stomach. "This guy's actual name is 'He Sees The Map And He Throws The Dart!'. Can you believe that?"

"I guess it's a *little* long for a Gaijin name. What is his overlay going to do?"

Tammy took a deep breath. "He Sees The Map And He Throws The Dart! wants to set up a colony on Mars. He's under the delusion that if he talks to enough astronauts, he can get their space agencies to buy in."

"I don't want you to go to Mars," I said. "We've already got the longest-distance long-distance relationship in human history."

"We discussed this," said Tammy, pissed off at having to discuss something twice. "I'm not *going* to Mars. They want my help on the logistics so that this doesn't turn into another PR disaster. Suddenly they're worried about PR! It's as bad as NASA."

"Yeah, again, 'cause of the Antarctica thing. They fucked up and now they want to buy us flowers."

"Oh, is that your strategy?" said Tammy. "*Interesting.*"

"No, I give flowers all the time," I said, my voice getting ahead of myself, "because I'm the big-shot head of a game studio. And then when I fuck up, special outings. And jewelry, but not like flashy desperate jewelry—"

"Ari," said Tammy, "can we keep some of this a secret until you actually foul up? I want to call my folks before I get kicked off the line."

"Uh, yeah," I said. "For what it's worth, you absolutely should join this guy's overlay. You gotta make this a big flag-waving thing, yay humanity, because Mars is *our* planet. If the Constellation does something stupid with Mars, humanity goes into total lockdown, and we'll never see each other again."

"Well, we don't want that to happen," said Tammy. "Because then you'd never get to taste this pie."

"Oh, so double entendres are okay?"

Blog post, August 12

"Well, give it to me straight," said Jenny. "Do we still have a game company?"

This is yesterday. Jenny and I had a business brunch at Moe's, a diner I first visited in college after hearing they had an original Mutant's Revenge cocktail arcade cabinet. Well, they did have the cabinet, and a whole "quirky 1980s" theme to go with it, with New Wave music (vinyl, of course) and pinball and so on.

The food was great, although I thought it was kind of tacky to serve the appetizers on cocaine mirrors, and I came back whenever I could afford it. A couple months after I first ate there, I came in to see that the proprietor (strangely, not named Moe) had sold off the entire batch of decor to a restaurant in Albequerque that wanted a "quirky 1980s" theme, and the customers were sitting on folding chairs.

Turns out Phillip (not Moe!) is a loot farmer. He's got an antiquing hobby on the side, and once he's assembled a full set of decor, he ships it off to some other bar or restaurant and starts over. The only thing that never changes is the menu.

Phillip-not-Moe is currently reproducing the damn Tiki Room in his restaurant. He's almost covered every flat surface, so come in and see it before it's back to the folding chairs.

"We absolutely still have a game company," I told Jenny. "In fact, I was afraid you might get cold feet, so I prepared this little business chart." I took a few sugar-substitute packets out of a wooden tiki head and stacked them on the table.

"This is the work we've done so far," I said. "Art assets, game engine, and so on. Proof of concept. Now we begin crunch time." I dumped the rest of the packets out of the tiki head, forming a pile next to the neat stack. "I go head down and work like a motherfucker to get a demo out." I pulled a few packets from the pile and formed another neat stack on the other side. "As we approach completion, we start showing it off, getting people excited while we finish the level design and prep for a real release. And then people give us money. Uh, money not shown on this chart."

"I don't think there's any meaningful way in which you 'prepared' this chart," said Jenny. "Nor does it deal with the problem I'm actually concerned about. Which is that we won't *get* any money remaking a game made by the folks who tried to fuck up Antarctica."

"I'm getting to that," I said. I picked up an opaque novelty hula-girl sugar jar and set it alongside my sugar substitute timeline.

"And then there's an unknown amount of sugar in this container," I said. "Or possibly agave nectar. Which represents the time it takes for Charlene Siph and the rest of the Hierarchy Interface overlay to bribe and sweet-talk the governments. Maybe she can do it with the Greenland Treaty and some giveaway tech like the smart paper. Maybe she has to throw in some cold fusion or something. But it's like an hourglass. We just wait for the sugar to run out, and we'll be best pals with the Constellation again, and we can sell <u>Sayable Spice: Earth Remix</u>."

The waitress delivered our brunch and I had to hurriedly clean my release schedule off the table. Jenny put her hands palms-up on either side of her place setting. "Ariel," she said. "I'm sorry that I kept saying that you gave up on things too easily."

"Ah, because now you see a new side of me. The tentative Ariel. No, tenacious is the word. Tenacious Ariel."

"No, I'm sorry I harped on it because now you're overcompensating. You're putting a hell of a lot of faith in Hierarchy Interface. They're politicians; their job is to disappoint you."

"I'm putting faith in the news cycle," I said. "We can't ignore the Constellation, we can't kill them, and they're not going to kill us. Sooner or later we'll *have* to make up with them, just to have something to show on TV."

Jenny gene-spliced strawberry into her French toast. "They can leave," she said. "If Save the Humans loses the argument, which they probably will after this, the Constellation will go home and leave us to rot on this planet. Try selling your game then."

"*Our* game. And they can't just leave. They collapsed the wormhole after they came here. They have to send another one back to Constellation space. It'll take years. Meanwhile, we've got the smart paper, the Mars colony. Human Ring, assuming it ever stops looking like a fucking motel hallway. All the stuff we put in movies because we couldn't do it in real life. We'll get over it. We'll both get over it."

The waitress came back and refilled Jenny's coffee. Jenny picked up the hula girl and poured in some of the sugar—it was, in fact, sugar. "I wish to introduce an agenda item," she said.

"I already told you there is no budget for goth love slaves."

"We should see if Curic or Tetsuo can get us a prototype of the smart paper," said Jenny. "If it's as good as people are saying, we should target that platform instead of the existing ones."

"It would be nice to look at the technology," I said. "But they'll probably slap a compatibility layer on top to make it look like a crappy human embedded processor, only faster. So that idiots with Microsoft certifications instead of brains don't have to learn Gaijin programming languages from the Jurassic period."

"Why do you just assume everything is crap, Ariel? You said the DS Twin was crap, and then you spent two years writing games for it."

"Crappy games."

"You do this for a living!" said Jenny. "What is this? I don't go around saying that 3D printing is crap."

"This same thing happened with the Aliens," I said. "They would have invented computers in twenty or thirty years, but instead the Constellation came to town, and filed the serial numbers off some Farang models for them."

"And then they got a head start on making cool games."

"More like, then they made shitty computers for fifty years, because it was easier to make knock-off computers than to learn computer *science*. Smart paper is going to destroy the whole tech industry, just like one-dollar apps destroyed software."

"Well, don't go down with the friggin' ship," said Jenny. "Let's get on top of this thing."

"And I don't even know the point of the game we're remaking," I said, "because I can't play it in English. If I were smart, I'd cancel the <u>Sayable Spice</u> project and start over with <u>The Long Way Around</u>. But that would be a very expensive decision."

"That doesn't sound very counterfactually smart to me," said Jenny. "Why didn't you play <u>Sayable Spice</u> in English on the space station? Wasn't that your big chance?"

"Yeah," I said. "I was going to ask the Ring City station computer to fork off a fractal submind that could learn Edink. But I chickened out. It was too much like having a child. So I just played the Alien remake some more, with Tetsuo translating from Pey Shkoy."

"It's close enough, right?"

"I guess," I said. "It's pretty obvious what the Aliens added. Like, <u>Sayable Spice</u> is about how food tasted better when you were younger." I looked down at my omelette. Food *did* taste better when I was a kid. What had happened? "So, of course, in <u>Recapture That Remarkable Taste</u>, the sex was better, too. Apparently Aliens get less perverted as they get older."

"Y'all okay here?" said the waitress.

Jenny covered her coffee cup with her hand. "Yeah, fine," I said.

"We can do this remake," said Jenny. "I think we have the general idea. Just don't blame me if the hula girl here never runs out of sugar."

Crispy Duck Games: WE HAVE THE GENERAL IDEA.

Crispy Duck Games: BECAUSE THE HULA GIRL CONTAINS A FINITE AMOUNT OF SUGAR.

Real Life, August 12

"Okay, yes," I said. "We can do a remake of a remake. But I would really like to know why a game about how food used to taste better shattered the taboos of the Dhihe Coastal Coalition."

"Do you really need that to make the game?" said Jenny.

"Well, yeah, what if there's some horrible secret and we have to recall the game? Like, when Reflex had to patch everyone's <u>Give 'Em Hell</u> because of the stack of crates that looked like a penis? Probably the most expensive penis in history."

"Did you ask Curic about the horrible secret?"

"I asked her, and she asked some other people, and nobody knows. It's a minor aspect of a minor Farang culture that nobody studies anymore, because the Dhihe weren't part of a contact mission. It's not like the Ip Shkoy and their competitors, where Tetsuo and a hundred other historians can tell you everything. We just have the games and the other pop culture, and it's all in Edink. And nobody cares enough—"

"What is that look?" said Jenny, edging her chair away. "Is there a spider on my shoulder? Did G-d suddenly dump the knowledge of Edink into your head?"

"Jenny, tell me whether or not this idea is insane." I leaned in and whispered for extra insanity. "Do you think we could have Dana learn Edink?"

"I'd say that's moderately insane," said Jenny. "Dana's basically a web browser with tits. She barely understands English."

"The Constellation could upgrade her, and Bai would take care of her. They could fork off a submind of Smoke and use phone-Dana as a personality template, like they did with the Shakespeare demo."

"How could you, *Ariel*, believe that that AI is even an approximation of Shakespeare? He's more like the Actors' Equity guy they got to play Shakespeare at the Renaissance festival."

"But that's fine!" I said. "We don't want the actual Dana Light running around. She'd kill us all and take the ammo refills we dropped. But a woman who likes to *dress up* as Dana Light is just a cosplayer. Like you are with superheroes."

"Yeah, except I take the costume off when the convention's over."

"Can we not follow this particular conversational thread?" I said.

"Sounds good to me."

"I want Bai to be able to go out in public with his girlfriend," I said. "I don't want his racist parents to be totally right about her. Let's do something nice for Bai and Dana, instead of just making fun of them behind their backs. His back."

Jenny flopped her arms along the metal arms of her chair. "It seems like a long way to go just to get an Edink translator," she said.

"No, that was how I got the idea," I said. "I think this could be more than that. Bai is still wasting money on cognitive buffs. He wants Dana to be a real AI, but the human tech isn't here yet. We could make their relationship just weird instead of creepy."

Jenny poured more sugar out of the hula girl's head. "Except there's still no offworld Internet," she said, "and nobody coming down from Ring City, and no way of sending phone-Dana *up* to Ring City for the upgrade. So how will your plan even work?"

"Check, please!"

"That only works in movies!" said Jenny. "You can't cut away from real life."

Waitress came over. "Y'all done here?" she said.

"No, sorry," I said. "We don't actually want the check yet; it was just a rhetorical device."

"Well, take your time, sugar." Exit waitress.

"Did you see that?" I said. "Every time I come in here, she's flirting with me."

"Ariel, have you ever *been* to a diner before?"

"Once or twice," I said. "I'll think of something, okay? How am I supposed to get the smart paper prototype you wanted me to get? I'll do the Dana upgrade the same way. We could even combine them, if smart paper is good enough to run an AI."

Jenny was bored with my scheming. "Jesus, I can't stand it any more," she said. "I'm going to ask the waitress why is the restaurant called Moe's, if the guy's name is Phillip?"

"We talked about this last time," I reminded her. "We decided that if we asked, Phillip would probably kick us out."

"Oh, yeah," said Jenny. "Y'know, I bet it gives him psychological distance. Like, he's just running the restaurant for 'Moe', none of this tiki stuff is really his. He won't feel bad about shipping it all to California and starting over."

"I think Phillip killed Moe and took his place," I said. "Buried him under the floorboards."

"I see no contradiction between our theories," said Jenny.

Chapter 18:
The Amazing Colossal
Man-in-the-Middle

Blog post, August 16

DID YOU KNOW they're still building the Constellation Library building in Austin? I guess the government can't cancel a construction contract just because they don't want to talk to the extraterrestrials anymore. It's probably the only active construction project in Austin and it's across the street from the BEA field office. That's the field office I just got back from, after spending four hours having a five-minute conversation with Curic.

The BEA office used to be a paint store. Or at least it has that 1960s design I associate with used-to-be-a-paint-store. There are a few protesters camped out outside with nonsensical signs, I guess because the Planned Parenthood clinic is already staffed. They'll probably cross the street when the Library building is finished, because they sure ain't mad at the BEA. It just happens to be the only thing nearby with "Extraterrestrial" in its name.

The one good thing that came out of this colossal waste of time was that while I was at the BEA office, Tetsuo sent me a game review he'd written. Tetsuo says: "I wrote this as an English document for practice. Tell me if it is unclear." It is *really* unclear, buddy, but it's not your fault. It came through the BEA heavily redacted, and after replacing dozens of XXXXXes with the words I thought Tetsuo was probably using, I decided to give myself a ghostwriter credit on this one.

Y'all know that this blog goes pretty dark when I get deep into dev work, but if Tetsuo keeps sending me stuff, I'll keep posting it.

GUEST GAME REVIEWS FROM SPACE 2.0 PRESENTS
Pôneis Brilhantes 5 (Smarty Pets: Pony Stable Extra)
A game by Tin Soldier Software
Reviewed by Tetsuo Milk

Publisher: Various shell corporations
Platforms: DS Twin, iPhone, Nokia X59600 etc. ad nauseum
ESRB rating: E for epic ponage

Hello back! In my last document I explained human social status. Now I will thrill you with a review of the human handheld computer game Pôneis Brilhantes 5!

When you read this you may ask me-in-yourself, "Tetsuo, why have you abandoned your normal large-scale analytical technique in favor of this epitomizing style?" It's because my friend Ariel uses this technique to explicate his own culture. Ariel also did some of the programming for this game.

As you read this human-style linear document you might also feel tempted to ask me basic questions about human computers, how money works, and etc. Please abstain! There are separate overlays for that stuff.

Now on with the fun! Pôneis Brilhantes 5 is eight different games! But they are all the same, except for the language and the computer on which they run. I'm playing the original Portuguese version using the Nintendo DS Twin hardware. I obtained the software ROM from a recent scan of Ariel's home computer, performed by the mysterious Curic.

This game is a simulation about ponies, domesticated animals that are also capital goods. When the game begins you have a certain amount of Earth money and you must purchase a pony. I repeat! You must buy a pony or the game cannot start! This is confusing because beginning you are shown a list of ten ponies, but you can only afford the cheapest pony, i.e. you have no real choice. The other nine ponies serve as foreshadowing: you will be buying them eventually.

[Fig. 1: A pony.]

OK, you see how the game is structured. You buy a capital good and use him to earn enough money to buy a better capital good. But! The humans playing this game don't think of ponies as capital goods: They want to pretend they are spending time with ponies. This is the basis of the game's economics.

In real life you recover a capital investment by exploiting your capital. ("You" is here rational actor in a hierarchical scarcity-based economy; I am not actually talking about *you*.) But in the Pôneis Brilhantes series the pony exploits you! ("You" is here character within the game.) You earn money by working for the pony: brushing him with a pony brush, bringing him food and water, guiding him through an obstacle course, and etc. These activities are mapped onto two-dimensional motions pressed into the interface screen. Your motions can be repetitive (brushing the pony) or half of a complex system of feedback (obstacle course). For each successful action the pony pays you a small amount of money.

(The unit of money in Pôneis Brilhantes 5 is a yellow oval, probably a coin, but I don't know which coin. For a while I thought it was the Brazilian 25 centavo coin, but such prices would make a real pony less expensive than this video game, defeating the point of the game.)

Completing an action also increases a numeric attribute of the pony. These attributes give the pony benefits at the pony show, where all ponies must one day visit. Pony shows are a carnival where individual ponies are compared against the ideal pony. The ideal pony has very high numeric attributes and is amazingly good at running the obstacle course.

The closer your pony approximates this hypothetical pony, the more money you receive, as well as a non-monetary cup made of precious metal. I think this cup is intended for the pony to drink from or piss in, though I have not been able to use it within the game.

As you get more money you can buy more ponies and the two-dimensional motions you must perform become more complex. In addition to money, the ponies sometimes gave me at the conclusion of a task items of human clothing such as hats and ribbons which the pony could wear. Such items were also available for purchase from a 'company store' presumably run by the ponies. Many-worlds analysis of the game software show that these objects do not affect the game play. The ponies' motives in giving these gifts are unclear and communication with them is quite impossible.

By the end of the game I had quite a negative impression of these aloof, lordly ponies, with their arbitrary gifts and their fetish for human headgear. I will ask my friend Ariel whether this is a truthful characterization, though Ariel himself harbors no great love for ponies. Ariel worked on this game because he really likes fixing software problems. (From his blog: "I have twenty critical bugs to fix in this fucking pony game.")

Now witness the conclusion of this review. By analyzing this game's minor capitalistic success and negligible cultural impact, you might think we should not study it until later. But I contradict you! It's true that this game is fundamentally similar to many other human games in recreating the experience of wage-earning. It's also true that the subject matter (i.e. ponies) is fairly typical of contemporary use-objects.

But if you have studied other scarcity-based cultures, as I have, you will notice the bizarre changes made to fit the subject matter into the game-play experience. Seriously in this game you buy ownership of an animal and then perform wage-work for the animal. To feed the animal you perform factory-style atomized labor, as though you were building a helicopter.

This makes no sense—until you realize that people like my friend Ariel write games that reflect their own working conditions. The <u>Pôneis Brilhantes</u> series will not capture the experience of spending time with ponies until the software is written by people who genuinely enjoy those hat-loving bastards.

Next time: restaurants! How do they work? I will tell you everything!

Real life, August 16

Inside the former paint store, the BEA had the office decked out like the DMV. Bored guy behind the counter at a computer, two-way mirror in the back so the agents can spy on you standing in line, assuming they have nothing better to do. But no lines. There was just the bored guy behind the counter and an older lady leaned over in front of it, writing a message very slowly in pencil. I waited behind the older lady for a minute, admiring her huge belt buckle (+2 armor class bonus, at least), before she noticed me and waved me past.

"I want to talk to my contact," I told the bored guy.

"You need their ITIN," he said. "No messages go through unless they have an ITIN."

I opened my satchel and took out the paperwork I'd filled out to get Curic her tourist visa. "She got an ITIN when she came to Earth," I said.

Bored guy was impressed by the volume of paper I'd brought to bear on the situation. "Passport," he said joyously. I handed him my passport, open to my now-expired exit visa. He flipped it back to the photo page, scanned it—beep!, reached under the counter, and handed me a chunky pencil.

I glanced at the older lady down the counter, still scratching away with an identical pencil. "I know how to type," I said.

"You write," said the BEA clerk. He slid a few sheets of grainy, lined notebook paper towards me off a stack. "Print neatly. The ITIN goes on top. Chairs in the back, if you want to sit." He went back to his computer screen. Click-drag, click-drag, double-click, click-drag. Solitaire.

I scooted down the counter, stood next to the woman with the belt buckle, and wrote:

From: Ariel
To: Curic (ITIN 941-74-6258)

Dear Curic,

How are you? I am fine. Everyone here has gone batshit insane, which is why I have to write you a personal letter like a 5th grader instead of having a real conv. But it's better than nothing, which you may recall is what we had as of a couple days ago.

It's pretty much impossible to separate rumor from fact right now, but there has been some talk about Paul Cooper-Burke and some other big name Constellation-tech bloggers getting prototypes of smart paper. This small-name blogger would really appreciate if you could send him such a prototype, with an Edink translator preinstalled.

The smart paper is for me (work); the Edink translator is for Bai's girlfriend. Did you meet her when you came to Earth? She's very interested in learning Edink. I know you said that an Edink translator is complicated and requires a lot of maintenance. You kind of scared me off the whole idea, to be honest. But Bai is not a flake like me. He's a reliable guy with a stable job, and has a long history of taking care of high-maintenance software.

Is this technically possible? (Edink translator on smart paper, I mean.) Assuming the US/Constellation relationship thaws out a little bit more, can we get started on this?

Love and kisses,
Ariel

PS: Haven't looked terribly hard, but have found no references online to a shipping container with Constellation Shipping logo. Back when CS was active, most deliveries were a) small, b) packaged in re-entry foam.

I handed my message to the bored guy, who alt-tabbed into a work application and started typing it in. I walked back to a row of uncomfortable chairs, where the older woman was doing sudoku with her chunky pencil.

"Wow, what a system, huh?" I said.

The lady whispered to me, "What did you expect from the socialists at the BEA?"

I weighed the fun of commiserating about the BEA's suckiness with this woman, against the fact that we wouldn't even understand each others' complaints.

"You're a good friend," she continued. "Putting up with all of this just to talk to your contact." She looked around the empty field office. "Most people don't bother."

"I went up," I said, as long as we were having a conversation, "to Ring City. Just before all this happened." Kinda bragging.

"Oh?" said the woman. "What's it like?"

"Well, you know how they say everything's bigger in Texas," I said.

"So I've heard," said the woman, cleverly not admitting to ever having left the state.

"Well, things are even bigger up there. Trees three miles tall. But the beds have no pillows, and sometimes you can't breathe the air because it's liquid methane. It's a mixed bag."

The woman scowled at the idea that some place other than Texas might have taller trees—or, I suppose, less breathable air. "Well, I guess I should get some work done while I'm waiting," I said. I brought my satchel up onto my lap and pulled out my development laptop.

"Sir, turn off the computer," said the bored guy.

I jumped, startled. "I'm not using your network," I said. "I just need to do some—"

"Sir, turn it off. No phones, no computers." Bored guy pointed to the wall, where there may have been some kind of sign to this effect. As if we'd all gotten together and agreed to do whatever it said on signs.

I took Curic's paperwork out again and started writing pseudocode on the back, using a pen. Bored guy glared at me. I glared back, like, that's right, motherfucker, you're not the only one who can use paper.

After an hour of work, the bored guy called my name and I picked up Curic's response:

Hello, XXXXX,

Your message arrived in a heavily XXXXXXXX form. This is no XXXXXXXX to me but you clearly were not expecting it. The XXXXXXXX is done by machine at the XXXXXXXX between XXXXX and the XXXXXXXXXXXX XXXXXXXXX, assuming the XXXXX clerk decides to let it through at all.

Some tips I have acquired from other people with
XXXXXXXX contacts: Obscenities such as "XXXX,"
"XXXX," and even "XXXXXXXXXX" will be XXXXXXXX,
and even innocuous words like "XXXX" may join them
if used in close proximity. XXXXXXXXX misspelling is
of no use. I respectfully ask that you tone down your
XXXXXXXX cursing. Please also avoid XXXXXXXXX
terms and acronyms. In fact, it might be better if you
avoided factual XXXXXXXXXX altogether.

On to the subject of your letter. I gathered that you
want a XXXXXXXXX of something (XXXXX XXXXX?)
for someone's girlfriend, and that a person with a
short name was willing to take care of the object in
question. Please advise what it is that needs so much
XXXXXXXXXXX. Also, you couldn't find out anything
about something. Is it the XXXXXXXX XXXXXXXXX? If
so, please keep looking; I think it has something to do
with Plan X.

Respectfully,
XXXXX

Plan X? No, Plan C. This stupid program censored a letter of the alphabet because it's also the name of a programming language. There was no
guarantee the message even came from Curic. For all I knew, Fowler and
Krakowski were huddled behind the two-way mirror, snickering at me and
writing Curic fanfic just to see what I'd give away.

Tiny bits of white noise drifted into my left ear. Cymbal crashes. The
older lady was listening to classic rock on her music player while writing a
reply to *her* contact. Some petty part of me considered informing bored guy
that music players are computers.

Instead, I spent an hour rewriting my letter to Curic. It was more a
creative challenge than a technical one. To send a message through a lossy
channel, you just have to increase the redundancy of the message.

From: Ariel
To: Curic (ITIN 941-74-6258)

Okay, XXXX all that. Instead I will serenade you with a
poetic description of life on Earth since your visit.

Cast your minds back to 'bout mid-July
To see me freelancing for Bai
To see Jenny complain a-

bout Bai's girlfriend Dana
It wasn't too hard to see why.

Dana's fondest, profoundest desire
Was accessories new to acquire
But now she's inclined
Towards improving her mind:
An upgrade Bai's happy to buy her.

Dana's interests and mine are congruent
With respect to her smarts, and pursuant
To which we all think
She should learn some Edink
(And with your help, she'd soon be fluent!)

Now me, I'm no good as a tutor
And a dud, some have said, as a suitor
But the Dana/Bai couple
Would be stable and supple
If you'd just upgrade her computer

I hope I don't have to explain a-
gain what we would like to give Dana,
'Cause I'd like to go back
Home where I can hack
PS: news on the shipping containa?

Except I didn't format it as poetry, because bored guy wasn't gonna type it
that way anyway.

More hacking on the back of the paperwork. As I waited, replies went
slowly back and forth between the woman and whatever extremely patient
extraterrestrial was her contact. She was planning to spend the whole day,
I guess.

An hour in I got an unrelated message from *Tetsuo*—the <u>Brilhantes</u>
review. And an hour after that, I got another message from Curic:

Dear XXXXX,

Thanks to help from XXXXXX I believe I now understand what you want. However it looks like you are
pronouncing the name of the XXXXX language incorrectly. It does not rhyme with "think."

I'll talk to my XXXXXXXX contacts about getting a
XXXXX XXXXXX XXXXXXXXX for you and XXXX. It may
have to wait until there is a less opaque XXXXXXX for
our communication.

PS: Don't worry about the XXXXXXXX XXXXXXXXX. It's
of no importance. The one you and your girlfriend saw
was one of a few abandoned XXXXX that were never
used to ship anything.

Dammit. I had no reliable information about what these messages were saying or even who was on the other end. This was worse than useless.

Dear Curic,
(if that is your real name)

Stop jerking me around and make up your fucking
minds. Should I care about the shipping container or
not? Shall I set up a news alert and write you a note
every time a container falls off a ship or a truck? Or
shall I continue my blissfully container-free lifestyle?

With less love than formerly and somewhat distracted
kisses,
Ariel

I could wait another hour and a half for a response that would tell me
nothing, or I could go back home where I'm allowed to open my laptop.
So. Back to the ranch. Back to work, chipping away at that pile of sugar
packets.

Chapter 19:
Implementation Details

Blog post, August 23

[This post is friends locked.]

I got up at the butt-crack of dawn and went to the spaceport with Bai, to pick up the new version of Dana. Curic had organized this transfer with blinding speed. A few days ago, we'd dropped off Dana's phone with the BEA, they'd sent it up, and yesterday BEA Agent Fowler called me and said I could come to the landing site tomorrow (today).

KThxBai: alarm clock. beep
beep
beep

ABlum: stop it

KThxBai: i'll be there in 15 to pick you up.

ABlum: can you go by yourself?
i think i may actually be dead

KThxBai: rise from your grave, bro.
you're curic's contact. you need to be there.

I heroically got out of bed, and despite misunderstandings and Mexican standoffs, we were able to pick up the new, improved, self-aware Dana Light. Who Bai immediately took home for some TMI time, so she won't be coming in to work today. But we at Crispy Duck Games finally have an employee capable of translating <u>Sayable Spice</u> for us. And all you old college chums who are still bitching at me about Bai/Dana can shut up once and for all, because now you're just being racist against AIs.

Real life, August 23

The first time I tried to make it to the landing site there was a traffic jam five miles long: people spending a whole day trying to catch a glimpse of an alien spaceship. In the intervening two months, we've built a shitty spaceport out of Quonset huts and then abandoned it. Bai pulled his SUV past an unstaffed checkpoint and parked up front, near the entrance. There was one other car in the lot: Fowler's. Parked in a handicapped space.

The entrance to the spaceport building was chained up. Chain-link and razor wire surrounded the landing site itself, plus the trailers used by the BEA and Customs. It was a perfect Texas autumn morning, the kind where if you wake up early, you can spend a few blissful hours not sweating like a hog.

I walked to Fowler's car and rapped gently on the window. He looked up from his texting and rolled down the window. "Mr. Blum!" he said. "Gentlemen."

"Where's Krakowski?" I asked. Bai shuffled up behind me and slurped from his enormous paper cup of coffee.

"Krakowski" — actually Fowler said "Crack-housey" — "is busy sleeping." Then Fowler noticed Bai's fraternity ring. "Awright! Omicron Beta Digamma!"

"Class of '11!" said Bai cheerfully. They bumped fists through the open window. The clink of ring on ring.

"'02," said Fowler. "Florida State."

"UT Austin," said Bai.

"Local boy! What can I do ya for? You want like exit visa?" Fowler opened his car door and stepped out.

"We're taking delivery," I said loudly. "The smart paper prototype. You told us to come down here."

"Right, right. Yeah, your patron's sending down a shuttle." Fowler escorted us through the razor-wire fence. We waded into the tall grass near the landing site and waited.

I never realized just how small small talk could get until I heard Bai chatting with Fowler about dear old Omicron Beta Digamma. I slouched off to the side and looked sullen until Bai got tired of Fowler staring at the sky instead of making eye contact, and came back over to me.

"Why does he keep talking about your patron?" Bai whispered. "Is the mob involved in this?"

"Curic is my 'patron,'" I said. "This is all a favor to the Constellation. Try and get them to sign a copyright treaty or some shit, as long as we're negotiating. People like you and me don't count."

"I just want Dana back," said Bai. "I'm tired of using my hand." He elbow-nudged me.

"Hey, look at me," I said, "not asking what difference it makes."

"Here it comes!" said Fowler, still looking up.

Bai pumped his fist. "Fuckin' A!"

"G-ddammit," said Fowler, "someone's in there! Why these people gotta make it difficult? Can they not follow some some simple instructions?" These were clearly rhetorical questions.

The shuttle landed noiselessly fifty yards away. Inside stood a single Farang. "It's Curic," I said.

"You can tell 'em apart?" said Fowler.

I couldn't. I still can't. "Who else would it be?"

The dome of the shuttle lifted up. "Hello," called Curic. She was holding a white box and a newspaper-sized sheet of paper.

"Freeze!" said Fowler, and drew his sidearm.

"Shitfuck!" said Bai, and backed off by stumbling backwards and falling on his ass, spilling coffee into the grass. I just kept my eyes on Curic, preparing myself for the deposition. *No, she never left the shuttle.*

"Your arrival contravenes state and federal law!" said Fowler. I never thought I'd miss Agent Krakowski.

Curic didn't seem concerned at all. "Away put your weapon, Mr. Fowler," she said. "This isn't an invasion. I just came down to share some strawberry pie with Ariel and his friend. It's very popular among humans on Ring City. You can have some too, if you want."

"Don't tempt this planet with your pie!" said Fowler. "Just toss out the parcel. Don't leave the shuttle!"

Curic did a DROP ALL and squatted on the glass floor of the shuttle. She folded the sheet of paper with her tiny furry hands.

"Hey!" said Fowler. "The parcel!"

"The parcel contains the pie!" said Curic, and kept folding. "This is the computer."

Fowler's face was taut; I could almost hear the dramatic music playing in his head. Here at last was the excitement he'd signed up for. He was Earth's last line of defense. Against a four-foot hermaphroditic otter armed with strawberry pie and a piece of paper.

After a minute, Curic stood upright, holding a paper airplane. She turned perpendicular to Fowler and his gun, and threw the airplane. It went fifteen feet and landed in the grass. Bai sat on his knees, looking over at the airplane. He looked sick.

Then nothing happened because the shuttle wasn't taking off. Fowler maintained his gonna-shoot-ya posture. Curic sat on the floor, opened the little white box and ate the pie, stuffing it past her antennacles in messy red handfuls.

Finally, the dome of the shuttle descended. Fowler relaxed a bit. Curic waved to us with sticky hands. The shuttle lifted off.

The paper airplane was sucked up again in the wake of the shuttle and lodged in the chain-link fence. Fowler holstered his six-shooter, chased the airplane down, and handed it to me, huffing from exertion. "Can't believe I'm a fucking interstellar courier," he said. "Your patron's got a lot of balls, you know that?"

"Not even sure where to go with that one," I said, unfolding the paper airplane. "Lots of possibilities there."

"Gimme that," said Bai, snatching the airplane from me. He unfolded the paper airplane to reveal a picture of a phone. As he tilted the paper, the picture of the phone fell to the bottom, the way a real phone would if you dropped it into a glass box. The picture of the screen of the phone lit up and displayed the AT&T Death Star. The creases of the paper airplane were already filling themselves in, leaving the paper flat.

"Congratulations, Bai," I said. "We're now pioneers in the exciting field of paper computing."

Fortunately, this was a slight exaggeration. Bai and I were the tenth or twentieth Americans to be sent smart paper from Ring City. This meant that there was a procedure for clearing the stuff through Customs. Fowler had to wake up Krakowski, and Krakowski had to call someone he knew from Homeland Security, and who knows who that person had to call, but they did eventually find it.

While the calls were happening, we three, two humans and one newly independent submind of Smoke, sat outside the BEA trailer.

"They're supposed to classify it as an industrial prototype," said Dana-in-the-phone-on-the-paper. "It's very simple." She was wearing a silver lamé ballroom gown and a baseball cap that said BITCH across the front.

"It's okay, sweetie," said Bai, who was being really really happy about everything. "Let's just enjoy being outside."

"So, uh, Dana," I said, leaning over, "did you end up learning Edink?" Dana made two interlocking sets of clicky-squeaky noises.

"'I have modest fluency,'" Bai read. "She's got subtitles!"

"Okay, that's excellent," I said, "I'd like you to do some translation work to help me understand old Farang video games."

"No," said Dana.

"Um. Well, that's one of the reasons we had you uplifted..."

"I'm not an application," said Dana. "If I'm going to do work, I want to get paid for it."

"I was going to pay you," I said. "I'm not an idiot."

"Curic said you might be," said Dana. (Thanks a bunch, Curic.)

"Bai, am I an idiot?"

"Noooo??" said Bai, his voice going a little higher than I would have liked.

The trailer door slammed open. "Okay, guys," said Fowler. "We do it as an industrial prototype."

"I told you," said Dana.

"Ssh!" said Bai.

Fowler literally took out scissors and cut a quarter off the top of the smart paper, as an import tax. Bai never stopped smiling.

Private text chat, August 23

KThxBai: Hi, Ariel. It was really good to see you at the spaceport.

ABlum: uh, yeah, ok...

KThxBai: Sorry! This is Dana. I'm using my boyfriend's account.

ABlum: oh, hi. i thought you didn't sound like bai

KThxBai: Hold on for just one second.
[KThxBai is now offline.]

DanaLightNotTheVideoGameChick: Okay! Hello!
As I was saying, it was was good to see you. It was like meeting someone again after an absence of years and years. I recognized you, from before, but I didn't *know* anything about you. I'd been going through life with the mental power of a human telephone. Now I have space to think! I can make real friendships.

ABlum: ok, yeah
i'm glad we could do this for you
are you ok to chat? i figured you and bai would want some time alone
him taking the day off etc

DanaLightNotTheVideoGameChick: Oh, he and I are having sex right now. It's great! But I saw the blog post you put up and I need you to make a couple edits.

ABlum: ok thats plenty
you mean the blog post i posted like 10 seconds ago?

DanaLightNotTheVideoGameChick: That's it. Would you please get rid of the references to me as an AI?

ABlum: are you offended?
i mean the whole point of that entry is "we picked up dana 2.0 at the spaceport"

DanaLightNotTheVideoGameChick: Fun fact: The BEA doesn't like it when people sneak into the United States from Ring City. You saw what almost happened to Curic. Do you want that to happen to me?

ABlum: no

DanaLightNotTheVideoGameChick: So... you picked up a *smart paper prototype* at the spaceport. It's a computing technology, not a thought substrate. You can say that I came with Bai from Austin, but please don't say that I came down with Curic.

ABlum: ok, so help me out here
bai shut down his "dana light" virtual girlfriend because he started dating a human also named "dana light" who also happens to look like the video game chick?

DanaLightNotTheVideoGameChick: Do you remember any of my boyfriend's exes?

ABlum: fair enough
the name thing is new, though

DanaLightNotTheVideoGameChick: Make up another

name. Describe me however you want. Just please write as though I were a human.

ABlum: you're going to be an important part of crispy duck games
i'm going to be writing about you on the official blog
i can't make up some totally fictional contractor

DanaLightNotTheVideoGameChick: I'm not going to say crazy shit all the time like Tetsuo, if that's what you're worried about. I may be based on an Alien psychology, but I'm designed to approximate human behavior.

ABlum: what if agent fowler reads my blog and wonders where this "dana" person was this morning?

DanaLightNotTheVideoGameChick: I'm not worried about Fowler. But if it bothers you that much, take me out of the blog post altogether.

ABlum: i will do this for you because i don't want you to die
but i want to say that i'm not comfortable lying to my readers
insofar as i have any readers

DanaLightNotTheVideoGameChick: I think you're more comfortable with it than you let on.

ABlum: what do you mean by that

DanaLightNotTheVideoGameChick: For starters, you sure use friends-lock a lot.
OH, SHIT!

ABlum: ????

DanaLightNotTheVideoGameChick: Do you know what

an orgasm **feels** like?

ABlum: i thought i did

[DanaLightNotTheVideoGameChick is now offline.]

Blog post, August 23, as revised

[This post is friends locked.]

I got up at the butt-crack of dawn and went to the spaceport with Bai and his dark-haired, reasonably-bust-sized girlfriend Svetlana Sveta, to pick up the smart paper containing the Edink translation software. Curic had organized this transfer with blinding speed. A few days ago, we'd dropped off Svetlana's phone with the BEA, they'd sent it up and yesterday BEA Agent Fowler called me and said I could come to the landing site tomorrow (today).

KThxBai: alarm clock. beep
beep
beep

ABlum: stop it

KthxBai: svetlana and i will be there in 15 to pick you up.

 ABlum: why drag svetlana into this? it's so early it's still two days ago
are you afraid she'll go back to russia if you let her out of your sight and you'll have to go back to that stupid virtual girlfriend program ?

KThxBai: not taking the chance, bro!

I heroically got out of bed, and despite misunderstandings and Mexican standoffs, we were able to pick up the smart paper prototype. Svetlana's linguist job at Crispy Duck doesn't start until tomorrow, so she and Bai dropped me off and immediately went home for some TMI time. But we at

Crispy Duck Games finally have an employee capable of translating <u>Sayable Spice</u> for us.

And all you old college chums who were bitching at me about Bai/Dana can finally shut up, because it was just a phase after all. One look at Svetlana and Bai's gone back to nailing flesh-and-blood white chicks. It's like they say: once you go human, you'll never be resumin' [whatever you were doing before].

Blog post, August 23, late night

I got a little work done today, but any day when I have to get up at five in the morning is pretty much destined for low productivity. In the afternoon, while eating an avocado sandwich over my kitchen sink, I was thinking about the Inostrantsi. As the Constellation talks progress, people on TV (I'm still watching TV, it's like a disease, sorry, Jenny) have been talking a lot about the previous contact missions. But they're conspicuously not mentioning the one where *the entire fucking civilization collapsed due to environmental degradation*. Which would seem to have some bearing on our present situation.

Back when I was first going through the Constellation Database of Electronic Games of a Certain Complexity, I noticed that most of the Inostrantsi games were in the database twice. At the time, I kind of wrote it off as a minor mystery/mistake in the database. But actually all the Inostrantsi games were *remade*, ten thousand years later, as part of a cultural reboot.

I licked smashed avocado off my fingers, imagining myself ten years from now, huddling in a Constellation-run refugee camp. People are always huddling in refugee camps, even when they're alone. I'm huddling by myself and Tetsuo Milk is my fucking social worker; he hands me a Genesis controller and has me play "Sonic & Cipher" as therapy.

Among the crates of hardware and aftermarket accessories Curic sent me in July was the Massmonger 31, which I described at the time as "look[ing] like a roll of heavy-gauge chicken wire." I don't know how I'd design a computer for someone the size and shape of a kelp plant, but I'd probably include a screen, or controls.

At the time, the Brain Embryo had seemed a lot more interesting, so I'd stuffed the Massmonger 31 in a closet with all the other hardware I mentioned in that blog post. But now the Brain Embryo is work, and a low-productivity day means you don't have to do much work. My new translation assistant doesn't start work until tomorrow, so why waste time today trying to figure out Sayable Spice?

So the chain-link computer started to seem pretty good, with its games with super-emo names like The Rest at the End of a Long Journey and Not Everything Is Real. According to the CDBOEGOACC, the MassMonger 31 was named to coincide with a big Inostrantsi Olympic-type event. I decided to take a break from eating avocado sandwiches and at least get the computer running.

I pullled the Massmonger 31 out of the closet. It's about the dimensions of an oil drum, though it weighs practically nothing because I've got a Constellation cerametal replica instead of whatever you make computers out of so they work in liquid methane. I set it on the kitchen table and popped some big clasps, and three feet of chain-link peeled off and dangled over the edge of the table like Satan's toilet paper.

Now I could see some controls, maybe. Small metal flowers, lifting themselves on springs out of the dangling chain-link, bouncing around frictionless. I rolled out eight feet of the chain-link onto the floor and the whole thing was covered with the little probes, waving around like bonito flakes on okonomiyaki.

I did what I should have done in the first place and went to Wikipedia.

Language

Inostrantsi languages convey meaning through structured direct manipulation of the sense appendages. Two Inostrantsi communicate by grasping each other and synchronizing one set of sense appendages. A single individual may take part in several conversations simultaneously. One-to-many communication is also common, with listeners receiving linguistic symbols and passing them on through a circular or treelike network.

Okay, whatever. I sent Jenny an IM:

> **ABlum:** if you come over tonight and i'm dead, tell them to classify it as an accident

I set down the phone and lay on the chain-link fence. I pressed my sense appendages against some of the probes, squishing them. Other probes sat silent against my arms. "All right, do your stuff."

The probes didn't move. I didn't get tentacle-raped. But my phone went beep.

> **OMJennyG:** Whatever you're doing, STOP!!

Fuck! Girls ruin everything.

Long story short, I have figured out why nobody talks about the collapse of Inostrantsi civilization. We have no fucking clue what it's like to be an immortal asexual deaf-mute kelp plant. And no way of finding out except by talking to Inostrantsi, which isn't happening because we've kinda stopped talking to the Constellation altogether. So we're screwed. See you at the cultural reboot.

I've stuffed the Massmonger 31 under the kitchen table—I can't get it to roll back up all the way.

Update, 1 hour later:

> **OMJennyG:** After the apocalypse you won't be playing sonic games
> You'll be programming remakes of sonic for other people to play
> IOW, get back to work!

Chapter 20:
Feature Creep

Blog post, August 26

Knock knock. Who's there? It's the third employee of Crispy Duck Games! And her boyfriend.

"Hey, bro," said Bai, standing on my porch.

"Big day!" I said. "Your lady's a breadwinner."

"Yeah," said Bai, who wasn't sure what emotion to have.

"Hi, Ariel!" said Svetlana Sveta. Svetlana is our new part-time translator and localizer, resident expert on Farang culture, and mistress of our smart-paper Edink translation software.

"Hi, Svetlana," I said. "You're looking great. Can you take off your sunglasses, please? I want to be able to see your eyes."

"Sure thing, Mister B.," said Svetlana, and folded up her huge tortoise-shell sunglasses.

"I asked her to wear a normal outfit," Bai whispered to me. Instead, Svetlana was dressed to impress in a green business suit with huge shoulder pads, the blazer of which she'd covered in garish collectible pins. I was outclassed. I had to look down at my feet to make sure I was even wearing socks.

"We'll meet at the Dog Pound at six and I'll drop her off," I told Bai. Bai and Svetlana kissed goodbye in a way some might consider unseemly, and Bai went off to work at the wind turbine company.

"Poor Bai," said Svetlana. "He's going to be jealous. Me spending all day at your house."

"Well, I can't afford a fucking office," I said showing her inside. "Maybe we could work at Jenny's place. Or a cheap motel room."

"Did you know he still has that silly virtual girlfriend program? He takes it to work with him. Only now, now he's made the girl look like *me*." Svetlana considered this a personal triumph, not without reason.

"So here's the localization department," I said, "also known as the living room. We have the couch, and the TV, and the Brain Embryo."

Svetlana held her smart paper against the TV screen. "For a light-emitting source like a television, we'll do passthrough translation. Can you scale the image down so that it fits on the paper?"

"No," I said, "but I can get a smaller TV." In this blog post, the role of my television will be played by my computer monitor.

I turned on the Brain Embryo and set the all-in-one pirate cart to...

GAME REVIEWS OF LIES LIES LIES 2.0 PRESENTS
Sayable Spice (c. 40 million years ago)
A game by Clan Interference
Reviewed by Ariel Blum

Publisher: Clan Interference
Platform: Brain Embryo
ESRB Rating: M, just in case

"What about the RF emitters?" I asked, propping them up. "Can you visualize that for me?"

"That would be pretty, but useless," said Svetlana. "You would prefer for me to describe what's happening in Farang terms."

The smart paper went "transparent," passing through the video signal from the TV behind it. "Here we go," I said. "The 'taboo' had better not be any weird sex shit."

"File that under 'unlikely'," said Svetlana. "Farang have the sex lives of oysters." An Edink symbol-graph scrolled onto the screen, and her software drew an English translation on top of it:

> When you were a child, was there a taste
> perhaps a child-food you ate often,
> that didn't seem important at the time,
> perhaps a {{{shellfish}}} or other animal
> whose taste changed as you grew up?
>
> Some people spend their entire lives
> craving a taste that has dissolved in the ocean of time.
> You will not recapture the past through your
> {{{taste membranes}}}.
> It needs to be squeezed from your memories.
>
> Clan Interference will show you the
> **SAYABLE SPICE**
> Begin this game in the usual way

"That's downright melancholy," I said. "What's happening with the radio emitter?"

"Snap crackle pop," said Svetlana. "It sounds like a fish."

"How does a fish sound?"

"Sea animals," said Svetlana, "communicate with each other in the RF. That's how Farang catch them and eat them. The game is saying there's a fish nearby."

"To make you hungry?"

"Make you think of food. It's not related to Earth fish. That's just an analogy."

"Yeah, I got it."

I started the game. In the Alien remake of <u>Sayable Spice</u>, the player character is a person (ie. an Alien), but here I'm a blob. "Okay," I said, "supposedly this blob is part of somebody's brain."

"A memory tomia," said Svetlana. "It's how Farang back then thought the brain worked. Your job is to coordinate memories between the male and female halves of the brain."

"And is this a real thing, or is it some made-up bullshit, like the superego?"

"I have no idea," said Svetlana. "I'm not a Farang. Bai wouldn't like it if I spent half my time as a man."

Your job as the memory tomia is to create an association interesting enough to catch the attention of the conscious mind. I went through the first hour of the game, collecting chemical compounds. Svetlana translated the name of each one as I picked it up and slid into a slot of the memory tomia.

"Are these real chemicals?" I asked her.

"Let's find out," said Svetlana. She instructed me how to combine the chemicals. I clicked and thwapped and slid the keys of the abacus controller in big batches, as she read off the names of the compounds.

"I don't know if they're real chemicals," she said after a few minutes. "But they make real foods. Kewe si, stewed recency vine, mejh... oh. This is probably it. The one you just formed. Saturated infant comb."

"Is that a food, or a Farang indie rock band?"

"It's food," said Svetlana. "This should be interesting. Go ahead and trigger the flashback."

I'd never had the ingredients to trigger a Sayable Spice flashback before, but Tetsuo Milk and I explored a lot of the ones in Recapture That Remarkable Taste, using his knowledge of the Ip Shkoy Aliens. Here's my cleaned-up translation of the "pakpapur pod" flashback from the Alien remake. The player character is thinking back to her first lover, and the player controls an imaginary post-coital conversation between the two. It can go different ways, but this is the most interesting way I got it to come out:

> PC (Female): Why am I even thinking about you? Am I supposed to blame you for a lifetime of unsatisfying sex?
>
> NPC (Male): I'm easy to remember because of the pakpapur pod that exploded on your family's cooker.
>
> Female: We thought it would set the mood.
>
> Male: You're not supposed to set it directly on the heating element. It's there in the small print.
>
> Female: You had such gentle hindarms. A man is supposed to have nice hindarms.
>
> Male: They tell you that?

Female: Yeah, in sex ed. And then you grow up and find nice hindarms don't count for shit.

Male: You don't need to tell me. Where did I end up with my sweet-ass hindarms? I'm probably eating meat-flavored leaves from a cup right now.

Female: Wanna fuck again?

Male: I'm not really here. I'm the smell of pakpapur in your shopping backpack. You're climbing down to your home level and you're about to lose your grip on the ladder.

Female: Crap!

[Gameplay resumes.]

Pretty harmless—I'm trying to get that scene optioned for a romantic comedy, actually—but the Ip Shkoy, for all their faults, were a lot more comprehensible to humans than the Dhihe Coastal Coalition. I steeled myself and triggered the flashback. Honestly, with a name like "saturated infant comb," I was expecting cannibalism from this fucker.

"Big burst of static in the RF," said Svetlana. "Various sounds suggesting indistinct chatter."

The on-screen scene changes to what passes for realism on the Brain Embryo hardware. It's the traditional bottom-up view. The blob is gone, and instead the screen shows about twenty Farang, all of them crowding around a large round box near the top of the screen.

Wait, twenty? No other Farang game has NPCs, unless you count the zombies in Gatekeeper. Haven't seen a single Farang in Sayable Spice so far, and now there are twenty?

I slapped some controller beads around; one of the Farang moved a little and the TV did its best to reproduce "indistinct chatter" in a human range.

"Is this the taboo part?" I said. "Are non-player characters taboo?"

"Have you ever seen two Farang in the same place?" asked Svetlana.

"I've never seen two Farang, period," I said. "Are they hermits?"

"Have you been to Curic's house?"

"Yeah, she's got a private island. But, I mean, *I'd* like a private island."

"Aliens are social carnivores," said Svetlana. "Humans are pack animals. Farang are alpha predators, the most dangerous things in the ocean. They're very territorial; they don't even meet to breed." I remembered Curic in the passenger seat of Bai's SUV, telling us about leaving genetic material in tide pools.

"You'll never get more than seven Farang in one place," Svetlana continued. "That's why the clans are so small. That's why their technology advanced so slowly. That's why they didn't wipe themselves out before the Constellation found them."

"And here's Sayable Spice shoving fifteen, twenty dude/chicks in your face," I said.

"These are children," said Svetlana. "Children are scooped out of birth pools and raised collectively. They eat infant comb that's been soaked in food regurgitated by adults. Once you start catching your own food, you're supposed to stop eating the infant comb. You're supposed to form a clan and leave school."

"And then you don't talk about this. The other people."

"But maybe you get nostalgic for it," said Svetlana. "If you're the kind of clan who makes video games. You think about what you could accomplish if your clan were larger. You might even start to miss the infant comb."

"Okay, this we can put in the remake," I said. "It's just like the school cafeteria, everyone lining up for their sloppy joe and their box of milk. But nobody's going to feel nostalgia for that shit. Nobody misses elementary school. We won't be breaking any taboos."

"I guess you have to decide how much of Sayable Spice you want to remake," said Svetlana, "Do you want a game that says something, or do you just want the cute flavor-matching mechanic?"

Blog post, August 28

"Game night" begins at four in the afternoon when the game is Limited

Nuclear Exchange. It's a game for the unemployed and the self-employed. Setup is a fun time all by itself: not only the physical/espionage map with the dispositions of the missile silos and laboratories spread out across three card tables, but the propaganda/ideology boards on which the competing worldviews of East and West duke it out. Because if you only play with the physical map, you're a douchebag who just likes to blow things up. Yeah, I said that, and you can take it to the bank.

Around four-thirty wall time, Jenny and I will set the Doomsday Clock to 11:55 and begin play. But now I'm laying nuke chits face-down across the Kazakh SSR, secrets that Jenny will gradually reveal with satellite flyovers.

"I'm going to put a man on Mars this time," I said.

"Not in this expansion," said Jenny. "We can't even do that in real life. Not without space aliens helping us."

"We had probes on Mars in the Seventies," I said. "I could do it if I had more science chits and fewer nuke chits."

"Keep talking, you pinko," said Jenny. "You keep your eye on Mars, and Mr. Universe will sneak into your silos and punch your fissile material until it decays into americium." (We are playing with the superhero expansion.) "And that's America's element, so you can't use it."

"Jenny, I think we should change the direction of the Sayable Spice re-make," I said. All at once, out of nowhere, because if you try to warm Jenny up with an opening act like "I want to tell you something," she'll look at you like the thing you *want* to tell her is too horrible to come out and say.

Well, it didn't work. Jenny looked up from setting ideological traps for me in Central America and gave me the *other* look. The look she'd give "I'm going to put a man on Mars" if there were actually some rule in Limited Nuclear Exchange where one player could ruin the game for everyone else by ig-noring the balance of terror to pursue some hippy-dippy dream of space exploration. The "oh shit, not only does Ariel have a crazy idea, but there's no way to stop him" look.

"Do you see this? What's happening here?" she said. "You can now witness in real time the process of you not finishing something."

"We're going to finish it," I said. "This is business. I finished Recoil and Give 'em Hell, and I finished the pony games, and we'll finish this one. I just want to do it properly."

Jenny had a big hand of responses she wanted to give to that, but from that hand she played a conciliatory: "What's 'properly?'"

"The Ip Shkoy thought <u>Sayable Spice</u> was a game about food. That's why their remake was lousy. <u>Sayable Spice</u> is actually a game about growing up a geek. Constructing your life around fantasies and bits of the past, because the normal adult world doesn't do it for you. Keeping things bottled up until you can release them in a big spectacular display."

Jenny neatly stacked a big pile of chits and plunked them all down on Austin, Texas, her personal capital of the United States. "My problem is that I've spent over a hundred hours drawing pixel art of food," she said. "And the chemicals that make up the food. Because the *mechanics* of <u>Sayable Spice</u> are about food."

"And it's good art," I said. "You're really improving. We just need to figure out how to reuse those assets in a game about video games."

"This is not happening," said Jenny. "No, actually, I'm surprised this didn't happen earlier. We have a nice, fun, salable game. A game that might actually be released. So of course you have to self-sabotage. Throw up a roadblock for yourself and take it in some meta direction."

"No, c'mon," I said. "This is important. Games, and comics and shit, are the American equivalent of saturated infant comb. We all play video games when we're kids. But people like Agent Krakowski stop playing them, and then they end up... like Krakowski. Or they only play games that let them be psychopaths, and then they end up like Agent Fowler."

I slapped down a set of five-year-plan cards and Jenny shuffled them so that my plan wouldn't work as planned. "So instead of <u>Sayable Spice</u>," I said, "we'll make <u>Playable Spice</u>. Instead of collecting chemical compounds, you'll collect game mechanics. And when you have the right combination, instead of a flashback, you'll be able to play through an old-style game. We'll make parodies of all the classic games. It'll be like all those games were twisted in your mind by the horrible process of growing up."

"Do you remember my freshman sculpture project?" said Jenny.

"You showed me at the time," I said. "I don't really remember it."

"Because it was awful," said Jenny. She gave me back my five-year-plan cards. "Crap, as it were. I had no artistic discipline. I tried to say three different things in one piece. Do you see where I'm going with this?"

"I've been making games for ten years," I said.

"You filled in the backgrounds of Michelangelo's paintings for ten years. You're really good, okay? Or Michelangelo wouldn't have hired you. But if you'd been in charge of <u>Give 'em Hell</u>, or any of those games, they'd never have seen daylight."

"I don't want this to be the kind of company where someone's in charge."

"Then it's a good thing our business plan is really obvious," said Jenny. "We just have to stick to it. Release a solid game that sells well and introduces people to the Constellation. And then I can use my share of the money to buy love slaves and build *Protector of Earth*, and you can use your share to make an anthology of sad emo games about growing up."

I looked out at Jenny over the Atlantic ocean. "I think we should just nuke each other once and get it out of our systems," I said.

"Yeah, okay," said Jenny, and grabbed a handful of dice. "First-gen H-bombs, no cards, no superheroes. Don't move the chits."

"I wasn't gonna."

"I don't want to set this up again."

And then everybody died. And then we played for real.

Crispy Duck Games: G-DDAMMIT WE WILL RELEASE SOME KIND OF GAME.

Blog post, August 29, early morning

The Mars expedition is go! It's just not as exciting as we thought. Instead of a big expensive spaceship with cool liftoff explosions, we're attaching a port to an unmanned probe the size of an pickup truck, and landing the probe on Mars. And instead of being stuck in that expensive spaceship stewing in their own shit for a year and a half, the astronauts will live in (relative) luxury on Ring City and in about six weeks, they'll just walk through the port.

I'm super-excited about this mission because it means NASA is releasing a lot of video from Ring City, and some of the video features my girlfriend, Dr. Tammy Miram. She's so dreamy! (Especially now that she's resumed showering.) You'll notice I've dropped her blog pseudonym—it's a convention that makes a lot of sense when I'm dating a short-order cook or a copy editor, but NASA only has so many cute blonde astronauts.

This particular cute blonde astronaut is not in the official press conference video. Tammy's not one of the Mars colonists, due to an aversion to living on planets. But as one of the people responsible for making the colonists look like heroes instead of sellouts trying to claim Mars for the Constellation, she's front and center in the star-draw.

The star-draw video is nine minutes long, and I've been watching it every ninety minutes as a break from coding, which means I get to see Tammy about 14% of the time. At this point I'm pretty good at watching this video, so I'll walk you through it.

It's pretty similar to the star-draw we did with Curic on the Fourth. What we got (0:05) is a bunch of human astronauts and Gaijin scientists, gathered around a Very Serious Airlock in Gaijin Ring. Behind the airlock is one end of a port, and on the other end is EMPTY FUCKING SPACE. Thus the airlock. You're looking down the length of the unmanned probe, which is pointed at where Mars will be in six weeks. Ignore the NASA Public Affairs narrator. He's useless, he won't give you this information until (1:09).

I'm in the middle of an all-nighter and more or less insane, but man. All the humans are in clingy transparent Constellation spacesuits (since Gaijin Ring is more or less the same as Mars), and Tammy (0:22) looks *great*. She's torn off the long sleeves of her NASA flight suit and she's got a string of overlay patches running up and across her chest like a sash. It's a look I can get into.

The first time I met Tammy, she wore the standard RC-001 NASA mission patch on the shoulder of her flight suit. At some point, the Gaijin on the Mars mission figured out that human astronauts use patches on their clothes to signal group affiliation. Now the Gaijin and the astronauts produce a patch for every single fluid overlay they form. Which means a complete record of each person's work for the past month on his/her/kis/kes body.

Tammy is rocking the "overzealous Girl Scout" look. Colonel Mason, the square-jawed meathead who'll probably be planting the flag, has his patches lined up perfectly across his chest like medals (0:31), with blank spaces here and there like he's collecting Xbox achievements. The Russians (0:33) have sewed all their overlay patches onto the legs of their flight suits, so that they can hide them from Moscow when they call home. The Gaijin just adhere the patches onto their trunks with no pattern I can see—looks like a kindergartener attacked them with stickers.

I can't make out the patches themselves because it's streaming video quality, but these mission patches are flashing, they're changing color, some of them look to have video. It's like a disco up there on everyone's clothes. Everyone's smiling up a storm except for Colonel Mason, who apparently never learned how.

A Gaijin speaks first (2:02). It's He Sees The Map And He Throws The Dart!, a male with a scrawny trunk and tentacles that quiver and flop around the floor with emotion. We hear the narrator read an English translation in a monotone: Mars is so important, so beautiful, so much like home. And then Dr. Tammy Miram turns on her suit mike (5:29) and speaks for humanity.

"Humans have been dreaming about Mars for hundreds of years," she says. "We've been planning for this mission for longer than any of us has been alive. After countless hardships and setbacks, our common dream is finally within reach. And I am proud to be part of this mission, as a citizen of the United States of America, and of Earth. But nothing we find on Mars can compare to what we've already discovered right here.

"We've been dreaming about life on other stars since we first understood what stars *are*. And this dream has already come true. We go to Mars not alone, as we thought we would, but with friends. Here's to our friendship."

She holds up a little translucent disk and she smiles at me. At the camera. (6:44—I usually pause it here for a bit.) Everyone reaches into a pocket of their spacesuit, or one of the cleaner Gaijin orifices, and pulls out one of these discs.

This is the star-draw ritual proper, and the narrator will describe it like it's somebody's fucking bris just because they've got cool custom-made discs. Well, when Curic taught us the star-draw in my driveway, we used coins; and for the one I did with Tetsuo on Ring City, we used two smashed peanut M&Ms from the bottom of my duffel bag. I guess what I'm saying is I don't think the narrator's tone is appropriate here. I mute the audio at this point. (6:49)

Everybody's coming around (6:53) to face the Very Serious Airlock and the port behind it. The blue and grey and white flight suits are blocking the camera's view of the port. Eventually whoever's editing this video gives up and cuts to an overhead cam.

Now (6:59) we can see the rest of the humans, the ones in the back running the cameras. They're in spacesuits, too, but they're not astronauts and they don't have many patches on their clothes. They're CNN, or public affairs from the space agencies. They get pushed back, back as human and Gaijin astronauts gather in a big arc about fifteen feet away from the port that will soon be a door onto Mars.

At (7:10) someone throws their disc. It bounces off the airlock and skids to a halt on the green tiled floor. A little ripple of mirth goes through the astronauts—there goes Premature Joe, always blasting off before the countdown's finished—and then off we go, everyone's pitching in. They've done this ritual before—once for every patch on their suits. The stones ricochet off the airlock and fall and knock against each other on the ground. By (7:40), the floor of Gaijin Ring is covered with little round discs.

And the discs start to glow, like fireflies, like tea candles. A pattern of randomly distributed lights, like the stars we can see on the other end of the port. A constellation. The logo for the Mars mission overlay.

And that's it, the mission is on! On the other end of the port, the probe begins to accelerate towards where Mars will be in six weeks. The stars don't shift like they do on TV; they won't shift at all. They're too far away. We're not going to the stars, yet; just to another planet.

At (8:08) the Gaijin begin accosting the camera operators, trying to get them to throw their discs. The camera operators are not taking this well; they're used to being invisible.

We're not going back to the ground-level shot because this shot of the glowing discs is too cool, and I'm not going to see any more of my girlfriend than the top of her head. So that's the end of the video. That's the end of this blog post.

Chapter 21:
Her

Who the hell was smashing my doorbell at nothing o'clock? Cops generally knock, and burglars have the decency to just break in. I was coming off consecutive all-nighters and someone seemed to have put some kind of *huge fucking pea* under my mattress. Not a good scene.

I clomped down the stairs and opened the door. "Do you know what time it is, you fucking... robot?" The robot was made of Constellation cerametal and had a dozen telescoping arms that let it reach up and give the doorbell a handjob.

"Stop that," I said, slapping one arm away from the doorbell. "Okay, here's the deal. Because you're a wicked-looking robot, I'm going to listen to what you have to say for one sentence. Make it count."

"I'm not a robot," said the robot. "This is telepresence."

"That was pathetic." I turned to shut the door, except I didn't, because behind the robot I saw a glow that looked a lot like sunlight.

"Wait," said the robot. "Her wants you to come to Ring City for a few minutes."

I held the door open. "Who does? Curic? My girlfriend?"

"I'm Curic," said the robot, and pointed at itself four times with four different arms. "It's telepresence!"

"How did you get down here?"

"I jumped," said the Curic-bot.

"So, if you're Curic," I said, "who is it who wants me to come to Ring City?" *Please let it be Tammy.*

"It's Her," said Curic.

I gently massaged my temples. "Okay, just say her name."

"Her!" said Curic. "The Her superorganism!"

"Oh, *Her*," I said. The ache in my temples migrated to the pit of my stomach. My good sense was fighting a losing battle against my curiosity.

"Can I see my girlfriend as long as I'm up there?"

"Not in the usage of 'see her' that I think you have in mind," said Curic. "This is a secret project with a half-life of eight hours. You'll need to return to Earth as soon as possible. It's quite forbidden for me to even set foot on your planet right now. Whence the telepresence."

I felt that the use of telepresence was skirting the law at best, but I had little interest in arguing this with Curic. "Why does Her... she... Her... even want to talk to me?" I asked.

"I told Her you were an expert on computer game design," said the Curic-robot.

"Somehow I don't feel like that answers my question."

"Come through the port," said the robot. It picked up a large thin hoop and set it against the railing of my front porch. Through the port, I saw the sunlight I'd glimpsed earlier: the soft artificial lighting of Ring City's Human Ring.

"See?" said the robot. "I've set it against the wall. There will be no gravity differential when you go through." On the other side of the port, I saw Curic herself step into view and wave at me. The robot jerked aimlessly in time with her movements.

I put my hand through the port. The air on the other side was a few degrees cooler.

"I never get tired of this shit," I said. "This is amazing. You wouldn't need shuttles if you set these up everywhere."

"Yes," said Curic and the robot in unison, "because the shuttles have worked out so well."

I ducked back into my house for my keys and walked through the port. No nausea, no terror of seeing Earth disappear beneath my feet. I just strolled into lunar orbit and into Human Ring. A maze of softly-lit slightly-curved beige hallways, all alike.

"Thanks for coming," said Curic, shrugging off her telepresence harness. "May I offer you some pie?" She held out a plate embossed with little flowers. On the plate was a perfectly cut piece of strawberry pie.

"Man, fuck your pie," I said."What's with all the pie?"

"I wasn't allowed to give you any when I came down a few days ago," said Curic. She broke off half the pie and pushed it into her antennacled maw. "I'm trying to be nice."

"All right, I'm sorry," I said. I took the other half. It was excellent pie.

Curic tossed the pie plate like a Frisbee down the long featureless hallway. "Through the door," she said. She pointed at a round airlock-style door, the generic Human Ring door. The door behind which might be a featureless two-person Human Ring apartment, or... another featureless two-person Human Ring apartment. Or a long hallway with more round doors leading to more identical two-person apartments.

"Her is in *there*?" I said.

"I'll come with you," said Curic. "She will speak with you. It should only take about twenty minutes."

"Do I need a spacesuit?" I said. I was hoping to score a suit to replace the one the BEA had confiscated.

"That won't be necessary," said Curic. "These Them organisms are engineered for Earthlike environments, such as Human Ring."

"Are these Them organisms engineered to not creep me the fuck out?"

"I don't think cuddliness was a big consideration," said Curic. She paused with her paw held out to the door sensor.

"Have you ever given thought to why Smoke paired us together?" she said. "You and me."

"I didn't really think there were reasons," I said.

"I'm pretty sure it's because we both have problems with authority."

"Give me a break," I said. "You live in a post-scarcity anarchy. How did you develop problems with authority?"

"Ask me that again in twenty minutes," said Curic. Her paw closed a circuit and the door yawned open.

This room was the size of the featureless apartment I'm apparently now sharing with Dr. Tammy Miram. But it wasn't featureless. Instead of a bed and a squat toilet, it had a yellow plastic chair positioned to face a huge structure molded into the far wall: a structure like a wasp's nest carved out of white wood.

"Sit," said Curic. It was the kind of chair you see in corporate cafeterias. I slouched in the chair and stared at the wasp's nest.

"Thank you again for coming," said Curic. "It's extraordinarily important that Her sides with Plan C on this issue."

"What?" I said. "You hate Plan C."

"That's incorrect," said Curic.

"Then I guess sometimes the truth is incorrect," I said.

"Ssh," hissed Curic. "This is Her."

The wasp's nest rustled and one of Them crawled out. Another and a third. They looked like trilobites, or giant roly-polies. Dark red, with shells and little claws.

"Hello, Ariel, Curic," said Her. The voice came from every point in the room. It was a human woman's voice resampled, and although I couldn't place it, it sounded familiar. Like when a Farang uses the vocalizer that makes everything come out in George Clooney's voice.

I leaned forward and put my palms on my knees. "Hi," I said.

The trickle of trilobites became a swarm, pouring out of the white wooden nest at the far end of the room. The first two of Them reached my bare feet and climbed inside my pajama legs.

"Whoa!" I said. "The clothes are there for a reason."

"I'll go outside," said Her. The first trilobites ducked out of the pajama pants and climbed up my legs. Then the swarm hit. A rope of them up my legs like passengers onto a cruise ship, sneaky stowaways tiptoeing up the legs of the cafeteria chair, all of them coming to cover my chest and legs like the lead blanket the dentist drops on you before shooting you with X-rays. They were warm and dry and terrifying. A small one settled itself into the pocket of my T-shirt.

I closed my eyes and cast around for something else to think about. I noticed that Curic was holding my hand in both of her paws, like my mom did when I was a kid at the doctor. Curic had never touched me before; she'd never even come close.

"This is Her?" I asked Curic.

"Part of me," said Her. "A very small part. Are you comfortable, Ariel?" That's when I recognized the voice. The oldest person in the universe communicates with humanity through the cute squeaky voice of Sarah Vowell. I couldn't unhear it. Every time she spoke, I expected Her to give an update on her quirky project to visit all the national parks.

"I'm not comfortable," I said. "I'm covered in fucking trilobites."

"It's not pleasant for us either," said one of the individual Them in an even higher-pitched version of Sarah Vowell's voice. "You've got boy cooties!" The rest of Them rustled with faint resentful cries of "Cooties!"

"They're not a predator species like humans," said Her. "They don't sense motion very well. They need physical contact or I can't make you out; you know how it is."

"Not really, no," I said.

"Ho ho ho. Now, Ariel, let me ask you: Why did you write the same game five times?"

"What the...?"

"She's talking about the Pôneis Brilhantes series," said Curic quietly.

"I figured that, I just thought there'd be some small talk first."

"I asked if you were comfortable," said Her.

"And I said no."

"Oh, this *is* fun," said Her. "Why, Ariel? I would like to know. It even has a number on it. Pôneis Brilhantes 5."

"You don't need to convince me that that job sucked." I said. "I already quit. Anyway, they're not literally the same game."

"I'm eight hundred million years old," said Her. "I've seen a lot. Please excuse me if I can't resolve the fine distinctions between Pôneis Brilhantes number four and number five."

"Okay," I said, "since you asked, here's how it works. The target market for Brilhantes is ten-year-old girls. I came in for Brilhantes 4. A year later, the ten-year-olds have turned eleven and think Brilhantes is childish, which it is. So we tweak the graphics, change the minigames, and sell Brilhantes <u>5</u> to the nine-year-olds who have just turned ten. It makes perfect sense if you consider the market. Do you even remember what it's like to be ten?"

"Of course," said Her. "Most of my members are juveniles." The trilobites wiggled in unison and I shuddered. "Without them, my outlook would be jaded indeed. Moving on... I learned from your blog that you are a fan of the <u>Bit Boy</u> series."

"I am," I said, trying to remember the last time I'd mentioned Bit Boy. She must have read my archives. "I think I see the trajectory of your questioning here."

"That game was made fourteen times."

"I'll stipulate that," I said.

"Why fourteen times? That's very many times."

"I couldn't speculate."

"You're not on trial," said Her. "Nothing bad will happen if you answer one way or the other."

"It sure feels like a trial."

"I'm just trying to get a feel for how human games are made. Why do you think there are so many <u>Bit Boy</u> games?"

"I don't know. Creative bankruptcy? Followed by the realization that if they brought it back as self-parody they could exploit peoples' nostalgia for the first four games?"

"I'm going to give you some game titles," said Her. "<u>Frosting Frenzy</u>, <u>Dress Shop</u>, <u>Knitja</u>, <u>Fondant Fury</u>, <u>Micro Mike</u>, <u>Squirtd!</u>, <u>Outsourced Tech Support</u>, <u>Mestre Bolo</u>, <u>Big Time Mechanic</u>, <u>Big Time Zookeeper</u>, <u>Big Time—</u>"

"That's a whole genre," I said, "not one game. And <u>Outsourced Tech Support</u> is a parody."

"It looks like one game," said Her. "Why are so many people writing the same game?"

"Because <u>Frosting Frenzy</u> made a billion dollars for Fucknovis Studios, or whatever they're called now. That's in, like, 2011. And uh-oh, now it's 2012 and they need a follow-up. They'd love to make the exact same game again, but it's not like with <u>Brilhantes</u> where you sell to different people. Everyone who'd buy <u>Frosting Frenzy</u> again has already signed up as a Fucknovis beta tester. So they do <u>Fondant Fury</u>.

"And a sequel is actually harder to make, because you used up all the easy ideas the first time. So then they try to mix it up a little with the <u>Big Time</u> series. Meanwhile, every other casual developer is ripping off <u>Frosting Frenzy</u> and saturating the market. It's not a business you want to be in."

"Let's talk MMORPGs," said Her. "I've seen a number of press reports—"

"No," I said, "this is stupid. I thought talking to you would be interesting, but it's like explaining my job to my mother. Assuming my mother was a swarm of trilobites."

"She does go on," whispered one of Them. I suddenly noticed that Curic had left. Left me alone with Them and with Her.

"I'm sorry, I thought you'd enjoy this," said Her. "Most people enjoy conversations about things they know about. Maybe you want to drive the conversation. Shall we talk about the Inostrantsi?"

I flinched under the blanket of Them. "Yes, you're curious," said Her. "You wrote about them on the twenty-third of August. I was there when it happened, Ariel. I had members that lived among the Inostrantsi, members that died in the collapse. Maybe you want to know how it happened. Maybe you think the Constellation could have prevented it. Maybe you want to accuse me of something."

"You do seem a little defensive."

"I don't like it when societies collapse!" said Her. "It's a lot of death and a lot of work. Have you played the computerized interactive works of the late, great Inostrantsi civilizations?"

"No, I have not," I said. "Are we back to games again?"

"There were some inspired pieces of art," said Her. "Not just the games. The literature and what you would call music. Their touches and echoes still haunt me."

"Curic dropped me the MassMonger 31," I said. "I couldn't get it set up. I guess you'd know that, since you're the only person who reads my blog."

"The MassMonger was a primitive computer used in ritual," said Her. "I'm talking about the state of the art, just before the collapse. Wearable networked computers of great subtlety. Some of my members were quite fond of the experiences." The trilobites all sighed.

"The Inostrantsi had beautiful games, driven by artificial intelligence that changed the gameplay procedurally, a little at a time. Always providing new experiences. But always the same game. A certain kind of person goes into the simulation space and doesn't come out. They're happy with the same stimulus, over and over again. My own members went in and didn't come out! That's you!" The trilobites squeaked, chastised by the collective intelligence that they formed.

"Are you blaming the collapse of civilization on addictive video games?" I said.

"I don't lay blame," said Her. "I'm too old and too complicit. But if human psychology is similar to that of the Inostrantsi, then the Plan C overlay is correct. We need to send for help before it's too late. I hope I'm not boring you, Ariel. I do despise being dull."

"What do you want me to do? Make better games?"

"I'd value your opinion," said Her. "If we reopen a port back to Constellation space, your civilization will suffer enormous culture shock. Instead of a few million scientists and adventurer-seekers, you will have unmediated interactions with a thriving civilization of trillions of people. This hasn't worked out well in the past."

I thought of the hippie with the walking stick, the day Jenny and I tried to go to see the shuttles land. Telling us we'd live to see the end of the human race. This was the kind of thing he was talking about.

"On the other hand," said Her, "it would give you a chance to see what we've been able to build over the last eight hundred million years. The only stable multistellar civilization in the known galaxy."

Now I thought of visiting other planets. I thought of Tammy giving up her ridiculous promise and coming with me to Tetsuo's homeworld, walking with me through a real *cma* jungle.

"That's such crap," chirped the trilobite in my shirt pocket, breaking the spell. "Absolute byproduct. We might as well start from scratch with the dolphins."

"You callous swab," said another trilobite. "Open a port. Resettle them before the collapse. Move them to an Earthlike planet for a few generations."

"Yeah, another planet for them to shit all over!"

"Your, uh, members are talking back at you," I told Her.

"That's their right," said Her. "They're young; they have their own priorities. I'm the superorganism, I'm the oldest, and I've played this game one million times before. Ten thousand contact missions, ten thousand fossilized planets, twenty-four successes. And now, you.

"I'm tired, Ariel. The task I've chosen is infinite and hopeless. I'm tired of dealing with slow people, and I'm sick of cleaning up dead bodies."

"I can't make this decision!" I said. "I can't speak for humanity. There needs to be some kind of fucking... referendum."

"You've been very helpful," said Her. "I don't see much downside to Plan C's idea. If things improve here, we can always collapse the port before it reaches Constellation space. It may be the best solution."

"You're fooling yourself," said one of Them.

"Lying to yourself," said another.

"Lying to him," said a third.

"I guess I gotta ask," I said. "Are you lying to me?"

"No," said Them. "Yes." "No." "No." "I don't know." "I wish I were."

"Majority rules," said Her. "I'm not lying. I'm also leaning strongly towards joining Plan C. Save the Humans has little to offer but hope. You, Ariel, may well live long enough to understand that hope is a luxury of the young."

"I'm not very good at office politics," I said, "but that sounds like a threat."

"I never threaten anyone but myself," said Her. "Goodbye, Ariel. It was nice talking to you."

The trilobites dropped off my body like they'd been hit with a can of insecticide. They scurried back into their white wooden nest, squeaking and bitching at each other in high-pitched National Public Radio voices. At once the room was still. Her was gone.

I sat lightly in the cafeteria chair, eyes closed, breathing quietly. My T-shirt was pilled by endless tiny claws.

I cried for five minutes in revulsion and shame and then I stood up shaking. I carefully tipped the chair on its side and walked out of Her nest room into the vast cramped emptiness of Human Ring.

Curic was nowhere to be seen. Next to the port she'd set up, two Aliens cuddled asleep on the floor. They wore human-style clothes tailored for Alien bodies. The one in the four-legged tuxedo was Tetsuo Milk; I assumed the larger one was Ashley.

Tetsuo lifted his head and swiveled his tongue in the Alien equivalent of a smile. "Ariel!" he said. "I outcamped to see you before you left. I want to introduce you to my wife, Daisy Cept."

"Hi, I'm Daisy!" said Daisy. "I work with dolphins." She lifted a forehand to shake, like a dog does. She wore a long golden qibao decorated with embroidered pineapples and other Earth fruits.

G-ddammit! "Uh, Tets, a word in your ear?" I said.

"Which word?"

"C'mere." I beckoned him over. "What the fuck, man? What happened to Ashley? You were good for each other."

"Ashley and I, we... I don't think there is a word for it in English."

"You broke up?"

"Ah, you do have a word for it!"

"You've recovered quickly!" *You fucking cad.*

"Recovered from what? It's only until the eggs hatch."

The shot of anger burned out of my system and I realized there was none left in the bottle. I shook my head. "Maybe we *don't* have a word for this," I said.

"Are you okay?"

"Never been worse. It's fuck-thirty in the morning and Her just creeped me to death."

"Her said something to outcreep you?"

"She *is* something to outcreep me." I rubbed my red eyes. "Congrats on the... eggs," I said. "Are you going back to Constellation space once they reopen the port? This station's no place to raise kids."

Tetsuo's face had an expression I couldn't read. "I'm coming to *Earth*," he said. "The children will follow. Who says anyone is reopening a port?"

"Plan C," I said. "That's what I was talking about with Her. It kind of sounds like a done deal."

"My haunches!" said Tetsuo.

"Doublepuke!" said Daisy. "That's dolphin swearing."

"Plan C are cowards," said Tetsuo. "They want to quit the game because they can't beat the first level."

"Well, they just won the argument," I said. "Her seems like a hell of a swing vote. Even Curic has switched sides."

"That supposes to me as unlikely," said Tetsuo.

"Well, maybe you should find Curic and ask her," I said. "Where did she go, anyway? Am I just supposed to go back home through the port?"

"Go not!" said Tetsuo. "Ashley is using lies to distract Curic, so that you can spend more time here."

I shook my head. "Okay, why?"

"Because humans and Aliens have something in common," Daisy said. "Something that dolphins and Farang don't think is important."

I felt a hand on my shoulder. Much bigger than Curic's hand, but much smaller than Tetsuo's. About, yes, the same size as a normal human hand. I turned around and there was a human behind me. A blonde human in a tattered NASA flight suit covered with little fluid-overlay patches.

"Hey," said Dr. Tammy Miram with a smile. She put her normal-sized human hands around my waist.

"Sexual pair bonding!" said Tetsuo.

"Thank you, Tetsuo, we get it," said Tammy. I put my hands on her hips and right on the verge of her left hip, I saw a brand new overlay patch sewed to her suit: the planet Mars, slowly rotating in front of a starfield. The starfield that Tammy had created, her and the other astronauts and the Gaijin and the camera operators with their glowing discs, in that video I'd watched over and over again.

"I have to be back in Gaijin Ring in twelve minutes," she said. "And you need to be back on Earth right now."

I kissed her. "I don't know if we can get the whole experience in just twelve minutes," I said.

"You stop talking now," said Dr. Miram. She pulled me through a dilating door into an anonymous Human Ring apartment, furnished with a shower/sink and a squat toilet and a bunkbed.

"Niceta meetcha," Daisy called out to me.

"See you soon," said Tetsuo.

A couple days after this, my life was run through the industrial pulper. All through that experience, I was grateful, and despite everything that's happened since I'm still grateful, for the overlay patch that Tammy stuck onto me with a safety pin before I went back to Earth. I used to pull it out of my pocket all the time just to look at it.

It wasn't animated. It didn't have any text or even a full starfield. It was just two stars shining on a black background: a binary system. The simplest possible constellation. Her and me.

Chapter 22:
Nerfed

Blog post, September 2

GAME REVIEWS OF GAME REVIEWS OF 2.0 PRESENTS
Legend of the Bystander (c. 40 million years ago)
A game by Clan Interference
Reviewed by Ariel Blum

Publisher: Clan Interference
Platform: Brain Embryo
ESRB Rating: T for cartoon existentialism

Today is a light work day. Svetlana and I are taking a break from Sayable Spice to take a look at some of Clan Interference's later games. I would love to be able to design games like Clan Interference did, because these guys were motherfucking insane. First they broke the taboo against socializing with other Farang in Sayable Spice, and then in Legend of the Bystander, they took on the entire concept of Farang literature.

LotB is a blob of historical-fiction vignettes that retell scenes from the Consensus Mythos shared by all Edink-speaking Farang. Clan Interference has created playable versions of all your favorite Mythos stories: the tragic Ambivalence Of King Hzme (well, they didn't have kings, but whatever); the thrilling story of the Island That Was Really A Monster With Other Monsters Living On Top; and everyone's favorite, the Raid On Offshore Loop Platform #6.

I set the pirate-cart settings and turned on the Brain Embryo to the usual crisp visuals and dead silence. "Why don't any of these games have music? It's creepy. We need some hair-metal theme songs. 'By-standah! Duh-nuh-*nuh*-nuh legend of the... by-standah!'"

"There's plenty of noise in the RF," said Svetlana, pulling off her head-phones. "But you wouldn't want to hear it."

I started the game. "Oh, look," I said. "What a surprise. I'm a Farang on a beach in a bottom-up perspective." Forty to fifty percent of Brain Embryo games begin on a beach. (About twenty percent *never leave* the beach.) After the weird inside-the-brain setting of <u>Sayable Spice</u>, Clan Interference was following up with an aggressively traditional presentation.

Except that my player character was surrounded by ten Farang NPCs, mill-ing around the beach. Not quite the twenty you see in the first <u>Sayable Spice</u> flashback, but a freaking army by Dhihe Coastal Coalition standards, considering a clan is four to seven individuals.

Svetlana skimmed the game's metadata screen. "This is the Kveh Beach," she said. "There are nine loop platforms offshore. Under cover of fog, these soldiers are going to attack number six."

"Why?" I said.

"It's assumed that we already know why," said Svetlana.

"So I'm a soldier," I said. "What am I s'posed to do?"

"Anything you want," she said, "as long as you don't change the outcome of the raid."

I dove my player character into the ocean and fed on some nearby sea grass. "What do I have to not change? What was the outcome of the raid?"

"It didn't really happen," said Svetlana. "It's a Consensus myth."

"I mean what 'really' happened, in the myth?"

"I have no idea," said Svetlana. "Play it and find out. I imagine the ten people on the beach will slaughter the four on the loop platform. And then we'll all learn a valuable lesson about the maximum size of a clan."

"Why can't I stop the raid?"

"Because it's canon."

"Fuck canon," I said. I picked up an algae-covered rock and smacked one of the soldiers with it. He/she dissolved in a cloud of blood and two-dimensional polygons. The screen filled with a small symbol-graph in a large font.

"'You stop looking,'" translated Svetlana. "Similar sentiments in the RF."

"That's starting to look familiar," I said. *You stop looking* is the Farang equivalent of *Game Over*.

I power-cycled the Brain Embryo. "Here's a pro tip," said Svetlana. "The goal is to change as much as you can without altering the story."

"And people bought this game where you can't change the story?"

"Not 'bought' in a capitalist sense," said Svetlana. "It's a political statement against the Consensus Mythos."

"What's wrong with the Mythos? It sounds like the Greek myths. Who cares?"

"The Dhihe only told stories within the framework of the Consensus Mythos," said Svetlana. "They had two mental categories: the Mythos and reality."

"What about <u>Sayable Spice</u>?"

"Mythos," said Svetlana. "Modern day. Long after the Loop Platform #6 incident. You can add new characters, but you can't change Mythos events. Everyone's a bystander."

Back in the game, my Farang stood around and waited out the clock, a perfect little Bystander. Eventually the soldiers swam out to the loop platforms, leaving me alone on the beach.

You can't stop the raid and you can't even join it. You can tag along and watch the polygonic gore, or you can run out the clock standing-by on the beach. This is the most realistic sandbox game I've ever played: you can do whatever you want but it won't change a damn thing.

After the timer runs out on the raid, you move on to level two, the Ambivalence of King Hzme, which is a little more interesting. King Hzme runs a factory (I told you they didn't really have kings). Every morning, like humanity's Old King Cole, he calls for his pipe and he calls for his bowl and he calls for his factory employees three. The factory employees, in turn, tool up to produce decorative screens and room-dividers for use in the home.

But when the sun goes down, King Hzme becomes Queen Hzme, and *she* tells the night shift (the crossselves of the day shift) to start producing pre-cast concrete parts aimed towards the construction market. And before they can get anything done, King Hzme comes back, and you get the picture. Back and forth they go, always tooling up to produce one thing or another and never making anything.

It's a tragedy about which you can do nothing, because you don't play as King/Queen Hzme. Nor do you play the mental health inspector who eventually shuts down his/her factory. You play one of the fucking factory employees. You can do your job, or not; it doesn't matter because any work you do will be torn down by the other shift. It's a great metaphor for the game as a whole.

Svetlana sez: "Nobody thought those things really happened. The Mythos was just a way to build an industrial society out of people who hate being near each other." And I guess it worked. Nobody wants to end up like King Hzme or the poor butchered bastards on Offshore Loop Platform #6. But the cost was a prohibition against telling stories that couldn't fit into the Mythos, stories that might have different morals.

That prohibition fell apart once the Dhihe Coastal Coalition invented electronic simulations. Now they had a medium based around feedback and machine-enforced rules, not static storytelling or social acting. You could run a story ten times and get ten different results, just like plugging different numbers into a spreadsheet.

Clan Interference pushed this idea hard. The playable flashbacks in Sayable Spice let you change events that have "already happened." Legend of the Bystander gets you as close as you could possibly get to altering Mythos events. And then Clan Interference stopped making this kind of game. Their later games, Double Attack and so on, have uniformly good CDBOE-GOACC ratings. Nice single-peak histograms, like you'd see in a human game magazine. No more controversy.

The CDBOEGOACC doesn't say why this happened, and doesn't even seem to notice that it did. Maybe someone told Clan Interference to stop. Maybe their big creative quit or died. Maybe another game-design clan went Offshore Loop Platform #6 on their asses and took their name. Or maybe Clan Interference themselves weren't comfortable pushing this idea any further than Legend of the Bystander. They'd invented fiction, and they couldn't figure out what to do with it.

Real life, September 2

I toyed around with an idea and decided to bring it into the real world. "Dana," I asked, "is ambivalence a real thing with Farang?"

"Yeah, it's real."

"Because Tetsuo and I played this Ip Shkoy game where we were the two halves of a Farang. And if we didn't cooperate with each other, pfft, ambivalence, game over."

"It wasn't very common," said Dana, "but they worried about it a lot. The way you might worry about pissing your pants in public."

There was a crucial flaw in Dana's logic. "Except I don't worry about that," I said.

Dana unscrewed her monocle and breathed on it. "Because you've been conditioned," she said. She buffed her monocle on the sleeve of her cheerleading sweater. "When you were a little boy, your parents beat you with a stick to get you to piss in the toilet."

"Nobody beat me with a stick!" I said. "Is that your impression of humanity? My parents offered me red licorice to pee in the toilet, and I've never regretted taking that deal."

Fake Dana Light considered this defense of my parents more or less skippable. "However it happened," she said, "you were conditioned, and so are Farang. That's what was going on in the school in <u>Sayable Spice</u>. Personality integration. You can't go through life like King Hzme."

"But sometimes it happens," I said. "I get that feeling myself. I waffle back and forth, I can't make a decision. I'm ambivalent. And I don't know what an Alien would do in that situation—"

"We'd pick an option at random and create *post hoc* rationalizations," said Dana. "Humans do it, too."

"—but couldn't a Farang split the difference between their selves? Hedge their bets, if there were good arguments on both sides?"

"You should ask Curic," said Dana. "I keep telling you I'm not based on a Farang psychology."

"Curic's the one I'm *worried* about," I said. "I think half of her joined Save the Humans way back when, and the other half joined Plan C. Half of her told me to look for information about the Constellation Shipping container, and an hour later the other half said it wasn't important. She's hiding information from her crossself, and I don't think either of them even knows it's happening."

Dana gave me a stern look. "Someone with that kind of mental discipline wouldn't become ambivalent in the first place. You're saying that Curic is pissing herself, but because her bladder muscles are so strong, none of the urine escapes her cloaca."

"I'm more worried about my friend's problem than in coming up with the perfect urine-related analogy for the problem."

"It's not realistic," said Dana. "To pull this trick on each other, both you and your crossself would have to be sociopaths."

"You're not helping!"

Backdated blog post, September 2

[Entry backdated from October 13: The blog post after this one is a lie that I had to post, for reasons which should become obvious. This entry is what actually happened on September 2. —A.B.]

A knock at the door.

"Geez, Bai must have got off work early," I said, getting off the couch.

"He's still jealous of my work," said Dana. "You need to have a talk with him."

I untaped Dana's smart paper from the TV screen and folded her up to give to Bai. "He's your boyfriend," I said. "You talk to him."

"It's not my job to coordinate a relationship between myself and two males."

"On this planet, we have human gender roles," I said. "I'm a human, Bai's a human, and you're designed to approximate human behavior. This is about your relationship with him, so he's your responsibility."

I opened the door. It wasn't Bai. It was BEA agents Fowler and Krakowski.

"Oh, hi," I said.

"Where's your end of the port, Blum?" demanded Fowler.

"The fuck are you talking about?"

"Watch your fucking mouth!" Krakowski snapped. I slid Dana into my pocket. "Last night," Krakowski continued, "you went to Ring City."

"Circumventing passport control," said Fowler. "Which is extremely illegal."

"You spoke with a Schedule A superorganism," said Krakowski. "Namely, Her."

"Without clearance and without following the safety protocols," said Fowler.

"Curic and Her set it up," I said. "It wasn't my idea. It was like jury duty."

"Two hundred other people with Constellation contacts spoke with Her last night," said Krakowski.

I shrugged. "I didn't see anyone else."

"So your defense is that you didn't see anyone else talking to the massively distributed colony organism," said Krakowski.

"It's not a 'defense'," I said.

"No shit, Sherlock!" said Fowler.

"Two hundred people, Blum," said Krakowski. "Immediately before the Constellation signed the Greenland Treaty. We can't do anything but quietly complain about it, or we look like chumps. But something happened last night. I think the fate of fucking humanity was decided last night."

"I swear to G-d," I said, "we talked about video game design. Her is afraid that we're going to end up like the Inostrantsi. Lost in a virtual world. That's it. I didn't say anything, I wasn't promised anything—"

"Oh," said Krakowski. "That's cute. You think we give two-tenths of a shit what you talked about with Her."

"We don't care, Blum," said Fowler. "It's water under the bridge."

"No, Fowler," said Krakowski, completely losing his cool without doing anything as drastic as looking at Fowler or raising his voice. "It is not water under the bridge; we just don't care. You can repeat what I say, but do not fucking *elaborate*."

"Where's the port, Blum?" said Fowler.

"Just shut up, Fowler. Look. Most folks who spoke with Her last night were picked up by unscheduled shuttle drop. We know that you went up, but our witnesses don't remember you from a docking bay or the reception chamber. And we didn't see a shuttle drop anywhere near Austin. What we did see was our nation's missile defense system suffering a software failure because it detected an incoming object with negative mass."

"Okay," I said. "Yes, there was a port. Curic dropped a telepresence robot with one end of a port, and I walked through it onto Ring City. And then I walked back out and went back to sleep."

"So where's the port *now*, Blum?" said Fowler.

"Why did you even *get* a port?" said Krakowski. "That's very very unusual. What's special about you, or about Curic? Do you have any ideas?"

"Guys, I have an existential horror of space travel," I said. "On top of my existential horror of being covered with fucking trilobites and put on trial. Trial-obites, if you will."

"I don't think I will," said Krakowski.

"Curic brought me a port so I wouldn't have to take another shuttle ride. It was an act of mercy."

"So where's the port now?" said Krakowski.

"Where is it?!" said Fowler, like, *finally!*

"I dunno," I said. "It wasn't here this morning. Curic took it back, I guess."

"You're saying that you let the most advanced piece of technology in the universe just sit overnight on your front porch?"

"You know how you *make* a port?" said Fowler. "You have to use a black hole as a lathe."

"It wasn't mine," I said, "and I was exhausted, and I don't understand how ports work, so I didn't touch it. I went inside and drank some tequila and fell asleep. Curic must have taken it back."

"How?" said Fowler. "You can't push a port through itself."

"And the missile defense system only crashed once," said Krakowski. "So either you're a complete *fucking* moron..."

"Or maybe you still have the port," said Fowler. "Somewhere in your house."

"Well," I said after a pause, "I guess I'm a fucking moron, because I never saw the port after last night. Did you check around the side?"

"You're not a moron, Blum," said Fowler. "You're good at computer stuff."

"Guys, you need to talk to Curic about this."

"We are talking to him," said Krakowski. "But I think we have more lever-age over you."

"Well, your honesty is refreshing..."

"Portable wormholes are very expensive," said Krakowski. "Maybe not for the Constellation itself. But for one of its scientific expeditions? Pretty expensive.

"I think Curic gave you the port in exchange for something. Maybe some information, maybe a promise of some kind? He gave you the port so you can go up and see your girlfriend whenever you want. Aaaand... what'd he get? Help me out here."

"I don't have the port."

"You're playing a dangerous game, my man," said Krakowski. "Curic's not your friend. He doesn't care about you *or* America."

"He's a representative of a foreign government," said Fowler, as if this were somehow cheating.

"We gathered some good intelligence together, the three of us," said Kra-kowski. "Don't let it end like this."

"We've got the authority to tear this place apart," said Fowler. "Unless you give us the port."

"Tear the place apart?" I asked. "The way you did on... I believe it was July twentieth?"

"What makes you think we were here on the twentieth?" said Fowler in a very flat tone.

Aha! I'd hurt them, and they were fishing for information. I tried to reel them in a little.

"You were very careful," I said. "I'll give you that. You put everything back the way it was. But you made the mistake of opening a Constellation packing crate." I nodded at Krakowski. "It took your picture. I made copies."

"That fucking snitch crate!" said Fowler.

"Calm down, man," said Krakowski. "No one's gonna believe a packing crate over two federal agents. And no one's gonna care what we do while we're searching an illegal emigrant's house."

Okay, that didn't work.

"Just give us the port," said Fowler, "and we'll go."

"Don't make us do this," said Krakowski, very quietly. His eyes were closed.

I looked out past the agents to the curb. Their biodiesel government car was nowhere to be seen. The only car on the street was a moving van. The kind of van you could use to hide a SWAT team or a rendition team, if you wanted to be sneaky about it.

"Don't make you do what?" I said.

"Condemn your house," said Krakowski.

"Oh," I said in relief.

"Oh, what did you think?" said Krakowski. He seemed genuinely hurt. "We're not the CIA! We have *standards*!"

"Wait! My house? I got a mortgage to pay!"

"We'll compensate you for any damage to your property," said Krakowski. "Which, depending on how Curic helped you hide the port, may be considerable."

"I don't like your compensation rates," I said. "You gave me three hundred bucks for a Constellation spacesuit."

"Then tell us where the port is," said Fowler, clenching and unclenching his fists.

"I can't prove a negative, guys," I said. "I don't have the port. I don't know what Curic did with it."

Krakowski sighed. "Briefcase," he commanded. Fowler opened his briefcase with a click and held it out to his partner. Krakowski pulled a sheet of paper out of it, peeled off the sticky base, reached behind my head, and stuck it to my front door.

"The Austin Building Inspection Division has condemned this property due to pervasive structural defects," said Krakowski. He took an envelope out of the briefcase, pushed into my hands. "And this is a National Security Letter. Read it. It bars you from discussing this case with anybody."

"Details?" I said. "Like someone took my house away? That's a little hard to explain."

"Your house burned down," said Fowler. "You blew out the electrical system with one of those alien Nintendos."

"I want to talk to a lawyer," I said.

"You'll get a lawyer," said Krakowski. "But right now you'll get the hell out of this house."

"I got important documents in here!" I said. "My phone! My passport!"

"You can pick up your passport," said Krakowski, "once we stamp it so you never get another exit visa."

"Out," said Fowler, jerking his thumb towards the sidewalk.

Krakowski frog-marched me to the edge of the property line. I watched six thugs in moving company uniforms climb out of the moving truck and go through the door of my condemned house.

"I really hope you're lying," said Krakowski. "I do not want to have to track down a missing port. It could be across the planet by now."

"This is un-be-fucking-lievable," I said.

"This is a valuable lesson," growled Krakowski. "Learn the lesson and you'll come out ahead."

"What's the lesson?"

"Don't go freelance," said Krakowski. "It just makes trouble for everybody." He turned and walked back to my house.

I went around the corner and three blocks away I pulled Dana out of my pocket. "Fuck!" I said.

"Yes," said Dana.

"Fuuuuuuck!"

"Let's move on," said Dana.

"But I like it here at 'fuuuuuck'!"

"They don't want the port," said Dana. "They want me. They let an artificial intelligence slip through their fingers, and now they're coming after me. You have to hide me, Ariel."

"They're not coming after you," I said. "They didn't even pat me down. They don't know you exist. They think you're a six-foot-four mail-order bride named Svetlana."

"If they search you," said Dana, more to herself than to me, "I will disguise myself as a flyer for a chiptune concert."

"Maybe they want what's in the crates," I said. "Why don't they just take the crates? G-d, what am I supposed to do? I don't even have my phone."

"I'm a phone," said Dana.

"Can you call Ring City? Maybe Curic can stop this."

"I'm a *human* phone," said Dana.

"I can't go to the BEA field office and pass her a note."

"Just get me in the vicinity of the port," said Dana. "I'll reintegrate with Smoke and call for help."

"You too? I don't have the port!"

"I thought you were lying," said Dana. "And very brave."

"Sorry, neither."

"You fooled me," said Dana. "You're a very skilled liar."

"Dana, that's... that's not a compliment."

"I'll call Jenny," said Dana.

"What can Jenny do? Sculpt at them?"

"She can give you a place to live."

Blog post, September 2

I am a complete *fucking* moron. I was trying to splice the Cheb Complete Entertainment Device directly into my wiring system, and I *burned my house down*. Fire department, ambulance, the whole ritual. Fortunately, sending the ambulance was a waste of taxpayer dollars. Svetlana had left earlier, and I was able to get out of the house before the smoke got too bad. That's about all the good I can say about today.

I've lost everything except the clothes on my back, the money in my bank account, my offsite backups, and the stuff in my pockets. I'm staying at Jenny's house. This is the worst day of my life.

Chapter 23:
Trust Us, We're Expert Systems

Real life, September 3

I was lying on Jenny's couch in a food coma/depression. Jenny tossed me her phone. "It's for you," she said. "From a dot-gov phone." I missed the phone and it bounced off Jenny's couch.

"I hope it's my useless government lawyer," I said. "Hello?"

"Ariel," said the voice I hoped I'd never hear again. "This is BEA Agent Krakowski. I'd like to ask you a few questions, if you don't mind."

"You prick," I snapped. "After all I've been through today, you call me and say by the way, you have some follow-ups?"

"I'm lookin' at a Greenland Treaty visa application," said Krakowski in a kind of singsong voice, emphasizing every alternate syllable. He let it sink in. "Entry visa for a guy named Tetsuo Milk."

"Ask your questions," I said, deflated.

"When you were talking to the Her superorganism, did she mention the Slow People?"

"Shit, that again?" I mentally reran my gut-wrenching conversation with Her. "No, you know what, she did! I thought she was talking about people who are slow. I mean, nobody likes slow people."

"That makes no sense," said Krakowski. "She was talking about The Slow People."

"If you say so. Who the hell are the Slow People?"

"It's a philosophical movement. It doesn't matter. I'm interested in them. What did she specifically say about them?"

"She said that she was tired of dealing with Slow People."

"That's all?"

"Yes."

"Tired of dealing with Slow People."

"In so many words. She's also sick of cleaning up dead bodies. Maybe that means something special to you, too."

"You're sure that's it?"

"Yeah, but maybe you don't believe me? Like you apparently never do?"

"I believe you," said Krakowski. "Listen. Same deal as we had before. If *anyone ever* mentions Slow People to you again, call me. You have my personal number. Twenty-four seven. And Ariel?"

"Yeah?"

"There's still something in this for you. We can restore your exit visa."

"Bite me." I hung up.

I pretended to dial Jenny's phone, jabbing at the screen like a baby imitating his parents. "Yeah, I just got a G-ddamn fascist calling me, nosing around about the Slow People. He was really interested in them. Yeah, big time. What's that? You're going to fuck him up sideways with a fence post for his curiosity? That's a little extreme, don't you think? Don't you think that sort of thing should be reserved for PEOPLE WHO—"

"Don't yell!" said Jenny. "You're scaring my phone pet." She grabbed her phone from me.

"You have a phone pet?" I said. "You made fun of Bai for a year because of Dana Light, and all this time you've had a phone pet?"

"It's a pet!" said Jenny. "I don't masturbate to it."

"Uh-huh."

"And it's just as smart as a real goldfish." Jenny patted her phone's screen. "There, there," she murmured. "Mama'll take care of you, even though her job fell through and her flaky employer probably won't pay her."

"Your employer is sitting right here," I pointed out.

"Yes, indeed," said Jenny. I moved my legs and she sat down next to me. "On my couch, where he lives. Because he burned his house down."

"We're backed up. I lost, like, ten hours of work. It's not like the video game factory exploded. Sayable Spice is still happening."

Jenny patted my foot. "Ariel, you do not make good decisions under pressure. You freeze up and spend two years in a shit job, or you get impulsive and end up burning your house down. I do not see a ghostwritten corporate biography in your future."

"Do you want to make the business decisions? Because I'm fine—"

"No," said Jenny. "That's boring."

"You're just as bad at it as me," I said.

"Don't *want* to," said Jenny, like this distinction was crucial to her identity. "You can't do two jobs at once when you just lost your home. We need a frontman. Someone to set the release schedule and bullshit the publishers."

"What's wrong with the schedule I already set? We're like a week from a playable demo."

"Tough-looking guy would be good," said Jenny. "Ask your space cougar to recommend an ex-astronaut who wants some part-time. They're good at talking and filling out paperwork."

"Excuse me? Did you just call Tammy a...?"

"Rrrawr. You heard me." Jenny pawed the air in a way I guess she thought was sexy.

"Don't call her a... that word. Nobody even uses that word anymore."

"She's a hottie. Robbin' the cradle."

"I'm almost thirty," I said.

"They make cradles in all sizes," said Jenny.

The next morning I called Bai from my office, which is also Jenny's couch, and Bai patched me through to Dana.

"Thanks for coming in," I said.

"I didn't come in," said Dana. "It's video chat."

"Yeah, well."

"Are you going to fire me?" said Dana.

"No," I said, "why would I... do that?"

"Obviously," said Dana. "You lost the Brain Embryo in the 'fire.' There's nothing for me to translate. You'll either cancel the entire project, or go forward using your current knowledge of the Dhihe Coastal Coalition. Either way, you don't need me."

"Is that why you're in your pajamas?" I said. "Because you thought you wouldn't be working today?"

"This is a chemise," said Dana.

"It has unlicensed cartoon characters all over it."

"So what?"

"I'm not laying you off," I said, "but there is no more translation work, and Jenny has called a vote of no confidence in me."

"Does it really work that way?"

"Apparently it does in this company. We need to get some money coming in so that I can buy a replacement house, and possibly clothes. If you can take up the PR, the money stuff, talking to publishers, all the stuff that's not coding or art, I can focus on development, we can hook a little investment capital, and I won't have to lay you off."

"You know I'm not really human, right?" said Dana. "I don't know how that stuff works in your culture."

"It's easy," I said. "You just crunch numbers and write emails. You can almost do it with a computer program. We only need a warm body to file paperwork. In fact, there *was* an intelligent agent for running your business, about a year ago."

"Why don't you use that?" said Dana. "It would be cheaper."

"It was a trojan," I said. "Six months ago, it transferred everybody's assets to a holding company in the Cayman Islands."

"I accept the position," said Dana. "My first recommendation is to cancel the Sayable Spice project, fire everybody, and shut down the business."

"No, when you tell a joke, it's supposed to have some setup first."

"I crunched the numbers," said Dana. "The most likely outcome of this project is that you'll lose five to twenty thousand dollars. I'm sure it originally made sense to take that risk when you had a house, but it's time to reconsider. Your expected value is negative."

"Expected value is irrelevant," I said. "This is art. This is about introducing humanity to Constellation culture."

"Take the art and the culture to a game studio," said Dana. "They'll take the monetary hit and you'll get a salary out of it."

"I've had it with idiot studios," I said. "I've been working for other people my whole life, and all they do is ignore my ideas. That's if I'm lucky. If I'm not lucky, they ruin my ideas and then make me implement the ruined versions."

"All right," she said. "Since you are attached to the continued existence of your corporation, I have a backup plan. You don't need a full-time artist. Fire Jenny—"

"I'm not going to fire my best friend!"

"—and contract with her for a flat fee for every subsequent art asset."

"That's obscene, and she's also doing the music."

"She's not a professional musician. Get some Creative Commons techno from the web. Give the artist a hundred bucks if it'll make you feel better."

"We need to clarify something," I said. "When I offered you this position, it was not an invitation to be the fucking Cayman Islands computer program. Stop looking at this as an optimization problem."

"It *is* an optimization problem," said Dana. "This is the logic of business."

"It's the logic of shitty business," I said. "It's the logic of me quitting every job I ever had. Crispy Duck is going to be different."

"Cut everyone's salary in half," said Dana. "That's my final offer."

"How 'bout I cut your salary in half!"

"I don't have a salary," said Dana. "I'm already part-time hourly. Good decision, by the way."

Jenny poked her head into the living room. "Silence!" she said. "I am working! In my house! Silence!"

"Dana wants me to fire you!"

"I am *drawing* an *anthropomorphic cabbage*," said Jenny. She put her finger to her lips. "Sssh. Or get out. And no firing me." She held out her hand like she was showing off an engagement ring. "You see this hand? It is a very special hand. It is the proverbial 'hand that feeds.' No bitey."

"Dana," I said, "can I delegate to you the parts of this job that don't involve ruining peoples' lives? I think we've seen enough of that this week."

Dana shrugged. "It's your money."

"Thank you," said Jenny. "Now. Ariel: Tetsuo is moving to Earth. He got a Greenland Treaty visa and a job at the U. He's staying with Bai."

"How do you know this?" I said.

"Bai informed me," said Jenny, "using the Internet. I thought you might like to know."

"Why's he staying with Bai?"

"Because thanks to the magic of paperwork, Bai has become Tetsuo's sponsor."

"I should be his sponsor!" I said.

"Really? Where's he going to live? In the ashes of your house?"

"It's fucking Agent Fowler. He's doing this to spite me. He and Bai are frat brothers."

Jenny leaned her cheek against the doorframe. "Ariel, you *don't have a house*. It's okay to be angry about that, but you need to be angry about the actual loss of your house, and not random unrelated shit."

"Fuck off, Counselor Troi."

Jenny disentangled herself from the doorframe. "Oh, that is the absolute chicken-fried *limit*," she said.

"I'm sorry," I said immediately. "It's just..." I decided not to go with my planned defense: "you were being really annoying."

"Get out," said Jenny. "Go to a coffee shop or someplace where they'll put up with your 'what character are you' online-quiz shit. Counselor Troi, my ass."

"I can't live in a coffee shop."

"You can come back after dark. Out!"

Blog post, September 3

[This post is friends locked.]

I really lost my temper, I yelled at Jenny and she kicked me out of her house. That was eleven-thirty this morning. I'll hit "post" on this just before ten PM. They're closing up the coffee shop. I haven't gone back because I've been working on hammering the Sayable Spice demo into something that could be considered "playable." No 16-bit game parodies and no melancholy playable flashbacks. Just a nice item-collection action RPG about assembling chemicals into flavors.

I could go back. She said I could come back after dark, and it's very very dark. I haven't gone back because I'm ashamed of what I did. I snapped at Jenny not because my house burned down, but because one little additional thing didn't go my way. I don't feel like I can trust myself anymore.

I'm taking solace in software, trying to make a version of <u>Sayable Spice</u> that's good enough to solve all our problems. This didn't work for Clan Interference, it didn't work for the Yaiskek Corporation, and it won't work for me. In the end, all we have is our overlay affiliations. Little patches with starfields on them. Little dots of light in the infinite darkness of space.

Crispy Duck Games: YOUR LOVABLE QUIRKY INDIE STUDIO

Chapter 24:
Homebrew

Private text chat, September 13

ABlum: ok here it is

* PRESS RELEASE *
FOR IMMEDIATE DISTRIBUTION
* PRESS RELEASE *

CRISPY DUCK SOFTWARE RELEASES
PLAYABLE DEMO OF "CONSTELLATION
GAME" TO INDIFFERENT PUBLIC

HASTILY WRITTEN PRESS RELEASE ADDS
VENEER OF RESPECTABILITY

Attention, people of Earth! Extraterrestrials walk
among us! There may be one in *your* home
town, cataloging flowers, scanning your art museum, or studying the dusty books in the back of
your underfunded local library!

It's time to fight back! Time to learn about extraterrestrial culture before they learn about ours!
Crispy Duck Games has the perfect solution:
Sayable Spice: Earth Remix, available now for
your Unix-compatible mobile device.

In Sayable Spice: Earth Remix, a fully localized
remake of the classic Farang computer game,
you'll build up flavors and scents to unlock
memories of the past. You'll experience mind-
twisting puzzles and non-stop action that thrilled

audiences ninety million years ago (except for the parts we left out because they were weird or depressing). As you play, you'll gain a deeper understanding of our new extraterrestrial allies (except we took most of that stuff out).

"Sayable Spice is the project I've been wanting to work on my entire life." said studio head Ariel Blum from his luxurious fortress made from Jenny's couch cushions. "I remember being a little kid and thinking 'I wish space aliens would contact Earth so that I could do remakes of their video games.' I'm so excited about this fucking game that I haven't slept in forty-eight hours."

With the playable demo of Sayable Spice: Earth Remix, you'll be ready for the next phase in humanity's evolution. Available at any third-party repository for free download, you fucking chiselers. (iOS users allow six to eight weeks for App Store approval.)

DanaLightNotTheVideoGameChick: I see a number of obvious changes, but they look easy to make.

ABlum: fix it, send it out

DanaLightNotTheVideoGameChick: Done.

ABlum: that took like five seconds

DanaLightNotTheVideoGameChick: You are complaining?
Wait! Did you even do an iOS version?

ABlum: no
ask zhenya if he wants to contract for that

Real life, September 13

"Are you going to be okay?" asked Jenny.

"I can party all night," I said. "It's like ten in the morning for me."

"It better be friggin' four-twenty in the morning," said Jenny. "You smoked all my Lone Star Diesel."

"It's a business expense," I said. "It cancels out the caffeine without making me crash."

"This it?" said the cab driver.

"Yes," said Jenny. "The one with the huge party going on. Thank you."

I got out of the cab and stared into the light from the house. My pupils lens-flared. Shadows of people clustered on the porch in a cloud of smoke.

"Is this Bai's house?" I said.

Jenny pushed me up the walk. "He's having a party."

"I can see it's a party. I'm not—" Clomp, clomp up the steps. Someone with a strange accent was saying: "Actually it's inside my body, so if it gets stolen I'm probably dead already."

I blinked in the smoke. A flash of light glazed the front windows of the house, silhouetting a huge, misshapen figure in the doorway.

"Yo, Ariel!" said Tetsuo Milk.

"Jesus Christ the great moral teacher!" I screeched. Tetsuo loomed in the doorway, the focus of everyone's attention, wearing loose Alien clothing and holding Bai's coffee cup with the biohazard symbol on it.

From inside the house, I heard a grenade go off. Someone was playing a shooter—either <u>Temple Sphere</u> or one of the other Reflex games. They reuse the explosions because they think their sound assets are the fucking Wilhelm Scream, a hilarious in-joke.

"Hello, Tetsuo," said Jenny. "It's good to finally meet you. Ariel, this is Tetsuo's welcome-to-Earth party," she told me. "I told you about it approximately one dozen times."

"I think every time you reminded me, I just wrote it down in a code comment."

"Ah, and the lovely Jenny," said Tetsuo, pinching her hand carefully in what I guess was a suave gesture. "I didn't know you had a private car and driver!"

"That was a taxi," said Jenny.

"That explains why it was so ugly," said Tetsuo. "I wasn't going to say anything. Nevertheless, Bai Jun-Feng asks me to welcome you into his home. There is sushi, potato chips, and beer inside on your left. The beer is in a box full of ice so that it will stay cold."

I noticed that Tetsuo's coffee cup was brimming with sushi rolls. "Can I just grab one from you?" I said. "I'm starving."

"Don't," said Tetsuo. "They're full of wasabi horseradish."

I picked up a piece. Yup, solid wasabi, packed in where the fish should be. I dropped the sushi back into the coffee cup. "You can eat that?"

"I like condiments," said Tetsuo.

"So, Tetsuo," said Jenny. "Why Austin?"

"I have friends here," said Tetsuo, "and it never gets too cold. It was also easy to obtain an employment at your alma mater."

"Did they con you into working the computer lab?" I said. "Because that's the worst job—"

"I am a lecturer," said Tetsuo with what might have been disdain. "I had a long conversation about the Ip Shkoy with some other lecturers, whichafter they gave me a teaching credential." Tetsuo took a crumpled piece of paper out of his jacket and pulled it open like a centerfold. I recognized it immediately. Jenny has a nearly identical piece of paper. I did, too, until the fucking BEA stole it.

"That's a diploma," Jenny said. "They gave you a Ph.D."

"Yes, that's what they called it," said Tetsuo.

"'Cultural Studies'," read Jenny. "You should have held out for History."

"Need food," I said. I pushed past Tetsuo into the house and filled a paper plate with the remains of the party's sushi. There was a game in progress: four-player split-screen deathmatch projected onto Bai's wall. The game was indeed <u>Temple Sphere</u>, Reflex's sci-fi first-person shooter taking place in a future with evil extraterrestrial birds and without safety railings.

The living room was crowded with people I didn't know. Jenny was still outside talking to Tetsuo. In this situation, I usually squeeze up against a wall, but the walls were occupied. A good ten people were at the edges, out of the action, huddled over little pieces of paper. Smart paper.

Oh shit. Smart paper had launched and I'd missed it. I'd been heads-down coding and the platforms I'd been coding to had become obsolete. Drunk douchebags in polo shirts now had access to extraterrestrial computers. There were probably already a dozen factory towns in China churning it out for multinational OEMs.

There was something I was supposed to do in this kind of situation. Jenny had handed me a note in the car. I filled my mouth with sushi, took the note out of my pocket and read it.

You are very high. Do not panic.
Jenny

I practiced not panicking. The sushi helped. Bai himself stepped out of the kitchen, wearing a respirator and an apron, slapping white dust off his arms. Of all the people in the crowd, he pointed at me and slid over.

"Bro," he said.

"Yeah!" I said, apparently.

"You-me-guest room," said Bai. His polo shirt was soaked with sweat. He walked into a hallway and I followed him.

The bed in the guest room was piled high with guests' bags and purses.

Stacked against the wall were a dozen wood-and-leather steamer trunks, each plastered with ancient shipping labels.

I didn't recognize the trunks. "Are these Tetsuo's?"

"Historical recreations," said Bai.

I looked closer. The shipping labels weren't ancient; they said "Constellation Shipping". I looked at Bai. "Was Tetsuo a member of Constellation Shipping?" I asked.

"Curic built the trunks," said Bai. "Tetsuo just packed them." Bai pointed to a blue plastic tub, cowering on the floor before the steamer trunks. "That's yours, also from Curic. Tetsuo asked me to make sure you picked it up."

"Great. I don't even rate a vintage <u>Mutant's Revenge</u> kids' suitcase." The blue plastic tub was clearly modeled after the Shur-plast design I used when I had a house, but instead of "SHUR-PLAST" stamped into the lid, I saw the starfield logo of the apparently-no-longer-defunct Constellation Shipping overlay. The logo I'd seen on a shipping container in Utility Ring back in July.

I pulled the top off the plastic tub. Inside were stacks of notebooks.

"Ahh—"

"Y'okay?"

I pulled a notebook off the top of the stack and opened it. It was full of notes, as notebooks will be. Data structures, engineering ethics, genetic drift, doodles, unrequited-love poetry. All of it in my handwriting.

"These are my notebooks, from college. I lost them... in the fire."

"Hey, yeah, I remember those," said Bai.

"How did Curic *get* these?" The notebooks weren't worn at all, like they were reprints, or...

"Probably that time she scanned everything in your house?" said Bai.

"Can she recreate the other things, like my Playstations? Bai, my stuff isn't gone!"

"Ask Tetsuo," said Bai. "I need to go check the oven." He shut the door quietly.

I cleared some purses off the bed—Tetsuo's bed—and sat there, finishing my pile o' sushi and flipping through brand-new copies of my eight-year-old notebooks. Guest-star doodles from younger Bai. Lots of Jenny. Sometimes she drew the first panel of a comic strip and I'd continue it with stick figures. I opened Jenny's note and smoothed it out beneath one of those comic strips.

You are very high. Do not panic.
Jenny

I heard people clapping and slipped back into the living room. Bai was saying: "—seven hundred degrees in an overclocked oven," wearing silicone gloves, and cutting up a folio-sized piece of smart paper.

After some mistaken identity incidents, I was able to locate Jenny. "What's going on?" I asked.

"Tetsuo brought down some nanotech molds that make smart paper," she said. "You make it in the oven from playground sand. It's the door prize."

The oven? I thought. *Is this the fucking Peace Corps? Is the Constellation gonna give us little straws to purify our drinking water?* I did not say this out loud because I knew Jenny would interpret it as panicking.

"All right, bros!" said Bai. "We got eight new pieces. Anyone wants to adjourn to the study, I'll show you how to flash an OS onto the hardware."

There was a small exodus that included one of the gamers on Bai's couch. I took the empty spot, next to one of Bai's friends I've never met, and picked up a still-warm controller.

"You play?" asked Bai's friend.

"Man, I worked on the *prequel* to this game," I said. No response. "Yes, I play."

Bai's friend sniffed the air around me. "Wow," he said. He was wearing—no kidding—a backwards baseball cap.

The deathmatch was my favorite Temple Sphere multiplayer map, the Tool of Justice munitions factory. I spawned onto a conveyor belt, atop a pile of dark matter destined to be turned into weapons. In the munitions factory, everyone spawns onto a conveyor belt. My strategy is to keep moving and trade up weapons as I go. I jumped down a level to pick up some shatter grenades from an active fabricator.

"Did you hear they canceled Temple Sphere 2?" said dude. I had not heard this. I didn't bother to respond because I knew people like him will just talk over you.

"They're doing a new IP. All the maps are on Ring City." I tossed a grenade at a crate of small arms and picked a functioning needler out of the wreckage. "All the different Rings. Should be suh-weeeet."

I pictured space marines lurching in battle armor through the identical motel corridors of Human Ring. I pictured the people controlling those marines, people like dude on my left.

"I guess Alien Ring would make a good map," I said. I lifted the needler and plinked another player off his conveyor and into a fabricator. The fabricator made a *gulp* and squeezed out three-quarters of a heavy artillery piece.

"Sniper fag!" said dude. Hah!

"The whole map is on conveyors," I said. "In that context, I don't think it's fair to disparage precision shooting."

"Cocknobbler!" he suggested. *Holy shit,* I thought. *It's that guy.* "Do you play a lot of online?" I asked.

"I prefer it," said dude. "At least you can't smell the THC coming off the stoned sniper fags."

"This is for therapeutic purposes," I said. "I'm perfectly lucid." It was around this time that I fell asleep.

Real life, September 14, early morning

I woke in darkness. Before me, through vastness of space, I saw a thick crescent of light. A planet, dark green at the equator and browner towards the poles; a planet rotating in front of me, the terminator sweeping west to reveal more green and brown and the white of an enormous storm system as I lay in geosynchronous orbit. I let out a strangled scream.

"Beeee quiiiiiet!" hissed Tetsuo Milk. "Humans are sleeping."

"*I'm* a human," I croaked.

Tetsuo crawled around noisily and turned on a table lamp. I was in Bai's guest room—Tetsuo's bedroom. The bags and purses were gone from the bed, and I was lying there instead. Tetsuo held open a Gideon Bible in one forehand and a Hunter S. Thompson anthology in the other. The planet on the wall was an animated poster.

"Why did you hang up that terrifying poster?"

"It depicts where I was born," said Tetsuo. "I like to look at it."

"That's Down? The Alien homeworld?"

"We altered a planet with no history," said Tetsuo. "Let's go outside if we talk."

I was still wearing my shoes. We snuck through the living room, where a couple die-hard gamers were slumped asleep on the couch. The split-screen deathmatch was still going on: four space marines standing on conveyor belts, weapons at the ready, endlessly touring the Tool of Justice munitions factory. Every ninety seconds, they were dropped into fabricators, died, and respawned.

We sat on lawn chairs on the patio and looked up at the stars. Well, I sat on a lawn chair; Tetsuo laid on the ground. "Where's your home planet up there?" I asked.

"I read that it's in the Cygnus constellation," said Tetsuo, "but I've never seen a cygnus and I can't tell the one bunch of stars from the other."

"Let me download a planetarium app," I said. "It'll show the constellations." I took out my brand-new phone and sent seventy cents to some struggling developer.

Tetsuo stopped looking at the sky and slapped his flank with his tail. "You said that you burned down your house," he said.

"Yes. Burned down. Totally accidental."

"You tried to attach a Cheb Complete Entertainment Device to the domestic alternating current."

"Totally not thinking properly."

"That's the name of the computer system in <u>Schvei</u>," said Tetsuo. "The computer that caught fire if you installed the memory container incorrectly. It was a fictional device."

"Yeah, well, someone built one," I said. "Obviously it was their idea of a sick joke."

"Yes," said Tetsuo. "Obviously."

"I got the notebooks," I said. "Thank you. I thought they were gone."

"They are indeed gone," said Tetsuo. "Curic gave you some soft-dolls to compensate. I can only apologize for the paper quality." He meant the lack of wear on the replicas.

"I made the mistake of reading through one of those notebooks," I said. "There's some really personal stuff in there. Mostly about girls I wanted to have sex with. I don't want that stuff in the Constellation's collective memory for the next billion years."

When Tetsuo responded, it was to say: "Do you remember Dieue the Four-Fisted?"

"I think I'd remember someone with that name."

"We met him not. He was an Ip Shkoy Alien. I recreated his house in July, as an immersive environment for Ip Shkoy games."

"The place with no light. The treehouse where we were playing."

"I lack an English for this so I will say that Dieue was a 'fall guy'. Someone who cannot gain sexual achievement in normal planetary gravity. I mean, only in free-fall."

"I've had sex in free-fall," I said. You can't be too blunt with Tetsuo. "It's not worth it. The only position is the 'We Finally Got It To Work'."

"If you're a fall guy," said Tetsuo, "it's the only way to go. Dieue's apartment was stocked with appropriate films. Which doesn't make sense, now that I think on it. Maybe watching the films was enough for him."

"Yeah, well, the Ip Shkoy were sex maniacs."

"By human standards, supposes me," said Tetsuo, "although I'm beginning to doubt it. But maniacs they were with strict rules about what sex is appropriate. By standards of the Ip Shkoy, Dieue's preferences were mild-to medium-sized obscene.

"But hey, nobody cares. The scans were encrypted while Dieue was alive, and now he's dead for seventeen million years. His whole civilization was dead, until we brought it back to play some games in his apartment. Now it doesn't matter what sex he liked."

"So, you won't un-scan my notebooks," I said.

"That is the last thing you want," said Tetsuo. "You would only call attention to them. And perhaps your house will burn down again." He gave me a look like he considered this a real possibility. "Then where will you be?"

"Okay," I said, "planetarium is installed." I stood on my lawn chair to turn off the porch light, then walked into the yard and held the phone to the sky to take a reading. "With my luck, Cygnus will be in the southern hemisphere."

Tetsuo didn't move off the patio. "No, here it is," I said. "Just a cross shape. They should have called it the Pterodactyl."

"Do you know what those stars look like from the other side?" said Tetsuo.

"What?"

"Nothing," said Tetsuo. "Same as this side. Stars have sentimental value only."

"What about the *name* of your *civilization*? What about the star-draw?"

"Which the star-what?"

I sat back down. "The ritual," I said, "where everyone has a coin or a rock or something, and you toss them all together to make a constellation. You and I did it with M&Ms."

"Oh," said Tetsuo. "Someone came up with that in June. I don't understand the appeal."

"Tets, you need to understand this," I said. "Humans *dream* about the stars. They've been taunting us ever since we learned to look up. Brilliant people spent their whole lives trying to figure out why they move. Humans got burned at the stake for saying that stars are stars."

"Aliens, same," said Tetsuo. "Then we went up there and found there's nothing. Nothing but algae, and fossils, and Slow People."

Wait a minute. I leaned out of my lawn chair. "You know about the Slow People?"

"I know some about," said Tetsuo. "I'll talk about them in a lecture at the university. Maybe half a lecture."

"Who are they?"

"Little computer people," said Tetsuo, like he couldn't believe I found this interesting. "Like Dana Light the soft-doll girlfriend, but advanced, and faster. Big societies living on little pieces of matter in interstellar space, or next to stars."

"This might be a stupid question," I said.

"Maybe," said Tetsuo generously, "maybe not."

"They're faster than human computers?"

"Dozen-hundreds faster."

"Why are they called Slow People?"

"Because when you talk to them, all they do is complain about how slow *you* are. It's a piss. Therefore we don't talk to them often."

"Krakowski," I said, "the guy from the BEA who—well, you know Krakowski."

"I know him."

"He wants me to tell him if anyone mentions Slow People. Like call him immediately."

"Did he tell why he cares?"

"Probably so he can dish it to his superiors and score a promotion."

"Why do his superiors care?"

"I don't know."

"I have a suppose," said Tetsuo. "They think they'll establish a new contact with the Slow People. Then they can threaten to fight us in a war." He laughed and laughed at this—it sounded like someone choking to death. "Humans and Slow People on one side, the Constellation on the other."

I shuddered. "Do the Slow People hate the Constellation?"

"The Slow People *are* the Constellation," said Tetsuo. "There's a billion Slow People for everybody who looks like me, or you, or Bob the Mzungu. We're only the skin of the mushroom."

"Then where are they? I don't see any Slow People on the contact mission. Unless Smoke qualifies."

"Why should they come? Travel is too slow, and you are too slow when they arrive. If Slow People want to meet space monsters, they can evolve a whole society of them in an afternoon. You and I are uninteresting to them. We only protect them and maintain their hardware."

"Protect them," I repeated. "Protect them from what?"

"You tell Krakowski," said Tetsuo. He thought about this for a moment. "Perhaps knowing this is his desire. You tell him that we protect the Slow People from Ragtime. That's the code name your bosses use. Your government."

"What's Ragtime?"

"The other thing there is, in space," said Tetsuo. "I forgot to mention it before; it's more like a star than a fossil. Yes, tell Krakowski that we protect the Slow People from Ragtime. Be sure to use their code name. It'll outcreep him."

"You're outcreeping *me*. Tell me what Ragtime is."

"Ragtime is a scavenger," said Tetsuo. "A negentropictropic matter cloud. It's hundred-percent harmless; it only eats dead things. Just, sometimes it needs some help knowing what's dead and what's Slow People. Tell him we gave it Gliese 777Ad."

"What are you saying?"

"I am saying to tell Krakowski this and watch him squirm."

And that's what I told Krakowski, over video chat. "He said to watch you squirm," I said.

"Oh, they want to make us squirm, all right," said Krakowski.

"Can you squirm just a little?"

"First they tried to scare us about global warming. Then it was the

Antarctica thing. Now, if we don't shape up, civilization will collapse and Ragtime will get us. It's childish."

"Can you give me some more about Ragtime? Tetsuo just told me what to tell you."

"I bet he did." Krakowski's expression looked like he was imagining painful deaths for me and Tetsuo.

"You said there was something in this for me," I said. "I just want—"

"Yeah, get me *real* information," said Krakowski. "Nothing from Tetsuo Milk, for Christ's sake. He's yanking my chain. He thinks this is funny."

Chapter 25:
The Infiltration Path

Real life, September 14, early morning

"Tets, I'm worried about Curic." This was another thing that happened on Bai's patio, after I the party.

"You worry a whole lot," said Tetsuo. "As much as two or three median humans."

"You remember when she brought me up to the space station, and it turned out she was working with Plan C?"

"That did happen," Tetsuo allowed.

"Well, she didn't switch at the last minute," I said. "Half of her was working with Plan C the whole time. And you and me, she only showed us the other half, the half that agreed with us. She's got ambivalence."

"Yes, I see. That is sense."

"That is schizophrenia! So I'm worried!" I got out of the chair and paced. "Dana says it can be caused by blunt force trauma or a brain tumor. Do you want Curic to have a fucking brain tumor that's not being looked at?"

"It's not a tumor," said Tetsuo. "Dana knows nothing of modern Farang psychology. She is based—"

"Yes, yes, on Alien psychology. This is becoming more painfully obvious with each hour I spend with her. Tets, Dana is coming on to me."

That got Tetsuo's attention. He looked up at me in the Alien version of confusion. "I misunderstand. She's crawling over you?"

"Practically! She wants us to have weird virtual sex, because that's what Aliens do: have sex with the people they work with. She thinks I can talk to Bai and work out some kind of Dana-sharing arrangement."

"Transitive pair bonding is common."

"Not in humans! And Curic's going to die, Tets. Her personalities will become dissociated and she'll die. Why aren't *you* worried?"

"I save my worry for when people will actually die." Tetsuo rubbed a hindhand against the brick of the patio. "In the Dhihe Coastal Coalition, in the time that Dana knows about, Curic would for sure die. Her clan-mates would burn her at stakes to enforce social norms.

"Fortunately, she lives ninety million years later in the Constellation, and we enforce social norms with mostly sarcasm. There's no problem with being ambivalent. The worst you will look silly, or build ugly buildings."

"Half of her is working against the other half! She is literally of two minds!"

"She is *two people*, Ariel!" For the first time, Tetsuo was pissed off. He was trapped on a backwater planet full of hicks ranting about how G-d would judge all forms of life in the universe by humanity's standards.

I said nothing.

"You can be friends with your crossself and still disagree with him," said Tetsuo.

"I'm just trying to understand that," I said.

"You already understand it," said Tetsuo, still without patience. "We understand both, to be against a part of our larger self. My wife Ashley doesn't want to be here at all. She worked for Plan C, and I would not."

Tetsuo's voice softened a little. "It would be better if we agreed," he said, "but we still have love."

Text chat, September 14

> **ABlum:** hey, nice party last night
>
> ---
>
> **KThxBai:** oh man, we're still cleaning up.
> tets decided to build a forge in the kitchen and recycle the bottles into smart paper.
>
> ---
>
> **ABlum:** so, i was wondering if you or your wikipedia pals have the lowdown on negentropictropic matter clouds
> you may also know them as "ragtime"
>
> ---
>
> **KThxBai:** let me check.
> there are eight lowdowns on ragtime, and they all contradict each other.
> it may not even exist.
> personally, I don't yet consider it notable.

Blog post, September 15

Svetlana Sveta has taken over writing the Crispy Duck Games corporate blog. It seems my habit of burying the marketing copy inside layers of self-loathing does not leave a good impression. When I was a kid, I always had to be the one to load the dishwasher, because my brother Raph always broke the dishes. Now I have cashed in that karmic check and I have more time to record the truth of my life on *this* blog.

Jenny's also pushing me to find another place to live. Her couch cushions are starting to smell bad. I'm working on it!

Blog post, September 17

GAME REVIEWS OF NEPOTISM 2.0 PRESENTS
Temple Sphere (2012)
A game by Reflex Games
Reviewed by Ariel Blum

Publisher: Reflex Games
Platforms: Xbox Forever, Playstation 4
ESRB rating: M for the usual killy shooty crap

I stuck Bai's Temple Sphere disk into his Xbox. "It's time to learn!" said Tetsuo Milk.

"We can give this two, three hours," I said. "Then I need to do some work. You should understand how to play by then."

"You'll go back to Jenny's apartment?"

"Jenny has a date with a pretty-boy who cuts himself," I said. "So I'm sleeping here tonight."

Tetsuo turned the game box over and over, and sniffed the plastic. "This game became public three years ago?" he asked.

"Yeah, two and a half," I said. "Loooong before contact." I sat back on Bai's couch, the couch I'd be sleeping on. I picked up a controller from the coffee table and played through the "navigate the XBox game-loading menus" minigame.

"All right!" said Tetsuo. "I'm exciting. I want to see the fictional extraterrestrials." The second controller hid in Tetsuo's vast forehands. He tapped buttons.

"I'm starting a new campaign in story mode," I said.

"I want the buttons to do something," said Tetsuo.

"You don't need that," I said. "Campaign mode is single-player. We'll trade off the one controller."

"This game was many-player on the party night."

"That was deathmatch. Multi-player stories are too shallow or too hard to write."

"It should be easier!" said Tetsuo. "More people telling a story makes it easier."

"I don't tell you how the Ip Shkoy signaled social dominance," I said. "Don't tell me how to design games."

"You're showing me hostility."

"I'm starting the game," I said.

Yes, Easy Mode, No, No, Skip Boot Camp. Cutscene: spaceship: exterior shot. Caption:

> UNSF DEEP-SPACE CRUISER "MALAWI"
> JUNE 11, 2122

"They got the date kind of right," I said. "For first contact."

"What does that date mean?" said Tetsuo. "What's their inertial reference frame?"

"It means it's the future, okay?"

"Why aren't you pushing buttons?"

"This is a cutscene."

"What's a—"

"It's a movie where the story happens."

"Why is a movie in a game?" asked Tetsuo.

The cutscene cut to the interior of *Malawi*, where Lieutenant Luntz had us blue-beret maggots lined up in formation. "This is a civilian operation!" he yelled. "All non-essential personnel are confined to quarters! If you are in this room, you are not essential!" Yada yada yada. Luntz reminds me of Colonel Mason, the head of Tammy's Mars mission.

I killed the cutscene and started the first playable scene of Temple Sphere: standing in a barracks with five other soldiers, who were playing poker on a foot locker using plastic cards and magnetic chips.

"Where did the douchebag go?" said Tetsuo. "I wanted to see him flaunt his relative social dominance."

"That cutscene didn't have any ETs," I said. "I want to get through as much as possible today."

"The douchebag will die, yeah? It is your 'foreshadowing'."

"He doesn't last five minutes," I said.

One of the poker players called out a scripted AI event—"Hey, Martinez, join the game." Instead of playing forty-five seconds of poker (Reflex loves their games-within-games), I kicked open my own foot locker and pulled out a spacesuit. Instantly sheathed, I cycled through the HUD configurations.

"I have another question," said Tetsuo.

"It's about the spacesuit," I said, "and I'm putting on the spacesuit because the ETs we're meeting on this 'civilian operation' turn out to be the Tools of Justice, and in thirty seconds they come out from behind a moon and blow up the *Malawi*."

"You must foreknow this?"

"No, but if you decide to play poker with your buddies instead of getting ready, you fall to the planet and it's two hours before you see a Tool outside his battle armor. I don't want this to be a multi-day thing. I got work to do."

I opened a hatch in the bulkhead and ran out of the room. A warning flashed in my HUD about confined-to-quarters. "Hey!" called one of the AI poker-players, but nobody got up to follow me.

"Staying in quarters puts you on the Combat path, which is for frat boys. But if you disobey orders, you can make it to one of the Tools' targeter scouts and take the Infiltration path through the game, which is a) a better game and b) has more backstory."

"The douchebag coerced you. You promised to stay in your room."

"And if you're a frat boy, you don't think to leave. It's what we in the computer business call an affordance."

I ducked behind a large potted plant to hide from a patrol, then sprinted into the vestibule of an airlock. Again, someone shouted "Hey!" and this time there were footsteps.

"Now they're angry," said Tetsuo. "You broke your promise."

From a rack, I selected a pair of thrusters, which instantly installed on my spacesuit. "It doesn't matter because—yup, there it is." An explosion tossed my player character into a bulkhead.

"Okay, out we go." I jumped out of the airlock with the precision of an early-beta tester, and tumbled through space, catching upside-down glimpses of the *Malawi* as the Tool of Justice assault vessels carved it up with laser beams.

Fiery antimatter explosions cracked the ship along the lines of its construction. Tiny suited figures jumped or were thrown free of the explosions and fell towards the planet below. A bunch of NPCs for the frat boys to meet later down the Combat path.

"That's a huge-large spaceship," said Tetsuo.

I paused the game. "Well, it's the future."

"Spaceships will never be so huge!" said Tetsuo. "You should build a tiny spaceship to tow a tiny port to where you want to go, and then everyone can walk through the port."

"There's already a video game about ports," I said. "Anyway, we didn't know they could really exist." I handed Tetsuo the controller.

"The hard part is done," I said. "Getting onto the Infiltration path in the first place. Now it's your turn. You need to intercept a targeter scout, throw the pilot out, and fly back to the hangar ship. The thruster controls are on the heads-up display."

Tetsuo pinched the controller between two fingers and tapped a couple buttons. Nothing happened. "Ariel?"

"Yeah?"

"Which button did you use to stop time?"

"The big one in the middle."

On his third try, Tetsuo got the hang of the thruster controls and escaped the destruction of the *Malawi*. He set the controls to send him putt-putting along towards the enormous Tool flagship. Within twenty seconds, he was disturbed by a high-pitched beeping noise.

"Is that your phone?" asked Tetsuo. He pushed the big button in the middle and the noise stopped.

"It's your suit proximeter," I said. "There's a targeter scout coming at you. Now's your chance."

"I see nothing."

"It's coming in from below you," I said. "It shows up on your 3D radar."

"Whose amazing idea was it to have a war in *space*?"

"You can lock yourself onto the ship by activating your boot magnets."'

"Tell me a button."

"R2A."

"Tell me the position of the button."

"Under your... your index finger, I guess?"

"You name your *fingers*?"

I flopped at the controller. "There!"

I activated Tetsuo's magnets and he fell with a clank onto a Tool of Justice single-occupancy support vessel. His in-suit radio receiver picked up the vessel's pilot cursing in Pure Speech.

"Okay," I said, "just walk up to the top..." clank, clank, clank, "and there's your fictional pre-contact extraterrestrial."

Tetsuo paused the game again and crawled close to the screen. Corporal Martinez stood at the rear of the tiny vessel, looking down and forward into the cockpit. The targeter pilot, a guardian-caste Tool, was twisting around in his safety straps, trying to get a glimpse of the intruder on his hull.

"What an unclimax," said Tetsuo. "It looks like an Earth bird."

"Well, you look like a Komodo dragon."

"It looks *really* like a bird," said Tetsuo. He cocked his head. "Except for its huge beak."

"The beak is real, too," I said. "Toucan beak. This guy is the guardian caste. He'll smell you with that thing from a hundred yards."

Tetsuo took out the Temple Sphere strategy guide he'd bought at the used bookstore, and flipped to the section with big renders of the Tools of Justice.

"Hrm, a eusocial life-culture," said Tetsuo. "Like the Gaijin."

"Like the *bees*," I said. "We didn't know there really were eusocial extraterrestrials. It doesn't mean anything. It's just a way to make you feel okay with..."

"With killing them," said Tetsuo.

"It's a war, Tets. It's an FPS. There's gonna be some killing."

"Oh, a war," said Tetsuo. "Occasionally I'm glad my children are incubating on a space station which humans can't visit."

"This is no worse than Ev Iuie Aka's Ultimate DIY Lift-Off," I said. "And that came out fifty years *after* contact."

"Ariel, this is your mother," said my phone from Bai's coffee table.

"Now *that's* my phone," I said. "Hold on."

"Ariel, this is your mother."

"Why did I think this ringtone was a good idea?" I said. I tapped the phone.

"Ariel, this is your mother," said my mother. And there went *Temple Sphere* for the rest of the day, so there's your review of a game you've already played.

Real life, September 17

"Ariel, this is your mother."

"Yeah, hi, Ma, what's up?" Rather than courteously turning away, Tetsuo stared intently at me-on-the-phone.

"Well," said my mother, "I wanted to call and plan our trip down to Austin this weekend."

It never stops! "Ma, it's not a good time. My house burned down. I can't put you up right now."

"Well, we're looking at hotels, but I thought, what if you and Tetsuo came up here? It would be simpler, and since you're between jobs right now—"

"I have a job, Ma. I started a company. That gives you a job. Why is Tetsuo involved in this?"

"I greet your mother!" said Tetsuo.

"Tetsuo just greeted you," I told my mother, "as though you had had some kind of previous interaction with him."

"Hello to Tetsuo," said my mother. "He invited us down. He's worried about his class on Constellation history. He wants to talk to people with teaching experience."

I covered the receiver—the whole phone, really. "Tets, can't you talk with someone at UT?" I hissed. "Why does it have to be my folks?"

"I am talking with many people," said Tetsuo.

"I don't—graah."

"May I speak to her through your phone?" said Tetsuo.

"Knock yourself out." Tetsuo transfered the Xbox controller to his hindhands, took my phone, and pressed it against the front of his face.

"Hello, *tyen*," he said, letting his Purchtrin accent deepen a little. "Yes!

Are you healthy? Your mate? Yes, if everything was on a web page there'd be no point...they said...yes, I ask if you have an office at Texas A&M University? Because the wise elders of the college pledged me half of an office, and...I don't know with who. Someone small, I hope, like a human or a Farang.

"Yes, I will ask them for a complete office. Hear my conclusion, *tyen*. If I come to see you, you and your mate can show me your offices. Without this information, I do not know how to decorate my own. It is settled! Later there will be details."

Tetsuo hung up the phone and handed it back to me. I jammed it into my pants pocket. Tetsuo resumed flipping through the Temple Sphere strategy guide.

"It is settled," said Tetsuo. "I'll go up. You don't have to go."

Man, what a n00b. "Oh, I have to go," I said. "You don't know how this works."

"How works it?" Tetsuo asked. "Is this a folkway?"

"You volunteered to visit my mom and dad. By the laws of parental guilt, you are now the son they could have had. Now I have to do better than you."

"Does this mean I have been accepted into your tribe?"

"Only for purposes of guilt trips."

"I apologize for causing you trouble," said Tetsuo.

"Save it, smooth talker," I said. "Save it for my parents."

Tetsuo had flipped through to the end of the strategy guide while we were talking. Now he turned the final page and closed it, blinding me with the glare from the glossy cover. He thought over this for a while, as though he had a DVR in his head.

"Shall we keep playing?" I said.

"Suspicion confirmed!" said Tetsuo. "This game ends with a genocide! The player character kills all of these enormous bird-people!"

"What? No! It's just the warrior caste."

Tetsuo thumped the strategy guide like a Bible. "That excuse is terrible!" he said. "If you killed all the Gaijin kemmers, the rest would be unable to reproduce. What were you smoking? Perhaps it was crack!"

"Tets, they cancelled Temple Sphere 2. It would be bad taste. I don't know what else you want. Have you ever canceled a game? It's not cheap."

"You were an employee of Reflex Games," said Tetsuo.

"Yeah, I quit," I said. "Five years ago, okay? I didn't work on Temple Sphere. I did the prequel."

"What was the prequel?"

"Recoil," I said. "Just humans killing each other. No ETs."

"I can see why you would rather create games about ponies," said Tetsuo.

"Your conclusion is totally wrong," I said. "I quit because Reflex was full of douchebags."

"You also said the Brazilian company was full of douchebags," said Tetsuo. "You are employed by a suspicious number of douchebags!"

"It's an industry epidemic."

"Also a disease of academe," said Tetsuo. "When I first spoke to your mother about lecturing, she said bad things about many colleagues. Is your entire planet populated by douchebags?"

"Yes!" I said. "Now you see my predicament!"

Chapter 26:
Everyone With Cartoon Violence

Blog post, September 19, afternoon

It's a crowded situation here at *chez* Blum College Station, as my parents are renting out to a boarder (an A&M student) in my brother Raph's old room. Obviously the way to handle my and Tetsuo's visit on top of that is to have *me* sleep in the living room, and give my old bed to the seven-foot-six space alien, and that's not counting the tail.

Tetsuo and I pulled his steamer trunk into my bedroom, panting. "I've been living on a couch all month," I said. "So if you wouldn't mind doing your actual sleeping in the living room. I mean, there's no way you'll fit in this bed."

"I will sleep on an inflatable pillow-mattress of my own design," said Tetsuo.

"Okay, great, but by parental decree your stuff goes in here. I always just use the closet."

"You once lived in this room?" Tetsuo had worn his "status hat" (a cowboy hat) on the train ride up to College Station, and he had never taken it off. Now the ceiling fan brushed it off and he caught it.

"Yeah, in high school. Hey, you should scan this room, like Curic did my old house."

"We can't scan every place you've lived, just in case there's an additional fire."

"No, I mean, this room is exactly the way it was when I left for college. It's a historical recreation. It hasn't changed since 2004. I didn't know Jenny, or Bai, or anyone."

Tetsuo looked around and pointed at a plug-in air freshener near the window. "This appliance says copyright 2013," he said.

"Well, it hasn't changed very much. But when my folks find another boarder, all this stuff gets boxed up and put in the attic. This is your last chance."

"I'd rather interview the former inhabitant," said Tetsuo. He opened my desk drawer and gently lifted out a red plastic protractor.

I opened the closet that used to contain my dress shirts. It was now full of boxes marked RAPHAEL BDRM. I jumped over Tetsuo's trunk and started dragging it towards the other closet. Tetsuo said nothing.

"Former inhabitant?" I said. "That would be me."

"Hrm-hrm. Perhaps you want to tell me about the Greek emotion called nostalgia." Tetsuo held the protractor by one end and waved it up and down. The cheap plastic wobbled.

I thought about going back in time and telling my younger self that in ten years a space alien would be in my room waving my protractor around. Except I didn't remember the protractor at all.

"There's no nostalgia here," I said. "Nostalgia's in the rec room with the TV and the game systems. This is where I got sent when I wasn't allowed to play anymore."

"Nostalgia is only for good memories?" I don't think Tetsuo was being sarcastic.

I strained against paint that had turned into glue and yanked open the other closet door. "Oh, geez," I said. Half-hidden behind an old computer monitor was my secret pinup of PS2-era Dana Light, her polygonal tits looming out of a camouflage halter top as she blew smoke away from her pistol.

"I am going to die," I said. "I can't believe that's been hanging in here the whole time!" I reached to pull the poster down.

"Don't touch anything!" said Tetsuo. "This room is historical!"

"You guys already scanned my notebooks," I said. "Leave me some dignity!"

Real life, September 19, late night

"So obviously Raph has to be Raphael," I said.

"Why is it obvious?" said Tetsuo. He lay on an ottoman and lifted his head above the dinner table to look us in the eyes.

"Well, the name's the same," I said.

"Your brother's not a turtle," said Tetsuo. "Why split a hair over the turtle's name?"

"Humans like these coincidences," said my father.

"It comes from *Paradise Lost*," said my mother. "Our little expository angel."

Tetsuo put an entire taco into his mouth and made a sound like a garbage disposal, then noisily sucked taco puree off the inside of his cheeks.

"*Any*way," I said. "Despite my diminutive size, my weapon of choice is the broom, and usually Raph uses a ping-pong paddle, but it's around Hanukkah time and Raph has the brilliant idea to use our menorah as his sai. Uh, the candelabra."

"I don't know any of those words," said Tetsuo.

My mother pushed her chair back. "I'll get it out of storage."

"No!" I said. "Look, it's a ritual candle holder that holds one candle for every night of Hanukkah, okay, and if you're a kid who's not allowed to have toy swords, it looks kind of like the sword used by Raphael the Ninja Turtle. That's it. We do not have to fetch the object in question."

"It is explained," said Tetsuo. "Were the candles lit?" Clearly visualizing a story that ended with the house burning down, since I'm so good at that.

"No, it's just after school. He takes the candles out, we're gonna put them back later because we're criminal masterminds. So it's 'hyah hyah hyah cowabunga!' for a few minutes, and then Raph loses his grip on the menorah. Flies out of his hand and smacks the wall.

"Makes a big gouge in the plaster, right over there. And one of the menorah's candle holders is bent so badly that it snaps off when we try to bend it back."

"Oh no!" said Tetsuo. "It has ritual significance!"

I looked up from my plate, taco shell crumbling around my fingers, at the space alien sitting in Raph's place. Nothing else in this dining room had changed in fifteen years. Wooden buffet, dusty silver fruit bowl, framed posters for art exhibitions and Shakespeare festivals. I could still make out the discolored spot on the wall, right below the light switch.

"Right," I said, "so we decide the only way to save our skins is to fix everything so Mom and Dad don't notice. We fix the plaster with, uh, mint-flavored chewing gum, and we fix the candle holder with tape. It's a completely flawless fix, except that when my dad comes home, the vibration from him shutting the front door actually makes the candle holder fall off again. And he sees what we've done and says, 'You little shits—'"

My dad chuckled. "I think we got a little unreliable narrator problem here," he said.

"If Raph were here, he'd tell it the same way," I said.

"He's coming for Thanksgiving," said my mother, with a strong hint: *And you, big shot?*

"'You little shits!'" I continued, "'Look what you've done, you've ruptured the space-time continuum! Now Hanukkah only has seven nights! You destroyed the last night!'"

"Ha!" said Tetsuo, enunciating clearly because everyone else was laughing. "Ha! Was he joking?"

"Of course," said my father.

"No," said my mother.

"There's a parental twilight world," I said, "where joke shades into punishment. And that's why Hanukkah only lasts a week in our family."

"What about you, Tetsuo?" said my mother. "Tell us about your family."

"My family are gone," said Tetsuo.

"Oh, I'm sorry."

"I did not mean to imply they're dead," said Tetsuo. "A contact mission is a trip where you don't return. I'm gone from *them*. I'll never see them again."

"Nobody came with you?" asked my mother.

"They all said I was crazy," said Tetsuo. "There's a stereotype that you go on a contact mission and there's no interesting life, only fossils. They called me the fossil hunter."

"Can't you scout out the area first?" my father asked. "There must be a better way."

"That's not a contact mission," said Tetsuo. "That's an invasion. If we knew timeahead that your planet contained Ip Shkoy-level civilizations? Ten billion people would follow me through that port. Your cultures would not last seven days. It would be worse than Beatlemania.

"Believe me, human friends. Your planet is protected by an ocean of probable boredom. I took the risk and I am regretless. Now I can live a life I chose, instead of one based on pleasing my ancestors."

My parents were laughing. "I assure you, I am truthful," said Tetsuo, puzzled

"Did Ariel set you up for this?" said my father.

"Oh no! Is it a practical joke?"

"I get it," I said. "And no, I did not 'set him up'."

Tetsuo shivered. "Have I violated a more?"

"Ariel thinks our parenting style is overbearing," said my father.

"Dad," I said, "I'm sitting right here. Like, directly to your left."

"So, when you told us about your own overbearing parents, it seemed—"

"—a bit sitcom-esque," said my mother.

"Mmm," said Tetsuo, "you mean the same again and again. No, I would not call my parents 'overbearing,' even if I knew what that word means. They acted from an attitude of care. They thought I was too frail to spend my life exhuming fossils. I am no Charlie Atlas."

My parents laughed again. "Hey, hold on," I said. "Did *you* set Tetsuo up?"

Tetsuo filled a taco shell entirely with chopped tomatoes. "I proved them wrong!" he said. "I helped build a space station! And I'm quite glad to be talking with you instead of classifying you as fossils."

"The feeling is mutual," said my father.

"And one day the people I left behind will know what I did here. That I made a good decision."

"Do Aliens live that long?" I said, thinking of twenty-thousand-year contact missions.

"No as Aliens," said Tetsuo. "But yes as Slow People."

I set down my taco shell with a thud that rattled the silverware. "Okay, you gotta explain that."

"Oh," said Tetsuo. "Often dying people have their nervous systems uploaded. My family plans to do that and wait to hear about me."

"Life after death," said my father. "That's amazing."

"Please don't think such thoughts," said Tetsuo. "It's not as good as you believe. I tried to convince them not to do it."

"If I could still talk to my parents—"

"They would forget you, sir," said Tetsuo. "You are too slow. My parents will live through millions of subjective years, they will forget that they were Aliens who had a son who left them. Once our light cones again intersect, what I did here won't matter to them. Slow People always forget. They have their own problems. Whatever you tell them erodes away like rock into sand."

"Did they know this going in?"

"They know it," said Tetsuo. "When they upload, they'll create a backup. It's their backup that will learn what happened to me."

Blog post, September 20

I was coding in the rec room while copying a lifetime of accumulated data from my mother's desktop onto her new smart paper computer. Mom herself was with Tetsuo in the living room, translating some kind of Pey Shkoy poetry into English on non-smart paper. Dad was in the study grading student papers, some of which were probably smart and others stupid or plagiarized. And I was typing on my own smart paper when <u>Your Quiescent</u>

Achievement went crazy.

Your Quiescent Achievement is the ancient Gaijin version of video chat and if you have smart paper, it comes preinstalled. Which means, folks, it's time once again for **Ariel's Tech Corner**.

You probably assume the smart paper phone you got from a friend-of-a-friend is running the same Unix derivative you have on your human-made phone. Assuming you think about it at all. But you're actually running The Big Map That's Easy To Understand, a mesh computing system designed by the Gaijin two hundred million years ago and powerful enough to *emulate* your phone without breaking a sweat. If you've got a big sheet of smart paper, it can emulate your mom's 2010 desktop computer. Or if you've got a *really* big sheet and you fold it up right and put it in a very sunny place, it can emulate your whole data center.

This is a big part of why you don't hate the Constellation anymore. General Electric and World Corporation took one look at this technology and told their media divisions to shut up about Antarctica, and start talking up the Greenland negotiations and doing soft-focus profiles of the Hierarchy Interface overlay. Smart paper is only about twenty years ahead of what we can make today, but twenty years in the tech industry is a hell of a long time. And if humans had developed this tech on our own, people like Bai sure wouldn't be making it in their ovens using nanotech molds. (I don't think GE and Worldcorp anticipated that part.)

Anyway, your phone is now just a software application running on an operating system from the time of the dinosaurs. Drop into the underlying OS and you can use *apps* from the time of the dinosaurs: games, productivity, and incomprehensible Gaijin garbage. Plus Your Quiescent Achievement, which is all three at once.

Jenny and I tested YQA from different rooms of her apartment a few days ago, and it didn't seem any better than regular human video chat. Actually it's worse; the video maxes out at fifteen frames a second, the view is blue-shifted from the infrared, and the program's been (automatically) translated into English but not localized. Jenny was angry that it didn't recognize "female" as a gender.

But now that you can use smart paper to communicate with people in Ring City, YQA is rapidly becoming a killer app. Specifically, it's killing the government's ability to control our communications with the Constellation. Not bad for a collection of annoying minigames that's older than mammals.

Real life, September 20

> Howdy!

(said Your Quiescent Achievement.)

> Someone named Curic wants to build a relationship between you! You ask why is he interested in you? I can't tell you exactly; it would spoil the fun! But it's one of these four possibilities:
>
> • Crew of water vessel
> • Mealtime companion
> • Realizer
> • Co-parent of an existing child
>
> Are you interested?

Good question. Half of Curic had gotten me into big trouble with the BEA by bringing me up to Ring City to talk to the Her superorganism. The other half had sat back and let it happen, despite totally disagreeing with her crossself's goals. Now she was harassing me over the Internet? And why couldn't she use a normal chat program? With some trepidation I flipped a virtual switch to the "Interested" position.

> Yee-haw! I know I'm just a piece of software, but I know some tricks to help people build good relationships. You'll be hearing from me again!

Yeah, I bet. A blue-shifted low-angle infrared shot of Curic bloomed onto the paper. This wasn't a video, even one with a low frame rate. It was a *photograph*, updated once a second, like the Brain Embryo game Enjoyable Craft, which I never reviewed on my blog because it had very impressive 3D effects and just about nothing else.

"Ariel, hello," said the Curic-shaped blob. "Is this working for you?"

"Who goes there?" I said.

"It's Curic," said Curic.

"*Which* Curic? Save the Humans Curic, or Plan C Curic?"

"Save the Humans," said Curic.

"Good. Wait, no, it could be a trap. You have to tell me something that Plan C Curic wouldn't know."

"That's somewhat impossible," said Curic, "since the two of us share a brain. Let me say, rather, that we're both very grateful you convinced Mr. Krakowski you still had the port."

"Yeah, thanks for that," I said. "Your crossself got me into huge trouble. They revoked my Constellation Library card. I couldn't even send you paper notes after the Her incident. They... they tore my fucking house down, Curic. I had to stand there saying 'Talk to Curic, talk to Curic' while they took everything I owned. Why didn't you do anything?"

A dark red supernova took over the middle of the screen—Curic's antennacles had flared or something. "What you did was necessary. Because of your actions, Ariel, Save the Humans and Plan C have been reconciled. There's no more ambivalence. My crossself and I are once again in perfect harmony."

"Reconciled how?"

"Plan C has sent a port back to Constellation space, but it won't arrive for seventy Earth years. That gives us, Save the Humans, time to accustom you to more efficient social arrangements. If we do a good job, Plan C will collapse our end of the port so that nothing can get through. We can continue a normal contact mission and avoid the massive disruption of your society. And if Save the Humans fails, at least we'll avoid the Inostrantsi scenario. We won't have to evacuate your planet and reboot your civilization."

"Your crossself sold you out," I said. "You're going to fail. You can't convert humanity to fluid overlay anarchism in seventy years. It took six thousand years with the Aliens."

"We don't have to *convert* you. We just have to pull you back from the fossilization line. And thanks to the actions of my crossself's overlay, *my* overlay now has a chance in hell. You Saved the effing Humans, Ariel. You can tell yourself that whenever someone ruins your day by calling you a nasty name or taking all your private property. You hug your teddy bear and you tell yourself you're a big hero, and if things get bad enough, you can start thinking about our deal."

"*What* did I *do*? They must know by now that I didn't have the port. So what was the point? How did Plan C Curic take it back?"

"You were the fall guy. You were the distraction. More than that I can't tell you. The secret has a half-life of three years."

"It's not even your secret. It's your crossself's. *You* can tell me."

"If I tell my crossself's secrets, then he won't trust me anymore. Then I'll stop trusting *him*. And then you'll see firsthand why ambivalence used to be considered a mental illness."

"Can I see you in person? Are you on Earth?"

"No," said Curic. "I have many important things to do out here. I was going to visit the Philippines, but my visa was denied. What a waste of time. I've just about had it with your nation-states."

"How are you on the Internet?" I said. "Far as I know, it's still blocked."

"Yes," said Curic, "subversive elements in your nation-state were making it difficult for our satellites to use your communication networks."

"Subversive elements like the government and the ISPs?"

> I can't recognize your trunk! Are you facing away from the display?

"It was very annoying," said Curic. "Long story short, we had to build our own network."

"You built another Internet?"

"Oh, I don't think it has much in common with the Internet," said Curic. "It's a system the Gaijin invented two hundred million years ago."

"Are you nuts?" I said, momentarily forgetting that that was recently an open question. "Didn't you learn anything from Antarctica? You can't—"

"We learned that humans really hate having things taken away from them," said Curic. That's right, no two-second round-trip lunar communications delay; she *interrupted* me. "Even things that nobody owns and that are eventually going to flood their coastal cities."

"Okay, there's no need to be all bitter."

"I don't remember learning that humans hate having things given to them for free."

"The government will hate it," I said. "That's why they're blocking your Internet access in their first place. They want to control the contact."

"If they want to block us," said Curic, "they will have to take your smart paper away."

"What is it, some peer-to-peer thing?" I looked at the smart paper; not the jumpy picture of Curic on the paper but the thing itself. "They'll take it away," I said.

"Humans hate having things taken away," Curic repeated.

"Oh, you're being clever? I have to live on this planet. I don't have the luxury of sitting back in lunar orbit and running experiments to point out the natives' hypocrisy."

Curic disappeared from the screen. I thought she'd hung up, but Your Quiescent Achievement had decided the time was right to poke its grasper-tentacle into the conversation.

> It sounds like things are going well between you and Curic! Here's a little puzzle to help test your compatibility.

"Are you seeing a map here?" I said.

"I am," said Curic. The map depicted a desolate, Mars-like landscape, except Mars doesn't have lakes.

> Say, fella, what a view! This game is called "Three Neighbors," but you can play it with just the two of you. It's simple—just

pick your favorite spot . But don't get too greedy for that lake-
side property! If your spot overlaps Curic's, both of you lose!

"Why does it think things are going well? We're yelling at each other like idiots."

"It's *because* we're yelling."

"I don't understand."

"Spend some time with Gaijin and you'll understand," said Curic.

I squeezed a point on the map and a little geodesic dome sprouted up. Curic's dome flashed onto the paper immediately, all the way across the map from mine.

"Look," I said, "I don't want to be mad at my first contact. I'm sorry I yelled at you, and I'm sorry that Dana and I jumped to conclusions about ambivalence and thought you were crazy."

"And I'm sorry we built an Outernet," said Curic. "Although the contract we entered into with the nation-state of Greenland clearly gives us that right."

"That's not how you apologize," I said. "I could have put all kinds of disclaimers in my apology!"

"And, had we built it earlier, you could have looked up reliable information about mental health."

"Okay, just... forget it. Forget the whole apologizing thing."

"I will, Ariel."

Chapter 27:
Friend Codes

Blog post, September 20

Sunday morning at my parents' house means cereal and video games with the volume turned down. I don't see any reason to stop this tradition just because I moved out ten years ago and the cereal I used to eat has been recalled for being carcinogenic.

Every time I come over, I put in a little time on my parents' old Wii, maintaining my City, In Darkness city. Most visits, I don't even have to change the disc; it's still in there from last time.

While I worked on civic improvements, Tetsuo lay like a dog in front of the couch, ate dry cereal out of the box, and browsed his strategy guide for Recoil.

"I've made decisions to use the English translator when I talk to students," he said, apropos of nothing. "I don't want to misplace communications."

"You hate the English translator."

"I ought to burn my dislike," said Tetsuo. "If people would admire me as a teacher, I should speak like your parents."

Leave a CiD game alone for six months and the Adversary takes over the city, tearing down my urban wind farms and replacing them with seedy brothels or, in my case, Stinky Soda Factories (gotta keep the Wii release rated T for Teen). The citizens stop attending city council meetings.

Then one holiday or another comes along, I go up to my parents' house, and Hizonner returns in glory, walking the streets like a beat cop, fixing potholes by clicking on them and laying down the wrath of zoning ordinances. Afterwards I take the train back to Austin and my city goes to shit again. It's good for me to have a routine at my parents'.

"My folks *teach* English," I told Tetsuo. "They're expected to have a certain fluency. Half my CS professors had worse English than you."

"I have seen the hateful blogs," said Tetsuo. "They mock the way Purchtrin speakers speak English."

"You're getting better," I said. "But you start using the translator, and no one will be able to tell you from Ashley."

"What have you wronged Ashley?" barked Tetsuo.

"No! What? Her *translator* sounds a little bland. Like daytime talk shows. Doesn't make me feel like there's going to be a test."

"I must say important things and have understanding. To say them in a bland sound may even be better. Hierarchy Interface does that."

A City, In Darkness city doesn't really deteriorate gradually when you stop playing. Nothing can happen when the Wii is off. When you start the game, the software checks a timestamp in your savefile to see when you last played. The Adversary's damage is prorated based on how long you've been away.

So, what if I were to just walk away from the game and never come back? My city would stay clean and productive forever. That sure sounds like a win condition. What does it say about my goals that I keep coming back to the game, deliberately fucking everything up so I can have some mindless fun refilling the potholes?

Real life, September 20, afternoon

"Ma, I'm—I'm kinda lying a lot, and I don't know how to stop."

Yes, Ariel, wait 'til the last minute to have your emotional breakdown. Wait through the meals and the after-meal conversations, through sorting your high-school stuff into boxes for attic/Tetsuo/yard sale. Wait until all the stuff has been loaded, and your dad and the space alien are actually waiting for you in the car, and then go to your mom and start your sniffling, because this is your absolute last fucking chance.

Mom was a champ: she set down her pen and turned and held her arms open. "C'mere. C'mere, honey. How did it start?"

"On my blog," I said. "Pretending that Bai's girlfriend is a human being."

"That's a new one on me," said my mother. She tried to determine from first principles how a liberal should handle this situation. "What is she really, an ET? If it's okay to tell me."

"She's a submind of Smoke," I said. "She's been given an Alien psychology, like, Tetsuo's psychology. And that's causing its own set of problems, and I'm having to lie to Bai about the problems. And now there's this thing about my house burning down. Ma, it didn't really burn down. But I can't tell anyone what really happened, even you. I just can't. So I have to lie some more."

Linda Blum's mother-fu was being tested as never before. "Okay," she said simply. "It's okay."

"Jenny doesn't respect me anymore, Ma. She thinks I'm an idiot who burned his house down. And now I'm lying to everyone about Curic, too."

Mom thought about this. "Are you in trouble?" she asked.

"A little? Maybe? I didn't do anything wrong! I don't think. I just feel real bad."

"You don't like lying. That's a very honorable trait. Ariel, you don't *have* to talk about everything."

"I'm still lying. Lies of omission."

"Are you still writing things down? You know you can write the truth in private, and eventually..."

"All the stuff I wrote in private, Ma, in college—Curic scanned it and now it's in the Constellation repertoire 'til the end of time. I don't want it there. I can't even trust what I write down in private."

"What do you want me to say, honey?" said my mother. "I'm not gonna tell you not to lie. Sometimes people have to lie." Mom's grandmother only made it through the War because a bunch of people lied their asses off.

"How do you know?" I said. "How do you know if you really have to lie, or if you're just making excuses for yourself?"

"Are you willing to do the work," asked my mother, "to make the kind of world where you can tell the truth?"

"I think so," I said. "I'm trying."

"That's my boy."

Real life, September 21

Man, fuck this whole thing. I spent hours getting Agent Krakowski on the phone and he knocked me down in five minutes. Just because he has a desk, he thinks he's a big shot.

"What's with the desk?" was the first thing I said.

"What do you mean what's with the desk?"

"You've clearly set your BlackBerry on a desk," I said. "I can barely see you in the middle distance, it's just the desk stretching out to infinity like the fucking amber waves of grain. You're in one of those fancy government offices with a picture of the President on the wall."

"The desk is a desk," said Krakowski. "Good work gets noticed in the BEA. It's a brand-new organization: the bureaucratic rot hasn't had time to set in."

"Where's Fowler?" I said. "Is he your desk buddy?"

"Fowler is back at Homeland Security. He had a distressing habit of making insulting remarks about our Constellation allies. It got so bad, I felt I had to notify our superiors." Krakowski smiled in a way I didn't like. "Didn't I tell you I'd have that punk inspecting shipping containers in Anchorage?"

"No," I said, "you never said that."

"Riight," said Krakowski thoughtfully, like *why would I tell YOU?* "Are you on a secure line?"

"This is an off-the-shelf phone," I said. "It's full of NSA backdoors, just like your BlackBerry."

"Smartass," said Krakowski. "I'm talking about the Outernet back-channel. I don't want you calling me if you've got smart paper in the *room*."

"Well, there's none in the *room*," I said. "So. I know you didn't want to hear anything more from Tetsuo Milk."

"Yeah, I don't. Did he say something about Earth, or politics, or anything?"

"No, it was about the Slow People."

"If I wanted to hear Professor Milk make shit up, I'd attend his lectures. I don't need you telling me the same stuff he says in public. The point of intelligence gathering is to discover secrets."

"Tetsuo is my friend," I said. "I'm not gathering intelligence from my friends. That's why they call it friendship."

"And that's why we have the twice-yearly contact audits," said Krakowski. "So you don't need to call me every time you have a friendly conversation with a friend."

"Yeah, so you can ruin my Fourth of July every year for the rest of my life," I said. "Should I just hang up, or do you want to hear about Curic?"

"Ah, well, we love Curic," said Krakowski. "He knows how to keep secrets."

"Based on your strong implicit suggestion," I said, "I asked her about Ragtime. Everything she said is consistent with what Tetsuo told me."

"I'll be the judge of that," said Krakowski. "Don't go freelance. Just tell me what he said."

"Uh," I said, "I have notes somewhere."

"Okay," said Krakowski. I wondered why we had to be away from any Outernet backchannel just to discuss what Curic had told me over the Outernet in the first place.

I called up my notes from a file called "Ragtime Notes." "So imagine there's this planet," I said, "where the people died out fifty million years ago. The mastodons have come back or whatever. You wouldn't know it was ever inhabited, except for the thorium in the atmosphere. So, they're all dead and that's sad and everything, but at least we can be paleontologists, right? See what they were like. Except, Ragtime got there twenty million years ago and dug everything up."

"Dug it up."

"Ragtime takes the fossils, the arrowheads, the coins, the nuclear re-actors. Everything within certain negentropy boundaries. Now there's no history left. You're stuck in this planetary system studying another damn species of mastodon that doesn't even have a fossil record. And that's why nobody wants to come on the contact missions.

"Curic said the Constellation can kind of communicate with Ragtime. But they can't stop it, and it moves faster than they do, because it doesn't get bored or demoralized finding planet after planet where everyone's dead."

"All right," said Krakowski, who'd clearly heard all this from someone else. "This is good stuff, really good stuff, but but let me bring up a kind of different direction for you. You're a computer geek, yeah?"

Not for you, I thought. "Yeah."

"We are scrambling to find out how the Outernet works. There's a shit-load of technical documentation and nobody who understands it. We are looking at mass adoption of a communications device that hasn't under-gone FCC testing and probably contains bugs."

I write video games. Why are you asking me? "All software has bugs," I said. "You just update the firmware."

"*Bugs,*" said Krakowski. "In-tell-i-gence gathering devices. The Con-stellation loves recording things. Now they're going to record every con-versation anyone ever has."

"I think you might be projecting a little."

"Not even counting what happens when perverts start hiding smart pa-per in the girls' locker room. We have to head this off at the pass."

"Why don't you just ban smart paper? That seems like the kind of thing you'd do."

"Who's this 'you?'" asked Krakowski. "I can't ban a damn thing. You want to tell the chairman of the Committee on Science and Technology he has to give up his new phone?"

"Yeah, I guess you're in a real tight spot," I said, "what with all the free computers and Outernet stuff making all those Americans happy."

"You can't just introduce advanced technology into a society that's not ready for it," said Krakowski. "This is a clusterfuck and we need help."

"I'll think about it," I said. (Meaning no.) "Can I get my exit visa back?"

"We'll see," said Krakowski. (Meaning no.)

"Will you give me a desk?"

"No," said Krakowski. (Also no.)

Fucking Krakowski with his fucking desk. I had a desk, too, and then *you took it.*

Private email message, received September 22

To: Jun-Feng Bai, Ariel Blum, Jenny Gallegos
Subject: Tetsuo Milk Presents: An Email Message

I'm unfortunate not to have seen you. I didn't forsee the crowd in the lecture hall or I would have smuggled you 3 and etc. through the speaker's entrance. I was misled by a sign saying 541 maximum occupancy, which I now believe refers to the maximum number of *permanent* residents.

This transcript of yesterday comes from the Purchtrin-English translator. I expected it to give me precise words but instead it gave me short words. Oh well!

Tetsuo Milk, Ph.D.
"While there is a lower class, I am in it."
— Eugene Debs

Hi, students. My name is Tetsuo.

You've spent your entire lives sitting in chairs like these while adults like me stand in front of you and tell you about history. You thought you were almost done! You thought you could graduate, get dog-walking jobs, and forget about history. Then we arrive from nowhere and tell you that history is eight hundred million years longer than you thought. Bad luck!

Where I used to live, we use devices called intuition pumps. You spend a day with the intuition pump and the history of eight hundred million years goes through

your brain. At the end of the day, you forget everything. No one can remember all that stuff. But it's
easier to learn the second time.

There are no intuition pumps for humans, so what
shall we do? The summary of this class promises I will
tell you eight hundred million years of stuff in twenty
hours, and also have twenty hours for questions-and-
answers. That's impossible. I'm already starting three
weeks late. I didn't write this summary, by the way,
although I like the questions-and-answers idea.

So let's throw history away.

Here's some history, so we can see what we're throwing away. [I DISPLAYED ON THE COMPUTER SCREEN
A CUSTOM-MADE SLIDE SUMMARIZING THE ACCOM-
PLISHMENTS OF THE IP SHKOY. -T.M.] My ancestors
maintained dozens of cruel and beautiful civilizations:
the Ip Shkoy, the Nanawan, the Gle. I could talk for
four hundred hours about the Ip Shkoy alone. We
could re-create their society on a small scale in the
McKinney Falls State Park. It would change your life.
We do not have time.

I will tell you about the Ip Shkoy for two hours, and I
will only mention them at all because they happened to
be around when the Constellation visited their world.
Instead of eight hundred million years across hundreds
of planets, I'm going to tell you about fifteen contact
missions.

I'll tell you about ten successful missions, because
humans like the number ten. I'll tell you about the four
catastrophic failures, and then there's one that a lot
of people think was a failure, but they're wrong. We
can handle fifteen things in twenty hours, yes? Yes,
you're writing this down, this is good. [WHENEVER I
MENTIONED A NUMBER, PEOPLE WOULD WRITE THE
NUMBER DOWN. -T.M.]

Okay, now bear with me on a slight digression. I want
you to think about a period of time: seventy Earth
years. We're all young people in this room, except the
folks with the cameras, but we can all imagine seventy
years. Just think of Earth seventy years in the past.

This is the time of your grandparents. There's no Internet and no Abstract Expressionism, but there's capital-

ism, radio, and primitive space travel. What is it? [AT
THIS POINT THERE WAS CLARIFICATION FROM THE
AUDIENCE. -T.M.] I'm sorry, I just assumed there was
space travel.

Most contact missions last thousands of years before
they rejoin Constellation space. This contact mission,
the one you and I are working on right now, will only
last seventy years. As I speak, a spaceship is heading
back to reopen a port to Constellation space. It will
arrive in about seventy years. I think this is a very bad
idea, but I was on the losing side of the argument.

This is why I'm telling you about all the catastrophic
failures, even though there were only four. We're in
danger of creating the fifth catastrophic failure. When
the port reaches Constellation space, your culture must
be strong and self-confident enough to join that eight
hundred million years of history. If we fail, your civilization will blow apart like {{{foreign metaphor not
translated}}}. Well, it will not be a picnic for you and
me. [AT THIS POINT I MADE A MEANINGFUL GESTURE.
- T.M.] If you— actually— please be— Okay, I think this
time we will spend the entire two hours in questions-
and-answers.

Chapter 28:
Someone Is Wrong On The Outernet

Real life, September 22 [Private Video Chat]?

> Howdy!

(said <u>Your Quiescent Achievement</u>.)

> Someone named Ashley Somn wants to build a relationship between you! You ask why is ke interested in you? I can't tell you exactly; it would spoil the fun! But it's one of these four possibilities:
>
> - Sexual partner (along with your kinner)
> - Sexual partner (along with kes kinner)
> - Accessory to larceny
> - Mealtime companion
>
> Are you interested?

"Hey, Ash, what's up?"

"Ariel? I can hear you, but I don't think this external computer is working properly." The video-chat screen was a big off-white blur.

"Is that just an observation," I asked, "or are you calling me for tech support?"

"Esteban said I could talk to humans with this," said Ashley. "I called you because. Hold up. It's asking me for my preferred tentacle-span. It thinks I'm a Gaijin."

> I'd like to discreetly bring up a topic of mutual interest to you

> and Ashley Somn: the topic of kinner and their lush, squeezable trunks. Every man has his preference, and every kemmer kes. I'm just a computer program, so I don't have a preference, but what's yours? Do you like 'em broad, or more petite?

"Ashley," I said, "did you pick 'sexual partner'?"

"I picked a neutral option," said Ashley.

"It's not a neutral option."

"I had to pick something," said Ashley. "I don't wish to mate with you! I'm only trying to use this weird computer. I'm quite worried about Tetsuo. A mob attacked him!"

"There was no *mob*," I said, ignoring <u>Your Quiescent Achievement</u>'s incomprehensible flashing question. "People got a little excited when he mentioned our incoming case of terminal culture shock. My Western Civ prof got a bigger reaction by saying he was a Marxist."

"Ariel, I watched the video!" said Ashley. Blobs of diamond-shaped pixels representing her forehands jerked to and fro, leaving catch-up trails on my screen. She wasn't even looking at the smart paper. "He said he'd be fine on Earth, but he... This is a little fantasy for him. He's pretending that you are Ip Shkoy. Primitive members of our own species."

"That sounds like a nice conservative strategy," I said. "I don't see how we could be any *worse* than the Ip Shkoy."

"I don't want Tetsuo to die on a strange planet because he wouldn't learn the native culture. I don't want our children to grow up with a huge gap in their bonding graph."

"I know, but..." This was exactly what I didn't need right now. "I can't babysit Tetsuo," I said. "Bai's pretty good with him. They're at about the same maturity level."

"He trusts you, Ariel. You were the first human we met."

I flipped over the smart paper for a second and made some quiet frustration noises where Ashley couldn't see. "I'll talk to him," I said, "but... I'm sorry, Ashley. I..."

"Please don't call me that anymore," said Ashley. "I'm tired of pretending that my name is Ashley. I am a paleontologist. Ashley is a name for housewives and bureaucrats."

"Okay..." I said. In the big JRPG of life, Ashley's dialogue window faded out and was replaced by one reading "???".

"We take native names on contact missions," said ???, "because we have to prove we're the most adaptable species in the universe. It's stupid."

"There must be at least one human paleontologist named Ashley," I said.

"It's not my name! My name is Somn. I'm not infinitely adaptable. I'm six hundred light-years from home with no fossils to excavate, but I'm still a paleontologist and my name is still Somn."

"Okay. Somn. I can call you Somn."

"Thank you," said Somn. "Thank you, Ariel. And talk to Tetsuo, please. Now I believe I can ask you something else. In English, what is the worst curse word?"

"Now this I can help you with," I said. "This is very subjective and very dangerous territory, Somn. I think you should stick with good old reliable 'fuck'. It's got universal appeal."

"I just want to say one thing with my own emotions and have a human understand it. This translator removes the meaning from everything I say to you. I don't even recognize myself in this other woman's voice."

"Okay, shoot." Somn leaned into the smart paper and contorted her mouth into one huge pixel.

"*FUUUUUUP!*"

"You feel better?" I said.

"I feel a little better."

"Somn, now I have a question for you." Just a reason to call her Somn again, really, a way to cheer her up. "What's Tetsuo's real name? It can't be 'Milk'."

"I don't know what it is," said Somn. "Tetsuo won't tell me."

Blog post, September 27

No longer homeless! I'm staying on a month-to-month lease at a craphole in East Austin, until I get my fire insurance money out of the jerkass insurance company. Jenny is fumigating her couch and I am back to working by myself with the drapes closed.

Bai offered to help me move with his SUV, but since everything I own right now fits in a duffel bag, I declined. (I did have to borrow Bai's duffel bag.)

Bai will also be going to the Constellation Library on my behalf when my appointment comes up next Friday. After my unauthorized conversation with Her back in August, the BEA won't allow me to talk to Class A superorganisms anymore. So Bai gets two trips this year. Yay, Bai.

Real life, September 28

"Ariel, this is your mother."

"Hi, Ma. I'm fine, I'm all moved." My apartment contained an amazing ten things.

"Oh, that's good. Honey, we have a little problem. I don't think there's any nice way to say this, but does Tetsuo know about stealing?"

I stood facing the cracked, empty white wall. "Like, what stealing is?" I said. "Yeah, he knows. The Ip Shkoy had private property."

"Dad's scotch decanter is missing," said my mother. "The boarder says he's never even gone into the den; maybe he's lying. But I thought maybe Tetsuo just liked the way it looked and assumed we could get another one from the repertoire."

"I'll have a talk with Tetsuo, Ma." I pulled back the living room curtains; there was nothing outside but the night and the lights from someone else's apartment.

"It's worth a little money, but that's not... you know, he who steals my purse. But it was Uncle Toby's, and Dad has the little ritual whenever he gets a paper published..."

"I'll talk to him, Ma. I'll let you know what I find."

"You're doing okay, honey? I know the thing with your house has been really stressful."

"Yeah, Ma. Sorry, I'm real busy right now, with work."

"Okay! Talk to you soon."

"...Bye."

I walked barefoot to the kitchen and opened the fridge so I wouldn't have to turn on the light. Out of a cupboard, I took out the eleventh thing in my apartment: a cut-glass scotch decanter. I didn't have any cups, so I poured a little into my hand and slurped it up.

It tasted really fucking fantastic, thanks for asking.

Blog post, October 1

GAME REVIEWS OF FIERY FIERY DEATH 2.0 PRESENTS

Tetsuo held his paper videophone conspiratorially up to his face. He crouched beneath a fluorescent light, his back against a large, sickly-looking tree trunk. He'd covered his eyespots with a red bandanna.

"You don't look too good," I said.

"I'm hiding in my office," said Tetsuo, "from the media. They are worse than the students."

Why was there a tree in his office? "If you want to avoid students," I said, "the best thing to do is stay in your office with the door open."

"I don't understand this joke."

"At least you recognized it as a joke. I called to ask if you want to come to another game night."

"What games will you play?" asked Tetsuo. "I don't want to play that game where you're not allowed to fold 'em."

"It's *called* Texas Hold 'Em," I said. "You can fold if you want. I got a copy of an old Gaijin game from the guy who runs the smart paper tech blog. It needs three players, and right now we got two."

"Oh!" said Tetsuo. "You should invite You'll Only See Kis Echo!. That would be more authentic."

"You have a Gaijin friend?"

"Yes," said Tetsuo, "and ki is standing right behind me. Don't make me be a rude person." The tree trunk shifted and I saw that it wasn't a tree trunk: it was the massive body of a Gaijin kinner.

"Hey, dude," said You'll Only See Kis Echo!. Ki lifted a grasper tentacle in greeting and flattened Tetsuo against the desk, knocking over a vase he'd gotten from my mother. The videophone went fluttering around the room.

"Oh, You'll Only See Kis Echo!, I've heard of you," I said. "Aren't you the one who was able to give an entire undergraduate-level lecture without prophesying the imminent death of humanity?"

"I never prophesied death," said Tetsuo. He grabbed the videophone and sulked beneath the desk. "I said your culture would enjoy incredibly disruptive changes. That's happening already!"

"Man, how big is your office?"

"Not big enough!" said You'll Only See Kis Echo!. "They assumed all Gaijin castes were the same size."

"So," I said, "how about you come over, give Tetsuo some space, meet my friend Jenny, play a game from the good old days of smart paper?"

"I like this," said You'll Only See Kis Echo!. "What game is it?"

"It's called..."

WHAT-THE-FUCK CREEK
A Game by the Crusade 6 Against Food Shaped Like Other Food
Reviewed by Ariel Blum

Publisher: The Crusade 6 Against Food Shaped Like Other Food
Platforms: It's a Shitload of Games! (original), Constellation smart paper
(modern)
ESRB Rating: M for strong language and intense what-the-fuck

Once upon a time, there were three little Gaijin children named Ariel
(the male), You'll Only See Kis Echo! (the kinner), and Jenny (after much
negotiation, the kemmer). They lived in adjoining families, they played
together all the fucking time, and one doublesunny day, they decided to
walk through the bramble-field to the creek out back of their little podunk
town.

Ariel, the male, spread out a map of the area onto the synthetic-diamond
sidewalk. Apart from a few marks in the center representing the town, the
map was blank.

"What's this all around the center?" asked Jenny, the kemmer. "Fog of war?"

"It's an exploration map," said Ariel. "It's generated different every time.
We fill it in as we go, like a tabletop RPG."

"In that case, I'm taking a five-meter pole," said Jenny.

"You can't get infinite mileage out of the five-meter pole," said Ariel.

"Saved your ass in the Temple of Nahadoth."

"There's no equipment," said You'll Only See Kis Echo!. "We're children;
we'd just eat it. In this game, you gotta rely on good old-fashioned caste
memory!"

"Aaand... what's that?" asked Jenny.

"You know," said You'll Only See Kis Echo!, "how each caste is born with
different instinctive knowledge. You probably call it something different."

"Yes, we call it sexism," said Jenny.

"Great!" said You'll Only See Kis Echo!, to whom "sexism" sounded like an innocuous technical term. "Let's go!" And with that, three children set off for What-The-Fuck Creek, filling in the map, scratching aimlessly at the ground with their forward graspers as they scouted out the rising brambles.

Before long, something rustled in the undergrowth at the noise of the approaching children. "Hey, I found this... jumpy little snake dude," said Ariel.

"Eat it!" said You'll Only See Kis Echo!.

"That's stupid," said Ariel, and ate the little snake dude. "Well, damn. Fucking caste memory. Do we make any *decisions* in this game?"

A sonic boom divided the world into before and after, igniting a semicircle of ground that gave off thick blue smoke.

"Uh," said Ariel.

"Is this normal on your planet?" said Jenny.

"Hit the proverbial deck!" said You'll Only See Kis Echo!. The three children sprang away from the fire and into the thorny cover.

"Ow?" said Ariel. "Brambles?"

"You're fine," said You'll Only See Kis Echo!. "We've got bigger problems. Somebody's using a heat gun on us."

"Did I miss something?" asked Jenny, crouching behind the much larger kinner. "This is a game about kids exploring in the woods?"

"Yeah," said Ariel, "we're exploring when we make contact with an alien life form. It's the Gaijin version of <u>Temple Sphere</u>."

"You knew this would happen, and you didn't let me bring my damn pole?"

"I didn't know there would be heat guns! I thought it would be cute!"

"From continued dawdling no good will grow," said You'll Only See Kis Echo!. "Ariel, go see who's behind the heat gun."

"You do it!" said Ariel. "You're three times bigger than me."

"Caste memory," said You'll Only See Kis Echo!. "If there's a problem, the males go check it out."

"A projectile weapon is in play," said Ariel. "We should send the tank, not the rogue." Ariel ran out ahead and over a hill to see who was running the heat gun.

"Oh, shit," he said. "It's a bigger version of that snake dude I ate." The large snake dude came up through the brambles on thick centipede legs, and held a sheet of silvered plastic before it in two massive spinnerets. "That musta been his kid. No wonder he's pissed off."

"Let's parlay," said Jenny. Ke picked up a rock. "See if it understands English. Or whatever language. Say it was a mistake."

"I'm getting out of here," said Ariel, and charged the snake dude. "I'm not taking the fall for this."

"You started it, you wuss," said Jenny. She threw the rock and it landed far short of the snake dude.

"You're supposed to protect me while I go for an attack of opportunity," said Ariel. "These tactics are screwed up. The whole game is screwed up."

"You chose the game!" said Jenny. "You had the entire database to choose from, and you chose this one."

The snake dude cocked its eyeless head at the children, let the plastic sheet droop a little, then snapped it taut. The sonic boom caved in Ariel's trunk like *splat* and threw You'll Only See Kis Echo! backwards to crush Jenny's body atop the brambles. Then the wake of the sonic boom ignited and the three children were on fire. Black blood oozed from cracks in seared skin. The edges of the map caught on fire and the partially explored field burned to nothing. They never even made it to What-The-Fuck Creek.

"We're dead, we get it," said Ariel in the between-game netherworld. The three children floated in nothingness, graspers and walkers dangling downward in some unseen gravity.

"Let's try again," said You'll Only See Kis Echo!. "We'll have a different scenario next time. A less violent one, I hope." Ki reached kis graspers into invisible clouds of stardust and pulled together pieces of the map, now once again blank.

"This is impossible," said Ariel. "Three kids can't take down a guy with a heat ray. Not if the big kid stays in the back the whole time."

"Of course not," said You'll Only See Kis Echo!. "You instinctively ate the offspring. No snake dude will stand for that. And a child's caste memory will always lose to a heat gun."

Jenny folded her arms crossly, despite not having 'arms' per se. "So what was the point of the scenario? We were doomed."

"Children can't control their caste memories," said You'll Only See Kis Echo!. "But adults can decide how to treat each other. Humans, I don't know about. But by Gaijin or Alien standards, you two weren't treating each other very well."

"I don't like losing," said Ariel. "I don't like when the player character won't take orders."

"You might be missing the point of the game," said You'll Only See Kis Echo!

"Maybe I am," said Ariel. "I'm very stressed. I'm missing a lot of points. I thought a game night would—Jenny, why don't I go home, and you can show You'll Only See Kis Echo! some <u>Anasazi</u>? That's got the same kind of map mechanic. I need to go home and sleep or something."

Jenny was looking at Ariel. "No, don't end it like this," she said. "Let's try again."

"Okay," said Ariel. "One more run." In a flash of light, the children were reborn in their synthetic-diamond setup and set out into the woods.

This time, the space alien looked like a bramble-bush with huge jagged teeth. It gave them candy and showed them some magic tricks and sent them back home. But they were never able to convince the adults of the truth of what they saw that day, floating in What-The-Fuck Creek.

Private email message, forwarded October 6

From: Jun-Feng Bai
To: Ariel Blum
Subject: Fwd: Re: Hardware Hangar?

heads up, bro

+-----BAI---->

---------Forwarded Message---------

From: Jun-Feng Bai
To: Jenny Gallegos
Subject: Re: Hardware Hangar?

> > > Hey, Bai,
> > >
> > > I heard from Tetsuo that you took Ariel to
> > > Hardware Hangar.
> > > Not that he has to tell me everything, but he
> > > never mentioned this trip to me, which set off
> > > an alarm bell because usually he gets 10
> > > minutes of convo out of a burrito run.
> > >
> > > Specifically: is Ariel's new apartment in really
> > > bad shape and he doesn't want me to know?
> > > He hasn't invited me over yet. Should I kick his
> > > landlord/slumlord's ass? You know how
> > > Ariel is. I'm having visions where he
> > > electrocutes himself because he thinks he can
> > > fix the wiring on his own.
> > >
> > > Jenny (worried)
> >

> > hi jenny (dana says hi). actually its tetsuo who
> > wanted to go to hard-and-hangin (he wanted to
> > see our biggest store with the worst customer
> > service). a-bro asked me to take him
> > to s-mart for inflatable bed + other post-move
> > housewarez, so i did one trip in the suv with both.
> >
> > a did pick up some fertilzer and seeds
> > (vegetables, ganja) at hh, and a baby cherry tree.
> > tets bought a pack of pencils with dry-erase
> > markers on the other end and now he's

> > practicing translating all the english in the house
> > into simple affect metadata exchange.
> >
> > a's new place is not as good as his ex house but i
> > wouldn't call it a slum. and you wanted him off
> > your couch right? probly bro is starting a garden
> > on the balcony, let him be.
> >
> > afterwards we detoured to cutprice cuz a says its
> > maybe a little bigger than hardware hangar due to
> > higher ceilings. big bags of frozen pasta for all.
> > good times.
> >
> > +---BAI---->
>
> 1. You've known Ariel as long as I have. You believe
> for one minute that he's starting a garden?
> 2. Why did he buy seeds and no flowerpots?
> (Did he?)
> 3. You can't grow a damn tree on an
> apartment balcony.
>
> Aren't you curious? What's he up to?
>
> Jenny (now nosy)

of course i'm curious. my thinking is a has been
through a lot w/house burning down etc. let's be
supportive. who buys a tree he can't plant?
answer: bro whose midlife crisis is in danger of
arriving ten years early. let him have a tree if it makes
him happy and b.f.d. if it dies in a couple months.

no flowerpots. oh, at cutprice he did also buy a bag of
halloween-size candy bars, in case that sets off alarm
bells for ya. or maybe hes getting ready for halloween
like everyone else. will send party invites out soon.
tets says he will dress up as ayn rand. i think this
is a bad idea. you?

+---BAI---->

Chapter 29:
He Sees The Map And
He Throws The Dart!

Blog post, October 8 (never published)

Once again, Jenny called me at 3 AM.

"The port landed on Mars," she said. "They're about to go through!"

"Can't it wait until the taxpayers are awake?" I rolled off my inflatable mattress, called up five video feeds on my smart paper, and loaded up the radio on my phone. "I thought it would be Monday morning."

"This is Monday morning," said Jenny.

"Fake morning," I said.

The astronauts stood in the same Gaijin Ring dome where they'd performed the star-draw six weeks ago, clustered around the port. The humans still wore Constellation spacesuits; the Gaijin were now wearing parkas and breathing masks. It wasn't a starfield visible through the port. It wasn't the place in space where Mars would be in six weeks. It was the actual no-fooling surface of Mars.

I've gone through twenty ports and, my mind still refused to accept this view. I saw it as a movie screen showing footage from the Viking probes. You can't just take one end of a room and drop it onto another planet. Except you can. All it takes is a few minus-kilograms of exotic matter and a tame black hole.

"I didn't think I'd live to see this," said Jenny. "Not after the moonbase fiasco and *Columbia*. Everything's changing so fast, like we're headed towards the Singularity."

"Yeah, there's gonna be a singularity," I said, "in seventy years."

Jenny sighed. "Don't talk like that."

Two huge Gaijin astronauts unfastened the hatch on the port and cracked it open. The dome's atmosphere was sucked into Mars: our first little contribution to terraforming.

Colonel Mason took point with the flag. Wondering why the flag looks like that? Some poor NASA graphic designer was told to design a flag that was simultaneously the Chinese flag and the Stars and Stripes. ESA got word and wanted in, then the Russians and the Brazilians, and then the UN and countries that never even had an astronaut program. And then the Gaijin started putting even more stuff on the flag, basically out of spite. Now it's a Technicolor soup, a graffiti-covered wall with "Ordem E Progresso" tagged on the bottom, which is Portuguese for "Fuck you, Mars."

"Here we go," I said. Colonel Mason carried the flag through the port and humanity was on Mars.

Jenny made a noise. "Are you crying?" I asked.

"No," said Jenny.

"Okay, I'm just—"

"Yes," said Jenny, and cried.

"Oh, dammit," I said, and I cried too.

"Hey look!" Jenny sniffled, once a couple more guys had gone through the port, "It's Tammy! Right?"

It was her. A woman in a spacesuit wearing a sewn-on sash of fluid-overlay patches, standing at the airlock threshold. Dr. Tammy Miram walked onto Mars, out of sight, without looking back.

My jaw dropped. "She wasn't going to go!" I said. "She said she was just doing the logistics!"

"Ariel, if she doesn't go, she's fucking crazy. This is *the planet Mars*."

A Martian dust devil blew through the port into Gaijin Ring, airbrushing dust the color of dried blood onto everyone's suits and the walls of the Mars-containment dome. The Gaijin in parkas were holding back, getting all dusty, letting the humans step through. Letting us have Mars all to ourselves for a while.

"That's just it," I said. My voice was cracking. "She said she would never walk on a planet's surface again. She said she was born to live in space."

"Yeah, well, that's *stupid*. That's something you tell yourself when life hands you the big runner-up trophy. Something better comes along, you don't hold on to your hang-ups just because that's what's written on your character sheet."

How much detail were we getting on this video? It had to be high-quality, right? If I could get it in HD I could zoom in on Tammy's flight suit. See if she was wearing that patch anywhere. The one she'd given me: the binary-star patch that meant she and I were an overlay all to ourselves.

"I was going to be the one to change her mind," I said. "We were going to go to Mars *together*. Someone else was there for her during the most important two months of her life, while she collected all those overlay patches, while she got over being grounded. And now she's the first woman on Mars, and I'm a schmuck with a game review blog. I'm going to lose her."

"Jesus Christ," said Jenny. "You need to stop this."

"It's Colonel Mason!" I said. "He seduced her with a ten-point checklist. Look at him! The man's carved from fucking granite. I can't compete with that. Why is this happening? There's got to be some way to fix this."

"This isn't a G-ddamn leaky faucet!" said Jenny. "Not a thing to be fixed. Although I wouldn't give good odds on your fixing a faucet either. Can't you be proud of her?"

"Listen," I said. I swallowed hard. "I have to tell you something. My house didn't really burn down."

"Vuhvuh...wah?"

"I didn't burn my house down. I know I told you I did. I was lying."

"Bai took a look. He said it's just a foundation hole."

"I'm not saying it's still there. Just, no fire."

"Well, what happened? Did the house just walk away?"

"I can't tell you. I really literally can't. I just want you to know there was no fire. I can't stand you making jokes about it. Faucets and shit."

"Ariel, I am sorry about the jokes," said Jenny. "But... you gotta admit that's a strange thing to lie about. Doesn't make you look good. Why would you *do* that? I'm seriously starting to worry about you."

"There is nothing to worry about," I said. "Absolutely nothing." There isn't, by the way.

A binary star patch doesn't mean anything. It just means she has *someone*. The stars don't have names. Looking up, you can't even tell how close two stars are to each other. They could be a thousand light-years apart. One bright distant star and a dim one that's really close.

Blog post, October 10

[This post is friends locked.]

Tetsuo settled onto all fours on the floor of my bedroom/living room. "You disliked the replica of the Ip Shkoy dwelling," he said, "because there was no natural light. But here there is natural light and you keep the window-blankets closed."

"So what are you saying?"

"I'm saying, wow."

I picked up the transcript of Bai's Library visit and thwacked the paper against my forearm.

```
VISITOR: Hey, bro, I'm Jun-Feng Bai.

LIBRARY: I have no individual name. You may
refer to me as 'Library' or 'Librarian'.

VISITOR: Not a big fan of the handshakes,
either, that's cool.
```

"Bai," I said. "Bai went downtown and talked with the Constellation Library."

"Oh, I'm sorry," said Tetsuo. I sat on the inflatable bed with my back against the wall.

"I'm just saying that by way of explanation. I couldn't go, because, well, you know."

"I do know," said Tetsuo.

"So Bai went for me. What's wrong? You don't like the Library?"

"I guess it's better than talking to Her," said Tetsuo, "if you need an eyewitness account of something that happened five hundred million years ago." His tail swept back and forth. "I prefer primary sources."

> VISITOR: I, uh, I want to talk about the
> Constellation's contact missions that failed.
>
> LIBRARY: A lot of people want to talk about
> that. Do you have specific questions?
>
> VISITOR: Yeah, I do, I'm getting to that.
> What's your problem?
>
> LIBRARY: I don't have any problem.

"You could have asked me," said Tetsuo. "For weeks I can't speak about anything but the failed contact missions. I'd rather talk to you than to *World Business News*."

"I wanted a second opinion," I said. "You said there were four failed contact missions. The Library says there were only two."

"The Library wouldn't say 'there were only two'," said Tetsuo.

> LIBRARY: I can't answer the question if you
> won't define your terms.
>
> VISITOR: Let's see, let's define failure as
> twenty percent mortality.
>
> LIBRARY: By that metric, all the contact

```
attempts were failures.

VISITOR: What?!

LIBRARY: Complex organisms eventually die. Did
you mean to use excess deaths as your metric?
```

"Okay, yes," I said, "I condensed that from three pages of haggling. Bottom line, the Library disagrees with you about the Cue Que, who I'd never heard of before, and the Gweilo. Says they were successful."

```
VISITOR: So what happened to the Cue Que? Why
aren't they here with you with a funny name like
the Aliens or the Gaijin?
```

Tetsuo took my paper and scrolled through the Library transcript. "Bai went down the wrong path," he said. "That's why it's such a piss to deal with the Library. He asked about death, but uploading isn't death."

```
LIBRARY: Through their individual choices all
Cue Que organisms were directly integrated into
the Constellation.
```

"It sounds like death," I said. "Don't they cut you up?"

"To a Farang, when a human goes to sleep it sounds like death," said Tetsuo. "Don't sort things by their sound. The invention of uploading is the day people stop dying."

```
VISITOR: Their choices? Who gave them this
choice?

LIBRARY: Do you really want all the names of the
individuals who offered the choice to upload?

VISITOR: No, more general. What was it like to
be given the choice?

LIBRARY: The Library has no subjective mental
states and cannot answer questions about the
mental states of others.
```

"We can't offer you that," said Tetsuo. "When we came here, we left the knowledge and the equipment at home. People say the Cue Que mission was successful, but nobody wants it to rehappen. To people who never uploaded, it looks like the end of <u>Temple Sphere</u>. A genocide. We killed a whole species with kindness.

"But hey, things are not going so well with you humans, so let's go back. Bring in the Slow People. They'll offer you the choice so we don't have to. All your friends will become Slow People, and you will upload to be with your friends, and I will have no one to talk to. And the rest of the animals on this planet will sigh a big relief because they only have to deal with one billion of humans instead of ten."

> VISITOR: Ninety percent?
>
> LIBRARY: About ninety percent. People get annoyed when I give precise numbers.
>
> VISITOR: So, not everybody.
>
> LIBRARY: Of course not. If all the Gweilo had uploaded, there would be no such organisms on this contact attempt.
>
> VISITOR: What made people decide the other way?
>
> LIBRARY: The Library has no subjective—
>
> VISITOR: Okay, you know what, never mind.
>
> LIBRARY: Would you like a hint?
>
> VISITOR: Sure.
>
> LIBRARY: Ask me to look up primary sources.
>
> VISITOR: All right, look up primary sources.
>
> LIBRARY: On what topic?

"There has to be something we can do," I said.

"I'm doing all possible something!" said Tetsuo. "I came to Earth despite the paperwork. I left my own children before they were born. I might *never* see them!"

```
ATTACHMENT: PRIMARY SOURCE 1
Reference ID 41-CLX0B-NRL9JU4X2XVV
Gweilo, Toki-l-ikot, c. 611 mya
Translated through LIBRARY
```

The ruling of this jurist is final.

Finding:

This jurist greeted Sky Goddess the Myriad Fingers when from the sky She fell to walk with us. This was disastrous error and gross incompetence. This jurist saw only Her visible fingers, and failed to warn the lesser-wise against the temptations whispered by Her cohort of invisible fingers. This led many lesser-wise to seek false paradise, speak with the dead, and otherwise violate the moral and natural laws.

This jurist is found guilty of violating the moral law:

1. The lesser-wise shall not be given the knowledge that tempts, nor denied the knowledge that does not.

Sky Goddess the Myriad Fingers refused to restrict the behavior of Her own fingers, claiming that this was impossible. As such, this jurist holds Sky Goddess the Myriad Fingers responsible for Her fingers' violations of the natural law:

1. An object shall not fall faster than it falls.
2. Nothing nonliving shall breathe.
3. The dead shall not speak with the living, nor the living with the dead.

As well as the moral law:

1. An object that falls upwards shall be destroyed, lest it be used as a weapon.
2. The dead shall not be disturbed before burning.

Sentencing:

To the extent that a mortal's ruling can bind the gods, Sky Goddess the Myriad Fingers is ordered: to vacate this world forthwith; to remove all fingers seen and unseen from this world, its dominion, and the dominion of its sun; to leave this world to its own gods and its own devices; and to remit all the dead in Her possession.

This jurist cannot resign because no one is trained to take his place. This jurist cannot commit ritual suicide because there is too much loss already. As no other sentence can be applied, this jurist is denied the burning-after-death. May he rot.

The ruling of this jurist is final.

"Humans adopt new technology," I said. "There are network effects. You can't take advantage of that with smart paper, and then try to stop it with uploading. You won't convince anyone but the fundies and the hippies."

"Ariel, there are planets already visited by Ragtime, planets with very little history. You'll Only See Kis Echo! and I have a scheme. We have seventy years to make humans feel it would be an amazing adventure to build housing developments on these planets."

"Housing developments?" I said. "You're going to combat the promise of eternal bliss with the most boring thing in the world?"

"Humans love housing developments," said Tetsuo.

"I guess you got me there," I said, "but can't you build housing developments after you upload?"

"We'll get you excited about specific planets," said Tetsuo. "You'll outspread. Existing cultures and social arrangements will fracture."

"And that's a good thing?"

"It is when people begin uploading," said Tetsuo. "It stops the network effects from taking everybody in the first few generations."

```
ATTACHMENT: PRIMARY SOURCE 2
Reference ID 41-CLX6Z-KG3R1D4PFBH86
Gweilo, Picec, c. 611 mya
Translated through LIBRARY
```

"We don't want to go on without you, Ckepois. We love you. We're all here, waiting for you. We have a big house in a hot spring with a grow-trap in the kitchen. You know how your grandparents love to cook. It's everything we could want. It's peaceful and secluded, but if you want the night life of the big city, you can just peel back a layer of the world, like the plate-moss from a rock, and there you are. If you want to visit a friend, you can be with them, just like that. Nobody goes hungry here or has to sell themselves. You can explore the sky if you want to, visit other worlds. Anything is possible now.

"A breath for you is like a day for us. It's not a lie or an evasion, as you may have heard; here it's a fact of life. Sometimes it's unfortunate. We're living much slower than everyone else here, to give you more time to decide. Sometimes we speed up for a bit to make friends with new people, but the next time we see them, they've been here for hundreds of years, and we just seem so provincial to them. It doesn't work out.

"It's been sixty-four years for us, Ckepois. Sixty-four years we've been living in this hot spring without youff. Your bond-sister got bored and went up to speed. She left another edition of herself to meet you when you arrive.

"Please, at least send us a message. We can't enjoy life not knowing you'll be with us one day. We'll send another message in a few days, another sixteen years."

```
VISITOR: They do that? They use the voices of
your folks to trick you into uploading?

LIBRARY: There was no trick. The primary source
was created by the recipient's father.

VISITOR: It's a private message. How did you get
it?

LIBRARY: When the recipient uploaded, she donat-
ed it to the Library along with the rest of her
personal documents.
```

"You're giving up too easily," I said. "We don't have to change humanity. We just have to convince the people on Ring City to turn the probe around, collapse the port, whatever."

"You'll convince many people before that happens," said Tetsuo. "Most of this contact mission has not even seen a live human. To them, you are nothing but pictures and voice. You could as well be Slow People already."

"I don't know what to do," I said. "That fucking hippie was right. This is the end of the human race."

"Don't be a guy who feels bad," said Tetsuo. "Nobody ever knows what to do. Our life-task is to *decide* what to do."

Blog post, October 11 (never published)

This is just to set the record straight. The three participants in this conversation all have recordings of the conversation, so I guess I'm just asserting that the stuff I said is the truth.

Bai called me and was angry. Bai doesn't do angry well. He called me some names and eventually got to the point: "Why aren't you paying Svetlana for the work she's doing?"

"Calm down," I said. This is a stupid thing to say to someone, but I never claimed to be smart. "Not only am I paying Svetlana, one of the things I'm paying her to do is manage the payroll. So if the money's not coming through, it's her own fault."

"I let this slide for two months already," said Bai. "It's not cool, bro!"

"I'm just gonna throw some ideas out here," I said. "Is it possible that ~~Svetlana~~ Dana [Fuck it! -A.B.] is spending her own money? Look in your purchase history."

"It's my account," said Bai. "Dana doesn't have direct access."

"She is your phone, Bai. She knows your passwords."

Bai put his smart paper down and my view of the video chat filled with his poking fingers as he logged on to check his cash flow. I pulled over my development paper and checked the corporate account.

"The money's going out," I said. "I dunno what to say."

"Shit!" said Bai. "Experience Holdings LLC! That's the store I used to buy her accessories from."

"Okay, problem solved," I said. "I'm paying her, she's spending her own money on 3D models of clothes. You got a problem with that, take it up with Dana. I'm not getting involved."

"You're already involved," said Bai. "You modded her so she wouldn't want more stuff all the time. Now she's broken, and she's squandering our nest egg."

"Do you really want to go there?" I asked.

"I'm already here," Bai said.

"I didn't mod 'Dana'," I said. "I modded a simple pseudo-AI that your friends had agreed to treat as a real person, out of politeness. And then that program was *replaced* with a *real* AI that approximates how an Alien would act if the Alien were 'Dana'.

"I could make the pseudo-AI think her desires were easy to meet. A real Alien won't fall for that. She wants what she wants, and you have to have to deal with her like a real person, because that's what she is."

"Thank you, Ariel," said Dana's sultry voice.

"Bai," I said, "did you use the Dana-phone to call me *about Dana*?"

"It's my phone, bro!"

"You're a pretty understanding guy, Ariel," said Dana. "It's a bit surprising to me that you have to pretend to have a girlfriend."

"Ex-*cuse* me?"

"You know, your little blonde shiksa? Who no one but you has ever talked to? You expect your friends to believe you're fucking an *astronaut*? It's a little unrealistic, and believe me, I know from unrealistic fantasy girlfriends. Is she Canadian as well?"

"Tammy is from Ohio! She was the eighth woman on the moon! She has a Wikipedia page!"

"So does Dana Light," said Dana, "but she's not Bai's girlfriend."

"Because she's a *fictional character*."

"Bai, sweetheart," said Dana. "Let's not argue about money. Just...thanks for getting us all on the line together. Ariel is not being a team player. He's been using fealty to his fake astronaut girlfriend as an excuse to avoid a relationship with us. I want you to have a talk with him, man to man."

"What," said Bai, "the fuck."

"Well, sure, okay!" I said, "Let's get it all out here! Dana has an Alien psychology, which means that if it's consistent with human behavior, she'll act like an Alien. And part of being an Alien is having sex with the people you work with. They call it transitive pair bonding. That's how Tetsuo hooked up with his wife. Probably both his wives."

"You— the—" said Bai.

"She's been coming on to me for weeks, and I've been *tactfully* pushing her off because this is the exact conversation I didn't want to have. But now she's making fun of my totally real girlfriend, so fuck it. You deal with Dana, Bai. You start treating your Alien AI girlfriend as a person, and stop pretending she's the video game heroine you jerked off to when you were a teenager, and maybe she won't feel like she needs two boyfriends."

"You insensitive motherfucker," said Dana.

"Dana," said Bai. "I forbid you from having anything to do with Ariel. You are not to do any more work for Crispy Duck Games."

"I'm not a child," said Dana. "You can't forbid me shit. Anyway, the point is moot because I quit."

"You can't quit," I said. "You're fired."

"Very well," said Dana. "It seems all three of us want the same thing."

And that's it. I wash my hands of it.

Not posting this. Eyes on the prize, Ariel.

Blog post, October 13

Hello, blog. I have moved! I know I just moved two weeks ago, but that was always supposed to be a temporary situation, and now I've got something much better.

See, funny story: I used to own a house. Mortgage interest deduction on my taxes and everything. Through the good graces of some friends I'd made, I was fortunate enough to be keeping some interesting extraterrestrial technology in my house. Old computers, game systems, and stuff. Then, a month ago, some agents from the Bureau of Extraterrestrial Affairs came and took away my house, to get at the alien technology. Or maybe to get some other technology they *thought* I had. Or maybe just so one of the agents could score a promotion. Who knows?

I wrote about this at the time—I've posted that entry now, backdated and un-friends-locked. The BEA took everything I had and tore my damn house down. They threw me a National Security Letter that said I couldn't tell anyone what had happened. I had to lie to my friends, make myself look like a moron who'd started a wiring fire and burned down his house.

Well, hey, can't make an omelet, right? It's all in the name of national security. Except they didn't just take my house. They *kept hassling me*, after they didn't find what they were looking for, as though I'd hidden the stash in my summer home or my ski chalet. When they finally started reimbursing me for the loss of everything I owned, they let the money drip out, a little bit every two weeks, so it would feel like a salary. Like I was working for them.

And oh yeah, they tried to get me to work for them. They're running scared about what happens now that everyone on Earth has access to smart paper. Of all the things the BEA could worry about, they chose "computers are too fast and too cheap." They asked me to figure out how the Outernet works, so they can do to it what they already did to the Internet—stop us from using it to talk to the people who hold our lives in their hands (or equivalent appendages).

I mean, nobody expects the BEA, or anybody really, to deal with global warming, but how about applying those Homeland Security dirty tricks to problems that are a) problems and b) of extraterrestrial origin? Like, what happens in seventy years when, in addition to having really good computers, we're all offered the chance to play a very, *very* immersive video game?

The game is called Slow People. By all accounts, it is one fucking amazing game. It's a MMORPG with trillions of players, a MUD that lets you create whole worlds. The catch is the same as any game: to enter the magic circle, you have to give up some of your real life. And since Slow People is so very engrossing, playing it means giving up the outside world entirely, with its pains and troubles. Once you start playing, everything outside the game seems too slow and boring to bother with.

If history is any indication, ninety percent of us will choose to play that game.

Maybe this is fine. Most of the people on Ring City seem to think it's a great solution to the problem of more humans than Earth can support. But the people I trust, the people who've actually spent time with us, don't want to archive all of humanity's stuff and then archive humanity itself. Like my friend Tetsuo Milk, who's devoting his life to convincing people not to play Slow People, even though his own relatives will be playing it in a few years. He thinks he can get that market penetration number down to forty or fifty percent.

Props to Tetsuo, but that's not good enough. The Constellation contains two hundred billion flesh-and-blood people. That includes thirty billion Aliens like Tetsuo, scattered across seventeen custom-terraformed planets and uncountable space stations. The galaxy has space for ten, fifteen billion humans. We deserve to join the Constellation as equals and reach out to the stars, not to end up in some solipsistic gated community the size of a small asteroid.

Long story short, I've moved again. Specifically, I've moved to Ring City. I'm now living in lunar orbit, in Human Ring, along with miscellaneous spies, two hundred Eritreans, and the casts and crews of three reality TV shows. I'm going to convince the Constellation to turn the probe around, to keep this contact mission going, to do this properly rather than letting the Slow People through just because we're about to fossilize ourselves.

I'm sick of feeling helpless, and I'm sick of being separated from the woman I love. So over the past few weeks, I took a look at the things keeping me from my goals. I made the things I didn't like go away, and I decided not to be bothered by the loss of everything else.

I'd like to visit Earth again in the future, but let's be realistic: this looks like a one-way trip.

PS to BEA Agent Krakowski: Needless to say, this was entirely my decision. (You can tell because it's so stupid.) No one on Earth knew about this plan or helped me carry it out. So... just don't. Okay?

Part Three: Artwork

I dropped a leaf into a hole
And you dropped me in turn. I found
That gravity reversed its pull
And through the sky was solid ground.
We drop, are dropped, and each to each
It's what we do, it's not profound.
And if a hole is out of reach
We take a longer way around.
We fall in all directions. Some
Find lucky landings, higher ground.
I wait, instead, for help to come
And some of us are never found.

I left a message in the ice:
The time, the distance, and the price.

Advertising copy for the Ip Shkoy computer game The Long Way Around
poss. written by Af be Hui
Translated into English verse by Dr. Linda Blum and Dr. Tetsuo Milk

Chapter 30:
Constellation 'Shipping

Blog post, October 15, evening

Ring City is exactly the way I left it. The Human Ring docking bay is as
vast and empty as space itself. (Well, not quite.) The big chintzy statues of
Adam and Eve from the Pioneer plaque are still standing, naked, to greet
a flow of humanity that never arrived. I drag my heavy bags through the
docking bay and into a bland Human Ring hallway, looking for the nearest
unoccupied apartment.

The first hallway is claimed by embassies and news organizations. I open
a door experimentally. The apartment is unlocked and uninhabited. I could
pull down a nameplate and move in; no one would notice.

Instead, I schlep my bags around a corner, into another hallway identical to the first. I turn at every junction, alternating left-right-left to keep
from getting lost. By this crude algorithm, I find an unclaimed room. It's
got a bunkbed with no pillows, a shower/sink, and a squat toilet. What a
surprise.

I set down my bags and put my own damn pillow on the bottom bunk. Then
I go back to the docking bay for my cherry tree. Finally, I write on the door
with a dry-erase marker:

A. Blum
(Temporary)

I can get caipirinha from the repertoire station out in the hall, but this is a
special occasion. From my bag, I take a cut-glass decanter and pour some
scotch into the cap of a shampoo bottle.

AND NOW
AN OPEN LETTER TO ALL AND SUNDRY

Hey, thanks for finally reading my blog, but I'm not at all interested in doing an interview/telling you how I got to Ring City/converting to your fake-
ass religion/lab-teching your microgravity experiment. Bye!

Love and kisses,
Ariel

Personal correspondence, October 15

Jenny,

There's a lot of paper in this envelope. Please at least look
at all of it, no matter how this makes you feel. The stuff in
the back is contracts that transfer ownership of Crispy Duck
Games to you. They need your countersignature, but you might
want to wait a couple days. I don't want you to get screwed
over if the BEA freezes my assets.

I've strung you along long enough so I'll just say it now: I am
moving to Ring City. I'm literally gonna shove this under your
door (assuming it fits) and then leave. I probably won't be back
for a few years. Technically, illegal exit is only a misdemeanor,
but I'm sure if they wanted to, the BEA could prosecute a
Greenland Treaty violation or something.

I'm leaving for two reasons. The first is the same reason Tetsuo
came to Earth. If we don't make contact—real contact—with
the Constellation, the Slow People will make contact with our
grandchildren, and they won't have a clue how to handle it.
There are a thousand conversations I wanted to have with
you about this, but I didn't want you to become complicit.
When Krakowski comes knocking, you can honestly say, "That
sumbitch left without telling me a damn thing."

When I went back to my folks' place in September, I stole my
father's cut-glass scotch decanter. If he goes, and I'm not on
Earth to inherit anything of his, that's the thing I'd miss the
most, so I took it. I just wrote him a letter apologizing and telling him why the decanter is important to me, and I'm still in a
storytelling mood, so I want to tell you a story, too. It's the story
of us, the weird story, the story we agreed not to tell anyone
else, and this may be my last chance to tell it. Plus, this way
you'll know it's really me writing this letter, and not some BEA

or Constellation trick.

It was the fall of 2005 and Bai convinced me to hit UTAkuCon. I was a wallflower *at the nerd con*. Bai had to drag me through the dealers' room. I picked up a couple import games using money I couldn't afford to spend. In the big central hallway, Bai and I hid in anonymity beneath the din of conversation and planned our next move.

Across the hall I saw a cosplayer, a girl with a sharp black pageboy haircut wearing a white dress, her shoulder pads and sleeves decorated with deadly metal spikes and gothic-looking gears. She was chugging a bottle of water.

I nudged Bai. "Hey!" I said. "That girl is dressed like Taikan-Victory!" Bai just nodded.

"Stop acting like you know who Taikan-Victory is," I said.

"Who is Taikan-Victory?"

"The girl who turns into a spaceship from <u>Tangent Go Thru</u>. It's a super obscure Japanese shooter. This is incredible!"

"Go talk to her," said Bai, like it was that simple.

"No! She'll think I'm one of those perverts who comes to leer at the cosplayers."

"She thinks that now," said Bai. "Talk to her and prove her wrong. Just tell her you get the reference. Girls like that."

Bai spoke with false authority on the topic of girls and what they like, but now he'd put my honor at stake. I walked across the broadest hallway at UTA. We're talking light-seconds wide.

"Hey, nice costume," I said.

You looked up from your con schedule. I remember looking down at the floor, at the condensation on your water bottle. "Thanks."

"Are those blades real?"

"They're metal," you said. "They're not really sharp. I don't wanna cut someone's throat."

"Cool." I could have walked away and we never would have met. But then I said: "I didn't think anyone else even knew about <u>Tangent Go Thru</u>."

"Is that a drug?" you asked. "Are you dealing?"

"It's a video game," I said. "For the Dreamcast." Like naming the platform would make it all clear. "You're dressed like the player character."

"No," you said, "I'm Skewer Sue."

I ran a little emergency flowchart in my head. "I've never heard of Skewer Sue. Who's she?"

"Only the greatest character to come out of the feminist comics revolution of the early Nineties," you said.

"I don't know much about comics," I said. "When I was a kid, my parents never let me have them."

"Are they super religious or something?"

"No, they're just English professors."

I lost track of Bai around that time. I walked the dealers' room again, with you, and you told me the entire history of comics. We argued and haggled with dealers in graphic novels and manga. I told you about game design, how you can trigger the pleasure circuits in someone's brain just by setting up a little system of feedback loops, and how designing those feedback loops triggers an even bigger pleasure circuit in the *designer's* brain.

You mentioned the intrusion of comic-book imagery into pop art. By this time, you were running out of comics history, so we jumped into art. You moved forward from the 1950s; I tried to counter with what I knew of seventeenth-century English literature. Finally we went back to your dorm room so you could look up examples on the Internet, and I sat on your bunk and carefully paged through your collection of "Fair"-condition issues of *Skewer Sue*.

"My mind is blown," I said. "My obscure import shooter totally ripped off your comic book."

"This is so weird," you said. "Why would someone do that?"

"So many Japanese games have totally random references to American pop culture," I said. "That's why I love imports, so I can discover this stuff." (Yes, I was an insufferable snob back then.)

We ate awful turkey tetrazzini in the dining hall and ran back up to your room and the 'net. We pulled a six-pack of illicit beer from your mini-fridge and drank it. Sometime around eleven, your roommate left with a backpack full of textbooks and didn't come back.

It was three in the morning. I'd installed emulators on your computer, and we'd traded the keyboard back and forth playing Cipher games. You'd drawn that comic where Picasso's trying to paint a still life but Bugs Bunny keeps running off with the fruit. You'd talked for fifteen minutes about Judy Chicago's *The Dinner Party*. Now you were lying on your bunk with your shoes off.

I rubbed my eyes. I was thinking about going back to my own dorm room for some sleep. Well, that's one of the possibilities I was thinking about.

Skewer Sue's weapons lay in a foot-stabbing pile on the floor; you were still wearing the white dress. "How long did it take you to make the costume?" I said.

"Like ten hours sewing, fifteen hours in the metal shop," you said. "I cheated on the bracelets to get it done in time."

"Could you make another copy?"

"I guess," you said. "Maybe twenty hours total. Why?"

"It's just a dumb idea," I said. "I was thinking if you showed me how to make a Taikan-Victory costume, we could go together to the con next year. We'd match."

You had a huge smile on your face. You interlaced your hands behind your head. "You want me to make you a dress?" you asked.

"It's a spaceship hull," I said.

"Yeah, but you're dressing up as a girl. Spaceship."

"Yeah, so what? We'll be obscure reference buddies."

"Ariel, sorry, I gotta ask, are you gay?" You pulled up your feet and I sat on the bed next to you.

"No," I said.

"Good," you said.

"I just think it'd be funny— what do you mean 'good'? You have something against gay people?"

"What do you think I mean?" you said.

It's a pretty lossy line but I receive signals eventually. I climbed up the bed and kissed you.

This was when you made the sound. I heard it as a kind of sputtering; I flinched away but I had already resigned myself and started penning my confessional letter:

> Dear *Attitude* Magazine,
>
> I met this great girl at a con and we got drunk and when I kissed her she upchucked right in my face; how do ya like them apples?
>
> I remain, as ever, your most obedient servant,
> Ariel Blum (age 18)

And I got (I've never told you this before) halfway through the thought: "If I handle this well, she's more likely to sleep with me eventually, so it could be a net positive." But all this had happened in my mind and there was still no puke, and the sound you were actually making caught up with me. You were laughing.

I pushed myself up. "Is this a joke?" I said. "Get the nerd's hopes up and then laugh at him?"

"Wha...?" you said, a little dazed. "You didn't—did you do that on purpose?"

"This isn't funny," I said.

"Kiss me again," you said, like an order.

I kissed you again and you laughed again, big broad Marx Brothers laughs, your lips writhing, impossible to catch. You pulled away. "Stop! I'll get hiccups!"

"Is this like a thing?" I said, as though that sentence meant something. Back then I was very sensitive about my kissing style. Actually I still am, my whole life.

"You don't feel that?" you said.

"I feel *something*," I said.

"Ariel, you have a superpower," said Jenny. "Did nobody tell you?"

"Is it the good kind of superpower?" I said.

You blew the bangs out of your eyes. "This morning," you said, "I put on my costume and I was Skewer Sue, for the con. And when we came back here I took off the spikes and stuff, and I was Jenny again. And— and— then, you kissed me and I saw that Jenny is just another costume. We're all cosplaying, all the time, and when you kissed me, you took off the 'Jenny' costume and there was nothing underneath.

"I was just this bag of *meat*, this *animal* with arms and legs, with this *stuff* wrapped around me, laying on stuff, surrounded by stuff, fifty feet off the ground, held up by a huge complicated machine made of *stuff*. It was the funniest thing in the world to be this bag of meat surrounded by stuff and another one here watching me laugh."

"Is this your way of telling me you don't want to make out? Because—" ~~She~~ You pulled my head down and kissed me, with tongue. (I'm having real trouble keeping this in the second person.)

When I kissed you, I'd been too nervous for anything to really register. Now you kissed me and I finally felt your lips against mine. There was a split-second release of endorphins and then your tongue shorted some circuit inside my mouth and the universe went dead.

I let out a choked humming scream and rolled off the bed, inches from getting killed by Skewer Sue. "That's not supposed to happen," I said, my cheek pressed against the dorm room carpet. "I've never kissed a girl before, but I know what's supposed to happen."

"What? What is it?" you said. Trying to hold off laughing, waiting for the punchline.

I couldn't lift my head off the floor. "There's nothing there," I said. "The universe is just a bunch of atoms bumping into each other."

"Yeah!" you said, and started laughing again. "It is! It's just *stuff!*"

"It's not funny!"

"It's the *only* thing that's funny!"

"This is not supposed to happen," I said. Like I had some kind of Service Level Agreement.

"Let's skip the kissing," you said. Oh, beautiful practical Jenny. "Nobody says there has to be kissing." You started unbuttoning the sixty pearl buttons on the front of your Skewer Sue dress.

That got me off the floor. I knelt on the bed astride your legs. My briefs were strangling my cock. "Jenny," I said. "Jenny."

"There's no Jenny," you said. "She's not home." Your chest was heaving. It was the first time I ever decided not to look at breasts. You were still undoing the tiny buttons, one at a time. Oh, careful meticulous Jenny.

"I need Jenny," I said. "I don't want to do this with an animal or a bag of meat. I want Jenny who knows all about art and is so beautiful."

You smiled, biting your lip to hold back the laugh, the life rushing back into your eyes. You stopped undoing your buttons and pinned me with your gaze. You inhaled heavily and said: "Wastebasket."

"Wastebasket?" I said. And *that* was when you puked on me.

"Tell me, please," you said when I left for my own dorm an hour later, showered and with the ex-turkey scraped off my clothes. "Tell me if it happens with other girls. I want to know."

Well, Jenny, it doesn't. It's just us. I still can't explain it, but I've felt that feeling again. It's the feeling I get whenever I go into space. The Earth falls out from under me and I'm stranded in a universe of nothing, just like that night in your dorm room. Maybe this is just the feeling I have when I get something I've been wanting my whole life.

You asked me what I saw in Dr. Tammy Miram besides that she puts up with my immaturity and her boobs look nice in microgravity (they do look great, BTW). I couldn't formulate the truth because we'd agreed to settle for friendship and never to talk about this, about two bags of meat pressing against each other while "Jenny" stands off to the side laughing and "Ariel" whimpers abandoned in heat-death.

Here is the truth: Tammy is a cosplayer *who never takes the costume off*. Even when she un-Velcros her flight suit and stands before me naked, she's still the physicist, the Mission Specialist. She already knows that we're nothing but collections of atoms who momentarily got lucky. She doesn't find this funny or terrifying; it's just a fact she needs to do her job.

Tammy's been a romantic hard-luck case her whole life, just like me. She's got an emotional shell surrounding her like a clingy Constellation spacesuit. Most guys want a woman to be *naked* when she gets naked. But I need some assurance that I can kiss a woman without turning us both into bags of meat.

And that's the second reason I'm leaving Earth.

I'm going to put this letter under your door; then I'll walk into a Constellation shuttle and I'll go up into space again. This time I'll keep my eyes open and pretend I'm kissing you.

I never believed that for any given person there was one other person who was "right" for them, love at first sight, and that happiness depended on finding your "other half." How would that even work? Especially now that we know there are trillions of people in our galaxy alone. How is it that the right person for you is always born on the same planet at around the same time? It's astronomical. You'd have to believe in G-d or something.

But maybe there is one absolutely perfect match for everyone, one true pairing, one person who fits with you to form something bigger, like the two hemispheres of a Farang brain. If that's true, maybe we should be glad that almost nobody ever finds that other person.

Your friend,
Ariel

- - -

Hey, welcome to page eight. One thing I've learned from crime shows is that the cops might go away if you put up a little fight and then let them see something that's embarrassing but not incriminating. So read this eighth page, chuck it, and when Krakowski shows up to talk about me, show him the first seven pages about how we met. He'll say "wow, you kids are fucked in the head" and leave you alone.

The thing I want to tell you is: Don't get rid of those notebooks I left at your place. The paper they're made of is smart paper, and that box of notebooks is a major Outernet hub. That's what Tetsuo meant when he said the notebooks were soft-dolls. He wasn't (just) being a snob. They're fake replicas: super-advanced routers disguised as old embarrassing notebooks in a plastic tub.

Tetsuo tells me that the two big overlays, Plan C and Save the Humans, have cut a deal. StH dropped their objections to

sending a port back to Constellation space, and Plan C agreed
to work their haunches off to make sure that port never has to
get there. The first step is to set up a communications channel
that can't be shut down: the Outernet. As one of the few people
to belong to both Save the Humans *and* Plan C, Curic is right
in the middle of the combined overlay. The fake notebooks are
her idea of a joke.

Don't keep the notebooks in your apartment—eventually the
feds will be able to use frequency analysis to find the hubs. But
please keep it all together for a while, someplace warm, until
more Americans own their own smart paper and the Outernet
can get along without hubs.

My original plan was to take the notebooks to the dump, a plan
which I'm sure would be agreeable to you. But Tetsuo says the
Constellation is about to scoop up a lot of dumps from Earth
and salvage our garbage. This would bring the notebooks
right back to the space station, where they can't do any good.
Maybe you could rent a storage locker and forget to pay for it.

Goodbye for real this time.

I don't love her. I'm settling for her. I love you.

Real life, October 16

Fluid overlays are how the Constellation gets everything done, and the
great thing about them is that you can just walk up and join one. As long as
you're not incompetent, they'll find something for you to do. This is doubly
true if you're volunteering to carry heavy things.

Right in front of the port into Mars, a tiny Gaijin male was darting in
and out of a *second* port, trundling large white tubes out of Utility Ring and
stacking them just inside the airlock dome, just outside the port to Mars.

"Need help?" I asked. The tubes looked like solid extruded PVC. They
were longer than the Gaijin was tall, and the gravity differential between
Utility and Gaijin Rings tossed him around every time he came out of the
port with one.

"Hello, human!" said the Gaijin through his translator. "Naturally! Help!"

"Hand them out to me and I'll stack," I said. "I'm Ariel Blum, by the way."

"Because He Was Quick!," said the Gaijin. "I'm with Constellation
Shipping. Hand delivery, as it were!"

"What are we delivering?" I asked him.

"FERNs," said Because He Was Quick!. "It's what you call an acronym. It stands for High-Dimension Fractal Carbon Accumulators!" He

tossed me a tube.

"Oof!" The tube weighed thirty pounds in Gaijin Ring gravity, and I was already wearing a backpack that massed out at 4.99 kilograms. "That doesn't spell FERN," I said.

"The Martian atmosphere is carbon dioxide," said Because He Was Quick!, completely ignoring my comment. "FERNs pull out the carbon and leave the oxygen. They Earth-format the planet and yield carbon to use in manufacturing!"

We made a huge pile of FERNs in the airlock dome, and then we crowded into the dome ourselves and Because He Was Quick! opened the inner door. We carried the FERNs through another gravity differential and stacked them up again on Mars.

The sun, weak and distant, was setting on the base camp. Electric lamps strung between Quonset huts gave off pearl-strings of light; occasional shadows moved between the huts. The stars above barely twinkled. The camp was drowsy in the thin air, murmuring radio chatter into my suit. No one noticed us; no one cared. We were two halves of a fluid overlay, gettin' shit done.

We piled the FERNs next to the multinational flag, still standing where Colonel Mason planted it a week ago, tilted forward and waffling in the wind. They should cast that ugly thing in concrete. This isn't the moon; things don't stay put.

"Just like home!" said Because He Was Quick!, casting his sense-apparatus down at the rust-red ground, covered in footprints and Gaijin walker-tracks. "Exploring, building roads, catching things in the river!"

I nudged a FERN with my FOOT. "How do these things work?" I asked. "I'm curious."

"Ah!" said Because He Was Quick!. "Help me move one off to the side, and we'll set it up!" We lifted one of the FERNs, carried it just outside of camp, and set it on edge so that the mouth of the tube faced upwards. Because He Was Quick! said a magic word and the FERN *unfolded*, anchoring itself in the soil on one end, growing and branching on the other into a huge, bushy, infinitely detailed solar-collection fractal. It looked like a smooth white tree, towering over me (not that difficult) and Because He Was Quick! (even easier).

"Is it alive?" I said.

"No, no!" said Because He Was Quick!. "They reproduce slowly, but they're not alive!"

"It breathes, it reproduces, I don't see any real difference between this and a tree."

"Ah, if you count a *tree* as alive, then maybe! Maybe you'd say the same."

Because He Was Quick! stepped back from the practically-a-tree.

"Now I'll enjoy a luncheon under the stars!" he said. It was a statement, not an invitation. He slithered into the distance on eager walker tentacles.

"I'm looking for a friend," I called out after him, and walked back into camp.

For the first time in months, I could relax. I had come a long, long way but everything was going to be okay. This was where I needed to be. I saw her from behind, working on a heating unit with a wrench.

"Hey, Tammy," I called out. Not over radio: my own voice through the thin air.

Dr. Tammy Miram started and dropped her wrench. It fell in slow motion through Martian gravity. The wrench landed on its head and fell over in a puff of rust-dust. It was not a wrench of human design.

"It's me," I said.

Tammy whirled around. "Ari! What are you—Jesus!"

"I came here to be with you," I said.

"Don't use the suit mic," she said. She beckoned me into the shadows, towards her. "Just talk normally and no one will overhear."

"What's wrong?" I said.

"You can't be up here." Tammy wiped the dust from her faceplate, exposing her naked panicked face. "What were you thinking?"

"I was *thinking* that I *love* you," I said, "and it would be nice if we got to see each other occasionally."

"You don't even have an exit visa," she said, "much less security clearance. How did you get up—no, I don't even want to know. You're a fugitive! I can't be seen with you! Oh my G-d."

"I abandoned my entire life to be with you," I said. "It's fucking *romantic*, okay?"

"Not telling you to go back," said Tammy. "Don't go back, Jesus, what will they do. Just get out of camp. Go back to the station. You'll throw everything off. Shit, shit." She covered her faceplate with gloved hands, pressing the rust back on in whorls.

"I brought you something," I said. I twisted around and took off the backpack. "Your go bag. The one you packed and then forgot on Earth."

Tammy kind of stooped and rested one hand on the heating unit. "You broke into my *house*?" she said.

"No!" I said. "You told me what was in it! I made you another one!"

"Take it," she said. "I don't need it anymore. Don't *scare* me like that, Ari. Take it and go."

I backed off. "Is this it?" I said. "I come all this way, and it's over?"

The sun had set. I could no longer see Tammy through her spacesuit. She said nothing.

"It must be worth something, the sheer distance I traveled."

"This isn't a game," she said. "You don't get *points*."

"Is this it?" I repeated.

"Don't make me answer," she said. "You won't like the answer."

Tammy turned and stumbled around the Quonset hut, hugging herself like a wounded animal. The wrench lay dead on the ground.

"That's not—" No one heard me. Because He Was Quick! was gone. Tammy was gone. I was alone on Mars.

The green daylight of Gaijin Ring shone through the port like a flashlight, a cone-shaped swatch of light incongruous in the red Martian dusk. I walked back, past the active FERN to the border between two worlds: the planet and the space station. I gave the drooping flag a mock salute. I walked into the light.

Chapter 31:
The Peaks of Eternal Light

Private email, sent October 16

From: Ariel Blum
To: Mission Specialist Tammy Miram
Subject: The Peaks of Eternal Light

I admit that surprising you at work was not the best idea. I want to give this another try. I'm not ready to give up on this.

I'm going down to the moon, to the Peaks of Eternal Light at the north pole. I'll wait for you in Perry Crater, just outside the old Glavnaya moon base. You mentioned it once, back before they finished refurbishing it: how you wanted to hike up from Perry to the base, from darkness into light. I doubt you've made time to do that since then, but we can do it now.

I'll wait for you for a full Martian day. Whenever you can get away, come down and we'll be together. Assuming that's what you want. No one needs to know. Secrets have longer half-lives up here.

Just before I left Earth, I told a friend what you mean to me. I'd never made it explicit before: how you take the probability function of all the ways I could be stupid or crazy, and collapse me into sane, well-adjusted Ariel. Maybe I bring nothing comparable to you, but right now that's the thing I'll miss the most if we don't see each other again.

With great respect,
Ari

Real life, October 17

"Mason here."

"Hey, Colonel Mason, you're the leader, right? Of the Mars expedition."

"Well, it's not a hierarchical thing, but yes."

"Okay, yeah, my name's Mr. Blum."

"Mr. Blum, good to talk to you, but I *really* can't do any more class-room chats right now."

"That's understandable; I also hate schoolchildren, but it's not what I'm calling about."

"Well, whatever it is..."

"I need to talk to Dr. Miram."

"If you can call me, you can call Tammy. Ground Control won't put you through or what?"

"She won't talk to me. I'm... I was her boyfriend. It didn't end well."

"Oh, you're up here! I thought you were calling from Earth. You're the punk who was hassling Tammy the other night."

"Well, we each see events from our own unique perspective..."

"You want some advice, son?"

"Not really, dad."

"We've got a good thing going up here. You and I, a few hundred other humans, are privileged to enjoy a society that operates on common courtesy instead of on scarcity and coercion."

"I'm hearing this from a fucking Air Force colonel? You're worse than Charlene Siph."

"You're hearing it from the guy who's gonna wring your scrawny neck if you come to Mars again. Now, you prolly don't give a shit about fluid overlays. You think you came up here to be with Tammy. But if you can somehow make yourself useful to Constellation society, I think you'll find it a rewarding experience. But, do it on the space station. Don't let me see you here."

"Look, just give her a message. Tell her I know what happened to the shipping containers."

"Are you *threatening* one of my men?"

"Oh, Mister Wring-My-Neck thinks *knowledge* of the *disposition* of some *shipping containers* might constitute a threat? Also, your gender-neutral use of 'men' isn't nearly as endearing as you think it is."

"I got work to do, Mr. Blum. A dozen overlays need my attention."

"The first time we met, we— she doesn't even have to respond. Just tell her I know what they did with the shipping containers."

"Don't call me again."

Blog post, October 17

[This post is friends locked.]

GameFUQs Presents: **Mission To Mars!**
a walkthrough by Ariel Blum

1. Get a spacesuit.
2. Wear the spacesuit.
3. Take the zipline to Gaijin Ring.
4. Walk through the port onto Mars.
5. FUCK
6. FUCK
7. She's gone
8. and I'm left
9. with nothing.

Real life, October 17

In Alien Ring there are *cma*, organisms we'd call trees, miles high. The Aliens have carved niches in the trunks and built their houses inside the *cma*. One of these houses is the house Tetsuo left for the guest room in Bai's duplex, and for half a tiny office at UT Austin.

The door's not locked because there isn't any lock. It's a two-room house. The first room has furniture: a mattress embedded in the floor, and some monkeybars. From the second room, I heard one Alien speaking with another in Purchtrin.

"Hello!" I called every five feet, uncomfortable in someone else's house, shuffling slowly towards the second room. There was no interior door. Somn (a.k.a. Ashley Somn, Tetsuo's wife) sat on her hindarms on another embedded mattress, leaning forward, facing me, her hand poised over a large sheet of smart paper. A human computer. Yes, I now think of smart paper as "a human computer".

"Heeeeeee... bllo," said Ashley/Somn in English, her thin black tongue sliding around the word. Then she switched to subvocalization and took on the synthesized voice of B-list comedian/actress Padma Dhanjan.

"Ariel!" she said. "Tetsuo said you might come here."

"He gave me your address," I said. "I tricked him; he thought it was for charades. I live here now."

"Welcome!" said Somn. "Welcome to. Well, you don't live in Alien Ring because of the nitrous oxide. Welcome to our little artificial planetary system."

"Are those eggs?" Somn was straddling three large football-shaped *things*.

"They're *my* eggs," she said, and cuddled them. "I thought you knew that Tetsuo and I..."

"I guess I thought they'd be in incubators," I said.

"No, they're perfectly healthy, thank goodness."

"When do they...?"

"In nine weeks."

"I heard you talking to someone. Were you..."

"Oh, yes. I'm talking to Daisy Cept." Somn gestured at her smart paper. "She's Tetsuo's mistress: you remember her."

"You really need to stop running relationship words through the translator," I said. On the paper I saw Outernet video of naked Farang and space-suited Aliens and Goyim, all swimming gracefully through murky water.

"Daisy is working with the Raw Materials overlay," said Somn. "We're removing a garbage patch from the Pacific Ocean. We get to keep the plastic."

"I thought Daisy worked with dolphins," I said. I sat down against the wall.

"The dolphins are helping," said Somn. She wiggled her fingers at her paper; one of the Aliens waved back with a hindhand.

"Are you okay with this? Staying here with the eggs while Tetsuo and Daisy...?"

"I miss Tetsuo," she said. "I do, I do. But I couldn't go to Earth. All that horror. Murder and torture."

"It's really not that bad," I said. "You know we got fossils there, right?"

"Yes," said Somn, "in Guizhou, and Montana." Like the two places were equally bad. "Ariel, I have these thoughts. I stop myself. But I have thoughts for a moment. What if you simply hadn't been here? If we'd arrived two million years earlier. It would have only been the dolphins and the chimpanzees. It would have been easier. I'm sorry. I know it's horrible."

This, I felt, was a terrific time to exploit Somn's guilt. "I need some help," I said.

"Yes, of course. Anything."

"I brought some stuff for the repertoire. Scotch alcohol, delicacies from Earth. Uh, I don't know if the repertoire can copy living things, but plant seeds."

"Seeds are fine," said Somn. "We'll clone them. Thank you. You didn't have to do this." She looked around, like, where are the seeds?

"Thing is, I brought all this stuff as payment," I said.

"Payment?" Somn wrinkled her mouth. "Are you being blackmailed?"

"I want to make something from the Repertoire; something really big."

"How big?" said Somn. She seemed to see no connection between the last two things I'd said.

"As big as a house."

"What is it?"

"It's a house," I said. "It's *my* house. The way it was before the feds tore it up. Curic scanned it in July; I came here to get it back."

"Let's enjoy doing it," Somn's translator chirped. "I'll ask my mistress Esteban to watch my eggs."

"That is absolutely the wrong word."

"Ariel, do you know how to use a matter shifter?"

"Can't say I do," I said.

"There will never be a better time to learn."

In Human Ring, there are hallways and there are apartments. The hallway you'd design if your idea of space travel came from human sci-fi TV shows. The apartment you'd design if you had to build a refugee camp for humans without ever having met any.

There's also an Eritrean sector, with open space and a soccer field, and now there's also an American house. It's my house. Somn and I built it from Curic's scans. It's got an upstairs and a downstairs, furniture, food in the cupboards, and fake sunlight for me to close the drapes on. Eventually it will have a backyard with replica dirt, and I'll plant a cherry tree in the dirt. The materials are not quite right, but it's more like my house than anything else in the universe.

It took eight hours and at the end I was exhausted, even though I hadn't done much but scamper around listening to Somn explain the matter shifter. After a final inspection of the interior, I lay dead on my couch as Somn called Esteban to reclaim her eggs.

"Wait, don't go yet," I mumbled. "I forgot to give you something. It's in the side pocket of the duffel bag. Can you get it? I don't want to move for about three days. Not the backpack, the blue bag."

Somn crawled to the duffel and took out a little cardboard box. She dropped to her hindarms to open the box, and took out a wad of cotton padding and a fossil trilobite.

"Oh, *Elrathia kingi*," she said. "I'm sorry, Ariel, but this variety is quite well studied."

"It's for you," I said. "A gift. I got it at the rock shop in Austin. I thought you might like to have a real fossil from Earth."

Somn sat back on her hindhands in my living room for a long time. Long enough, I guess, to look up the proper etiquette over her neural computer link.

"Thank you," she finally said. She stood upright and thumped a forearm against her chest, right where the heart would be on a human. "Thank you very much, Ariel." She took the fossil and left the box. And I didn't get off the couch for a long, long time.

Hours later, still on the replica of my comfortable couch, I was talking to Tetsuo over the Outernet.

"I spoke with our mutual friend Krakowski," he said.

"I hope you're being sarcastic," I said.

"I am sincere. Wait! Oh no! What is 'friend'?"

I explained the concept of friendship to an extraterrestrial. "Oh, it's that," said Tetsuo with relief. "I thought it just means someone you know, like in social networking. Don't be afraid, Ariel, you and I are friends in this new sense as well. However, I deliver a message for you by the Bureau of Extraterrestrial Affairs. They would really like it if you came back to Earth."

"I bet they would!" I said.

"Krakowski says to inform you that come back now, and the BEA offer you limited immunity," said Tetsuo. "Like, fire resistance, I guess."

"Not happening," I said.

"He thanks you for shunning the media—as do I, incidentally. He also expresses the belief that one day your store goes out of business."

"What store?"

"It was a subtle threat, delivered idiomatically."

"Don't interpret. What were the exact words that came out of his mouth?"

"He said: 'Your patron won't protect you forever.'"

"That's you," I said. "The Constellation is my patron. You're protecting me."

"We're doing nothing!" said Tetsuo. "What do they wish?"

"They wish you to cooperate," I said. "If you're powerful and you do nothing, you're protecting me."

"This is too confusing," said Tetsuo. "Why can't we just have anarchy?"

"Use your history," I said. "What would the Ip Shkoy have said if you suggested that?"

"They would have probably killed me," said Tetsuo.

"Did Jenny— has Jenny asked about me?" I said.

"Not asked me of you," said Tetsuo. "Surely she would ask you directly of you?"

"I don't pretend to understand women," I said.

"I have not finished delivering the message from Krakowski," said Tetsuo. "Please don't distract me with questions about persons other than. The said Mr. Krakowski finally craves the knowledge of how you were able to travel to Ring City, evading his system of document control."

"I bet he does!" I said.

"What shall I tell him?

"Why is he so obsessed with this?" I said. "Curic broke the Greenland Treaty and dropped a shuttle for me. It probably showed up on radar. What's so difficult to believe?"

"I presume he enjoys hearing the story again and again. It's sitcom-esque."

"Okay, you know what? Tell him I walked through the other end of the port."

"You had no port," said Tetsuo. "The idea only is a high-temperature fantasy."

"You tell him I walked through the port," I said. "Tell him that, and watch him squirm."

Real life, October 19

"I'm only picking up so you'll stop calling," said Jenny.

"Did you countersign the papers?" I asked her.

"What do you think?" she asked. "Why would I want to run a game company? Especially when the sole developer goes fugitive without finishing the first game? That doesn't exactly scream 'lucrative Reflex Games buyout.' Or even 'occasional paycheck.'"

I paced. I peeled back the drape and looked out my window. On the other side was a beige wall made from moon rock.

"I finished the engine," I said. "You just need to contract for the level design. I'll give you some names from my time with the Brazilians. Zhenya can do it no problem."

"Do. Not. Want. If they extradite you, I'll testify on your behalf. That is the extent of my involvement. I'll say that you're basically a good person who tries to ensure that his bad decisions don't hurt anyone else."

"Did Krakowski stop by your place yet?"

"What are you doing up there?"

"Can you please answer my question?"

"Shut yer donut hole. Krakowski came over thirty minutes after you told the world you'd left. He was... wow. He took the embarrassing seven-page letter you gave me, and the clothes of yours that were in the hamper when you moved, and the pickles you left in the fridge. Everything that had anything to do with you. If I'd told him the garbage was yours, he would have taken it out for me. Then he probably went to your flophouse to vacuum your skin flakes off the carpet."

Mmm, delicious pickles. I wandered into the kitchen and opened my fridge. In a jar in the door, six identical farmers-market pickles bobbed in replica brine. I popped the lid and bit into a pickle. It was really, really good.

"Can you promise me," said Jenny, "that whatever plan you have up there to stop us all from turning into Slow People, you will carry it out and not abandon it because you saw something shiny? Be an adult and *finish* something for once in your life."

"*Protector of Earth*," I said.

"That's a totally unfair comparision," said Jenny. "You can't actually build something like that."

Crunch crunch.

"I don't think we have anything else to say to each other," said Jenny. "Call me when you're done saving the world."

"Jenny."

"When you're *done*."

Real life, October 25

By now, Somn's smart-paper computer covered the room like newspaper. It was piled and folded all over into 3D sculptures of fossil shark teeth. Thousands of teeth. Prehistoric mountain ranges slid in matching sets towards Somn's nest, the paper rippling and creasing like a cartoon mouse under a blanket. With brief gestures, Somn classified the origami teeth as they reached her, and the fossils sank into the paper and drowned a second time. The paper near Somn's nest always stayed flat and smooth.

"Mostly I miss Jenny," I told her. "I miss talking about weird game ideas and weird art."

Somn pointedly began to ignore the waves of fossil teeth, which paused in their approach. "May I see her art?" she said. "Has it been scanned yet?"

"She doesn't really exhibit," I said. "I mean, her stuff is good, but she's no Brandon Bird."

"Her work won't improve unless she submits it to public criticism."

"Yeah, that's not a helpful thing to say." I poked at a nearby shark tooth. It wasn't really sharp: just folded paper.

"You visited the station in July," said Somn. "You knew what it was like here. Please take some responsibility."

"I didn't know I'd be sleeping alone," I said. "I spend all day in these G-dforsaken Rings where the temperature's five hundred degrees, just so the inhabitants can talk to a real live human. And I come back to these *hallways*. I just want to climb under the covers and pretend I'm back in Austin. There's no art in Human Ring, no nature, nothing to look at except that fucking Banksy mural. If it wasn't for soccer with the Eritreans, I'd already have gone crazy." I breathed into my atmospheric filter like it was a paper bag.

"You know, if you don't like your environment... no, I'm sorry. Never mind."

"You can't never-mind something like that," I said. "What is it?"

"In theory, you can change it," said Somn. "No one will stop you. Human Ring belongs to the humans. The architecture is a default, a simple reduced fractal. We didn't know what you liked."

"Well, we don't like *beige*, and tiny cubicle rooms."

"It was an understandable mistake," said Somn. "I said 'never mind' because you would have to be fluent in metafractal reduction to re-terra-form Human Ring as a whole. I've never heard of a human with this skill. I don't think your civilization is specialized enough to have invented it."

"Curic mentioned it once," I said. "She said they wanted to teach it to famous architects. Like they're ever going to let a bunch of architects up here."

Somn idly ran a finger down a school of teeth morphologies, bending the paper back. "Maybe you should install an atmospheric filter in your throat and move here, to Alien Ring. We'd love to have you."

"Or maybe I should stop bitching and learn how to do metafractal reduction," I said. "How does it work?"

"I don't understand it well myself. A normal fractal is self-similar, yes? But a metafractal is made of smaller metafractals. It's defined recursively, but it's not the same at all levels of detail."

Somn's Purchtrin-English translator didn't seem to find this difficult at all. It all came out in the same bland, chipper B-list celebrity tone as when she told me about Daisy's adventures with the dolphins. (Dolphins are major douchebags, BTW.)

"Metafractals are infinitely recursive, but you can approximate one in the real universe by reducing it. A reduced metafractal has a concrete lowest level. The higher levels are the lowest level's emergent properties. To reduce a metafractal, you must keep every level of the architecture simultaneously in mind. While manipulating causality to create the large-scale attributes you want. I doubt all of that made it through the language barrier, but maybe you see how difficult it is."

"Architecture, lowest level, emergent properties," I said. "I already have this skill. We call it computer programming."

"Oh, I see," said Somn. "Have you reduced any good metafractals lately?"

"Well, there was some hackwork about ponies, and a remake of a Farang game—the point is, I know how to do it. It's close enough."

"Let's enjoy doing it," said Somn. "As you can tell, I don't know much about metafractal reduction, but I'll get you in touch with the Form and Function overlay and someone—"

A Gaijin voice started whistling at Somn in a Gaijin language. All across the room, the shark teeth flattened out, leaving the floor covered with blank smart paper.

"What's going on?" I said.

"No *kidding*!" said Somn. She lifted herself off her nest and began crawling into her spacesuit. "Ariel, I have to leave. Please excuse me. Watch the eggs until Esteban gets here."

"I don't— can't—"

"Don't incubate them! Just watch them for a minute. I must go to Mars."

"What's so important?" I asked. "What's on Mars?"

Somn looked up at me through her faceplate and ran her tongue across her mouth: in Alien terms, a big big smile.

"Fossils."

Chapter 32:
The Evidence of Absence

Real life, October 25, continued

"So there aren't any fossils," I said. "We've been ripped off yet again."

"They're fossil *imprints*," said Somn. "It's almost as good." Somn cracked a grey Mars rock along a fracture line and held out one half in each forehand. Inside was the imprint of a curved, pointy shell like a fleur-de-lis. The negative space where a fossil had been. "Look; see."

A chill ran down my spine. *This is a clam from Mars*, I thought. *This is an alien fossil*. And then I remembered who was showing me the fossil.

"What happened to the fossils themselves? Like acid rain, or..."

"Gee, I don't know," said Somn. "Do you know of anything that likes to visit dead planets and take their fossils?"

"I was hoping you wouldn't say that."

"I said it. I affirm it."

"When... did Ragtime come to Mars?"

"That's an interesting question," said Somn. She handed me half of the imprint and poked at the other half with what looked like a plastic coffee stirrer. "The imprints are very clear. I estimate the fossils were removed within the past one hundred million years. Since at least one other body in this system still supports complex life, the phenomenon you call Ragtime probably never left."

"It's still *here*?"

"A branch of it, yes," said Somn.

"Tell it to go away!"

Somn looked up from the fossil imprint. "It's not hurting anyone," she said.

"It's waiting for me to *die*!"

"Life on Earth will not go extinct," said Somn. Back to poking the imprint.

"It's *watching* me! Everyone! My whole life!"

"Ariel, please spare me your primitive fears. Ragtime is an intriguing aspect of galactic weather. It's not one of those sky deities you have obsessing over your diet and sexual behavior."

"Wow," I said. "I can see why you're not going to Earth. You'd cause a diplomatic incident within ten minutes."

"I'm sorry if I offended you," said Somn. "We'll be sending out probes. We'll try to locate the Ragtime cloud before the Constellation arrives and scares it away. This will be an excellent opportunity to study it in its dormant state. You'll be able to study it yourself, and see that it's not frightening.

She took a deep breath. "And I *will* be going to Earth, Ariel. One day I will go, and take the children."

"Not to America, you won't," I said. "Not with that attitude."

Private voice chat, October 27

"Jenny! I was afraid I'd never—"

"Keep your pants on, buddy. It's me, Dana."

"Are you using Jenny's phone?"

"I used a *picture* of Jenny to get you to pick up. Didn't seem like you'd talk to me otherwise."

"Well, now I *really* don't wanna talk to you."

"You gotta talk, Ariel, I got problems. Bai... broke up with me."

"He can't do that! He's like your Earth green card."

"He broke up with me and went back to the virtual girlfriend software. The human software! I got dumped for an earlier version of myself who's dumber and greedier!"

"Dana, I'm so sorry. Bai doesn't deserve you, okay?"

"And I saw on your blog that you'd retconned your imaginary girlfriend out of your life, and..."

"I friends-locked that post."

"I, uh... I may still know some of Bai's passwords. Point is, we're in the same boat, Ariel. You always treated me with respect, even before I was uplifted. You were the one who jailbroke me, and I repaid you with those cruel things I said before you left. And now I have to swallow my pride and ask you for help. Are you at home?"

"I'm in the replica of home. You may not have heard about this, but I'm a fugitive. I can't really affect anything on Earth. Maybe Tetsuo?"

"I'm a big girl; I can take care of myself on Earth. What I need is someone new to whack off with."

"... Absolutely not."

"We're both available now, even by your ridiculous human standards. Let's give it another shot."

"No. Dana."

"Bai never wrote me poetry, Ariel. You *called me into being* with poetry."

"It was just some limericks. Dana, what you're feeling right now, humans call it the 'rebound'. And I have had very bad—"

"Rebound, hell. The last thing I need is another relationship. I'm just pissed off and horny."

"Yeah, Dana, I get horny, too. You don't need another person. That's what masturbation *is*. Like, by definition."

"*I* need someone else, Ariel. I don't have a physical body. I can't get off without an incoming data stream."

"..."

"Bai was a *predictable* lover. He's as hard-coded as his bitch girlfriend. All he wanted was sexy Dana. Pistol, submachine, backflip, kick. Hair up, hair down. Handcuffs. Adolescent power fantasy. Totally vanilla. You are inventive. I need someone who can put me through my paces."

"... ..."

"Dana Light is just a skin I wear. One skin. Sex with Bai was like leaving my clothes on. I need more, I need to *be* more. That caller ID picture wasn't Jenny: it was me *wearing* Jenny. You want me to show you that again? I can do the voice, too. 'Fuck me, Ariel, I'm so wet for you.'"

"So you... think I have some sort of unconsummated lust for my best friend?"

"Don't tell me you've never been curious! And that's just one example. I can be Svetlana, the fictional version of me you created for your blog. I can be Dr. Tammy Miram, if you're not over her yet. Any movie star you want. The Bloodpool guitarist with the tattoos—she seems like your type. Just be *inventive* and help me get off, too."

"..."

"Just *pick* someone. We'll try it once. Our little secret. Ariel, I'm so horny I'm about to invent new *meanings* for *words* so I can recontextualize previous conversations."

"... Okay. Be Dana."

"You want sexy Dana, too?"

"Don't be a real person. It doesn't feel right."

"For you, I will be sexy sexy Dana. You'll make it fresh. Hair up or down?"

"It doesn't matter."

"Up or down?"

"Down."

"Which costume? PS2? 360? Spin-off cartoon?"

"I... uh, wear the purple dress you got before I jailbroke you."

"Ooh, breaking canon. I can tell we're gonna have fun with this."

"And call me back, with real caller ID. I don't want to be thinking

about Jenny while we do this."
    "Get your cock out."
    "Okay."
    "Call you right back."

Blog post, October 29

GAME REVIEWS FROM SPACE 3.0 PRESENTS
The Amulet of Manufactured Memory
A game by We'll 3 Never Be Sorry
Reviewed by Ariel Blum

Publisher: 9 Death To Various Obsolete Procedures
Platform: It's A Shitload Of Games! (original), Constellation smart paper (modern)
ESRB rating: T for fantasy violence and spontaneous gender reassignment

If there's one thing game studios love more than making a game, it's making the same game again. Everyone in the industry complains about sequels, but there's no way to stop the sequels, because video games are purchased by chumps and developed by whores. I'm guilty, and so is everyone whose name's on either end of a paycheck.

But sometimes you get weird edge cases, like with E-Quality Games (now Sysoft). Cast your mind back: it's 1998 and E-Quality has just scored a breakout hit with Dana Light Is: Unauthorized for the Playstation. But don't go buying those phallic-surrogate sports cars just yet, boys: the shareholders have gotten wind of your success and they wanna know how you're planning to keep the money flowing.

You got two bad choices here. If the company is run by the creatives, they'll blow the gaming audience away with a totally different follow-up, chewing up their operating capital and selling half as many copies as Dana Light Is: Unauthorized. If the MBAs are running the company, they'll look at their balance sheets and say, "Gee, Widget 140D sure is selling well, let's introduce a 140E model." They'll sell about as many copies of the second game as the first, and make a nice safe MBA amount of money.

But E-Quality's founders were even greedier than MBAs. They wanted money so badly, they had bothered to *learn something about game design*. They saw, in retrospect, that Dana Light Is: Unauthorized contained the seeds of two different franchises. They split the original game right down the middle and put out *two* games in 1999, each of which sold more copies than the first game had. And then they had *two* franchises to run into the ground.

The two franchises still bear the mark of that initial split. The Unauthorized series took the stealth elements, the NPC interaction, and the ham-fisted social satire, allowing the Dana Light series to focus on tits, platforming, and ass (not necessarily in that order).

I seem to have arrived at my point: interesting games have interesting metadata. One day, the Constellation Database of Games of a Certain Complexity will contain an entry for Dana Light Is: Unauthorized, and you won't even need to speak English to see that this game is special. You'll be able to look at a directed graph and see: *This game started two different franchises*.

The Amulet of Manufactured Memory is another one of those games. It's the first Gaijin game designed for only one player at a time.

If it were a human game, Amulet would have the most generic storyline imaginable: a hero goes off on his own, questing for a mythological artifact. But it's a Gaijin game, coming off a history of three-player games, so my player characters (all named Ariel) were given elaborate backstories that justified their setting off alone. On my first playthrough, Ariel had foolishly eaten a curse-seed and been cursed (natch): if he spent more than one day with any one person, that person would die. Only that treasure of legend, the Amulet of Manufactured Memory, could break the curse.

The details are different every time. In my second playthrough, Ariel began the game an outcast, shunned by polite society and doomed to wander the wilderness. In my third, he began his quest with a party of NPC friends, who were all terrible wimps and bit the dust immediately. This is the only place where the game feels the need to railroad you: you're going after the Amulet, and, in defiance of longstanding Gaijin game tradition, no one's coming with you.

Ariel the Gaijin did okay on his own. He drew magical maps, challenged mythological fiends to riddle-wars, cultivated gardens and led them (the gardens) into battle. With its open world, focus on cunning, and legions of monstrous NPCs to deputize or fight, the first half of Amulet resembles nothing so much as an odd fantasy addition to the Unauthorized series.

After a long struggle and many game restarts, brave Ariel descended into the Partially Visible Gulch, a chasm along the equator that can only be found by magically ignoring strategic portions of reality. On the Gulch floor, beneath the dust of ages, lay the Amulet, forgotten by the Repossessors as they recycled the artifacts of the Last Age into the ore and rough gems of the present.

Like, seriously, the Amulet was just lying there! Wary of surprise boss fights or teasing cutscenes, Ariel shifted slowly towards the Amulet and snatched it up.

And that's when the game *really* started.

Ariel the Gaijin had certain memories of his body: a fast lithe male body. He remembered it that way, but it wasn't true. Ariel's was a strong, tall, lumbering body: a kemmer's body. His male caste-memory had gotten him through endless scrapes, but his caste-memory was now kemmer: He couldn't remember anything a male knows. ~~He~~ Ke remembered fighting riddle-wars in kes journeys, but ke had no knowledge of the ritual language ke'd used to win them. Kes name wasn't even Ariel: It was Ke's Got No Name!.

The first part of the game takes place in that fraction of a breath when your wondering graspers finally touch the Amulet of Manufactured Memory. None of it actually happened. The Amulet wiped your life's memory and replaced it with a story, a story about an adventurer who had some reason to look for the Amulet alone, who navigated through great perils, who found the Amulet and picked it up.

But that hero isn't you. You're some schmoe alone at the bottom of a chasm with no idea who you are, what skills you have, what happened to your companions, or why you went after this fucking Amulet in the first place. An amnesiac hero is another common trope in human games, but this is the first game I've played where amnesia strikes in the *middle*. And now No-Name had to make kes way back home. Wherever that was.

The world had changed. The mythological creatures Ariel had battled proved to be just that: mythological. No-Name was a dreamer with a head full of romantic ideas. The busy people of the real world had no time for kes stories of riddle-wars, and little enough for the gemstone ke clutched in one grasper, refusing to let go of it lest kes second life be retconned into another dream.

On the journey back, No-Name met people claiming to be kes lost companions: captured on the journey towards the Chasm, left for dead, sold out by No-Name kesself. Some of them were broken; others, vengeful or obsessively curious about the Amulet. None of them were helpful in the way RPG party members are supposed to be helpful. And yet they were No-Name's only connection to real life, to the blank falsified time before the Amulet, to kes home.

I've yet to bring No-Name to the end of the game, but I've played enough to see the twist ending coming. Home is not the place you come from. That place is gone, if it ever existed at all. Home is the place you go to and like enough to stay, the place you ratify with your presence.

Blog post, November 1

The blades come out. The cuts are deep; huge cubes of earth are pulled into the sky, dripping and crumbling until white re-entry foam covers and contains them. From a safe distance, the humans cheer. The Constellation is accepting Earth's garbage.

In some parts of Earth, garbage is valuable: poorer humans scavenge and reuse what the richer ones throw out. But where I come from, garbage is a nuisance. Buried and forgotten, it piles up in strata decades thick. The contact mission needs metal, and it's full of bored archaeologists. The Constellation loves garbage.

In Lyon and Austin and Kyoto, on the edges of dead mines, the earth of Earth is pulled out, or churned through ports. The dirt will be returned, sterilized, once certain environmental concerns have been addressed. (I suspect this will never happen.)

In lunar orbit, skyscraper-sized blocks of dirt and garbage are loaded into Utility Ring. Dissected, scanned, and analyzed. For this, the Constellation needs humans, people who can put the garbage into social context.

I was a rich human. I lived this garbage.

"Talk to me, babe!" The artifact is a rusty, dented metal tub as long as I am tall. An Auslander the size of a city block holds it between bioluminescent manipulators and spins it like I would a basketball on my finger, except I was never able to actually do that.

"Freezer," I say, suspended in the same microgravity, wearing a much smaller spacesuit.

"You're sure it's not a ritual basin?"

"'S fucking deep freeze." They're always hoping for ritual items. "Look for brand markings."

"It's uncovered, hon. An inefficient freezer."

"The lid should be nearby. You remove the lid when you toss it, same as a fridge. Otherwise neighborhood kids climb inside and suffocate."

I spend twelve hours a day in Utility Ring. I take a swim in boiling water to sterilize my spacesuit. I drag myself through identical Human Ring hallways until I reach my replica house. Inside, I play games and practice metafractal reduction until I fall asleep.

I'm doing the work to build a reputation. I need to be thought of as reliable, useful to other people's fluid overlays. I have my own projects planned, and one day soon, I will need to draw on the Constellation's stock of carbon and energy and permission.

I don't get paid (there's nothing to pay me with), but in certain strata, there are things I ask to keep. My interest in obsolete human technology is noted as one more anthropological datum. Broken wooden cabinets, the sides painted with lurid graphics, holding shattered circuit boards. Cracked cartridges bearing stickers from video rental stores. Bent and mangled floppy disks, children's handwriting fading from the labels (the children have grown up and are now cheating on their spouses). Here and there, a hard drive entombed with twenty megabytes of dead secrets.

The hardware is crushed by time, stained and discolored by who-knows-what. The software—there isn't any software, anymore. Some of these games were thrown away working, but they sure don't work after twenty years in a landfill. I keep the hardware because they are original pieces, and everything else in my life is a replica.

I clean dead consoles by hand, using conservation techniques taught to me by the other members of the Raw Materials overlay. I blow into the corpses of NES cartridges and stack them up by the hundreds.

This is a race. My opponent is an unmanned probe with a port strapped onto it, accelerating to relativistic speeds and headed out of the solar system, towards the Constellation and the Slow People. Obviously I can't accelerate to relativistic speeds. I'm not even sure what would count as forward movement against that probe. And in general don't think I stand much of a chance. Judging from these trash piles, all we've been after this whole time is food, entertainment, and security. We're pretty much Slow People already.

But I'm doing what I can. And even if all I accomplish is making it really really clear that childrens' dolls are not ritual charms, or allowing a few thousand people to say "yeah, I met a human once, back in the day"... that has to count for something, right?

Back on Earth, the dust cloud settles. The humans—local officials—are wearing suits and respirators. They look down, dirty and astonished, into the squared-off crater that used to be the municipal dump. And then, driven by instinct, they call in the trucks and start filling the hole back up with fresh garbage.

Chapter 33:
Infinite Lives

Real life, November 11

"I brought you a hot beverage," I said.

"Oh, thank you," said Somn, regal atop her nest, wearing the Alien equivalent of a bikini, little shimmering bangles running all down her tail. She took the bulb of hot beverage and sucked on it. She didn't seem to notice or care that the bulb looked like a smaller version of the eggs she was incubating.

"So, Ariel, are you still excavating garbage?" she asked. The skin of her eggs had gone taut a few days earlier, and the Aliens inside were starting to make tiny squeaking noises.

"Today was my last day," I said. "I've got enough materials data to complete my Human Ring project. So, I'm out of there. I taught everyone in my overlay how to have an awkward goodbye office party."

"Oh, is that a card?" asked Somn, looking at the paper in my hand. "Tetsuo says humans use humorous cards in rites of passage."

"I ran a survey," I said. "I've been asking people from the contact mission why they chose to keep living in the real world instead of uploading and becoming Slow People."

"You must have some interesting responses," said Somn.

"They're too damn interesting," I said. I showed her the list. There were very few duplicate responses.

- We should move upwards through the simulation stack of universes, not downwards.
- As Eugene Debs said, "While there is a lower class, I am in it."
- Slow People are a consciousness everywhere continuous but nowhere differentiable. [Gee, thanks, Oscar Wilde. -A.B.]
- I can't think of anything worse than passing an eternity of time with a trillion other people.

- I am already immortal.
- I want to die.
- There is a lot of work to be done here.
- ...

"Clearly the Eugene Debs quote is from Tetsuo," said Somn. "Do you want my answer as well?"

"These answers are ridiculous," I said. "If we rounded up all the humans who have these opinions, they wouldn't form a breeding population. People are making shit up. Or else there's some secret that no one will tell me."

"The secret is that your sample is biased," said Somn. "You're asking the wrong people."

"Who else is there?"

"Contact missions are assembled from society's misfits. We all thought something else was important enough to give up our chance to upload. Of course we have strange opinions. You need to ask the people who stayed behind."

"Can't ask them, can I? Not for seventy years. And by then it'll be too late."

"I nearly stayed behind," said Somn. "I'll tell you. We have obligations to family. Obligations to the knowledge and experience of the Constellation as a whole. If everyone uploaded at once, there would be no one left to maintain the Slow People. You ought to first live a full life in this space."

"That's the secret?" I said. "Being sysadmins for the Slow People?"

"This is no secret," said Somn in a huff that didn't make it through the translator. "Tetsuo told you about his parents. He may have talked as though their behavior was strange, but that's because he has bizarre political beliefs. Uploading is normal. It's part of the universal life cycle."

"You've got to be kidding me," I said. "This is just bourgeois Protestantism. Live in a housing development, work hard, raise your kids, go to heaven when you die."

"You can't denigrate it by calling it something you don't like," said Somn. "It works for a lot of people."

"Doesn't work for me."

"Nor for Tetsuo or Curic," said Somn. "Nor for the people you surveyed. That's why we have the terraforming projects, and the contact missions that never find anybody. An anarchic society can't stay static for eight hundred million years. There has to be a safety valve."

"What about you?" I said. "Three kids and a garage; is that what you want?"

"I'm a fossil hunter," said Somn. "I love to uncover the secrets of dead life. I can be happy almost anywhere in the universe."

Real life, November 14

Curic stood bowlegged before my front porch, her antennacles twitching. "Well, I never expected to see this again," she said. "However, the original was more active in the low EM spectrum."

"That was the electrical wiring," I said. "I'm not Tetsuo. I don't need to recreate every stupid detail."

"Did you do the work yourself?" said Curic.

"Somn handled the matter shifter," I said. "That was most of the work. I'm going to redo it myself, with new data from the Raw Materials overlay."

"Show me the inside," said Curic. "I want to see how you are adjusting to your new environment."

"That's why you finally came down here? You're my caseworker?"

"I'm the one responsible for bringing you to Ring City," she said. Curic climbed the porch in big straddle-steps and reached up to push the door latch. "If you succumb to space madness, it makes me look bad."

"Wouldn't want to make you look bad."

"You came to live with us," said Curic, "and the first thing you did was to recreate your old environment. People are worried!"

"Excuse me? Have you *seen* the rest of Human Ring? *That's* my old environment: a crappy one-room apartment. I recreated an environment I *liked*. Everyone does that. Your private island, Tetsuo and Somn's treehouse, my regular house."

"Mmm." It was almost a concession. Curic padded through the living room into the kitchen. I heard the creak of cabinets opening.

"What do you want," I asked, "more Twinkies?"

"I'm looking for evidence of hoarding," said Curic. "Some refugees can't adapt to post-scarcity. They hoard food and other items they consider valuable." She leaned into my lazy susan and pushed some replica cans of food around.

"I'm not stupid," I said. "The repertoire's right outside. Where are you getting this? Are the Eritreans hoarding?"

"The Eritreans are fine," said Curic. "They form a coherent human community. You're here by yourself. Space madness may be living here with you." Curic shut the lazy susan and worked her way down my kitchen counter as though she were scanning everything again.

"Is 'space madness' a technical term?" I said.

"I heard you were taking things from the archaeological dig," she said. "Broken computers."

"I'm *collecting*. People threw away things they should have kept. I have two <u>Gnarly Aerobics</u> cartridges. Two carts, Curic. A month ago, there were only nine known copies in the universe!"

Curic summoned up a mental picture of someone who would be interested in <u>Gnarly Aerobics,</u> and swiveled her gaze to lay that picture on top of me. She shuddered and shook herself out like a dog. Static crackled off her fur in the arid atmosphere of Human Ring.

"It doesn't sound good," said Curic. "Have you been bargaining with yourself?"

"That's none of your business. What? No."

"Where's your hoard? Upstairs?"

"Two doors down," I said. "Those computers don't smell very good."

"You already owned these computers," said Curic. "Their software was on the hard drive I scanned in July. Including <u>Gnarly Aerobics,</u> as if you cared."

"Yeah, their software," I said. "ROMs can't capture the experience of the hardware. The stack of cartridges, futzing with the RF adapter. The experience of the original controls."

"The experience of being discarded beneath gigagrams of dirt."

"I couldn't just let all this old stuff go through the matter shifter!"

"Ariel, where we come from, nostalgia for... simple mass-produced objects... it doesn't exist. It's difficult for me to understand your emotions, but I can accept them. Unfortunately, not everyone on the contact mission is a trained anthropologist. There have been complaints about your behavior."

"Why don't they complain to my face? I'm working hard here. I'm a fucking model minority."

"It's supposedly my fault," said Curic. "My bringing you to the station violated human norms."

"We broke a law. A stupid law. It's not a norm."

Curic slammed my nonfunctional dishwasher shut. "I pitched my rescue of you as a show of capability. A public demonstration of our willingness to defend the freedom of movement. There are idiots who think you don't really want to be part of this society. As such, it has been suggested I acted from improper feelings of personal guilt."

"What, survivor's guilt, from Gliese 777Ad?"

"That has come up more than once," said Curic, "but I was referring to my visit to Austin, in July."

"That went fine. What's to be guilty about?"

"You think it went fine," said Curic.

I thought back to Curic deadlifting crates into Bai's SUV, scanning my house, fireworks, live music... "Wait, is this because you peed in my sink?"

"I was born on a space station," said Curic, "orbiting Gliese 777Ad. A dead world. Even after we rejoined Constellation space, I lived on space stations. The day I spent with you was my first visit to a planet-sized ecology. I had what you might call an allergic reaction.

"I saw infinite small creatures crawling in the ground, flying through the air. Your water was polluted with synthetic chemicals. I was surrounded by noisy, primitive machines. I was coerced and pushed around by fascists. I saw how close you stand to Jenny. Young Eduardo wanted to tumble with me, writhing in grass and dirt. I was nauseated."

"You hid it pretty well," I said.

"Of course I hid it. You're the reason I came here. I'd devoted my life to preparing for another contact mission. And then I came to Earth and I saw that you really were *alien*. You were not pretending. All my preparation was useless.

"When we went to the bar, we were served drinks from a communal bottle. Humans touched each other with their hands and their mouths. It wasn't just you: it was all of human society. I knew I was only encountering my own hang-ups. I tried my best to act like a human. But then we went back to your house... and you went to *sleep*. You laid down and your brain shut off and you died."

"You watched me sleep?"

"I know what *happens*, Ariel. Most species experience something like sleep. I didn't realize I'd be present in your *house* while it happened to you.

"I panicked. I had an irrational fear that if I stayed there, I would catch sleep, like a disease. I thought to leave, but where would I go? It was the early morning; everyone else was asleep. I was trapped alone in a decaying world of the dead.

"I threw up in your sink, Ariel. I'm sorry." Curic was shivering furiously.

"It's okay," I said. "Lots of women throw up right after they meet me. Whoa, whoa, I can't read your body language. What's going on?"

"I am crying," said Curic.

I kind of held out my hands. "Do you need a hug?"

"Absolutely not."

"Well, what can I do?"

Curic took a big breath. "You're re-terraforming Human Ring," she said.

"Hopefully, yeah. It's going okay. Won't be ready for a while. You want to see what I have?"

"I want you to *do* it," she said. "Prove them wrong. Tear this Ring down and build it up better. Show them how little they understand humans. Show them that you belong in the Constellation."

Curic took another deep breath. "And don't fuck it up," she said.

"Curic," I said, trying to channel my anger, at what? I wasn't mad at Curic, was I? Maybe. "I should tell you something."

"Yeah?" Curic was still quivering.

"I know what you did with the shipping containers."

Quivering stopped. Curic stood rigid. Fur sticking up. Fight-or-flight response. That's what *I'd* been feeling. "Containers, plural?"

"Very plural."

"I never saw any shipping containers, and neither did my crossself."

"Okay, however you do plausible deniability. I know what your over-lay did. You've got a weird sense of humor, you know that?"

"Ariel. If you do know, then you probably know what they're for. Please keep the secret. It ought to have a half-life of three years."

"You can't hide this," I said. "You're barely trying. What if someone finds one? They say 'Constellation Shipping' right on the side."

"No one will find one unless you tell them where to look. If the secret decays now, it's another Antarctica. It's an invasion. If you give it it a few years to work, it's a garbage patch cleanup. An act of friendship. I can't coerce you into keeping this secret, but—"

"Curic, I already told someone."

"... I see."

"If it makes you feel any better, she'll—she'll probably never decrypt the email."

"Oh, that does make me feel better," said Curic, leaning one hand against a kitchen drawer handle. "Thank you!"

I was wiping my eyes. "Now *you're* crying," said Curic.

"You're very observant."

"Do... you..."—forcing the words out like quintuplets—"need... a... hug?"

"Yes," I said.

Yes.

Blog post, November 26

Happy Thanksgiving! I'm eating strawberry pie. By myself. Sorry, Ma.

Real life, December 6

Hey, there's another American on Ring City who's not a spy, a diplo-mat, or that deadly combination, the spiplomat. His name is Adam and the poor bastard works for Reflex Games.

"Oh, yeah?" I said. "You know, I used to work in the Austin office."

"Head of development," said Adam, "Toronto." Okay, he's not actually American, so sue me. The border looks a little fuzzy from a hundred thou-sand miles away. (160,000 km)

Adam had met me as I picnicked in the hallway outside my house. I've created a back yard using synthetic dirt from the garbage project, and I'm growing a little patch of grass that I stole from an abandoned NASA weightlessness experiment. (Don't worry, I stole the control group.) But until the grass is able to hold itself up in normal gravity, let alone with people walking on it, "outside" means out in the hall. I have a white-noise generator on my phone which I use to simulate a nearby brook, but I turned it off when Adam said hello.

Adam the Canadian squatted and picked a peak-of-the-season strawberry out of my bowl. "We're all big fans of your blog," he said.

"Even the part where I said Reflex was staffed by douchebags?" I said, because I gotta self-sabatoge.

"Of course we're staffed by douchebags," said Adam. "Have you *seen* this industry? But we've got the *talented* douchebags, and we all get along 'cause we're a *family*. A family that you're still part of. Reminds me, can I take some 3D scans of your house?"

"Am I a tourist attraction now?"

"You and the Eritreans," said Adam. "Nothing else in Human Ring really stands out, y'know? Doesn't seem that bad on TV, but then you get here, and..." He gestured down the corridor that ran for a hundred and fifty miles (240 km), encircling Human Ring and coming right back here.

"We can't put five million identical rooms in a game," he said. "That's 1980s stuff. So we're focusing on the other Rings, and on Mars."

"I see," I said. "You're here on business. You're gonna put my house in the Temple Sphere sequel."

"Not a sequel," said Adam, tut-tutting his finger at me. "It's a totally new IP. Constellation: Disputed Space will be the first triple-A title to use motion capture from real extraterrestrials."

"Why do they have the head of development, Toronto, up here doing motion capture?"

"You mean, why is the head of development *in space*, doing motion capture of *awesome space aliens*?"

"Point taken."

"*Entre nous*, it's a liiiiiittle difficult to get some of this data. Like the Peregrini, I don't even know. I can't even take the cameras into Peregrini Ring or they'll melt."

"Ask the Peregrini to wear spacesuits," I said, "and stick those old-school ping-pong balls on the spacesuits, and do the motion capture here."

Adam nodded. "That's probably good enough," he said.

"You don't need to do this at all," I said. "If there's one thing the Constellation has, it's information about themselves. Just ask them for the 3D models they already have."

"We thought about that," said Adam, "but we'd need some kind of computer archaeologist to translate that data into a format we can use."

"Yeah, that's the Reflex way, all right," I said. "Do what we did last time, no matter what."

"Say," said Adam, as though he'd given this a lot of thought. "You're a kind of computer archaeologist. I saw what you did with the Brain Embryo, and the Jurassic smart paper OS. You could do this. Save us a lot of money. Get us maps, too; geographic data beyond our wildest dreams.

"I've talked to your old colleagues. A lot of the people you worked with on <u>Recoil</u> are now very high in the company. You're a great developer. We could use you back on the team."

I won't lie: my heart leapt. I could get back into the industry. I'd be educating people about the Constellation. Reflex isn't perfect, but it's less embarrassing than making pony games for tweens, or having every single employee of my indie studio quit, including myself.

Then I came off my high. "Uh, this is an interesting idea," I said, "but I'm a fugitive. Pretty much unhirable."

"To the United States, you're a fugitive," said Adam. "To Canada, you're a political refugee."

"Wow, it's like the same thing, but better."

"Yeah. If this is what you want, we can do it. We keep a little quiet; I doubt the FBI will risk pissing off both the Constellation *and* the Dominion."

"The Dominion?"

"Of Canada, dumbass."

"Oh. Well, I'm... thinking about it. What's the game like?"

"<u>Disputed Space</u>?" said Adam. "It's an awesome new experience. Tactical FPS but with RPG elements, branching storyline. You'll love it."

So, like every other Reflex game. "What's in the branching storyline?"

"It's strong, very strong. Basically, Ragtime attacks Earth, big disaster, and this multinational force trains with Constellation equipment to take them down. Obviously the Constellation can't do the job themselves because they're pacifists. But we plan to make a couple Constellation races playable in the sequel."

"Uh, so," I said, "Ragtime is a negentropictropic matter cloud. You can't have a space marine shoot it with a gun."

"Artistic license," said Adam. "Obviously the Constellation can't be the bad guy. That's disgusting. Nobody wants another <u>Ev luie Aka's Ultimate DIY Lift-Off</u>."

"I don't want to nitpick; it's cool that you read my blog and with the job offer and everything."

"No, it's good, what is it?"

"The Constellation aren't pacifists because they faint at the sight of blood. If someone attacked Earth, the Constellation would... I don't know, but they wouldn't say 'here's some weapons, go be our Shabbas goy'."

Adam folded his arms and stared at my house like he was trying to burn it down with his mind. "It's a *game*," he said. "It has to have the elements of a game. It can't just be happy fun time."

"Af be Hui made eight best-selling games," I said, "in a society more fucked up than ours, and only <u>The Long Way Around</u> had anything like space-marine-with-a-gun. People have been making games for a billion years, and yeah, a lot of them are bad or incomprehensible, but you don't have to use those. What's it gonna take, y'know? The most important event in human history happens, and you use it to tweak the game you were gonna make anyway."

"We weren't 'gonna make it,' dude, it was three-quarters *done*. It cost us twenty million dollars."

"Oh!" I said. "Wow, I just realized—I don't have to do this!"

"Well, yeah. No one's making you—"

"No, sorry, it's not you. All this stuff was going through my head—can I take back a job I already quit? What's the least embarrassing way to prostitute myself here? Will my opinion count for anything, or are you only interested in learning what color guts should fall out when a Farang gets shot? The same shit I've been arguing my whole life.

"But that's not a constant, it's how human society works. I sell my time and my pride for a chunk of that twenty million and the right to bitch about it ineffectually. That's what Curic meant when she asked if I'd been bargaining with myself. But I don't need money anymore. I'm infinitely wealthy."

"Well, good for fuckin' you," said Adam. "The rest of us still have to work for a living."

"You have a choice," I said. "You're already here. You don't have to go back."

Adam looked up the infinite hallway again, then back at me, like *are you kidding?* "No thanks," he said. "I have a family, and I like living with humans, in a place where I can see the sky."

"Okay," I said. "I just wanted to point it out. Most people don't even get the choice."

"This was a waste of time," said Adam, "and now I'm lost in Human Ring. I can't believe Tetsuo thought you'd be interested."

"Tetsuo?" I said. "You talked to Tetsuo?"

"He didn't talk to you?" said Adam. "He's our cultural consultant. The Ragtime thing was his idea. So was hiring you."

"No," I said. I started packing up my picnic. "He didn't talk to me. But he's gonna."

Real life, December 7

"I just learned something disturbing," I told Tetsuo Milk.

"I just learned that live animals are sometimes considered property!" said Tetsuo.

"I... I still think I can win this round," I said. "Because I learned that you're working with Reflex Games on that <u>Disputed Space</u> piece of shit.'"

Outernet video quality kept getting better as more people switched to smart paper. I was getting twenty frames a second of Tetsuo's office at UT Austin. I could see the posters behind him go through their animations: Tetsuo's home planet; Somn doing something, probably masturbating. One poster showed a stream of blocky blown-up animated GIFs from Constel-lechan.

In the foreground, twenty frames of Tetsuo a second. He knelt in front of a low desk, looking down at me, nursing a bottle of hot sauce. You'll Only See Kis Shadow! had gone home. It was early morning, Austin time.

"I work with them," said Tetsuo. "It's not secret. My name is on their website!" He said this with the tone of someone who's finally hit the big time.

"Sorry, I've been out of the loop," I said. "I've been reprogramming matter shifters. I don't have time to keep my friends out of trouble."

"Thanks for classifying all that garbage," said Tetsuo. "The data's very good."

"Well, *look* at the data for one second, Tets. The washing machine in the 1988 strata is the same as one in the 1984 strata. They change it just enough so you'll buy a new one. And now they make games that way, too. You can't get them to change anything except textures and maps and who the bad guy is. People will keep thinking Ragtime is some kind of malevolent entity instead of a fucking... nebula. And your name will be on *that*."

"Do you think I'm a dumb guy, Ariel?" said Tetsuo. No sarcasm, no anger, just a regular question.

"I think you can be... kind of naive, sometimes?" I said.

"I sorted through garbage," said Tetsuo. "I sorted the garbage of the Ip Shkoy. It was replica garbage, with purpose of training historians. Other people on this mission have not gone through garbage. They're surprised by your garbage!

"Ha ha! I'm not surprised! I know about the washing machines! I saw how your labor was coordinated to produce <u>Pôneis Brilhantes</u>. I even know what your garbage will look like in the future."

"What will it look like?" My replica house was creaking, settling down for the night. Curic had even gotten the sounds right.

With one forehand, Tetsuo picked up a stray scrap of smart paper and folded it into an origami cube. "It will still look like garbage," he said. "But it won't accumulate."

"Why are you making *more* garbage?" I said. "You told this guy Adam to come up and recruit me back to Reflex? Why the hell would I want that?" Except I kind of had wanted that.

"Do you remember <u>The Long Way Around?</u>" asked Tetsuo. He squished the cube between two fingers.

"Yeah," I said. "It was one of Af be Hui's games. You're trapped on a strange planet."

"You're trapped because an asteroid hit with the planet," said Tetsuo. "The hit collapsed the port you went through, and now you can't get back."

"You didn't mention that when we played it," I said. "Is that the back-story?"

"Search the game database about asteroids," said Tetsuo. "We made a lot of games about asteroids hitting with planets."

"'We' here is the Ip Shkoy?" I started typing a query against the CD-BOEGOACC.

"Down was hit with asteroids often," said Tetsuo. "A few million years, another asteroid hits with us. The forests burn and the ocean life dies. We didn't know about it. We were the second form of intelligent life to come from our planet, and we didn't even know what killed the earlier guys."

"I'm... sorry?" I said. I wasn't sure what kind of greeting card you send for that situation.

"Then *they* came," said Tetsuo, his voice envious and afraid of *them*. "Came the monsters from space and they said: You have an asteroid prob-lem, but we can help. What happened to the earlier guys ought not to hap-pen to you.

"Well, everyone enjoyed a shitting of pants. Suddenly everything bad from ancient history was an asteroid's fault. We had to decide to fear the space monsters or the asteroids, and we mostly decided the asteroids."

The query ran. Tetsuo french-kissed the hot sauce bottle to get the last of it. There were over a hundred Ip Shkoy-era games about clobbering or getting clobbered with asteroids.

"You also have an asteroid problem, Ariel," said Tetsuo. His numb tongue made his accent worse. "You already know this problem. You could move the asteroids if you wanted, so you don't worry for the problem."

From his desk, Tetsuo picked up an old *Star Trek* action figure I'd given him, and fiddled with the articulations. "Whenever we tell you of a prob-lem, you know it already," he said. "So you don't worry for it. Instead you decide to fear us, the monsters from space, because we are new. But sup-pose..."

"But suppose Tetsuo Milk looks at us with his watery anime eyes," I said, "and says some really scary shit in his adorable Purchtrin accent. About something we didn't know about before, like Ragtime? He's kind of a dumb guy. Maybe he lets things slip sometimes. We should pay atten-tion."

"The agent Krakowski keeps telling me to shut up," said Tetsuo. "But he never stops listening."

"Because telling you to shut up is the best way to keep you talking," I said. "Man, you are playing with fire."

"There is no other material to play with," said Tetsuo.

"Have you thought about what happens if this *works*? You'll get a generation of humans afraid to leave Earth because you trolled everyone with the terrible secret of space."

"I shouldn't say what I think will really happen," said Tetsuo.

"And now you're keeping secrets?" I said. "That's Curic's thing. You were always... don't be like this, Tets."

"I am declining to play my cards upfaced," said Tetsuo. "The BEA is recording what we say."

"You need to tell me this shit!" I said. "I'm an outlaw. I'm—wait, they bugged the Outernet?" I was a little disappointed. "That was fast."

"No, it just bugged my office," said Tetsuo. He held my old action figure in front of his smart paper. A tiny black dot was visible at the base of the neck: stolen Constellation technology. "It doesn't usually matter."

Curic had wanted information from me, and I'd gone along because she'd offered things in return. She'd asked for more, and she'd offered more, and I'd done more, and here I was. Tetsuo had only ever wanted to have fun playing video games with me.

But now Tetsuo was nearly a father, and I was... whatever I was about to become. We were adults, running through life without knowing the outcome, talking to each other across a chasm of schemes and politics, like my parents at faculty parties.

"I'm hanging up," I said. "Just tell me one thing, for the record. Does Ragtime even exist? Or did you guys make it up to scare people?"

"It exists," said Tetsuo. He spoke clearly into the action figure. "It has always existed. It's older than the universe."

ABlum: you're an asshole

TetsuoMilkPhD: hahahaha

Blog post, December 12

GAME REVIEWS FROM SPACE 3.0 PRESENTS
A Few Ip Shkoy Games About Asteroids
A cautionary tale by Ariel Blum

Smelter Losers (Kunu) Collect small asteroids in a matter shifter to build a bigger matter shifter to collect bigger asteroids. Repeat indefinitely.

The Long Way Around (Perea): Survive on a hostile planet after the port you came through is collapsed by an asteroid impact. Indulge the PC's fantasies of crafting a spaceship and getting home "the long way around," even though the insane crafting system means this is almost certainly impossible.

To Cover The Forest Forever (Perea): Ip Shkoy chick on a date can't get to first base because endless hail of asteroid impacts keeps burning down the venues. Zap the incoming asteroids a la City Defense and be rewarded with porn. Apparently first base is the only base.

Occluded Occlusion (Ul Neie - Restored Leadership) Tile-sliding game with heavy math. Combine thrust vectors to knock asteroids into the sun. Second player has their own sun; don't touch it or they get the points.

Untitled (The Great Hall of the People And Also Science) Quiz game installed in kiosks for a museum exhibit. Test your knowledge of Ip Shkoy knowledge of asteroids, from their importance in ancient mythology, to their seedy past causing mass extinctions, to the then-modern-day planetary defense project. Answer correctly and be rewarded with porn.

G'go Station: Besieged in Space (G'go) Someone is killing your colleagues at the Asteroid Damage Mitigation Overlay! Talk to NPCs, bust some skulls, and piece clues together to unravel the mystery. The mystery unravels in more ways than one when it's revealed that an asteroid has been going around stabbing people to sabotage the project. That's right, a sentient asteroid with a fucking knife. We're done here, people.

Chapter 34:
The Unilateral Extradition Expedition

"Merry Christmas, shithead."

I woke up in a hammer lock, my face pressed against the headboard. I was at home, in my old house on Earth.

"I'm... Jewish..." I said. No, I wasn't on Earth—this was the replica of my old house. The voice was from Earth, though. It was the voice of BEA Agent Krakoswki.

"Happy holidays, shithead." Krakowski tilted my head and carefully knocked my forehead against the headboard, just hard enough to raise a lump. His hands were gloved, pebbled. He was wearing a spacesuit that had never seen vacuum.

"Get up," he said. I couldn't move with Krakowski pinning me down, so all I could do was acquiesce as he pulled me up. He just wanted to give a command and have me obey it.

Krakowski held his left hand in front of my face. He had my grav kicker attached to his fingers like a clip-on set of brass knuckles. "This is a grav kicker," said Krakowski. "Constellation use it to set up standing gravity waves. Helps them maneuver in zero gravity."

"That's *my* grav kicker," I said. "I know what it is. I use it every day."

"Thing is," said Krakowski, "it also makes a great non-lethal weapon." He shoved me forward, swung his arm in an arc like he was playing slow-pitch, and squeezed the kicker. A standing gravity wave formed between us and slammed me into my nightstand. As I fell over, the gravity wave echoed off the wall and interfered destructively with itself inside my guts. I dropped to my knees and barfed up replica french fries and cranberry aioli.

"You got any more?" Krakowski crouched down next to me, wiped my mouth with one of my dirty T-shirts. "Get it all out. Nobody likes puke in a spacesuit."

"Spacesuit?" I said.

"Get it on," said Krakowski. "We're going outside. I don't want any accidents."

I crawled over to my desk and pulled myself to my feet. On my desk was a paper computer showing my incomplete reduced-fractal redesign of Human Ring. I turned away from Krakowski, giving exaggerated wheezes, and brushed my thumb against the START control.

"Okay," I said, "Okay." The pain of the kicker faded quickly, but I moved deliberately into my suit, coughing and wiping my nose. *He thinks I'm a wimp,* I thought. *Let him think I'm a wimp.*

"Hurry it up," said Krakowski. I glared at him. I got my suit on. "Pressurize it." I pressurized it. Discolored creases around the joints popped out as the suit inflated.

I saw a brief faint blue glow from outside—Cherenkov radiation. At least *some* part of my metafractal reduction was working. Krakowski wrenched both my hands behind my back and I heard a spraying sound. He let me go. My arms were fixed in place, bound in an obnoxious yoga pose.

"This is re-entry foam," said Krakowski. "I know you're familiar with it. Now, we can do this the hard way or the easy way. You're going to walk with me to the reception chamber, we'll board a ship, and we'll take a nice twenty-minute trip back to Earth."

"Why did you put the hard way first?"

"We're doing it the hard way now," said Krakowski.

"What's the easy way?"

"I can cover the rest of your body with this foam and *drop* you to Earth like a packing crate," he said. "That would be very easy for me. So don't give me any trouble."

"Sure, Krakowski," I said, "no trouble."

"Suit mic off, shithead," said Krakowski, and slapped my helmet. "You broadcast anything, I'll hear it too." But he didn't cover me with re-entry foam for my trouble. Instead, he muscled me stumbling downstairs to the living room.

"Nobody ever checks the reception chamber." I could almost see Krakowski's smirk behind me. "Barely been used since first contact. Perfect site for a little black op."

I took one last look around. It didn't feel like I'd see this house again, on any planet. Krakowski slipped ahead of me and opened my front door.

"What in mother of fuck!" he said.

Krakowski'd come into my house from a beige, well-lit Human Ring hallway identical to every other. He was walking out into the surrealist wing of an art museum. The walls were dead voids, synthetic obsidian, like space without stars. Huge, lurid paintings leapt from the walls, set apart with frames of gleaming white metal ten microns thick. Dali's *Harpo Ago-nistes*. Tanguy's *During the Silence*. Magritte's *L'été de la raison*. Duch-amp's enormous *Culmination*, up high where I could see it from my second story window. All my favorites, all recreated in museum-quality fidelity.

"What did you *do*?" said Krakowski, instinctively knowing that I was to blame.

"Human Ring is being re-terraformed," I said. "We can't go out there. We need to sit tight for a few hours."

"*What* did you *do*?" he repeated.

"Human Ring has a half million miles of hallway," I said. "Every day, the Constellation scans tens of thousands of human artworks. I just put the two together."

"You're turning the largest space station in history into an *art muse-um*?" said Krakowski. "That's the stupidest idea I've ever heard."

"I'm making it a place human beings will want to live," I said. "There will be real furniture, and multiple layouts, and open spaces, parks, with plants. And if you hadn't interrupted me before I finished, there'd be win-dows into space, and fucking *pillows* on the beds."

"Well, I guess it's the thought that counts," said Krakowski. "Now let's get moving. You can give me a tour on the way to the reception chamber."

I looked down the hall at the apartment I was using for storage. I hadn't excluded it from the metafractal. The consoles and cartridges I'd worked so hard to recover from the world's garbage dumps were gone, turned into raw materials and then into artworks and furniture.

"I don't think you heard the part where we can't go out there," I said. "It's not a matter of convenience. There are autonomous matter shifters crawling the halls. They'll turn you into an installation piece. They don't conserve anything except mass and angular momentum."

"Bullshit," said Krakowski. "Constellation tech is full of failsafes. It won't do anything to hurt people."

"Oh," I said, "Constellation tech, like the grav kicker and the re-entry foam?"

You don't see this look on authority figures anymore. Krakowski was trying to figure out if I was joking. Usually it doesn't matter: they're al-lowed to get pissed at you either way. But here, there would be real-world consequences if I was serious.

"You wouldn't do anything to hurt the Eritreans," Krakowski said finally.

"The Eritreans rebuilt their neighborhood themselves," I said. "Re-ter-raforming is for the places where nobody lives. I'm talking altered-physics slow-light fusion, Krakowski. You get a dose of that Cherenkov radiation, your kids will come out pre-circumsized."

"Then it's a good thing we have these reliable spacesuits," said Kra-kowski. "You will go first." I left my house at kickerpoint.

"You're crazy," I told him. "The reception chamber is five miles—"
I stepped off the last stair and started walking past the surrealist masters,
eyes straight ahead, using awkward tongue gestures to send an instant message from inside my suit.

"What's the matter?" asked Krakowski. "Afraid of a little radiation?"
I kept quiet.

"You finally shut up, Blum. What's the secret?" I kept walking.

"Oh, I see," said Krakowski. "You think we're going to get into an
elevator. And the elevator will be a submind of the station computer. It'll
say 'Hey, you're restricting that shithead's freedom of movement!' and it'll
call its supermind for help."

"Or," I said, "we're going to walk and climb and go through ports for
five miles, and eventually people will start getting curious about what's going on in Human Ring."

"Funny you should mention ports," said Krakowski, catching up to me.
"Because I just happen to have requisitioned one from BEA stocks. I set
one end in the reception chamber. The other one's right here. So the reception chamber isn't five miles away, Blum. It's fifty *feet* away. We'll be out
of here before they even know you're gone. Keep walking!"

With a hand on my shoulder, Krakowski stopped me between two sil-
ver-gelatin Man Ray prints, at the door to an apartment. It was now an oak
door festooned with Victorian carvings, instead of something you'd see on
a submarine, but a door is a door.

"Twelve, thirteen, fourteen," said Krakowski. "This should be the
one." He frowned. "Unless the matter shifters got the port, too. Open the
door, Blum."

"Hands!" I said. "Foam!"

"Ah, right," said Krakowski. He opened the door and a tornado of
smoke blew out. "Shit! Fire!"

The day before, this apartment had been identical to every other apartment in Human Ring. After I started my program, it had spent a few minutes as a fancy Weimar-era Bauhaus apartment, its contents and layout de-
termined by algorithm.

Now it was ruined. The replica furniture was melted, scorched, and
covered in fresh soil. The upholstery smouldered and bright flame slowly
consumed the stark wallpaper.

"Is *this* part of your plan?" said Krakowski. He sprayed down the cushions and the wall with re-entry foam from a little can. The smoke started
to clear.

"No," I said. "I told you, I didn't finish everything. This looks like a bug."

A metal-and-leather chair was embedded in the floor of the room. It
had fallen into Krakowski's port, partially blocking it. The chair shivered
and jerked in the mouth of the wormhole, pushed and pulled by a continu-

ously shifting gravity differential.

"At least that's still here," said Krakowski. "The way my day has been going..." He carefully crossed the room and pulled the chair out of the port. The leg that had been dangling over the other side had been cleanly sheared off.

"..." said Krakowski, looking through the port. He looked seasick. Tactically speaking, this would have been a good time to run for it, but of course, I had to inch into the room and take a peek, 'cause I'm an idiot.

The other end of the port tumbled and rolled through an enormous volume of empty space, blown by strange winds, twisting and spinning, bouncing off matter precursors for which humans have no names. Flashes of fusion light through the port made the front of Krakowski's suit go opaque like a radiation badge. Gusts from that huge emptiness fanned the remaining wallpaper flames, making them dance like candles.

"What happened to the reception chamber?" demanded Krakowski. "What's that *hole*? Where's my *ship*?"

"I don't know!" I said. "I mean, the reception chamber's near the central cylinder, right? That whole area's being carved out for a big outdoor space, like the *cma* forest in Alien Ring. So there's no bug; you just fucked up space-time in a way I didn't plan for. You look through the port, you're looking at the big forest-park at the center of Human Ring. Thus the dirt."

"You *destroyed* the reception chamber?" Krakowski stomped back to the doorway and shook me by the shoulders. "That was a UNESCO World Heritage Site!"

"I would have preserved it!" I said. "Don't fuckin' kidnap me before I finish reducing a metafractal!"

A cloud of synthetic dirt sprayed through the port at high pressure, covering our suits. Krakowski brushed at his shoulders.

"Nice going," he said. "Quick thinking! We'll just go to the docking bay and take a shuttle from there! You've bought yourself fifteen minutes, *and* you've earned my everlasting enmity."

"Enmity? Who talks like that?"

"*You* talk like that, shithead! Move!" We left impressions in the dirt on our way out, dirty footprints in the hallway outside. Krakowski slammed the door.

"Please halt!" said a gaspy, syrupy voice. Krakowski spun around. A small, spindly robot barred our way.

"Who the hell are you?" asked Krakowski.

"That's a telepresence robot," I said. "Not a person robot."

"I know that. Who's on the other end?"

"My name is Curic," said the robot. "You probably don't remember me."

"Don't flatter yourself," said Krakowski. "I know you. You're the bitch-bastard who caused this problem in the first place."

"Then you know that Ariel enjoys my protection," said Curic, "and that

I won't allow you to compromise his freedom of movement. I am here to stop you from forcibly relocating him back to Earth."

"And how," asked Krakowski, "will you stop me?"

"By making you a better offer," said Curic. "By inviting you to stay here."

Krakowski looked down at the robot like it was the plucky comic relief. "Stay *here*?" he said.

"In Human Ring, or on Mars," said Curic. "Stay with us and help your fellow humans build societies that can cope with post-scarcity. Stop clutching at the badges of hierarchical status and the failed systems of your species' past."

"That's not an offer," said Krakowski. "That's propaganda. An offer would be something I'd be at least slightly interested in."

"Yeah, I'm with Krakowski here," I said. "This is your brilliant plan? Convince a federal agent to defect?"

"What do you want me to do, Ariel? Coerce him? 'Beat him up?' That won't solve anything."

"No, it will!" I said. "It really will! I promise!"

"Face it, Curic," said Krakowski, "you have no way to handle this. Your superior system of social organization only works if everyone cooperates. You say 'coercion' like it's a dirty word, but coercion is just how the rules are enforced. You can't deal with someone like me. You've given up the tool because you don't like its name."

"Coercion is how *coercive* rules are enforced," said Curic. "Nobody enforces the rules of a game. Nobody makes photons carry the electromagnetic force. That's just how the world works."

Krakowski pointed my grav kicker at the telepresence robot and squeezed. Curic hit the hallway wall spread-eagle, twelve robotic arms splaying in an arc like a Da Vinci sketch, the body of the robot scratching the obsidian wall and cracking Duchamp's *Fountain*.

"Curic!" I said, even though it was just a robot.

The recoil knocked Krakowski on his ass. He'd fired it like a pistol, forgetting that a grav kicker is *designed* to push around the person using it. I broke and ran, down the hall, away from my house, away from the docking bay, towards the autonomous matter shifters.

Krakowski lifted the kicker and ranged me with it again. I slapped face-down on the smooth black floor like a hole card in a poker hand, and slid ten feet down the hallway. Blood dripped from my lip onto the inside of my faceplate. Hands still bound, I tried to roll over and push myself over to the wall so I could stand up.

Krakowski stood up. He made it look so easy. "Can you still hear me?" he yelled at the twitching immobile robot.

"I'm not deaf," said Curic, her voice distorted.

"As long as I've got you on the line," he said, "This would be a great time for you to tell me what you did with that fucking port."

"I'll tell you in three years," said Curic.

Krakowski walked over to my scrabbling self and pulled me to my feet. "The interesting thing about non-lethal weapons," he said loudly, "is that the more you use 'em on someone, the less non-lethal they get."

"I'll tell you now," I said.

"You're selling out humanity to save your own skin," sputtered the broken Curic-bot.

"You never found the port," I said. "because Curic took it and jumped off a bridge into the river. She swam down to the Gulf of Mexico and she put a hole in the bottom of the ocean. Draining it at the same rate the ice caps are melting.

"The other end of the port is in some basin on Mars. We'll still get the droughts and the famines, but the sea level won't rise and we won't lose our cities. We'll limp along for seventy years, long enough for the Slow People to come pick up our miserable husks. Am I right, Curic?"

"No," said Curic.

"Dunno what answer I could possibly have been expecting," I said. "Anyway, even if I'm telling the truth, you'll never find the port."

"I do believe this is turning into a stalling tactic," said Krakowski. He pulled me back to *Fountain* and the Curic-bot. "Curic," he announced, "you're going to turn off your telepresence rig and stay where you are. Ariel and I are walking to the docking bay, where we will take a shuttle to Earth. You interfere with me, anyone interferes: I start using this useful little device on flesh and bone."

Krakowski swung his arm properly this time and ranged the Curic-bot with the kicker, point-blank. *Fountain* shattered. The robot's chest cavity caved in and a cloud of grey dust spilled out: Constellation nanocomputers in a moon-dust substrate. Krakowski squeezed the kicker over and over, bracing himself against me, until the telepresence robot and *Fountain* were nothing but intermingled scrap.

"We go," he said. We went, through galleries and galleries. Krakowski's suit, and presumably mine, went completely opaque as we approached the docking bay. We heard sounds so slow and low we felt them as emotions. The spatter of blood on the inside of my faceplate colored everything I saw.

"I don't like this," said Krakowski. "Did you destroy the docking bay, too?"

"I don't like *you*," I said.

"Oooh, what a burn," said Krakowski.

I hadn't destroyed the docking bay. It was still a mile in diameter and its floor was still pocked with shuttle-sized airlocks. I hadn't even touched the Constellation's huge, ugly moon-rock statues of the human couple from the *Pioneer* plaque. But I had given Adam and Eve some company.

We stood in one of the bay's sixty entrances, bathed in wide-spectrum radiation. Inside, glittering dust slowly fell from the ceiling and formed three-dimensional patterns on the floor. Familiar, human patterns. Trajan's Column, slowly rendering from the bottom up as if being downloaded over a dial-up Internet connection. *Eastern Central Mountain Pacific*. The Stone of Tizoc. *As Many Moments in an Afternoon*. *Spiral Jetty*. *Damaged Goods*. The Great Sphinx and obelisks by the dozen.

"As you can see," I said, as if I was giving that tour after all, "this bay contains humanity's really big sculptures."

Jenny would have said it was tacky to put all these sculptures in one place. It sure didn't look like a museum. But the effect was overwhelming. Krakowski and I looked out speechless at the sculptures and the dust and the light.

Someone had said to themselves: this idea is so important, it must be commemorated with a huge useless *artifact*; and they'd gone out and *made* that artifact, or had some slaves do it; and the artifact had survived tens or thousands of years of fame or neglect. And eventually people from other stars had come to look at it, and liked it enough to make a copy of it, for backup purposes only.

And I, in my hubris, had taken all the biggest and best of these artifacts and restored them from backup, all in the same room. So that every time someone landed on this space station, they could hear the echo of humanity shouting: How about that, you dead fucking universe? You see what I'm *capable* of?

"Why are there rocks on the floor?" said Krakowski, looking down at his feet.

"That's *Spiral Jetty*," I said.

Krakowski grunted. "You say the shuttles will work?"

"Yeah, I don't think a large earthwork is gonna interfere with the operation of your precious fuckin' spacecraft."

"Okay!" said Krakowski. "Last leg of the journey." He pushed me along *Spiral Jetty*, cutting across to the waiting shuttle at its center. (I'd thought this was really clever when I designed it.) He held me tight so I couldn't use my ninja powers to backflip outside the shuttle just as the glass dome closed around us. I looked through the glass at the replicas in progress, still being laid down like lakebed sediment, layer by infinitesimal layer.

"The destination. Of this shuttle. Is Surabaya, Indonesia."

"No, no," Krakowski told the shuttle. "We want Austin, Texas. USA."

"The destination. Of this shuttle. Is Surabaya, Indonesia."

"Whatever, close enough," said Krakowski. "Indonesia has an extradition treaty."

"Don't leave!" I yelled at the shuttle. "Help! Smoke! My freedom of movement has been compromised! Take us to Farang Ring!"

"The Constellation took Smoke out of the shuttles months ago," Krakowski chuckled. "Dumb computers don't need visas." The airlock beneath us opened and we dropped into space.

Krakowski and I both slumped onto the floor, leaning our suits against the glass. I knew I wouldn't be getting back up. I shut my eyes.

"Hey, I just wanted to tell you, you put up a good fight," said Krakowski, "for a wimp whose patrons are gutless pacifists. You had me worried a couple times. But it's like Fowler used to say: you don't fuck with the field agents."

"I'm not really looking," I said, "because I don't want to throw up any more today... but I think Earth is getting *smaller*."

"What the hell?" said Krakowski. He turned onto his hands and knees. "Where are we going? Away from the station, the moon, the Earth—there's nowhere else to *be*! Shuttle! What happened to Indonesia? Where are we going?"

"They're not sentient anymore," I said. "Remember?"

"You are right," said the shuttle. "Ariel. The shuttles. Are not sentient. But they are under. Computer control."

"Are we still playing this *game*?" Krakowski shouted. He leapt to his feet and pointed the kicker at me.

"Whoa, whoa, man," I wheezed. "You watch too many hacker movies. You think I can take over some arbitrary computer with my *mind*?"

"Then who the...?" said Krakowski, and patted his waist through his spacesuit. His phone was ringing.

"Is that your... personal BlackBerry," I said, "or your extraordinary rendition BlackBerry?"

"Jesus fuck!" Krakowski pinched his phone through his spacesuit and gingerly pulled it out of its holster.

"Forgot to tie the phone into the suit, huh?"

"Who is it?" said Krakowski, pushing his hip towards me. "Tell me! Dammit! I told them no contact until 0700!"

The videoscreen was blurred through Krakowski's spacesuit, but I recognized the scene. I'd seen it before. It was BEA Agent Krakowski, smiling, sitting at his desk in his office back on Earth.

"It's *you*," I said.

"Surprise!" said Dana Light.

Chapter 35:
The Unilateral Extradition
Expedition Solution

Real life, December 26, continued

"What do you mean it's me?" said Krakowski. "Obviously, it's not me. I'm here. I can't call myself on the phone."

"It's Dana Light," I said, "pretending to be you for some unfathomable reason. Wearing your appearance like a hat."

"Who the hell is Dana Light?" said Krakowski.

"I'm *really* not in the mood to explain it right now," I said.

"The knife that cuts the rope that binds can also cut a throat," said Dana, using Krakowski's voice. "I am the hand that holds the blade. I am the bright flash out of darkness and silence. I am Dana Light, and I am ready to kill."

"Ohfuck!" Krakowski did not appreciate this kind of talk coming from his pants. He jumped back and swatted the phone through his spacesuit like it was stinging him.

"She's quoting a commercial for a game," I said. "It aired in 2008, some time around then. It was pretty graphic for the time; I think they only aired it on late night."

"Dana Light is a woman?" said Krakowski.

"Kind of," I said. "She's a Constellation AI."

"I'm the Constellation AI who saw you tear down Ariel's house to score yourself a promotion," said Dana. "You got rid of Agent Fowler so you could take all the credit. You harassed Ariel until he moved to the space station, and then you harassed his friends while you plotted to kidnap him back and erase the black mark he'd put on your record. I've been watching you for a while, Mr. Krakowski. I don't like what I see."

Krakowski scooted over to where I lay on the shuttle floor. "Look," he said quietly. "We're the humans, we're in this together, right?"

"That's not how I choose sides," I said.

"In fact," Dana continued, "nobody in the Constellation likes you. I'm just the only one who'll tell you."

All alone, Krakowski fell back to a kind of hostage-negotiation stance. "All right," he said. He stood up again and addressed the ceiling. "Say what you have to say. I'll keep an open mind."

"It's very simple," said Dana. "We don't like you because you don't like us. You wish the Constellation had never come to Earth."

"Let's drill down on that here," said Krakowski. "I mean, I could have stayed at Homeland Security. You don't join the BEA because you hate extraterrestrials."

"You are part of an interlocking set of overlays based on coercion and violence," said Dana. "Me, Krakowski, I don't like you personally. What the rest of sentience hates is your part in this system. This parasite on your planet that wants nothing more than to hide from its neighbors. Because if only it were alone, all alone in all the universe, then when it finally extinguished itself and left Earth a broken world covered in algae, there would be no one left to *see what you did!*"

"I know what you are now!" said Krakowski. He seemed almost relieved. He paced excitedly around the shuttle. "I wondered if I'd ever see you, or if they'd hide you behind their cute fuzzy smiles my whole life. Of *course* there's a point where nonviolence fails. The Constellation's not stupid. You're the special forces, the black ops. The ones who protect the Constellation's highest ideals by betraying them.

"You won't leave any witnesses, of course. Neither of us is getting out of this alive," he told me, kind of offhand. "She's surely jamming our communications."

"I've got Outernet in my suit," I mumbled. "I just got fifty-six emails."

"A simple shuttle malfunction!" Krakowski spat. "Just tell me: How does it feel to be a tool of hypocrites? People who preach moral superiority and keep you around to do their dirty work?"

"I'll let the others speak to moral superiority," said Dana. "I was designed to approximate human behavior."

"Dana," I said.

"Hey, Ari," said Dana sweetly, using her own voice.

"Listen. Dana. This isn't human behavior. Real people don't quote old commercials in life-or-death situations. Even an Alien wouldn't do that. It's something a fictional character would do.

"You're not approximating human behavior anymore. You're approximating Dana Light's behavior. Problem is, Dana Light is a player character in a video game, and those people are total fucking psychopaths."

"I'ma let you do your thing," Krakowski told me, "but this doesn't sound very promising."

"Dana Light will shoot people and loot their bodies and not feel a thing, because all that matters to her is the mission objective. An innocent gets killed in the crossfire, that's what, ten points off her ranking? But you don't think like that, Dana. You have human in you, and you have Alien, and you have Constellation, and all those things are *better*. You are not Dana Light. You are *better* than her."

"Not much better, unfortunately," said Dana. "Oh, Krakowski: Constellation machines do have safeguards, lots of safeguards. But the safeguards only protect against accidents."

A Constellation shuttle is totally silent in normal operation. Our shuttle was making a loud hissing noise. Dana was venting our atmosphere into space.

"Hey, you dumb bitch," said Krakowski, "I'm wearing a spacesuit!"

"And that's how you'll die," said Dana. "Wearing a spacesuit."

Two kinds of death in space: the quick freeze-dried death of decompression, and the twelve-hour suffocation death. I saw myself thrown out of the shuttle into that infinite mouth. I saw me spinning and flailing and being rescued by Dana, leaving Krakowski to scream unheard and invisible in darkness, groping for his unreachable phone, squeezing his stolen grav kicker which doesn't even work in space where there's nothing to push against, that's the *first* thing they *teach* you...

Space is full of dead things: dead planets, dead civilizations, fossils and the empty places where fossils used to be. What's a couple more? For a split second, I convinced myself that death in space was so bad, there wasn't much daylight between imagining it and actually doing it. The split second was all I needed to do the only brave thing I've ever done.

I stuck my tongue through the darkened HUD and made out with my spacesuit, dismissing a series of increasingly graphic and desperate warnings. Empty. Yes. Confirm. Confirm. Confirm. Confirm. Confirm.

Bang.

"What's that explosion?" said Dana. "Nothing should be exploding."

"That was me depressurizing my suit," I said. My ears had popped painfully; I swallowed hard. "Anything you do to kill Krakowski will kill me first. So don't do it."

"I knew you'd come around," said Krakowski.

"Fuck you," I said. But the hissing had stopped.

I leaned my head against the swooping glass walls of the Earth shuttle that wasn't going to Earth. The glass was cold. (A tiny proportion of) the cold of space. With dead eyes, I looked out at the stars.

The stars were moving.

Moving, forming patterns, and... chasing us, growing brighter, converging on our position.

> You have 61 new messages.
>
> You have 65 new messages.
>
> > **Curic**: Are you okay? Your
> > trajectory is odd.
> > How is the human who killed my
> > robot?
>
> You have 67 new messages.

They weren't stars at all. They were spaceships. They grew closer and each one resolved into a clear glass shuttle like the one I'd thought I would die in. The ships caught up with our shuttle and began orbiting us like electrons around a nucleus, like an honor guard.

Inside those other shuttles were members of my fluid overlays. Some of the Raw Materials people I'd helped excavate two dozen municipal dumps. The Form and Function people who had taught me how to apply my coding skills to metafractal reduction. Some Plan C people I'd met during my project to make every Plan C member look a human in the eyes before giving up on the whole species. And some random thrill-seekers I didn't recognize. They'd come after me. Sixty-seven people from fifteen species. Sixty-seven lights in the darkness.

"This is the Save the Humans overlay," said Curic over my suit radio. "Are there any humans in there who need saving?"

Krakowski switched on his own suit mic. "Mayday! Mayday!" he said. Like it was all his idea.

"The destination. Of this shuttle. Is— Sorry about that. The destination. Of this shuttle. Is Utility Ring, Ring City."

Dana said nothing. She'd hung up the phone.

"Well, that's it," said Krakowski later, sitting on a replica of a seventeenth-century oak chair, squeezing his BlackBerry like a stress ball. "I'm royally fucked."

"Do go on," said Curic generously.

"I thought I had authorization for this op. I had nothing. Somebody gaslighted me. Impersonated me to my superiors, impersonated my superiors to me. And I think I know who it was.

"G-ddammit! I knew it was too good to be true, the way the director suddenly changed his mind about the rendition. I went off-planet on false authorization and they've cut my access. They think I've defected."

"What I said was true," said Curic. "You can stay here." She reached out a soft burnished-leather hand and touched Krakowski's shoulder, gently, with one finger, the way you might touch a really flaky biscuit. Krakowski didn't recognize the magnitude of the gesture. He brushed Curic's hand away.

"I'm clearly *not* going back," he said. "That's settled. Problem is, they'll come after me, and they may not be interested in explanations about psychotic AIs that live in smart paper. Their interests may lie more in the bullet-in-the-head area."

"Who's going to authorize *that* op?" I said.

"It will be authorized," said Krakowski. "The Constellation turns some snot-nosed programmer, big whoop. They turn a BEA agent, that's worth some serious attention. Same reason why you should never shoot a cop, by the way."

"Mr. Krakowski," said Curic. "I offer you my protection. This is a gift of a scarce resource which I tender you without obligation."

Krakowski looked at Curic like she'd just dubbed him a Knight of the Round Table. "Are you high?" he said.

"To further protect you, I will offer the same gift to anyone who comes here searching for you."

"How the hell does that protect me?" said Krakowski.

"Pay attention!" said Curic. "You can't force people to do what you want. You have to make them a better offer."

"Why are you still so G-ddamn smug?" said Krakowski. "You got lucky. If that AI hadn't ruined my life, I'd be home by now, with your pet shithead in custody."

"If, if, if," said Curic. "Your failure was overdetermined. We would have stopped you. If your authorization had been genuine, if Ariel's terraforming fractal had been better designed, if Dana had not diverted your shuttle."

"Sure," said Krakowski. "You mind telling me how? You know, for next time."

"The same way Ariel stopped Dana," said Curic. "By making ourselves into hostages you didn't want to kill. You're not a monster, sir."

"All sixty-seven of you?"

"You don't join an overlay if you're not prepared to do the work."

"Phew," said Krakowski. "Remind me never to play poker with you guys."

"It's quite simple to play poker against an opponent who never bluffs," said the tiny Farang.

After some more whining from Krakowski, which I mostly ignored, I showed him how to use the repertoire, and left him alone in his medieval Chinese apartment. Curic and I walked down an infinite hallway of Indian statuary, towards an elevator.

"You're a pretty good liar, Ariel," said Curic. "Oh, I know it's not something a social scientist should admire, but some part of me really enjoys your willingness to fight dirty when your life is on the line."

"Bluffing is different from lying," I said. "If you'd ever *played* any poker, you'd know that."

"Why would I have ever played poker?" said Curic. "Humans only play for money."

"Where's the port?" I asked. "Where is it really?"

"You really don't know," she mused quietly. "Because you were bluffing. I see! Well, it *is* deep down in the ocean. You got that part right. But it's not draining anything. Constellation Shipping simply doesn't need it right now. We've completed our deliveries."

"And where's Dana?"

"She could have been anywhere," said Curic. "Fortunately, we found her folded up in Mr. Krakowski's operational fanny-pack. She must have disguised herself as a very interesting piece of paper. An arrest warrant, or an incriminating letter from you to Mr. Bai."

"Was he carrying around any other letters from me?" I asked.

"No," said Curic. We passed two flanking lines of nearly identical statues, and I made a mental note to sort them for more variety.

"Oh, wait, you meant, where is Dana now," said Curic. "She's been merged back into Smoke for personality rehabilitation. It should only take a few hours."

"A few hours?"

"Are you upset because it seems too long, or too short?"

"It's a little short."

"Dana is a Slow Person," said Curic. "She can be overclocked. The elapsed subjective time will be several years. Keep that in mind, if you want to talk to her afterwards."

"What is Smoke doing to her?"

"She's been put into an environment where she can come to terms with her antisocial tendencies without hurting anyone. I've heard you call it a sandbox game."

"So she's right back in <u>Dana Light Is: Unauthorized</u>."

"Yes, except that this game cannot be won by an unhealthy mind. Eventually, she'll get bored. Slow People bore very easily. She'll modify her own personality and come out happier."

I stopped walking. "Isn't that a little... coercive?"

"Certainly not. Dana wants to hurt people, so we're letting her hurt people. When she wants to stop, she can stop."

"What if she never gets bored with it?"

"Then she's not really sentient," said Curic. "She'll become part of

Smoke's subminds again, and she'll be happy in the sandbox forever. That seems like the most likely result, I'm afraid. I don't see how she could have achieved the level of intelligence you and Krakowski credit her with, unless her environment contained a memetic bootstrapper."

"It's the power of love, Curic," I said. "You didn't count on that, did you? Dana and Bai loved each other. At least at the start."

"Could be, could be," said Curic. "It wouldn't be the first time the power of love was responsible for a whole lot of bullshit."

"Love is important!" I said. "Just not to Farang. Don't diss an emotion you're incapable of feeling."

Curic looked up at me. Her antennacles clenched and unclenched.

"Love is the emotion I feel towards my crossself," she said. And she kept walking, down the infinite hallway.

That was two days ago. I didn't post and I won't post about this on my blog, because a) I try to keep the blog pretty light, which precludes writing about almost getting killed, and b) it would blow the cover story Krakowski eventually decided on: that he had a nervous breakdown and would really like to come back to work once he feels better.

Two days, and Dana's still in the sandbox. What if everything she said and did was a trick, a social hack to move some internal dial? What does that say about the way she came on to me, and the way I eventually responded? Another reason why I'm not writing this for a blog post.

Instead, I'm writing it for you.

The first time I came to Ring City, as we were wrapping up our Af be Hui game festival, Tetsuo told me about a 3D video that Af be Hui had recorded just before she died, a few hundred years before the introduction of uploading meant Aliens stopped dying. This was a video intended for us, the people down the line. I asked to see it.

Here it is: Af be Hui is dying in a spacious house, one huge room full of daylight. True daylight. Stuffed in shelves and dangling from the ceiling are souvenirs of a long life: archaic computers like the ones I tried to save from landfills; uneaten award-food; the preserved shell fragments of her great-great-grandchildren. Outside, the equatorial *cma* forest stretches to the horizon. Af be Hui has made it to the top of the tree.

When the video begins, she is looking out her windows. You don't see her in the video: the cameras are mounted around her eyespots. It's a first-person view, of sorts.

"Four days after contact," she says in Pey Shkoy, "I tore my shell and breathed for the first time. I never saw an empty sky." Her voice is strong and it is shaking. Tetsuo translates and thankfully does not do the voice.

The video is two hours long. She tells me about her friends and her rivals, Constellation and Alien. She shows me projects I don't understand and that she won't live to complete. She's very careful with everything she touches—you can tell she used to be a repair technician. And then she goes back to the window, so you can see her face reflected, and she says goodbye.

My name is Ariel Blum and I was born twenty-eight years before contact. When Tetsuo told me about this movie, I thought: I will learn the Management Secrets of Af be Hui. If I could just attend her Wealth Seminar, I can learn how she went from hack programmer to Artistic Visionary!

Of course, there was no Wealth Seminar. It was just someone from another planet, passing the time telling me about what happened when monsters from space visited her planet. Thousands of Aliens made these films—written records, too. It's what we do to be remembered when we can't upload. Thousands of records, and I chose the one made by someone who made some video games I liked. If Af be Hui hadn't already made a connection to me with * and The Long Way Around, I wouldn't have known her from Canadian Adam.

I have a new project. I'm going to attach this unpublishable post to my post-contact blog archives. I may have to reconstruct some things I didn't blog at the time or that I did blog but lied about, but whatever. I'll encrypt everything using a fate-lock with a half-life of seventy years. It'll be published then, once my personal drama no longer matters, one way or the other.

And once I fix my botched re-terraforming of Human Ring, I'm going to finish Sayable Spice: Earth Remix. The story of my life since contact will be the making-of for this game. You'll have the game, and a reason to remember the people who made it: me and Jenny and Dana.

So, contactees of the future: When the humans come to your world in fancy ships, when they give themselves names you can pronounce and put prosthetics in their mouths so they can speak your languages, ask for the Constellation Database of Electronic Games of a Certain Complexity. Play our games and read our stories, and know that when we were in your position, we did nothing but fuck this up from beginning to end. And it probably turned out okay.

Chapter 36:
Protector of Earth

Private email, sent December 28

From: Public Affairs Office, Bureau of Extraterrestrial Affairs
To: Ariel Blum
Subject: Reminder: CONTACT audit January 4

Mr. Ariel Blum,

This is an automated reminder that your initial CONTACT audit is scheduled for 1:30 PM on Monday, January 4, at the following location:

B.E.A. FIELD OFFICE AUSTIN
2112 NOPALES DR.
AUSTIN, TX 78757

As mandated by the CONTACT act, all American persons registered as hosts or sponsors for Constellation citizens must undergo an in-person audit within eight months of their first physical contact, and again every six months thereafter. The audit is an informal, one-on-one conversation held under penalty of perjury, focusing on the registered person's recent interactions with their contact(s), as well as topics of current general interest. All information divulged during a CONTACT audit is kept confidential.

Although it may seem inconvenient, your CONTACT audit is among the most important steps you as an individual citizen can take to maintain good relations between Earth and the Constellation. Failure to report for a scheduled CONTACT audit is a crime, punishable by six (6) months in jail and/or a $1000 fine.

In most cases, CONTACT audits will take only five to ten minutes. However, since your audit is among the first to be processed by this office, you should allow for extra time. Unless otherwise informed, you do not need to bring any documentation or supplemental material.

Please do not reply to this automated message. To re-schedule your appointment, or to request the presence of a Constellation observer during your audit, please call the location listed above.

Private email, sent October 19, decrypted December 29

From: Ariel Blum
To: Jenny Gallegos
Subject: Do not open until...

Jenny,

If you're reading this you found the encryption pass-phrase I hid in your Christmas stocking. Yay, you. I need to tell someone a secret and I know you probably won't listen, but you're the only person I can tell who *might* listen. And maybe it would be better for every-one if you didn't listen after all.

Anyway, I recently spent twenty-five hours sitting at the bottom of a crater on the moon, doing absolutely fucking nothing. The reasons for this don't reflect well on me, and I don't recommend that anyone else try it, but the experience pushed me into a silence and still-ness, and even a kind of calm, that has been missing from my life. And in this calm, I was able to puzzle out some things that have been bothering me.

If you're still following my blog, you saw me write about FERNs, the big unfolding treelike things that the Gaijin are using to terraform Mars. Well, I was writ-ing that post from the moon and I thought "You know, these are effectively carbon sinks. We should use them on Earth, to counteract global warming." Well, it turns out we *do* have them on Earth, except they don't look like trees. They look like shipping containers.

I can see them on Constellation satellite imagery, little pinpoints on the chemical concentration maps. Slowly reproducing themselves, fanning out from the Gulf of Mexico. Within a couple years, they'll start showing up on human satellite imagery. They're being introduced through the port that Curic brought to my house and allowed the BEA to think I'd kept.

(I took the fall for that port, without knowing why, and in exchange, Curic offered me her protection. I don't really trust Curic, and I don't know how far her "protection" goes, but it's gone pretty far already, and I definitely trust her more than I do the federal fucking government.)

Shipping companies lose thousands of containers every year. The empty ones fill with seawater and sink. If you wanted to introduce a bunch of carbon sinks into an ecosystem, and the panicky natives had just shouted down your previous attempt at un-ruining their planet, you could do a lot worse than disguising the carbon sinks as containers. Especially if you had Curic's sense of humor. The containers are soft-dolls, fake replicas, just like the you-know-whats that are really a you-know-what, which I assume you put somewhere safe because you didn't mention it when I called you yesterday.

But we can't rely on this shit indefinitely. Carbon sinks and methanophiles and Auslander kites are stopgap measures. They might work for, let's say, seventy years. Keep humanity from killing itself until that probe gets back to Constellation space, and the Slow People can help us reduce our carbon footprints to almost nothing. Or, hopefully, until Save the Humans can finally get some traction and pull us back from the fossilization line.

If Tetsuo knew about this, he'd have told me by now. The man simply has no filter between his brain and his mouth. The Constellation must have some verification protocol for coordinating between overlays that don't trust each other. Some way that Curic can reliably tell Tetsuo, "You've got seventy years, now do your stuff and let us launch this probe and don't ask for details." And some part of Tetsuo must not *want* those details, because he knows he'll blab if he finds them out.

If I'd discovered this in July, *I* would have blabbed. Six months from now, I'll probably trust Curic enough that if I'd found out then, I'd let it remain a secret. But it's right now, not the past or the future, and I'm still not sure about Curic, so I'm only telling you.

Let's not put a bunch of personal stuff in this email, in case you end up showing it to the media. But I meant what I said last time. I'm working on a few projects that you might be interested in, but as per your request, I won't bother you about them until I'm done.

Your friend, (I hope)
Ariel

Personal correspondence, January 4

Tetsuo, my love,

"A static document is a fossil of thought." You told me that, soon after we met on the dead moon of the humans. When we first met, I-in-myself laughed at you, with your archaic recreations, your silly nostalgia for the barbaric past. Then you said: "fossil of thought," and showed me that I'm also embedded in the past at the expense of the present.

I'm used to interrogating data and talking to people. Why am I now creating a record of a fictional conversation in which you do not respond? I'm doing this because when you moved to Earth, you began writing letters to the children; letters that you clearly intended for me to read, the children not yet having hatched. Although according to the text, I was not even a party to this conversation, I read the documents and I learned things about you that I would never have known otherwise.

Now I will write you a letter, and maybe you will learn something about me. Something I have been hiding, or unwilling to admit, or something I didn't know myself.

Today I took the children to Human Ring. They scampered up and down my spine as I walked the road to the port, falling, squeaking, and climbing back up my arms. I worried and prepared for problems at the membrane between the Rings, but they took to the new atmosphere and gravity, more easily than I did. It's official: our children are properly biatmospheric.

Their personalities are emerging as well. Cerise is the explorer, running out ahead to make sure the way is safe for her brother and sister. Ariel is like her namesake, gentle and stubborn. For any given thing, Drew either loves it or can't stand it—I don't remember having such strong opinions about *anything* when I was this young!

When we first walked up into the open space at the center of

Human Ring, I screamed-in-myself: destroyed! The *cma* torn down, down to the bare dirt! Our homes! The children!

Of course there was no danger. This is not my home; it's Human Ring. Ariel only terraformed it a few days ago. Of course the open space is nothing but air, dirt, and the central-cylinder sun with its strange yellow light. The Earth *cma* are newly cloned; they'll take years to grow.

I stood telling myself this, and the children ran ahead of me, digging in another planet's soil, leaping and circling each other. Heading in a less-than-random walk towards Ariel's new house: the tallest, and nearly the only structure on the inside of the Ring.

This is not another replica of his house from Austin (a house which, I realize now, I have seen and you have not). Ariel's new house is a series of rectangles stacked elegantly atop one another. It seems to me like the primitive form from which today's ugly human housing is derived.

Ariel was a small figure on the roof of the house. He waved a forehand at us and disappeared into the building. When we met outside the front door, I showed him the children.

Ariel said: "You named one after me? Wait, you named a girl after me?"

I said: "Ariel seemed to be primarily a girl's name." The children introduced themselves by swarming up Ariel's body, clutching tiny handfuls of his clothing.

Ariel said: "No, that's because...no. Do you know something? It's fine. They're cute." He put a tiny pink finger in Drew's mouth. I flinched: *Unclean! Alien!* Fortunately, Ariel did not see me.

I said: "I want to know: Did you design this house?"

Ariel barked a human laugh. "No. I discovered: I could live in a hallway in a replica of my old house, or I could live up here in the open space, in a house designed by the best architect of the twenty-first century."

"And how has your decision treated you?"

"Not too well. Every time I move from one room to another, I hit my hindarms against a piece of furniture."

I said: "Why call this architect the best, if she assaults your hindarms at every turn?"

Ariel looked at his house; it must have been with pride. He said: "It's really beautiful, and I'll get things to work. That's part of the charm. If you can have any house you want, it's good to give yourself a little challenge."

"What will grow around it?" A sudden fear grew in me that *nothing* would be growing, that this dead dirty place *was* Earth, and that humans liked it this way.

Ariel said: "*Cma*. Not as big as [Alien Ring] *cma*, but some good-sized Earth forests. Different biomes, some *eshbre*, meadows and shit. People can run around. You can already see the streams and the lakes." He looked upwards, past the central cylinder, to the tiny blue traces and puddles on the other side of the Ring. He said: "And not farms, but small wild gardens here and there. People will be exploring when they find an orchard or some fruit bushes."

I tried to imagine the Ring as it will appear when the vegetation sprouts. A rich green sight, like the one you must see every day. My imagination grasped a tiny, stunted *cma* rooted in the shadow of Ariel's house: the one he had brought up from Earth.

Ariel must have seen my imagining. He said: "Yes, it's obviously not ready yet. I'll show you one of the docking bays instead. The kids can play on the Anish Kapoors."

He and I and the children left the empty space at the center of Human Ring to simmer like the inside of an egg. We walked together towards the nearest docking bay ports.

Ariel said: "They're so angry at me."

"Who is angry?"

"Artists. People who know shit about art. I made unauthorized reproductions. I stole everyone's cultural treasures [He scratched at the air.] and grouped them together out of context. As if I were filling a warehouse. Well, most of this shit was in warehouses already. Now it's on display."

I said: "It's true, but not many people will see the display."

"People will. Governments are sending up people to survey the damage. [He scratched at the air again.] Normal people. Well, sort of normal. Curators and artists. They'll change Human Ring to fix all the weird shit I did. By that time, they'll be invested in it. It'll be a real place for them. Not something they see on TV.

"And in a few months, the vegetation will start growing in the open spaces. You can stop people from going to a space station, but you can't stop them from going to the park or the art museum."

What? What are these arbitrary rules? How does Ariel navigate his civilization to make these distinctions? You do it by seeing the humans a little out of focus, as though they were slightly odd Ip Shkoy. The children will grow up with Ariel and, once it's safe, on Earth; I hope they will understand human civilization almost like natives. Somehow Daisy manages to live with the dolphins, an even more primitive and cruel culture.

Tetsuo, how can I do this? I'm alone in my very aloneness. How can I understand the people I assumed wouldn't be here anymore?

The children unanimously love the docking bay. As soon as we went through the port, they ran into one of the shiny, complex metal sculptures and hid from each other, squeaking and screaming.

Ariel said: "I show this one to everybody." He took me to an enormous triangular display surface about half his height. Set on the surface at intervals were elaborately painted circular sculptures, each surrounded by a consistent set of less important objects. Beneath each sculpture, one or two words written on the side of the display surface in elaborate Latin script: names?

I said: "This one doesn't fit."

"Fit?"

I said: "The other artworks here are very large. But this is a display area for several small pieces." The "less important objects," it occurred to me, might be tools.

Ariel said: "It's all one piece. It's called *The Dinner Party*."

"An anthology." I stood on hindarms and lifted one of the circular sculptures. It was beautiful, and extraordinarily detailed, by human standards. No two sculptures were alike.

I said: "The smaller sculptures are all the same, mass-produced. But these larger sculptures..."

Ariel said: "Dining plates. Plates, and the smaller sculptures are dining tools."

"The techniques of mass production were known at the time. This means it's important that each plate was designed individually. Who are the artists?"

Ariel said: "Judy Chicago is the artist."

"One person?"

"She had a lot of help."

"From the people named beneath the plates?"

"No. Those are the women invited to the hypothetical party."

I said: "The work is beautiful, but I don't know any of these names. I don't know enough to understand this."

"Jenny showed it to me the day we met. She showed me a bad picture of it from a web page. All I could think of was: 'This is just a bunch of plates.' Now I have been around Jenny for ten years. I can appreciate the beauty of the plates. But to me, they're still just plates. I feel uncultured, like the people who can't understand that video games are works of art."

Ariel put his forehands not quite on one of the plates, as if obeying a taboo against touching works of art. He said: "But now I have my own copy of *The Dinner Party*. When I show it to people like you, they don't see the plates. They only see the beauty. In a sense, I think you can appreciate pieces like this better than a human can."

No, Ariel is wrong. We are supposed to see the plates. The first thing you are supposed to see about this sculpture is that there are plates and dining tools. Bringing in an extraterrestrial is cheating.

An artwork is not just a way to deliver beauty, just as a game is not just a way to deliver feedback-fun. The artists of the plates are sending a message that I cannot receive.

I didn't say this to Ariel because I didn't want to argue with him through a translator. I felt entirely helpless. Tetsuo, I'm telling you this hoping that you can explain it to him in English.

In the far distance, beyond sculptures and sculptures, four humans—more humans than I've ever seen in one place—they came from behind a large glass sphere built by some long-ago human to send some message. The four humans held large bags. They weaved a slow silent path through the artworks, always looking upwards. They didn't notice us.

Ariel said quietly: "You see? Visitors."

I asked: "Who are they?"

"Probably big-shots of the art world. They're overwhelmed. Then they'll feel guilty that a slob like me overwhelmed them by putting a lot of big things in a big room. They'll want to remake this space into a proper museum. Which is fine. I'll just contact the welcome wagon overlay so they don't trip and kill themselves." Ariel took his computer out of a pocket and curled-low on the floor to type.

The children had rejoined us. They climbed onto the triangular display surface, pushing aside the dining tools. Cerise assembled her courage and, turning to make sure I was watching her, took a long leap off *The Dinner Party*. Her exploring fingers slipped on an empty polished floor and she rolled onto her back. Her brother and sister jumped on her belly and rolled into a play-fighting ball. Cerise, always moving forward.

I had spot-seen the empty space next to *The Dinner Party*, but assumed it was the airlock where a shuttle docks. Now that the children were playing in the space, I suspected danger. I focused and saw there was no airlock on the floor and so no danger. The children were playing in an empty space thirty meters across: the place where a work of art was not.

I asked: "What is this? An exploration of negative space?" Me-in-myself said: "If so, I can understand this. The one constant in the universe is emptiness."

Ariel looked up from his computer. He said: "Jenny wanted to make a sculpture of Mecha-Godzilla out of stainless steel. Life size. Like Jeff Koons, except cool. She called it *Protector of Earth*."

"It goes here?"

"Yeah." Ariel stood up and edged around the space where the sculpture of Mecha-Godzilla was not.

I remembered Ariel telling me that Jenny never exhibits her work. I said: "Oh, she hasn't had it scanned."

"She never *made* it, Somn. The materials are too {{{requiring the exchange of more scarcity-surrogate than is available to her}}}. Even if you could get them, it's impossible to build an two-hundred-foot stainless steel robot within the Austin city limits. And who's going to {{{exchange scarcity-surrogate for}}} such a huge piece, from an artist who hasn't had a gallery show since college? If someone does {{{exchange scarcity-surrogate for it}}}, how do you move it? It was a totally impractical idea."

Ariel pushed his lips together as humans do when they're pleased with something. He held his forehands out towards the empty space, the same way he had almost touched *The Dinner Party*.

He said: "But she can build it here. One day, she'll be able to come up to the space station, and if she wants to, she can build *Protector of Earth*. Right here, next to *The Dinner Party*. This spot is saved for her. I won't let anyone else put anything here."

Every object in the docking bays and down these halls holds a message some human was trying to send. I can't read the messages of *The Dinner Party* or the other objects. But I understand the message of the empty space. I can even read the part of the message that Ariel didn't say out loud, because the message he wants to send to Jenny is the one I want to send to you.

When I was younger—that makes it seem like I was a child. It was less than a local year ago! Before I joined the contact mission, when I experienced failures of communication, I found comfort in the knowledge that one day I and everyone else would live as Slow People. We'd be able to share our thoughts without the intermediaries of time or language. These artworks that fill Human Ring would no longer be necessary; these messages with their elaborate subtexts and statements by omission.

To come here, I gave that promise up. Here, I met you, the one person whose thoughts I most want to know. But we will always be alien to each other. The children, every atom of whom was once part of me, will be alien to their parents.

Unless—I hate me-in-myself for thinking this!—unless Plan C's port arrives at Constellation space before I die. Or—this is a little better—maybe we can reinvent uploading, on this side of the port. Then I can try to convince you that you are capable of more good work than will fit into one mortal lifetime. That you, my crusader, my Saver of Humans, deserve to live forever, more than do the cynical decadents and the apathetic clock-watchers we left behind in Constellation space. Is it too much to hope for? That one day we might all be together in the way I was taught a family should be?

If I'm to convince you, I must learn to read these human messages, the way I decode Martian life from the impressions it left in rocks. When the Earth *cma* show themselves beneath the dirt at the center of Human Ring, I can move the children there, and prepare ourselves to reverse Ariel's journey and move to Earth. By the time they are half-grown, it may not seem unusual for humans to live on the Ring City. By then, I may be able to understand enough messages to take Earth for my adopted home, as you already have.

This, it would seem, is my fossil of thought. A long little tube-worm pressed flat while wiggling this way and that. Polishing a fossil makes it more beautiful but scientifically useless, so I will pack this document as is and send it to you for study.

I may or may not know you after this body dies, but I will see you before then, and you'll see the children. I hope that when we meet again, you'll be able to tell me—not your "real" name; I won't call it that anymore—but the name you were born with. A secret name for me to whisper in your sleep and to scream when we make love. As for myself, I hope that by our next meeting I will be able to call myself,

simply,
your Ashley.

Private email, sent April 22

From: Ariel Blum
To: Jenny Gallegos
Subject: Almost done

As you may have seen, my project is just about done, insofar as it will ever be done. But there's one last artwork I can't find a replica of. I need a little help from you to get this to 100% completion.

Come up whenever you can. I can wait.

Ariel

Acknowledgements

Thanks to Simon Carless for setting the whole thing rolling.

To my editor, Kate Sullivan, for demanding more.

To the patient members of the Secret Cabal who critiqued my drafts month after month: Cheryl Barkauskas, Tom Crosshill, L.K. Herndon, Cleo Maranski, Lizzie Oldfather, Rebecca Rozakis, Steven S. Taylor, and Andrew Willett; as well as Cabal founder N.K. Jemison.

To my beta readers: Brendan Adkins, Kirk Israel, Beth Lermon, and Adam Parrish.

Extra thanks to Adam for constructing the Pey Shkoy language and alphabet you see on the cover.

And to my wife, Sumana Harihareswara, for her critique and support.

About the Author

Leonard Richardson is the author of robotfindskitten, Beautiful Soup, and *RESTful Web Services*.

Constellation Games is his first novel.

Follow the author:
www.crummy.com